D0278561

DERMOT BOLGER

A Second Life

VIKING

This is a work of fiction and any resemblance to any person, living or dead, is purely coincidental.

VIKING

Published by the Penguin Group
Penguin Books Ltd, 27 Wrights Lane, London W8 5TZ, England
Penguin Books USA Inc., 375 Hudson Street, New York, New York 10014, USA
Penguin Books Australia Ltd, Ringwood, Victoria, Australia
Penguin Books Canada Ltd, 10 Alcorn Avenue, Toronto, Ontario, Canada M4V 3B2
Penguin Books (NZ) Ltd, 182–190 Wairau Road, Auckland 10, New Zealand

Penguin Books Ltd, Registered Offices: Harmondsworth, Middlesex, England

First published 1994
2 4 6 8 10 9 7 5 3 1
First edition

Filmset by Datix International Ltd, Bungay, Suffolk
Printed in England by Clays Ltd, St Ives plc
Set in 12/15pt Monophoto Sabon

A CIP catalogue record for this book is available from the British Library

Hardback ISBN 0–670–85634–7
Trade paperback ISBN 0–670–85787–9

For Donnacha and Diarmuid

The author is deeply indebted to E. Charles Nelson's and Eileen M. McCracken's *The Brightest Jewel – A History of the National Botanic Gardens, Glanvenin, Dublin*, and to Hazel and Leo Duffy, of Broadstone, Dublin, under whose roof this novel was written.

Chapter One

Whoever had resprayed the ambulance had missed the top rim of the doors. From above, the flaky rusting cracks in the paintwork looked like a dried-up riverbed. The top of the paramedic's hat was speckled with flecks of dandruff and when he lifted his head from my chest I could see my face staring up, crisscrossed with streaks of blood. The old trees were bare between the gates of the Botanic Gardens and yet from somewhere within the brown depths of their branches I seemed to hear a blackbird lilting.

How long had it been since I felt as serene as this? It was hard to remember the petty agitations of breakfast time: the phone ringing, Benedict refusing to eat, starting to bicker about his Christmas toys. All that had occurred only minutes before, but I no longer felt any connection to it. I was surprised to find no pain either, or any sense of grief or loss. Instead I observed the scene below with the same sense of casual engrossment that I remembered feeling as a tiny child turning some new curiosity over in my hands.

Weeds filled the gutters of the house in flats on the corner. There were roof slates cracked that would cause problems in winter. A girl stood behind lace at a top window. I could see party balloons Sellotaped to the glass and the top of her hair, still wet from the shower, when she leaned forward to stare at the cars stopped like an old-fashioned funeral procession outside the home of the deceased. How utterly terrified the faces looked through those windscreens, how strained and vulnerable. Where had they been going in this limbo of days between Christmas and New Year, with offices and factories closed? I felt sorry for the drivers being forced to stare at me. I did not feel sorry for myself, or indeed have any particular emotions towards my body lying half in and half out of the crushed car. It was like coming across a discarded overcoat which I had once clung on to but could no longer remember why.

The bus driver was in the initial stages of shock. He lay on the tarmacadam beside the gates, his face white, tufts of black hair in his nostrils. His legs were twitching involuntarily. It was not his fault. It had been me, late for a shoot as usual, taking the corner wide where the cars were parked outside the Addison Lodge.

Two officials from the Botanic Gardens came to the gate to watch. One was balding, a ridge of greying hair circling the freckles on his skull. The ambulance men had now got my body on to a stretcher; they worked frantically, thumping at my chest. All that futile effort and concern. Why could they just not let my corpse be? Already I was moving away from them, the morning turning to evening, then darkening and dissolving into night. I felt my body glowing, like in a sexual climax, only more gentle, until the heat became an intense tingling wave which I was consumed within. I had drifted beyond the gates of the Botanic Gardens. There were gnarled, ancient trees below, Victorian glasshouses to my left, the white glint of water beyond. Glasnevin cemetery was to my right. I thought of all the people I knew there. Then it became too dark to see; the old trees became shapes, the shapes in turn faces. Then the moon was up, so cold and brilliantly bright and yet casting no light in the blackest of skies and, as I began to be sucked towards it, I recognized the faces now.

How long was it since I had last seen the man whom I had

been taught to call Grandfather? I had been only three when he died, yet I knew him at once, and all the other faces which I had never thought I would see again. They were crowding in towards me now, growing ever closer and more numerous. My two children were there too, only now with the faces of adults, faces that were older than mine, faces smiling in welcome. I did not even feel the need to question their presence. There was such a sense of well-being, of finally coming home. What had I ever been afraid of, why had I waited so long to die?

You'll like it here, son. I knew that whispering voice, I could sense myself smiling. The white moon was cold no longer. It dazzled and spun, radiating heat, drawing me in. I knew I had only to pass through it to be able to reach my hands out to those faces that were gathering me up, spinning ever faster into vibrating colours now. All of them blurring except for that one young man's face. I knew his features so well, his sneer, the surly turn of his head which was so out of place in the joyous welcoming crowd. And then everything else was gone except him. Blocking me. Everything blackening. Ding, dong, dell, pussy's in the well. Is there water below me, how far am I falling from the sky? Snatches of life I had once, flecks of memories like a television flicked between stations. How far down . . .?

A wife, two children. Responsibilities. Business to finish. Pain to face. I had been a person once. I had used a camera for a living. Click. I'm lying here on the ground. Click. I'm lying here in pain. If I could only focus . . . if I could only climb back . . . Where do I know his face from? If I could only make peace with that one face which is unfriendly, that one face unblurred. *Go back down to hell, go back.* Am I saying that to him or is he saying it to me? Is it my voice I'm hearing and why then is it so strange? And why has the moon climbed so high and so far; why does he keep pushing it back up away from me? Out of light, spinning down into a black tunnel. Why must I plummet down this vast height, with the moon suddenly falling on to my face, splintering against it, turning everything white and then grey? A grey pavement with cracks, a grey morning with cold grey mist, a man with greying hair banging on my chest. That most awful of thuds like falling in sleep. I'm screaming now and I recognize my own voice, though it is barely audible. I'm screaming so loud that it's filling up my head and still it can't expel the pain. The sky begins to blacken as an ear, huge and expanding, starts to press down. A voice from the darkness says, *He's breathing again. He was gone from us for so long, how the hell can he be still alive?*

I'm breathing. The curse of God on them all, why am I breathing? I don't want to breathe, I want to fly to the moon. I want those welcoming faces back. I'm sick of struggling, I want to be weightless. I had never known such rapture in my life. The ambulance is jigging from side to side. I think of those lines of stalled cars we are hurtling through: stress inside bubbles of chrome; lists of appointments, destinations, deliveries, deadlines, drivers chasing their tails. Two figures lean across me, pulling on straps. I had been free, existing in a pure moment of bliss. Which of these two bastards had brought me back to this?

My body feels numb. The needles have done their work well. But there must be a drug to stop me from thinking. Do they honestly think I can fit back into this life? Maybe I'm paralysed, thirty more years ahead of me, vegetating in some ward. Give me back my death, I'm trying to tell them. We sway sharply left, then right again. The sound of another siren, a police escort. I think of the funniest joke of all, that this was what I was always petrified of. Check-ups every year, imagining a cardiac arrest every time a speck of heartburn touched my chest. I am filled with an utter sense of grief, of inconsolable loss. This is what cold turkey must be like, or a newborn prised from the nipple of its mother. My history repeating itself. The tears have not got the strength to fall down my face. They lie on my eyes like weights. Above those trees I had been wrapped in a blanket of love. I cry for myself brought back to face this life.

The ambulance stops. The doors open and there is light. I remember the story which a shy giant of a Gaelic poet I was photographing had once told me about himself: Máirtín Ó Direáin as an old man being brought to the operating theatre by a young nurse who leaned over as he was blacking out and said, 'My sister failed her Leaving Cert because you were on the course.' My nurse's hair is blonde: I can smell perfume or deodorant. *He's laughing*, I hear her say. I'm crying, you little bitch, I'm crying. The words will not come out. I do not remember being carried from the ambulance.

There were enough flowers around the bed for any man. The funny thing was that I knew all their names, or at least at those moments when I drifted towards consciousness, I knew names from nowhere which seemed to fit them. There were holiday golfers beyond my window giving golf a bad name. I could not raise my head but I could sense the trees and open space outside and hear agonized shouts of *Fore*. My wife came, sat by me and left. Benedict, my eldest child, came and touched my hand, hesitantly. I sensed his fear of tubes and masks, knew that he'd be pushing back against Geraldine, wanting to be away. He would block it from his mind before he had even left the hospital, talk only of the tractor glimpsed on the golf course from the window. If I did not pull through would he remember anything? I would not even be a photograph. I had never let myself be photographed. I felt for Geraldine and him and yet I felt nothing as well. *You're so lucky, lucky*. The feel of my wife's hand. I could have tried to say something to her in reply. I could have opened my mouth, even if no sound came out. Her lips were wet. I could feel them on my flesh long after she had left.

Then it was night. Nurses came. I was suddenly suffused with absolute pain. Long days ago I had a life, had been happy or unhappy or whatever those terms meant. Two days ago it had been Christmas. We had knelt by the tree, Sinead in her rocker, Benedict as interested in the coloured paper and the boxes as the presents inside them. Two days or was it ten days? What was a day any longer? How could I ever leave the safety of this bed?

If I moved my head I could see a bag dripping slowly down into my arm. I had stopped cursing the medics who brought me back to life. I knew it was him, that surly face which I still could not place, it was he who had blocked my path.

When I was growing up an old man on my street had gradually turned senile. At night he would waken, gripped by an obsession to recall some obscure name or date. At first he could ask his wife beside him or knock apologetically on the bedroom door of his widowed daughter who had returned to help care for him. But soon his affliction grew so random and absurd that he would be found at five in the morning, clad in pyjamas at the phone box on the corner, trying to contact men he had not spoken to for thirty years. He'd stare at his daughter, bewildered, while she tried to soothe the angry voices coming through the receiver. Now, a quarter of a century later, I had become him.

That face came between me and everyone. I knew it, I had met it in some corner of my past. It could not have been anybody important or I would have remembered. A workmate, schoolmate, somebody I had photographed among a crowd at a corner, somebody who had found their image stolen and printed in a magazine, somebody seeking redress? How far back had I to go?

Once I woke fully. I could see myself, not indifferently from a height, but this time inside the wad of tranquillized pain which I had become, by just tilting my bandaged head to glimpse the smashed shoulder and plastered arm. I am using him, I thought, as a shield to keep this at bay. I have to focus on the present, people need me, I have to rebuild . . . But my mind was gone already, scavenging through the past. When I blacked back into sleep I saw his head turning as always. I woke to hear a party in the streets outside the hospital. There were church bells ringing, car horns, New Year celebrations. I felt his name about to come to my lips. I passed the eternity till my next blackout like a man choking on something in his throat.

Mostly I could not say that I really knew the difference between day or night there. I knew only a limbo of white ceiling, a dripping bag and faces passing over like clouds. Or else I slept, experiencing the most vivid of dreams. There was no year of my life that I did not partly relive. Communion on my tongue, bare knees offering their pain up for the souls in purgatory. Stained glass in winter, brass plaques on each varnished pew . . . *Pray for the souls of the Miss Healys.* The first taste of coned ice-cream from the van parked outside the unentered gates of those gardens where I had briefly died. A wardrobe falling on me and my being consoled with an overripe banana. Being held on my father's shoulders among the Shelbourne fans in Tolka Park while the visiting goalkeeper, convicted of receiving a stolen wireless, was taunted with chants of *Give it back!*

That first, unfocused memory of sitting on a ridge of dug earth, staring at the wriggling worm in my hand, with a sickly feeling in my mouth as if after having swallowed something unpleasant. The spinning wheel in the cramped cottage in Wexford where we once holidayed, the sense of damp, mildewed thatch and the sudden utter terror which I had felt, as though abandoned, as I stood on the stone flags while some local woman stared spitefully at me.

I am calling excitedly from the top of the stairs at home for the woman I called my mother to inspect the two light-brown turds which sway in the bowl, waiting to hear her say that I am her best little man. I begin to drift back further, but even in that state I stop myself, scared of what I might find.

Then I wake from nowhere. A nurse is calling for assistance. The drip has slipped from my vein. There is somebody standing near the bed, a woman, my wife. I sense her patient anxiety. I struggle to fully crest the surface of sleep, then cease trying. I become seventeen instead, at night in late summer on an overgrown verge beside the bridge across the canal. *What did it feel like when you found out you were adopted?* The girl can sense my resentment at her words like a force-field. For half an hour she has been using her hands and still she has not been able to make me come. I am holding back, frozen by her question. I want her to suck me in her mouth, where that hated word has come from. I move up her body, rocking back and forth, but when I look down in the moonlight it is not her

8

tight lips I am pressing against but the underside of her neck.

My first child is being born. They have taken my wife away and I am left alone in a filthy waiting room. Trapped smoke refuses to leave. Nurses are at a break in a building across the car-park. I can glimpse them passing a window with trays. I want to be with Geraldine, to share her pain in whatever way I can. I have never felt such cold sickness. I remember the frozen avenue I had run down in search of a taxi, how the driver had joked about never seeing me anywhere before without a camera, the way we let him talk on, too scared to speak ourselves as he drove through empty streets. My body is glass which any movement could shatter. A child of our own. I still cannot grasp the actuality of it. I have photographed blood a thousand times, yet when I see the first trace of it now will I faint? I am filled with intense physical love for the child to be born, boy or girl. I try to pray for the first time in years but am too scared to remember any words, except to repeat over and over *May it be healthy in mind and body, may it be safely born.*

As the nurse calls me in to join Geraldine, from nowhere I think of that anonymous woman whose features may perhaps echo my own. My real mother experiencing the pain which I am about to witness. Nobody would have been waiting for her in some isolated rural convent, except for the other girls in that same predicament. Mothers allowed to hold their children for a few seconds before the nuns took them away. From a curtained cubicle my wife tries to smile at me. *I want an epidural too*, I joke with her, wanting to be strong for her sake. But I find myself haunted by something I have not thought of for years: my total ignorance about my own birth.

Now I find myself trying to imagine my mother's face, the agony of her conflicting emotions. Frightened to feel love for the child she would be forced to give up, yet carrying me inside her like a precious gift. How did I know what she had felt? Maybe she had cursed me into birth, left me discarded on the table for some nun to clean away? A bloodied, unwanted ball of flesh. I have to stop myself thinking. The only detail I knew was that she had been nineteen. My wife gasps at a quickening contraction. I feel guilty for not focusing on her pain. The nurse comes and adjusts the dials beside her. *I just want to go home*, she keeps repeating in a constant moan.

And then my wife's face is replaced by that face which is haunting my sleep. A man of twenty-five with black hair and sallow skin. His smile is a knowing sneer, yet it is not unfriendly. I know him. I am more frightened of him than of anything I have ever feared. He is my real father, I think suddenly, the nameless bastard who ran away. I feel a quivering excitement, the exhilaration of release. I have him now, that figure I know nothing of, not even if he knew of my existence. That is how he must have looked the night I was conceived: sly and boorish, deceit in his heart and lust in his balls. That was why he looked familiar and I could not place him. They were my own features I was staring at, distorted and borne forward by genetics.

I stare at him in hatred. His sneer only broadens. He is not my father, I am not rid of him so easily. I want to wake from this drugged sleep, but even if I do he will be there with me. The obsession to place him takes over again. Those fragments of my past no longer seem mine. *Who are you, you bastard?* I want to say. He turns away, his hair becoming the dark unconsciousness which I am consumed back within.

I am being lifted on to a trolley by two men. I know I have

just had an injection without being able to remember receiving it. *Just a short journey, Mr Blake*, a female voice says. *It's Ó Direáin to you*, I hear myself begin to mumble. A shadow leans across to listen and tells her, *He's asking how your sister did in her Leaving Cert.*

There are lights, more voices. Try to stop breathing, I hear myself think. *We cannot put you out fully*, a male voice says, and then there is darkness, denser and more luxuriant than one could ever conceive. When the colours come flashing I find that I am just an eye observing, an unleashed pupil cruising inside my own brain. It could be outer space except that I know I am travelling inwards through layers of magnified crusts and textures, a patchwork universe of blood cells and fibres with one infinitesimal cleft which I gradually float towards.

Yet I know this time I am not dead. There will be no faces waiting, I am in the power of their drug. The initial euphoria fades. The journey is inescapable and impersonal; a dog, given the same drug, would experience these same wonders. And this is what makes it more frightening than dying. Because I am no longer even a soul, I am a mere speck free-floating through a fantasy land of chemistry. Above me I sense that masked men are working at my skull. Yet I cannot think of myself in proportion to them. There are palpitating coils of colour interloping about me, water wheels of static sparks, rings of arid planets turning inwards majestically. How quickly or slowly they revolve and dissolve is impossible to fathom. Could I think in human terms I would feel utterly lonely, but this landscape is bereft of emotion. Here I can only drift impetuously through the heart of each imploding star, straining to connect back to the opened body I had once been.

I try to focus on any memory: a wife's face, Sinead's

birth, carrying Benedict up a flight of dark stairs, unlocking the back door to fetch coal on a frost-sparkled night. Once such things meant something but now I am so removed that they just pass beyond my grasp, rendered meaningless. Death is as distant as life here. I know that I must leave this state and yet it seems impossible that I will ever fit back into my body again. I can begin to sense cold white lights blazing an infinity away. I become angry and frightened, desperately wanting to feel human once more.

The lights die. I am lifted on to a trolley, but it cannot be the same one as before. Because I have come back the wrong size. I am Gulliver now, a huge blubbery figure dwarfing everyone. Except that the two figures who wheel me are giants as well. I cling on to the trolley, terrified that if I fall I will crush the ordinary men and women in the blurred corridor who have stopped to stare upwards and then scatter before the trolley's rubber tyres that are turning like huge Ferris wheels.

I woke up. It was night-time. A new room in a new hospital. A phone was ringing somewhere. I could not tell how much time had passed. The pain inside my head was fierce but bearable. I could move it and see my injured shoulder and arm. My brain was clearer than at any time since the accident. I tried to move my toes, aware of them but worried that the sensation might be a phantom pain. It was impossible to see if anything moved. I prepared myself for the worst.

A mobile receiver hooked up beside me had two yellow buttons with light bulbs sketched on them and a red one embossed with the outline of a nurse's head. I tried to reach my good arm over but failed. I opened my mouth, straining to make the faintest sound. To my surprise a scream came out. There were footsteps and the door opened.

'You're back with us, Mr Blake,' the night sister said.

'My legs? Tell me, are my legs still there?' As I spoke I realized how blurred my voice was.

'We've had the odd pickpocket here in our time,' she smiled, 'but nobody's ever stolen a pair of healthy legs. Rest yourself now, you're after a serious operation. They had to drain fluid from your brain, but you'll make a full recovery if you'll only rest.'

My mouth was dry. I wanted water, but needed to speak more.

'What else did they do to me?'

'The doctor will see you in the morning.'

'Tell me now.'

'You mightn't feel it, but you got off lightly. Any scars will be above the hairline. Nobody will see them unless baldness runs in your family. Two ribs cracked, a fracture of the arm and one of the shoulder. It will take a while but you're going to be fine.'

There was a television and a crucifix facing me in the wood-panelled room. A plastic bottle of holy water with a blue cap looked incongruous among the drips and cables near the bed. The lights of north Dublin were below me. I recognized the blazing floodlights of Dalymount Park.

'The Leinster Senior Cup Final,' I said. 'The fifth of January. Bohs are playing at home. I wish I was there.'

'Do you follow Bohemians?' she asked.

'No, Shelbourne, born, bred and buttered. I hate Bohs. But I'd sooner be watching that shower of wasters than lying here.'

'Somehow I think you'll recover.' She smiled at the old joke. 'Now try to go back asleep.'

'Sister . . .?'

She had turned to go back to her desk. My brief cockiness

was gone. I had to tell another person, but felt somehow ashamed. She waited, still smiling.

'I don't know for how long, but I was dead, wasn't I?'

'Your chart says so. Your heart stopped briefly. It's actually not uncommon.'

'How do people feel . . . afterwards?'

'There was a priest here earlier. I think he hasn't left the hospital if you'd like me to . . .'

'No, I want no truck with those fellows. You must have met people like me before. Tell me.'

She looked behind her. The corridor was empty. I could see the open book on the desk where she had been sitting behind a monitor. Her professional smile was gone. She looked more relaxed without it.

'There's proper counselling you can get,' she said. 'We can arrange for you to start it tomorrow.'

'Talk to me, please. Tell me what you know.'

'Jesus, I really shouldn't be doing this.'

She shook her head and smiled again, only now it was natural and slightly uncertain.

'Any I've met have all felt the same at first. Bitter to be alive, cheated. Don't ask me why, I hate the thought of death, but they . . . you . . . we have to watch people like you carefully in case you try to go back there. You're alive, Mr Blake, think of all the hundreds of thousands every year who never get this second chance at life. Now try to sleep, please.'

She closed the door. I felt less alone for her words, for the thought that others had felt this same overwhelming grief at being brought back to life. From the view I could pinpoint where I was now: a private room in the Bon Secours on Washerwoman's Hill. Only two hundred yards from here my car had crashed into a bus at the gates of the

Botanic Gardens. One of the last things I could remember was passing these discreet hospital gates, glancing up the long sweeping lawn towards these high windows. Moments later I had been clinically dead. I relived the collision in the same slowed motion with which it had occurred. It could have taken only two or three seconds, but within that time there seemed a long sequence of emotions, from utter terror into a mesmeric fascination. Yet now it felt as if the crash was a rendezvous which I had been racing for half a decade to keep. My life over those years seemed to have been spent soaking up pressure, sliding imperceptibly out of control, frantically seeking some way to halt its own momentum.

There was a remote control beside the bed. I pressed the buttons with the volume down. The ABC news from America was being relayed on a satellite station. There seemed to be a slow-moving foreign film on another channel. Geraldine's voice came back to me, the first time I brought her to see a Bergman film: *It's like watching Athlone Town play at home.* Geraldine. Her voice was real, but she wasn't. I was afraid that she would come in. The reception on the television was murky, the image slightly out of focus. It was a white altar with a wooden crucifix above a tabernacle draped in purple. Gradually I realized that it was a video camera trained on the altar in the hospital chapel so that patients could pray in their beds. A cleaner in an apron came into view and began to hoover the carpet around the altar. I felt uncomfortable, like a voyeur.

I turned the television off and found myself trying to smile. This was the nearest hospital to my home, but still, for an atheist like myself to wake up on my first time in hospital and find that the nuns had got me in the end . . . The smile faded.

It was not my first time in the care of nuns. But it had

been no luxury private room back then, no call bell for nurses to come running. Pregnant girls on their knees scrubbing floors or put to work in the laundry; infants in iron cots, like post in a sorting office waiting to be dispersed; the beeswax scent of shame and disapproval. Suddenly I wanted to know my real mother's name, why she had given me up, what had become of her. Perhaps I was being given this second life as a second chance not to turn my back on her. This time I managed to press the call bell.

'Water to drink,' I told the night sister, 'and take that hocus-pocus holy water the hell out of here.'

She held the glass to my lips and helped ease my head back on to the pillows. She went to close the curtains and I asked her to leave them unpulled. A taxi passed the hospital gates with their twin globes of light. A few lights shone in the apartment blocks by the river. A crane was discernible to the left of the black shapes of the arboretum of the Botanic Gardens. I remembered how they had been working all winter on restoring the largest cast-iron Victorian glasshouse; and remembered also that, after I had died, the same Great Palm glasshouse which I had gazed down on had no hoardings around it, no scaffolding and no crane. The memory was more vivid than my conversation with the night sister a few moments before. Behind the arboretum the O'Connell Monument was lit up in the cemetery where my adoptive parents were buried. I had always hated the desolation of that place, its mosaic of headstones beneath the bent yew trees. Now it seemed welcoming, like a doorway through which I knew the finest of friends were gathered, wondering what was keeping me.

A mile to the north, in an old estate between Griffith Avenue and Ballymun, a woman slept alone in the bed where we had conceived two children. I was being given this second chance, for her also and for their sakes. Then why could I not focus on the love I felt for them? My eyes had come to rest on that black mass of trees. His surly face came back and it seemed to belong there. *Aesculus.* I did not know where the word came from, only that it belonged out in that darkness of trees as well. I closed my eyes. I saw the old yew-tree walk there as it must be now in that moonless night, the two green benches covered with bird shit, the gnarled intertwining trunks that had withstood centuries of storm.

But the place seemed to involve me now. When I was ten a gardener had told me that the yew walk was haunted by a monk from the time when the ground was part of a monastery. Ever since then I had loved to pause there on the narrow sloping path. But now I felt that my fascination with the tunnel of ancient trees went much further back, that I had used the gardener's story to explain away the curious sensation I always felt there, that another story existed, buried like that young man's face somewhere in my past, and if I could only unlock it everything would make sense.

Chapter Two

Elizabeth heard the crash and woke. It was so close that she thought a car must have taken the corner wide, sliced through the railings and struck the wall of the bungalow. The cold light beyond the double glazing told her it was late, maybe ten o'clock in the morning. She stared guiltily at the bedside clock, wondering if anyone had been in to spy on her and guess from the fact that she was still sleeping how she had gone walkabout the night before. It was Sharon's husband, Steve, who gave them the phrase: 'Your mother's Irish, not Aborigine. This is Coventry. She can't just go walkabout with her spear.'

She moved to the window and stared out at the untouched square of lawn and the painted railings. The estate was empty, as it always was at this time. The lights of Christmas trees flickered in a few porch windows. The procession of older women was already gone beyond the corner, the slow thread of their shopping trolleys as they stocked up on milk and bread. The younger couples who had moved in recently would not be back at work, but still there was no sign of children playing out on the street. Thirty years ago how different it had been: skipping ropes, the thud of footballs, the bootsteps of young boys always haunting her.

The street was still, yet she knew that she had heard a crash, so close and so real that her nerves were jangling. It had not been a dream because the drugs meant that she no longer dreamt. It had been something real, beyond this house, a noise which had cut into her. Now the echo of chrome striking chrome was trapped like a missing name in her head. She took her hand away from the window, watching the moist outline of her fingers vanish from the pane.

She had to be gone from the house. It did not matter what the nurse might say or what threats her daughters would make. She had to be out walking. She dressed with furious concentration to overcome the pain, glaring at the wall phone, defying it to ring and prevent her. The street was still empty, but none of the neighbours would speak to her now anyway. Mr Grace was the only one there as long as her; those faces which appeared in the last decade had remained only faces.

The playground of the school by the Airport Road was empty. There were normally more coloured boys and girls than whites now. Often she would stop to watch them, still trapped into that habit. She walked on, her hair blown by the slipstream of the trucks, searching to find the crash. When the police discovered her that evening, walking along the motorway in her slippers, the woman constable wrote down the only words she could discern from her mumbling: *It was him. I know it was Paudi. My baby's dead and he'll never find me now.*

Above all back then in the fifties she had hated the London underground, the way people pushed forward as the lights of the train came out from the tunnel and how the tracks loomed temptingly before her in those seconds before the carriages careered to a halt. Even when you left the Slieve Blooms you married back into them, you met boys from Roundwood and Dunross and Ballyfin and Cooltrain in the Ierne in Dublin or the Big Top in Cricklewood, you became yourself with them again. Letters were sent home, the two families meeting on market day in Mountrath, standing in the rain among the tractors and ponies and racks of boots and great coats, marvelling at how you had found each other and how wise it was to marry into your own.

Even when you left home you re-created home elsewhere. The *Nationalist and Leinster Times* coming torn through the letter box, the calls made from phone boxes on Christmas Eve to the post office and Mrs Branagan screeching at one of her children to race across the road for your mother.

Lizzy Sweeney boarded the tube and tried not to stare at the black man towards the end of the carriage. She climbed up the steps into the night amongst a shoal of alien voices. There was jazz music and minerals and a balcony. A globe of mirrors sprinkled coloured light over the dancers. Down below she still hurt, her flesh felt twisted and she winced when passing water. But the hollow ache inside her stomach was what consumed her, begging to be filled. Across that foreign city girls she had run to school with in Dunross were now gathered before a smudged cloakroom mirror, boys were talking about her brother Tom in the seminary, asking about sightings of her.

'Everybody on to the floor,' the MC was saying into the microphone. 'There's only thirteen minutes to go to 1958.' Someone grabbed her arm. Before she had turned her head Lizzy Sweeney decided to give herself to an Englishman.

The maternity hospital in Coventry was cheerful but cold. In all its disapproving greyness the convent in Sligo had been warmer. A sinner among her own. The screams of the Roscommon girl in the next bed almost synchronized with her own. Here, in this half-rebuilt city, she had not been able to tell what Jack's family thought of her or of the fact that nobody from her family was at the Register Office. 'Elizabeth' was the name Jack told her to give people. She was his wife now; Lizzy was a skivvy's name.

'Catholics', she had heard someone say at the party afterwards as if that single word could explain everything about her. She held her stomach in and tried to cope with their accents. *When my boy is born it will be different*, she told herself, *when this longing has eased, when I know that nobody can snatch him from my arms this time*. She had not expected Jack's offer of marriage. Those few thrusts in that laneway with the cold stone against her buttocks while a single green firework drifted into the slot of sky between the two dark buildings and the bells of London rang out. One hand grasping his shoulder and the other holding her skirt while she pressed her face away every time he tried to kiss her. And when his breath came shorter her nails had dug into the seat of his trousers, as if to thrust his seed deeper into the empty void in her womb. The pain did not matter any more, or the stains on her skirt, or how he looked at her when he stepped back and said, 'Christ, you're no more than nineteen. I bet it's your first time, isn't it? I can tell by the tightness of you, girl.'

The Sunday after they were married he had shown her the same photograph printed twice in the *Sunday Express*. It was of Joseph Stalin with a group of Soviet generals. 'Look,' he said, 'how simple it is to make somebody vanish.' In the second copy of the photograph one of the generals had been airbrushed out and a pillar superimposed in his place. 'Poor blighter's either shot by now or else digging up the salt for our dinner.' Lizzy half listened to him explaining show trials, knowing how much he enjoyed passing on scraps of knowledge, as though he could shape her mind to blend into his world. She thought of all the homes in Dunross, the photographs of the eleven girls who made their confirmation in the 1948 class with a space which had appeared in the centre; and how in the photograph, cut from the *Nationalist* and framed above the teacher's desk in the classroom with the three high windows, the Laois county cup for camogie was left hanging in midair now that the Dunross captain in her green skirt had vanished.

'Do I look thirty?' he used to say before they were married, coming up to London to visit her at weekends. 'Do I? Eleven years between us. There's nobody would ever know. I'll look after you if anything goes wrong, I promise I will. Penis. Say the word. I love it when you blush like that. Penis. Say it. I want to hear the way you say it in your Irish accent. That's a sin to you Catholics to even say, isn't it? No need for your priests here. Lie over that knee. I'll be gentle. One little slap, see, and all's forgiven. Lie back, close your eyes, pretend I'm a nigger . . .'

Her eyes were already closed. She saw the nuns' car ascend the crumbling mountain road over the Slieve Blooms and the long sweep of valley behind her where pricks of light glimmered from milking sheds. That silence they drove in, squeezed between Sister Theresa and her father, each sitting in the grainy hint of first light as though cased in cement, and how the only colour left in the world had been the red bruise from her father's belt, which had loosened two of her teeth.

If Jack did not love her, then he loved what he thought of as her. He loved the way that she obeyed him. He loved the notion of having been the first to have her body on that New Year's Eve in London. He loved her unEnglishness, though he hated Frogs, Wops and niggers. English girls wanted everything. They came with families who made him nervous that he would not be able to keep up with them. He loved Lizzy's isolation without questioning it and, Christ, how he loved her body.

And she loved the feel of a child inside her and loved him for giving that feeling back to her. And if he ran away, then this time she would keep the child; even if she had to claw at them with her nails, nobody would force her to sign away her own flesh again. And she loved Jack because he did not run away, because – when he found out – he stopped coming to London and made her take the train to Coventry instead. And when he showed her the room in the bungalow which he had done up for the child to sleep in she broke down and could not stop crying, while he hovered about feeling awkward and masculine.

'Your first baby?' the nurse in Coventry asked. 'Forget everything you've been told about it, because nothing can prepare you for what's ahead.' The ward was filled with flowers and cards, English accents. There was dance music from a wireless in some room off the corridor. Where were those girls now? she asked herself. The girls who had worked with her in the convent kitchens in Sligo, the girls who scrubbed the floors in the laundry, the bloated girls who had stopped work only when the labour pains came? Where were the other girls who were sent by the nuns to work for their board in rich homes in Dublin and Cork? The ones who cooked and washed the houses and were never let out of doors? And where were all those babies? And, though she tried to stop the thought coming, where was her own? Padraig, Paudi. A boy with the bluest eyes, a boy who had cried while she struggled to teach him to suck at her breast.

The screens opened around a woman's bed and she was wheeled out into the corridor. *Little Boy Blue*, Lizzy said,

Little Boy Blue. She stroked her stomach, willing him out. During the labour the English midwife said to her suspiciously, 'Are you sure this is your first?' She pushed through the pain, she screamed the boy out. She closed her eyes, Sister Theresa and the other nuns came into her mind, she felt panic. 'Give him back, give him back!'

'Shout if you want,' the midwife said. 'Any nonsense. Just shout with the pain and push.'

'Bitches . . .!' The scream was so long that nobody could decipher the word. It was like trying to pass a camogie ball from her body. And in the searing heave of pain she saw his face, the morning she had put Paudi into his cot, the morning she had not known he would have been taken by the nuns to prepare for his journey when she returned from her duties. She felt the panic again with which she had ripped at the blankets that were cold.

'The head is out,' the midwife said. 'A last push, a last . . . you have a beautiful, beautiful little girl.'

Elizabeth's eldest daughter, Sharon, was waiting at the doorway of the bungalow when the police car arrived. This area had changed so much since she was a child. Even at Christmas things that could happen to her mother walking the city at night were not thinkable. Those new council flats were trouble. There would be riots here yet.

There had been nothing to suggest that this would happen to her mother. But maybe there were signs which their father had kept hidden. The house was spotless, as it had always been. Sharon could not remember a time when it was unclean. Even when she met people from the estate today they still said, 'You're the *Irishwoman's* daughter.' Never Mrs Wilkins's daughter. As a child she had hated the perpetual inspection of hands and nails, the way her mother refused to let her go back out to play if her skirt was even flecked with dirt. Any relation of her father who called without warning was left standing on the path while her mother ran about the spotless house, cleaning and polishing things that were already clean, shoving their heads under the sink to wash their hair, working herself up into a state before she opened the door.

Sharon knew her mother's life had been a constant inspection, but an inspection partly inside her own head. Her father was a quiet man. She had only ever seen him weep once, when Coventry finally won the FA Cup. He had never been able to discipline them, bringing them crisps on Fridays, leaving everything else to their mother. He had his tool shed and the solace of grease and spanners. An avalanche of rusted washers and screws poured from wooden presses when she had begun to clear the shed after his sudden death. She found pipe tobacco mixed with orange peel to keep it fresh, the placard he had carried in the 1972 strike carefully wrapped in plastic. Snapshots of his three grandchildren were tacked to the shelf at head height. She heard their delighted laughter again when he gave them swings around the lawn. There were wood shavings on the floor from the rocking horse he had been finishing for her youngest child. Something told her that she should stop, should put his ashes in that shed and the padlock back on and then set it alight, like Aunt Ellen had told her Irish tinkers did when someone died. She opened a plastic refuse sack and began to clear the old tins of congealed paint from the higher shelves, lifting down the newspapers, biting her lip but not crying as she handled the mildewed copies of *Janus*, *Blushes* and *Spanking Letters*.

She had never asked him about her mother's disappearances. Four times in her childhood she had woken to find her missing, her father shaking her shoulder, telling her to get her two younger sisters dressed. Sitting in class, convinced the teachers knew, hissing at her sisters to say nothing as they raced around the playground at break. The first time she had been only five but she remembered that week: neighbours in to cook their dinner, standing in the dark bedroom to peer through the lace curtain at the squad car parked outside the house, reciting their ages like a nursery rhyme to everyone who asked – *five, three years, eight months.* And the sense of being abandoned, so terrifying that she had retreated from it, had played with her toys in the front room the night that her mother was brought home by Aunt Ellen, had refused to kiss or be kissed, had woken and felt the warm gush of urine spreading out to drench the sheet with a vengeful thrill.

Aunt Ellen had been the one to find her mother, that time and every other time. Aunt Ellen, who had joked with Sharon and coaxed her to climb the fence and steal the daffodils from next door to run in and give to her mother. And how good it felt to be wrapped up in those arms once more, asking between sobs, *Where were you, Mama? Where were you?*

Aunt Ellen, who came to stay after every disappearance. *Lough Derg on pilgrimage,* she'd reply to all questions. *The woman's a saint. Beating the stones with her bare feet!* And it was Aunt Ellen who gave their mother a past for them, who called her Lizzy and made her a girl like themselves, only a dozen times bolder: running out into the moonlight to sit on a tombstone in Dunross graveyard for a bet; screaming with laughter as she played camogie – 'hockey where you could beat the heads off each other without it being a sin' – in a field full of weeds and sheep shite; swimming naked in the lake by the trees where they dumped the carcasses of stillborn calves. And when the girls ran in to ask if it was true, their mother would come out to glare at Aunt Ellen, who would light another cigarette and cackle with such laughter that they all joined in, watching the different person their mother became as tears filled her eyes and she leaned against the kitchen door, bent over as though a key had just unleashed the laughter locked deep inside her.

The squad car came to a halt and the door opened. Sharon came forward to take her mother by the arm.

'Your painkillers, you haven't taken them for hours. For God's sake, Mammy, are you trying to kill yourself?'

Her mother's eyes were very clear. She stopped on the path, looking back towards the road.

'Maybe he's not dead, it was just a bad fright. Maybe my Little Boy Blue is still alive after all.'

Sharon's anger was gone. She moved her mother towards the door.

'Daddy's dead, Mammy,' she said softly. 'You agreed to let us cremate him. You know that, Mammy. These two years dead now.'

They would get Ellen down from Reading. Like they always did. Ellen was the only one who could bring her back to herself, the only one who understood the two worlds she lived in. She would be here in the morning. Now the agency nurse was reading her paperback in the kitchen under the Christmas decorations, the television on with the sound off in case it disturbed her. When the nurse looked in she would feign sleep so as to be left alone.

She remembered the Christmas Tom Maguire from the forge at Clonincurragh lured them in on their way home from Mountrath, the horses patient and steaming as he beat shoes from the metal. Tom Maguire, who dug graves for Protestants, had scared them with stories as a frosty dusk took its grip on the road they had to travel up past the forest. The man he dug up with wood beneath his finger nails, the knocking you could hear from the vault by the east wall of the graveyard. And she and Ellen and the others had run past the winking trees, their bare legs cold, their stomachs empty and each shrieking to frighten the others, petrified and thrilled as the dogs barked across the valley.

This was how the man in his coffin had felt. Elizabeth had to be out of that bed and back on the streets, walking in the lights of trucks on the Airport Road, standing hunched by the gates of the school where a ghetto blaster blared from somewhere in the dark yard, circling the estate in the middle of the road where the cars no longer even beeped at her. She felt the room suffocating her, the curtains pulled against the street lights under which she had dreamt that she would meet her son when he came to find her.

Ten years had passed since she had dreamt that dream twice in one night, waking beside Jack to find her arms stretched out in greeting, her body swamped with exhilaration which faded to disbelief. Wanting to wake Jack and say that she had dreamt Paudi was coming, except that in all those years she had never been able to tell her husband the truth. She had fallen asleep again to have the same dream repeated. The young man at night asking her directions to the estate and she, with her heart beating, inquiring which house number he wanted. When he had just smiled and walked a few feet on she had called the name the nuns had let her give him, and as he turned she had woken again and known it would come true, and crept down the stairs to phone Ellen in Reading.

'I know he's coming to find me, I dreamt it, I know, I

know.' Half laughing and crying on the phone in the dark hall while Ellen tried to calm her down. The last of the girls had left that year. Susan in white walking up the aisle to be handed over by her father to a black man, and later at the reception how comic Jack looked, agreeing with the bridegroom's father about how England had changed: two grey heads, one white and one black, bent companionably to complain about Asians.

The house was empty then, no one to upset its silent order. Jack, home from work, hammering away in his tool shed after *Coronation Street*, not even noticing when she slipped out for milk that she was gone for hours. It was embarrassing being seen there by the boulder with the estate's name in gold lettering that the new Residents Association had erected. But this was where he would meet her. She could not wait in the house, she had to be there, a sign on his path like the candle they used to put in the window on Christmas Eve. Wearing the same old coat as in the dream, even though when winter came she caught a cold from not choosing something heavier.

But maybe Paudi could not find the estate, maybe he wasn't even sure of her married name, maybe he just knew which city she had settled in. She began to create a circuit, always walking in the one direction, always waiting at certain spots, afraid to go any further in case she missed him.

Sharon's husband didn't live in that part of Coventry. What right had he to start following her in his car? The family conference, the three married couples dropping in on the one night as though by accident. If she wanted to walk it was her own business. She did not have to be going anywhere, she could wear that old coat if she wanted to. She could see Jack dwarfed by his sons-in-law, bewildered, wanting to be back out under the bare bulb in his tool shed. Even Susan had been changed by a year of marriage. She felt a disappointment which she could never confess to them. They were her flesh and blood and yet they were foreigners, dulled by Englishmen. She had cared for their every need, going without sleep willingly when they were young, rocking them on her knee when they first discovered the fickleness of boys, crying at their weddings. Yet none of them had ever replaced her first-born.

She heard the light click off in the kitchen. The nurse would be curled up in her sleeping bag on the sofa now, the alarm clock set to give her her medicine at six in the morning. *Cry out if you're in pain*, the nurse had said. How long more would it be before they put her into the hospital? Six months the doctor had said; that could mean anything. *Let me die at home.* They hated her using that word. It gave her power over them, caused them to feel a guilt which allowed her to be left alone.

Ellen would be here in the morning and Ellen would make her laugh. Ellen with three months' back copies of *Ireland's Own*.

'Come up to Reading and visit the Irish Club,' Ellen would say. 'God, you might even bring me luck at the bingo. Mary McCann who married that buck eejit from Kinnitty is always asking for you. Remember he used to always be mooching about in the great heavy coat in summer to disguise the arse out of his trousers?'

'Paudi's going to come, Ellen. I know it. I can't leave here. I have to wait for him.'

And she would know by Ellen's face that her sister did not believe her.

'Lizzy, you're dying. Come away back to Ireland for a visit with me. Down to Dunross just once. Sure people have long forgotten that business. Most of the babies born these days in Mountrath wouldn't know a father if they fell over one. Joey Hammond has the farm now, but everyone would welcome you with open arms. We'll visit Father Tom up in Cavan even, it's time these things were patched up in the family. It was Mammy's funeral the last time you were home. Would you not come back with me this once?'

And she would give Ellen the same reply as she always did, that she would not go home without her son. The day he found her she would hire a car from Dublin airport to the door of the post office at Dunross, but she would not go home after all this time alone and shamed.

The drugs were drawing her under. There would be no dreams tonight, just darkness, and when she woke Ellen would be coming. She would tell Ellen about hearing the crash in her mind and beg her to phone every hospital in Dublin. She had no name, just a date of birth. But that might be enough. If she could only pray she would pray that he was not badly hurt and that any pain he was feeling might be passed on instead for her to suffer. And that Paudi might be one day closer to finding her. Tomorrow.

Chapter Three

This is the first portrait: a moonlit hallway with a brass chain on the locked front door. Above it the street glimmers in through a hammered pane of glass. Framed photographs, high enough up to be child-proof, line the wall leading down to what was once a tiny kitchen, where I squat on a toilet seat, naked and barely discernible in the shadows, as I stare back out down the hallway.

I occupy only a corner of the lens. It is the meagre shaft of January moonlight down the narrow hallway which draws the viewer's eye, the angular shape of the picture frames, the pale glint of taps in the background. Only at the third or fourth glance would the viewer notice what might be a figure gazing out at them peering in at him, and even then they would still be unsure if it was not just a trick of the shadow-strewn half-light.

Perhaps it was because I had never taken one myself, or had never allowed anyone else to take a photograph of me, that I spent so many idle moments after coming out of hospital setting up imaginary self-portraits in my mind.

After the stay in hospital my house no longer felt like mine. Geraldine had been told that the important thing was that I totally rested, at least until I went back for more tests on my heart, and so I slept in the spare room, where I would be least disturbed. Sinead was teething. I would half wake to the noise of crying which stopped when Geraldine's footsteps reached the cot. I always meant to rise and go into her, to help by holding the child or the spoon, but I would

A Second Life

drift away again and find that it was morning when I woke. I listened to the house rising without me, Benedict being dressed downstairs, Geraldine rushing up with a tray when the baby was fed.

The spare bedroom doubled as my storeroom, filled with old lens boxes, contact sheets and unanswered correspondence. A desk was piled with material which I was perpetually promising to sort through. It felt curious to wake up among all those things which had seemed too important to throw out even though I had known they would never be used again. And yet, through that month of January, I found it easier to adjust back to life there than in the bedroom next door which we had so carefully decorated together.

In the spare room I was both a part of the house and yet outside it. Often during the day I might have been a ghost at the window, listening to the sounds of life below me, knowing that the daily routine would still have occurred if I had not survived. After the time in hospital my legs had little strength. I found it disturbing that, even during the day, I kept drifting between consciousness and sleep. I would wake up, disoriented and vaguely afraid, to find my wife coming into the room with a tray. Although Geraldine had promised to let nobody near me, whenever cars pulled up I would sweat, plucking at the curtains irrationally and yet afraid to stare out. The nurse had told me it was not uncommon, but still I felt a freak. The Walking Dead. I wanted to be left alone among that bric-à-brac and not be forced to celebrate the miracle of my survival with anyone.

If the caller remained at the door for any period my breathing would quicken, a tightness starting to grip my chest. I would feel my fingers stiffen and buckle into cramped shapes, my legs starting to twitch before Geraldine closed the door and ran up to calm me down. Panic attacks, the doctor called them. She held my hand, fighting her own fear as she slowed my breathing down.

For four years my life had been neatly divided in two. Three days a week I worked on contract for the newspaper, doing whatever jobs I decided in advance, coexisting more easily with Gerry and the other journalists than with the staff photographers on the photo desk. Those evenings I came home joking, happy to laugh with Geraldine and swing Benedict in my arms. The other days were for my own projects. Geraldine learnt to leave me alone when I came in on those evenings, knowing that I needed time to adjust from the intimacy of my private world back into the one I shared with her.

When I began a series of photographs I was superstitious about discussing them with anyone, afraid that, brought prematurely out into the world, my unfocused ideas would appear cold and retarded. Now everything I had experienced since the crash seemed as precious and unformed in my mind.

Even with Geraldine I could not speak of my grief. I knew how much my silence hurt her, how desperately hard these weeks had been and how, every time she closed my door, her smile would fade away into a look of glazed exhaustion. At night sometimes I woke to find her kneeling beside the bed, checking that I was all right, wanting me to wake so that she could put her arms around me. *Go back to bed, you big chancer*, I would say, and her smile would be filled with relief and elation. This was the time to talk, the way we first used to when our bodies were drenched after sex, but I knew no words to share this isolation with her.

It was usually late at night when my thinking was really done. Often I woke with a pain in my bladder which, although it eased after I passed water, never seemed to fully disappear. Ten years ago a new kitchen had been built on to the house and the cell-like old kitchen was converted into a spare toilet. Squatting there at night, I remembered the day when we had bought the house and the deeds were pressed briefly into my hands in a pretence of ownership before being taken away again by the building society.

Glancing through the names of previous owners, I had felt that the house could never be mine or anyone's. The house existed independently as itself, the walls absorbing the various lives which had been lived within them. The Garda sergeant who had owned the house before us seemed to have taken an evening course in advanced architectural vandalism. The old banisters had been knocked down and a partition erected so that upstairs could be set in flats. The fireplaces had been removed and dumped, the old windows taken out and cheap new ones with picture-frame glass inserted in their place. He had built the new kitchen himself by working at night under floodlights. When he was finished the house had been rendered characterless. Our four years there had been a constant struggle to restore as much as we could.

Yet squatting there at night it did not seem to matter what I or anyone else had done to the house. I know that the painkillers had left me disoriented, but it felt as if the walls were breathing those lives back out, the way leaves expel oxygen at night, and that this moment, which I took to be the present, was just one random fragment of a progression stretching backwards and forwards. If I could only see it, the hallway would be one continuous blur of movement. Children in black boots stomping across patterned lino; a toddler proudly shuffling out in his father's shoes; a woman cooking a pig's head, passing right through me to open the back door at the sound of a bicycle in the lane; a girl allowing herself to be pressed back against the door and kissed, her skirted legs opening and closing around a boy's spread hand.

For eighty-five years people had been passing in and out of that same front door before me – women with the stigma of childbirth leaving the house for the first time to be cleansed by being churched; scrubbed children waiting to join the Corpus Christi procession at the church gates; a jigging boy cursing his sister before rushing out into the frosty morning to climb over the wall of the roofless toilet in the park; a father and son joining the throng walking down to see Drumcondra play Shamrock Rovers. All those lives which I could only guess at by names and dates on the deeds, and all the others, the sergeant's tenants whose names were not recorded, their sounds of laughter and of poverty, of bulging pay packets and of tickets for the boat train to London.

In those seconds after that crash my life had been taken away from me and then given back. Every moment from now on was a bonus to be savoured if I could only focus on the present. But, although I knew that it was a mixture of painkillers and imagination, at those times sitting in that half-light, straining to release the final trickle of urine, I felt a numbed version of the irrational terror I remembered as a tiny child standing alone in front of that woman in the cottage in Wexford.

That was why I would sit for hours, framing an imaginary photograph in my mind, filled with a sudden and desperate need to leave some proof that this moment had existed.

Critics always confused me. Those columnists confidently talking about concise meanings and themes in an exhibition. I never consciously thought in those terms. My photographs were simply photographs. They were moments which I had cheated from time, which I had framed from my own will out of the randomness of life. This was a personal and intimate war, not between me and the people I photographed but between my will and the headlong slippage of time. The feel of a camera had always absorbed me totally. It frightened me at first, as though the clinical yet passionate figure I became when holding one was a second self who had been waiting to be unleashed.

Even as a small child I had seen the world in frames. It was what had made me seem odd and fuzzy to others. Confronted by a teacher, I would put my hands up to my face and frame a section of him with my fingers.

When I was four the two girls next door brought me to the pictures and I cried among the darkened seats after the show began. I had expected real pictures on the walls – Donald Duck, Pluto, Popeye the Sailor Man – and that I would be able to walk from one to the next and stare at them like the Stations of the Cross. I felt cheated by the film, each image snatched from me by a succeeding one before I had time to absorb it. I wanted the film to go backwards, to be able to control its pace and see it all again slowly and properly. The girls hushed and hissed at me and finally had to bring me home, complaining to my mother.

There was nothing of my father's work in the house. Once, as a very young boy, he had lifted me up into the attic, where I had glimpsed the neat stacks of negatives and the darkroom chemicals which he no longer used. But I never thought of him in relation to photographs or that those bottles labelled *developer* and *fixer* contained the alchemy of light and shade. I saw him only as a van driver and mistook his modesty about photography – the second of his two loves, after Shelbourne – for shame.

The only pictures in the house were two cheap prints on the living-room wall – both idealized glimpses of rural England. One was a large house with stone flowerpots and rows of steps, the other a sleepy turning with an old inn and a church spire shaded by mature trees. They were the earliest details I could recall about my home. There seemed no time in my life when I did not close my eyes at night and, by savouring the most minute detail of them, feel a solace which real parks and real trees never gave.

Yet I never asked for a camera. When I was nine I began cutting the coupons from the back of the cornflakes boxes and storing them in my bedside locker. It was several weeks before my mother noticed.

'A camera,' she said. 'Isn't your father a photographer, for God's sake? Why didn't you ask him? I'm sure he has an old one up in the attic. He might teach you to use it if there is something you want to photograph.'

But I went on collecting the coupons. My father's name was never on any of the postcards he sold, just the Italian-sounding name of the company he worked for. Very occasionally in town he would stop in front of a rack outside a shop and point out which images were his. They were bland images of Ireland: lakes and cliffs at sunset, O'Connell Street with dark-green open-decked buses. They were printed garishly, the glaring colours adding to the static air of unreality about them. He would show me how they had carefully airbrushed Nelson's Pillar out after it was blown up. He always seemed slightly embarrassed telling me about his work and I would stare at them with the same dull sense of duty as I always felt knotting my bright red tie to wear with a white shirt to Mass on Sundays.

I wanted my own camera with which to take my own

photographs. I didn't want him bringing them home developed, spreading them on the table to inspect like a school report. Walking around, I imagined the shots which I would take in my mind. One morning two horses came wandering down the street, leaving a motif of hoofs on the neat lawns. I cursed the camera for not arriving, watching the younger children standing timidly on the doorsteps while the older ones ran about excitedly shouting after the animals.

When the camera came there was a free film with it. I had it used up within the first hour, but I still went on pretending that there was film left, getting neighbours to pose in their gardens, waiting at the corner for the bus to pull away and the conductor to toss a bus roll to the shouting boys, my finger clicking away as they jeered me and the long coil of blank paper fanned out in the wind.

The chemist had his Christmas display of Old Spice and Talc already in the window, the bottles arranged on a background of red crêpe paper. A tall machine told your weight for a penny. There was a smell of dust and dried wood. He was never visible when I entered the shop. I waited in the dim light beside the trays of combs and barley sweets, listening to the clank of pills being counted into coloured bottles behind the partition.

'Can't your father develop this for you free in work?' he asked when I handed it to him. I said nothing and the chemist winked. 'Secret documents photographed, is it? The Man from U.N.C.L.E. wouldn't be up to you.'

It took four days for the film to be developed. Each afternoon I called to the chemist in case it came early. I had my pocket money saved in two slim piles of silver and copper on the ledge beside the Sacred Heart lamp at home. The pictures were bitterly disappointing. The objects which my eyes had focused on were only small blurs in the black and white background. The chemist told me that they cost four shillings and seven pence. The man was stout, with a perpetual cough and grey threads of hair on his white coat. His face looked like granite. I promised to bring the money tomorrow. Instead I bought another roll of film from a chemist in the village. I put the photographs down a drain on the way home and told my mother they had not come out. For the next year I ran to the village every time I was asked to get something from the chemist and pretended that I had been to the local one. When I finally had to go in with my mother the man had either forgotten or else had decided not to give me away.

This is the next portrait: a converted attic over a shop. The skylight hints of clouds. There are blackout blinds which can be pulled to make it a darkroom. The figure kneeling cross-legged on the floor seems totally immersed in the piles of contact sheets spread around him. It is only when you stare closely that you discern the glazed, withdrawn expression in his eyes.

The middle of February came and still I wasn't working. I was hiding, I am not sure from what. The newspaper kept up my contract, their cheque still came in the post, and every day I went to my private studio. I felt that if I could only start taking photographs again, then two decades of instinct would take over. I could work through this lethargy. But I felt disconnected from every photograph in my files.

In old movies men wake up from accidents with amnesia. They stare at the women who claim to be their wives, the children who call them father. They wonder, who is this stranger gazing out from the passport found in their pocket? If only they could remember names, they think, everything else would come back as before. With me I could remember names, birthdays, every detail of my first life before the crash. But in some way none of it seemed to have happened to the person I was now. They were more echoes of memories than memories themselves. Half awake most mornings, I would find myself rubbing the palm of one hand over the back of the other, touching the skin with the same disconnected wonder with which Benedict often touched a strip of snake skin displayed in the zoo. It would take me several moments to adjust to the idea that I was inside that skin. My mouth always felt sour. I would put my hand out to feel Geraldine's warmth, then remember where I was, in the spare room, still unable to face the intimacy of sharing a bed with someone else.

She did not like me going out by myself, but I kept up the pretence of being busy, leaving the house as I had done before the crash, walking with the help of a stick to the studio full of resolution and then slowly being sucked into an endless sifting through realms of contact sheets on the floor. The deadline for the Berlin exhibition had already gone, as had that for the photo supplement for a magazine in Norway. I had always thrived on deadlines, but now I let them pass, becalmed, unable even to respond to the urgent reminders which kept arriving in the post.

I had known periods before when I just could not work, when the compulsion had been replaced by fear. I tried to hide the crisis from myself by organizing the studio, perpetually starting to index negatives, to shift boxes of contacts from one corner of the room to the other.

Sometimes I tried to find the scratched negatives of that first roll of film taken in the Botanic Gardens when I was ten. I had presumed them long thrown out until they were found in my father's papers after his death. I realized now that they were the only photographs I had ever taken there, although there was hardly any other part of the city I had not shot. I had not returned since the crash, yet the most vibrant shades of green remained with me whenever I woke from the frequent dreams which I now had of those gardens.

My day in the studio always ended up with the same random combing through old boxes of photographs, scanning the backgrounds for that one face which had confronted me when I was clinically dead, becoming more and more gripped, as the light faded above me, with unease as I glanced over my shoulder, unable to articulate what was disturbing me. My breath would start to quicken, my chest growing tight. The first symptoms of a panic attack. My doctor had told me how to counter them, but I was terrified of being trapped alone in the studio, at the mercy of some uncertain illusory presence. I would leave the room, taking my stick, not looking back as I limped down the stairs.

I remember one evening in late February when fork-lift trucks filled the narrow street outside as I came down, sacks of carrots and onions being loaded into vans from the Victorian fruit and vegetable markets. Plywood cartons lay smashed on the pavements that had been worn down by container trucks. A businessman in a crombie coat came to one of the doorways, joking with the two suppliers beside him. An old street trader in an apron pushed her battered pram down the centre of the street, cursing cheerfully at the fork-lift driver who beeped behind her. My panic eased as I watched her call across to the businessman that he had always been a mean wee scut like his father before him. But at least his father had only cheated half of Dublin, whereas now he was poisoning them as well. The businessman grinned back, asking her how many times she had sold the same bunch of flowers outside the cemetery that day.

'You might have the decency to wait at least until the poor bloody mourners have left before sending your son in,' he shouted after her. 'Sure they're passing the same flowers on the way out as they bought on the way in.'

The abuse was a nightly ritual. I watched him take the roll of notes from his pocket and count them out carefully into the palms of the men. One of the suppliers passed around cigarettes and they lit up, their heads framed by the electric light that had come on in the loading bay of the warehouse. Their confident masculine world brought back the memory of my father with a sharp and painful sense of loss. In this state he seemed more real to me now than the house I was about to return to. I could see him at the bar counter, that summer when I worked with him, could feel the sickening taste of a third unwanted lemonade as he laughed at the Donabate shopkeeper's terrible jokes and agreed that Blaney was the man to put manners on the Brits. I could remember wondering would he pull the stunt that McHenry, who drove for the rival postcard firm, was such a decent man that you would never dream his father had been a B-Special thug in the North, or would it be the one that you would never dream he was head of the British Legion in Leinster? And I could remember my father's laugh as we drove over the bridge by the railway station and he kissed the crumpled order in his hand, and then pulled in behind the parked Tayto crisps van to swap the driver two postcards of Howth Head for two packets of the cheese and onion crisps that he was addicted to.

You'll like it here, son. How happy his voice had seemed in that limbo after the crash. *You'll like it here.* Where was 'here'? No oxygen getting to the brain, the body releasing hallucinogenic adrenalins, having a farewell party for itself before oblivion. There was a logical chemical reason for it all. The voices I wanted to hear, the faces I had loved. The final perfect dream, fooling myself to the last. But then what about that face which haunted my sleep?

The businessman had climbed into his car. Lights were being switched off, steel shutters clanged down. How could I go back home to Geraldine and the children, to focus on nappy rash and teething? I wanted my father back as he had been that summer, the certainty of his strength, the thrill I had felt at being allowed to ride on the open footplate of the van as it careered past hedgerows in small lanes with insects crashing into my face and my hair blown back. I entered the shop on the corner and bought Tayto crisps for the first time in years. I limped home, closing my eyes occasionally to savour the taste of them in his memory.

On the afternoon of my tenth birthday a bus turned over on the main street of the village. My class had been unleashed from school and we ran shouting through the church grounds to push our way through the crowd. There were shards of glass everywhere, some speckled with blood. A woman screamed hysterically while the ambulance driver tried to reassure her that her daughter would be all right. A man with his head bandaged sat on the pavement with his back to a lamppost. His eyes were closed as the cigarette smoke came out from his nostrils. He inhaled again with intense concentration. From the way his foot hung it was obvious that it was broken.

There was a man in an anorak walking slowly around the scene. People made way for him, the police and ambulance men never putting their hand out to stop him like they did with the rest of the people. When he came near the figure slumped against the lamppost the injured man straightened himself up. His hand unconsciously tidied back his hair. He inhaled, his good leg stretched out, his eyes staring up into the camera lens. The man in the anorak clicked three times, then lowered the camera. Both men grinned, as though sharing a private joke, before the photographer moved on to photograph the smashed windows of the bus.

'Which paper?' the injured man called after him.

'*Evening Herald.* You'll be there.'

'Do you want my name, do you?' The injured man had shrugged off the ambulance men, who were trying to lift him on to a stretcher. The photographer kept walking, his silence making the man's question seem childish. Then, as if sensing my eyes staring after him, he turned to wink.

At home that evening I waited for my birthday present, growing more excited as I realized that whatever the gift was it was so significant that my mother was waiting until my father came home before giving it. Yet even after dinner, when I had blown the candles out, nothing was produced. I was dressing for bed when my parents came in to the bedroom. Seeing them, my excitement was replaced by anxiety. I could sense their nervousness, the way that both were waiting for the other to speak.

'You know that we love you more than anything in the world,' my father began.

I had always taken their love for granted. Now something in his tone made me feel cold. My bladder seemed filled with icy water.

'And you know how proud both of us are to call you our son. That's what you are and that's what you'll always be. And in years' and years' time, when we are dead, this house and everything in it will belong to you alone.'

My father hesitated and looked at my mother, who was

sitting at the end of the bed. She took my hand, leaving my father to continue.

'Remember when you were a little boy and you asked us where you came from? We always told you you were found among the leaves in that potato bed beside the greenhouse. You're older now, I know the way lads your age talk in school, you probably know a lot by now.'

'Mammy's tummy . . . I know.'

I was embarrassed. I did not want a present, I just wanted them to leave. This was talk for the shed, Doyler drinking orange and letting it piss out of him at the same time, the copy of *Titbits* Sheridan had hidden in his bag.

'No. Not your mammy's tummy.'

My father stopped, utterly unsure of himself.

'I mean, yes. Yes, your mammy's tummy, but . . . Oh, for Christ's sake, son, I'm no good at this sort of thing. Listen, we have to tell you this now. Most people on the street know and, well, we don't want you to be hurt, to find out from their children. Now sometimes men and women, they want children with all their heart, but God's a peculiar class of being . . . I mean, He has his own reasons and we don't know what they are, but He doesn't let those men and women have their own children. And then there are others, you see, who don't want children at all and they only have to spit sideways before God blesses them with what He doesn't give to others.'

My father was not a man of many words at home. I watched him stand there, hardly aware that he was banging his right fist into the palm of his left hand as he spoke.

'Do you understand what I'm trying to tell you, son? You're of an age to know. You are as much our son as if you came from your mother's . . . I mean . . . it makes no difference to us . . .'

46

'I have another mother?' I asked.

'No, not now. You had . . .'

My mother gripped my hand tighter.

'Yes, you do, son,' she said. 'And always will. You have two mothers and I can't tell you who she is or where she is now, beyond that she was nineteen and from Laois and I wasn't even supposed to know that. But I pray for her every night in my prayers because she brought you into the world for us.'

'And why did she not want me?'

The bitterness in my voice startled me. My father was silent, anxious to shift the responsibility on to my mother. I suddenly realized these terms were inaccurate. I no longer knew what I should call them.

'Maybe she did want you,' my mother said. 'Maybe . . . We're trying to be as honest with you as we can, Sean. I know it's hard, but you're ten years of age now. I don't know why she gave you up. She was a young girl, she was in trouble, she was . . . well, she had no husband. All I know is that you were six weeks old when the woman in the agency gave you to me, you were all wrapped up in a light-blue blanket and you were the most beautiful sight that I had ever seen. We could give you a life here. That poor girl never could.'

'What woman from what agency?'

'The Catholic Assurance Agency . . . Mrs Lacey.'

'Your friend from Cork? What has she got to do with me?'

My voice was low, yet there was hysteria in it. Twice a year Mrs Lacey came to visit and I would stand in the sitting room before her, confused by my mother's nervousness.

'She comes . . . just to check that you're okay.' My

mother squeezed my hand tighter. I prayed that she wouldn't start to cry.

'Could Mrs Lacey not come and take me back? Who owns me? How do you know my . . . my . . . that other woman won't find me again?'

'Your other mother knows as little about us as we know of her,' she said. 'It's been ten years. Even if she did try she would have no legal claim. You were . . . well, signed away. But sure she has her own life now, her own family maybe. She would never dare to tell her husband about you.'

'We have a present for you,' my father butted in, as though he could no longer bear the conversation. 'That old cheap thing you got is no good. If you're a big enough boy to tell things to now, then you're big enough to work this.'

He went out to the landing and came back with a new camera which he placed on the bed. The lens glittered in the light. There was a steel shutter and all kinds of markings and lettering like on a telescope. It felt heavy in my hand and solid. I raised it up to my eye. My parents stood caught in the viewfinder, distant now and reduced to adoptive parents, trapped into hesitant smiles.

Chapter Four

The next portrait is outdoors in March: a juxtaposition of past and present, life and death. The stark slant of light from an early spring sun, the long shadows cast on the grass by capsized Protestant tombstones. The black gates below the wrought-iron sign in white for Drumcondra Church are locked but the small side gate is open. Older stones are laid against the wall, listing the indecipherable virtues of eighteenth-century gentlemen of the city of Dublin. An overgrown gravel path twists beyond the small church and, beside the tumbledown wall, a man in his thirties, using a stick now more from habit than necessity, stands with a small boy on his shoulders. The child points with intense concentration at the earth-movers and mechanical diggers that are working on the foundations of a new block of apartments in the derelict site beyond the wall.

Even at three Benedict knew there was something special about this place. On our walks he would stop at the Cat and Cage pub and point down Church Street. *The tstrannge place*, he would insist, pulling at my arm. I never told him what this place was used for and why nobody else ever walked here. He loved to play with the gravel, making mounds of small stones on the path and breaking them up again with a stick. Or else we just stood by the wall, watching the construction work.

Sometimes workmen with hard yellow hats would stop and call up to him. Without being able to see his face I could imagine it, buried down for safety in my hair, both shy and thrilled at being addressed. When I had been in hospital Geraldine had pretended to him that I was leaving for work before he rose and coming home after he had gone to bed. Each morning another plastic zoo animal would be left beside his breakfast plate as a present from Dada. But he knew that something was wrong from Geraldine's voice on the phone or from the callers to the door. On the third evening he had suddenly begun to pull out of Geraldine's arm, sobbing over and over, *Give him back to me, give him back*, as though she could produce me like a soft toy from a wardrobe. He had grown whiny, wanting to keep a nappy on all day even though he had worn one only at night for the previous three months. Yet when she drove to the hospital to collect me all he said when I knelt to kiss him in reception was *I saw a tractor outside*. At home he found a stick in the garden and I watched him from the window, walking to the shops with Geraldine pushing the pram, leaning on the stick like Dada did, refusing to be parted from it even at bedtime.

Now every morning before facing the purgatory of my studio I brought him for a walk around Drumcondra. We sat on the bench outside St Patrick's College, both utterly immersed in spotting motor bikes and big trucks with trailers among the heavy traffic on the main Belfast Road, or else we searched the corners of Griffith Park for men working on the two tractors that were in use there. His concentration was total, his delight at finding his favourite red tractor completely illuminating his face.

In the last week in February I had finally brought myself to develop the last shoot I had done before the crash. It had been intended for a feature on homelessness in Dublin at Christmas time, a look at a day in the life of a middle-aged man sleeping rough in winter. The images were stark and technically skilled: the burst of light through the crack in the corrugated iron over the window frame in a derelict joinery and how it lit up a model's face and blonde hair on the broken wooden advertising hoarding under which the man slept, wrapped in newspapers; daylight coming like a train down the tunnel under the bridge where he raised the flagon of cider to his lips while his friend beside him lifted his face from the shadows after vomiting; the close-up of those eyes with their cold stare into the heart of the lens.

The final shot was the most successful. With that stare the man had ceased to be just himself. The mixture of resignation and defiance, of utter loneliness and haunting absorption, made him seem to momentarily become every man who ever stood outside in the rain – the Kurd by his fire on the hillside of bodies after the bomber planes departed, the Bosnian behind the barbed wire whose child had been raped, the Cambodian who had starved at sea in a crowded boat and was now waiting in his metal cage to be deported.

Yet looking at the contact sheet I knew that I had failed. There had been no communication between the pair of us as I worked and he stood waiting to be allowed back into his loneliness. The feature would appear opposite the fashion page of a newspaper with an interest only in circulation figures. My shots were just another catch for them, a fashionable name sucked in to fill the space between the advertisements. I had children now, responsibilities. For three days of the week my camera was for hire. That was what made the stare so frightening. The man knew he had my measure.

Ten years ago I would have spent the day with him, would have lifted his flagon to my own lips without wiping it and drunk. I would have taken in his quiet rage without even being aware of doing so and begun to imagine that room in the abandoned joinery as my home. And he would have opened to me, not out of any sense of shared experience, but because I would have come on an old girl's bicycle, would have been working only for myself and quite obviously not been successful. Gradually he would have grown relaxed and a little contemptuous, confident as he let me click away that these shots would never be seen by anyone.

For a moment as I drew the wet contact sheet out from the tray those eyes seemed to be my own on that day, working against a deadline, needing to remember to collect the cream for the baby from the chemist. I had been shying away from the misery on display, so busy focusing on the light in the joinery, and on how the curvature of the bridge echoed the bent heads of the two men, that I had ceased to focus on the human beings I was meant to be photographing.

That roll of film had been in the boot of the car when I crashed into the bus. I had set fire to it, watching the flames splutter into blues and greens in the half-light of the studio. I went back through the dozen shoots before it. All of them were stale and I was too good a photographer not to have known it at the time. The question troubled me again. Could I have turned the wheel out of the path of the bus? In that slowed motion, freed from responsibilities and deadlines, had I watched the crash occurring with terror or with relief?

But now, through Benedict's eyes, as on all those March morning walks, the staleness with which I felt I had been looking at life would evaporate. He leaned forward on my shoulders in the graveyard, his interest infectious. The webbed wheels of the JCB glinted in the winter light, rainbows of oil rocking slightly in pools among the stones and muck. One could almost smell the freshness of the timbers that were stacked against the wall. Every detail was of equal validity and fascination to him. I taught him the names of what we looked at, but he was teaching me how to see those objects again. His gift was the eternal freshness of a world without death. The misshapen tombstones in the graveyard were no more than funny crooked stones to him. He pointed to the cross on the old roof behind us and called it *broken God's house*, as though Christ was some sort of careless absentee landlord.

And it was with him alone that I felt fully at ease now, where all questions could be answered with a new name, where there was no pressure to do anything other than observe. With Benedict the moments did not come when I was suddenly swamped with loss at having been brought back to life again.

With Geraldine it was different. For two and a half months she had been keeping as many decisions from me as possible, but now there were everyday problems which we needed to discuss. Car insurance, hospital bills, my forthcoming court case, the names of schools for Benedict. I tried to listen to her but we both knew that my comments were half-hearted. I agreed with everything, putting it all back on her shoulders, impatient for Geraldine to be finished. I knew how unfair it was, but I had a phobia about being drawn into the present. I had been waiting weeks for her to say it before the night she finally broke down.

'Sometimes I think you wished you had never survived that crash. Apart from the scare about your heart and a couple of minor injuries you walk away scot-free. It was a miracle and yet half the time you just sit there, not even bothering to try and talk to me. I think you're just sick that we've all been landed back on you.'

A Second Life

How could I start to explain to her what wasn't even clear to myself, how I had come back to life changed, no longer able to focus on the world we had built up, cursed and haunted by gaps in my life?

Away from her, on those morning walks with Benedict, I began to dwell on my mother. For six weeks she must have nursed me, slept with me in a wooden cot beside her bed, woken to feed me in some night-lit dormitory. No matter what life she had made for herself she could not have just forgotten me.

Was I born of rape or incest? Had she seen the eyes of a hated man in my unfocused pupils? Or had my birthday been celebrated secretly in another place ever since, a woman alone in a locked bathroom furtively eating a slice of cake while her family moved about the house, oblivious of her tears? Perhaps she never married, drifted into drink and loneliness, until she was found frozen under cardboard outside an English railway station? I remembered Peter McHugh, the millionaire I had once photographed, who told me about being reared in an orphanage. *Your mothers were all prostitutes*, a nun had told them. *If you meet them outside these walls you should spit in their faces.*

When I was young my hatred of her had been laced with fear that she could somehow snatch me away from my home. I had felt abandoned whenever I allowed myself to think about her. There was no room in my mind to want to understand what had happened to her. Before Benedict was born I had rarely bothered to think of her, although on the one occasion I had won a press award I had a sudden desperate desire for her to be watching the news in whatever country she was in, for her to know that this was her son flown in to Brussels to speak in broken French with the taste of calf's brain and champagne on his tongue.

A Second Life

Once or twice I had wondered if perhaps she had wished to contact me, but even though I knew it was not possible for her to do so I convinced myself that, if she did, she would have found some way of making contact. But generally she had never entered my thoughts. The unspoken fear that if I did find her I might be rejected again allowed her to exist only as a callous invisible woman in my subconscious.

It was only now, after becoming a parent myself, that I could begin to guess at what my absence might have been in her life. In those first months of Benedict's life I would wake and kneel beside his cot, straining to hear him breathe, and feel such a sense of elation at the faint sound of his breath that nothing else seemed of any consequence. Even if she had signed me away with her own hand, for years afterwards whenever she woke her body must have instinctively listened for my breathing. She had been nineteen and from Laois. That was all the information my parents had told me. In all my travels I had never even stopped the car in Laois, always increasing my speed till I was safely into Kildare or Tipperary. Could there be other information that I had never been aware of?

Beyond the graveyard wall the JCB tilted its bucket downward into the brown muck. The sun had gone in behind rainclouds. I lifted Benedict off my shoulders as he began to cry in protest. I stopped. Instinctively I knew that she had been waiting all those years for me to find her.

'Tomorrow,' I told Benedict. 'We'll go walking again tomorrow. Where would you like to go?'

He stared at the cat who had crawled out from the railings of an old vault.

'The *Botogasis* Gardens,' he said, pulling at my hand to go home as the first drops of rain came.

*

The first gull landed on the concrete and tore at the plastic Downes Bakery wrapper. The gull had worked the crust of bread out when another snatched it away from him. The two birds rose, squabbling in the air, as others landed to devour the scraps left after lunch in the school yard. The class was arrayed by height in five rows on the steps, boys pushing each other and pulling faces as the teacher bent to speak to the photographer. The man had crouched over the tripod when I stepped out from the back row. I walked a few steps away towards the prefabs, sensing the heads of the other boys turning, the whole class dissolving into disarray. Even when the teacher screamed at me I refused to step back into place. I was scared of the attention, terrified of the leather in the teacher's pocket. But the fear of staring at the lens was more overpowering. It was irrational and primitive. I knew that only the presence of the photographer was saving me from being beaten, but still I refused to be part of the photograph.

The light was dim in the headmaster's office. My legs would not stop shaking. The man turned his back on me. I could imagine my mother in the hall of the neighbour who had a phone.

'So you only told him the news recently,' the man said.

Everybody has always known, I thought, talking behind my back in the shops, at school, in church. That's why the chemist had said nothing, what else could he have expected from a boy who came from God knows what class of people? Outside in the corridor a brass bell was ringing. I knew that I would not be beaten.

I watched the note suspending me for three days bob and swerve in the red waters of the Tolka. There was a slaughterhouse on the far bank across from the pitch and putt course where raw offal and bright blood splattered from an open waste pipe into the river. I waited among the trees until the others were let out from school, then walked home, marked out and surrounded by an excited cluster of boys. Two of them had money. Everyone crowded into the narrow shop where they chose sweets from the jars on the counter. I kept my arms behind my back, rifling chocolate bars, chewing gum, matches, anything that I could get my hands on down the seat of my trousers. I had never stolen before. In the laneway I distributed them out. 'I'm adopted, you know,' I said. The boys nodded as though this excused me everything.

The old album was kept in the press downstairs. The night after I was suspended I held my breath and waited to see if the click of the living-room light had woken my parents, then opened it. My life was laid out, dutifully recorded in black and white snaps. On the second page there were three spaces where photographs had been removed. I ran my finger over the dusty grey cardboard as if it could somehow give me a clue about what was being kept from me.

I had trusted photographs always, badgering my mother to take the album out and retrace each year of my life with her. I turned to the first page, where the first ever photograph of me was pasted in by itself. Sand dunes on Dollymount beach in summer. My mother has a swimsuit and a bathing cap. I am three months old. She holds me up for the camera, her face showing both pride in her son and an anxiety to make me smile. But my face under the sun-hat has an angry, sunburnt look. Now I knew that the photograph was lying. I was not her son. Her anxiety was not to make me smile but how to maintain this pretence. I felt no anger towards her or my father, it was the photograph which I blamed. It would never cheat again. I left the shredded pieces on the table for them to find, then changed my mind and ran back down to draw the bolt on the front door and stand in my bare feet in the front garden, watching the wind scatter the pieces away beneath the crooked yellow streetlamps.

The Botanic Gardens was the one place that I was never allowed to visit. The next morning I left, as if for school, but went there instead. A guard was reading a newspaper in the hut inside the gate. I kept my head down going past him in case he asked why I was not at school. I walked for five minutes before I heard the Tolka surging in from the grounds of the convent and then forking out in a millrace which joined the river again opposite the rose garden. I began to run excitedly towards the noise of white water. A gardener with an armband pushed a barrow past me. I stopped and lifted the camera. I felt both strength and cold excitement as I squeezed the shutter. The click was loud and absolute.

How often had I asked my mother to bring me to the Botanic Gardens and how many excuses had she made? In the end I stopped mentioning the place, but it had become like a secret garden in my mind, brighter and greener for being forbidden. A squirrel bobbed quickly through the grass beneath the trees. I knelt like a hunter, drawing him in, patiently waiting until he was only feet from me before pressing the shutter with a stab of triumph before he scampered away.

Before I had always wasted film, but now I set up every shot with a precise passion. This was a declaration of my difference, a way of showing that I had the power to hurt them. I knew that I was going to give the roll to my father to have developed in work, that they would know how I had disobeyed them in going there. I stalked every corner of the gardens, getting lost, finding paths which looked half familiar, perpetually ending up sitting in the tunnel of old branches which formed the yew walk. I was hungry, unsure of the time, waiting for the shouts from the convent to know when it was safe to go home. I leaned my hands back against the dry bark of one of the yew trees and felt content for the first time since they had broken the news to me.

Three nights later my father laid the folder on the oilskin cloth of the kitchen table. The photographs spilled out. My mother picked them up, her hands increasingly agitated as she flipped quickly through them. She glanced up at me, her eyes hurt and confused, then silently began to go through them again. My father looked into my face over her bent head.

'You have the knack, son,' was all he said. 'These are good shots.'

This is the last portrait from those becalmed months, imagined from high up near the ceiling. The crowded spare room, which I had gone back to sleeping in after a few nights with Geraldine, with the bed wedged between the wall and my desk. A single weak spur of streetlight through the gap in the curtains. My body is curled up, blankets wrapped between my legs as I rock in sleep. My breathing is rhythmic, growing deeper. My body twists again and abruptly I wake. My mouth is open. I begin to suck the night air in as if drowning. This is where the shutter should click, with my eyes staring up, coming sharply in focus. But the image breaks free of my control.

As always upon waking there is an echo of that incalculable ache of disappointment which I had felt at being dragged back to life, my mind scrambling to remember the dissipating dream. But this time my breath comes faster and my chest starts to hurt. My mouth opens wider, my face twitching as I snatch in oxygen. Still the air I am sucking in is not enough. My arms are sore now, my fingers knotting into cramped shapes. This is a panic attack, I think, trying to keep calm. But it feels different from those other times, more like a heart attack. They're coming back for me, I think, those faces waiting like ghosts in the wardrobe, more real than this house, more real than my family.

I look down. My stomach is like a piston, expanding, exhaling. I'm going to die, I know that I am going to die. My chest has become a tight wedge of pain, my heart feels about to burst. A few more moments and I will be back among those faces. I feel that I am pushing myself towards them with each deepening breath. Except that now I know I want to live. I'm struggling against the blackness which is taking over, but my hands seem to have taken on an autonomous existence. They flop and wave beyond my control. My torso is lifting itself off the mattress, banging back down as though my back is about to break. And now I am no longer fighting against my breath. I'm going with it, hearing the rasping inhalations as though from a long way off. My ears hurt. An all-prevailing whiteness comes, a feeling of sinking, and then the whiteness turns blue.

The blue of the sea. I know that I am still physically in the bedroom but yet I am also swimming through dense blue water. I am neither cold nor warm. I am without weight. I turn my head. A seal swims beside me. I turn the other way. A seal noses against my naked shoulder. Above me and below a whole shoal is swimming and I do not need to be told what way to turn. My body moves with them automatically, surging up towards the green light above the waves, then plunging down towards the rocks where flat fish glide. I am part of something greater than myself as I feel them brush against me, companionably, sensually.

I hear Geraldine's voice above the waves. There is fear in it as she calls. I am cresting too fast, my body buckling like a diver with the bends. I feel the crash against my forehead as I break through the waves. Arms are trying to hold me, to draw me in. This bedroom seems so distant. I want to go back to Geraldine, yet something is making me go on. I have to see this experience through. I fit back into my deep-breathing, pumping in the air, straining my mouth open. I'm plunging down into space again. Geraldine's scream sounds like a radio being slowly turned off.

All is quiet. The shape of night-lit trees. I can see myself, I know it is me, only now my face is different and yet familiar since the crash. My feet are bare. I know this place also although it does not look the same. How many times have I stopped beneath this canopy of sloping yew branches? But now there is gravel here instead of tarmac. I look perhaps seventeen, my head lolling, my mouth slightly open. My back is resting against the knotted bark of a trunk, my arms stretching behind it as though they were tied. But they are not. I draw them up towards the high branches, then slowly down to rest in the cropped hair of the man who kneels below me. I cannot see what he is doing. I am both inside my body, staring at the dark roots of his hair, and yet also up among the yew branches, watching as I push him backwards and turn, trying to straighten my breeches as I begin to run. He is behind me, gaining, and I both want him to catch me and yet am afraid of what will happen when he does. I cross a path into brief moonlight, glancing around for a hint of the nightwatchman's lantern, and vanish again up a steep slope beneath the narrow tunnel of yews, racing although I know the walk ends here in a cul-de-sac. My body hits the wooden fence at the end. I know as I try to climb it that he will catch me. He is stronger, older, easily able to turn me in his arms. I feel the stubble as he presses his lips against mine. I open my mouth wide. Something presses thick and hard against my stomach. There is terror and giddy excitement. Distantly I can hear Geraldine calling. His right hand comes up, pressing my head down. I am sinking, my mouth already open. I can feel something being pushed over my face. I am choking now. My breath is coming back at me. There are voices. I raise my hands, my face crinkles like thick brown paper. My breathing is slowing down. The side of my face hurts. I move my hand towards my forehead to feel the edge of a thick paper bag. I know that face now which has haunted me since the accident. Geraldine takes hold of my hand, drawing it away from the bag.

'It's okay,' a man's voice says. 'He's stopped hyperventilating. That's all you have to do when a panic attack gets out of hand. That quick breathing over-oxygenizes the brain. Keep a strong brown paper bag in the house and make him breathe into it. It means he's breathing his own breath back in without getting any fresh oxygen.'

The bag is lifted off my face. I am lying on the carpet in the landing. The light is blinding. The ambulance man stands behind Geraldine.

'Sean,' she says. 'Are you all right, my love? You had the heart crossways in me. You smashed your face against the wall and I couldn't leave you in the bed. I had to drag you out here where I could reach a phone to call an ambulance.'

There is blood inside my mouth. I look at the ambulance man again. I know his face.

'Bedad, you're keeping me in a job,' he says.

'I should stay away from buses and walls.'

'At least you won't get your licence endorsed for this one.'

I close my eyes. I feel sick. Could I really have been that young man or anyone else once? Could I have lived before? Had I worn those clothes, perhaps sucked a man's penis in my mouth? I retch suddenly. I remember sitting in that toilet downstairs and thinking that this house could never be mine. Was it the same with my body or spirit, was I just another passing tenant allotted my quota of years? I feel cheated of everything that I had thought I was. Geraldine keeps her arms around me as I cry.

'Hush, darling,' she says. 'It was a panic attack. You're still not right since that accident. This is just trauma. You can learn to control it.'

My body curls up, pressing against her stomach. Sinead is crying in the bedroom. I no longer care about trying to maintain some composure before the ambulance man. I keep sobbing the same words to her.

'I don't know who I am any more.'

I open my eyes. Benedict is standing at the door of his room, his face terrified.

'Mind me, hold me,' he says like a chant. 'Hold me, mind me.'

Chapter Five

My childhood career as a thief was short-lived. After my second heist the woman from the shop came running behind us into the lane. The other boys scattered as she chased with unerring instinct after me. I careered between the cars on the main road, almost getting killed before I managed to lose her. She never went to the headmaster, but soon the whole school knew. I was too scared to ever try it again but it no longer mattered. For the following two years I had the name of being dangerous: clashing with teachers, getting blamed for trouble whether I caused it or not. I welcomed it as a distraction from the name of being adopted, but I discovered how people could find ways to work my past in. Corcoran, the oldest teacher there, with a yellowing toupee which clashed with the grey remnants of his hair, patrolled the yard using his trained voice as a weapon. His roared threat, 'I will speak to your mother about you', would paralyse any boy with fright. When I ran on to the grass after the bell every boy understood the subtle insult in his words bellowed after me, 'I will speak to Mrs Blake about you.'

Some of the older boys, confident they were old enough to beat me, took it up. 'What sandwiches did Mrs Blake give you for lunch?' They leaned back against the shed wall, casually defying me to throw the first fist or boot.

My difference scared me, yet also gave a sense of power. Football was the currency of the yard, boys weaving between the piled coats which served for posts, scoring goals for Leeds or Arsenal. The English team you followed defined you almost as much as the street you were from. 'Shelbourne', I replied to anyone who asked me who I supported. Shels' brief glory of the early sixties was long over and the last time I had been in Tolka Park a desperate voice on the loudspeaker before the kick-off had requested that anybody in the ground with links to Shelbourne and a pair of football boots should report to the main stand immediately. When the goalkeeper had taken the ball down on his chest and kicked it upfield I could see a white paint stain left on his jersey. Soon they were even to lose their tenancy on that ground. Yet when the other boys persisted, incredulously demanding to know who I followed in real football in England, I would defiantly repeat the name of Shelbourne.

Finally, at twelve, it was my father's sister, Aunt Cissie, who decided to take me out of primary school. 'He has his entrance exam done to secondary,' she said. 'Leave him there any longer and he'll be expelled with a blot on his record.'

And it was in her kitchen, three streets away from our own, that Aunt Cissie gradually worked on my father to fake my age and get me a job as a van boy working with him under a bogus name for four months that summer. What did they expect that those months would do for me? Straighten me out, cure the disruptive streak which had me in trouble every week? But did his wife or sister really know anything of the other life of my father? Of the bright waistcoats he kept on a coat hanger in the back of the van, of the way his whole face changed when he passed the gates of Pezzani's every morning?

'Hang around outside here for five minutes,' he told me at the gates that first morning. 'I don't want us to be seen going in together. And remember now for the last time, you're not my son. You're just a van boy I've taken on, right?'

If I was not his son, then he did not seem like my father, cursing and joking with the three other salesmen, stopping the van around the corner and sending me across to the shop for cream cakes. I stood at the shop window to watch Pezzani's printer sneak through the gap in the wire fence and smuggle a box of rejected postcards out to my father. My first morning was spent in the back of the speeding van, carefully replacing one good postcard from each packet of twelve with one from the reject box and making up new bundles of twelve for us to sell on the black.

Even on that first morning our relationship began to change in this new masculine world. I had been hurt when he insisted that I pretend not to be his son, convinced that he was ashamed I was adopted, but I discovered that in places like Drogheda, Slane and Bettystown he wasn't even married.

'It's well for the pair of you bachelors,' the women behind the counter would say and wink at me. 'If you listen to that fellow long enough, you'll break every girl's heart in Ireland.'

After a week it occurred to me that I was seeing my father as he had been before he ever married, that he was not ashamed of me or his present life, but that it simply ceased to exist when he stepped up into the cab of the van. Here was a world of illusion where perhaps only he knew what was fantasy. With old ladies in Skerries he was a devout Catholic, talking earnestly about his work in the Legion of Mary. In Balbriggan he stamped his fist on the counter along with the young bearded shopkeeper and swore that the seventies would be red with Labour.

A Second Life

The Beatles were after breaking up that summer, the New Seekers saying *goodbye, my own true lover*. The grim queue of pensioners for the early dinner in Butlin's Holiday Camp scowled across from him as he sang *Happy Days are Here Again* to them through the open window. The world we drove through was more vivid than any I had ever known and the two words which reigned supreme in it were *the fiddle*. It wasn't just the money they made, it was a religion to many of the van drivers working that coast. They seemed to live for the same illicit thrill which I had felt running from that shop with chocolates behind my back. But out on the road it was soft drinks, crisps, ice-cream, plastic sunglasses, fish fingers, postcards, and once even six goldfish in a plastic bag which my father and I eventually left tied to a bush on the roadside.

We were a race apart, meeting at lay-bys to swap contraband, comparing notes on which shopkeepers were the sharpest to deal with, sitting in the rain each evening on the edge of Dublin to doctor the real and the bogus invoice books. Three Cross Doubles, Lucky Fifteens, Accumulators, Trebles, Yankees. I learnt more about maths running bets for them in a week than I had ever learnt at school. My father and I called at chemists to collect films to be developed, at hotels and shops to sell views of Ireland. And outside every shop his question would be the same: 'Did you count McHenry's shagging postcards?'

McHenry was his obsession. He was a quiet man with a Pioneer pin to proclaim his status as a teetotaller. My father claimed he turned the windscreen wipers off passing under bridges to save money. We met him once as he was coming out of the gates of Butlin's. My father insisted on stopping the van in the middle of the road to go over and shake his hand.

'Two of a kind, man. There's room for us both and more. It's great to see you looking well. Mrs Devine up there in Laytown was saying to me last week that if I saw you I was to ask had you a spare one of those green pennants of yours with *Quality Irish Postcards* in gold down the side of it. Sure, throw one out here and I'll pop it into her myself for you.'

We drove on through the gates of Butlin's, past the glum queue of pensioners, with me riding on the footplate, my right hand inside the open window to grip the handle for support and my left hand thrust up into the air to hold the burning remnants of McHenry's pennant as my father and I sang *Happy Days are Here Again*.

After focusing so hard on not calling him Da at work, it was hard to remember not to call him Eddie at home. Whenever I did my mother would call him into the kitchen. I could hear the hurt anxiety in her low voice through the door and, once, the words 'lose him'. The money I now had made me flippant towards her as I tried to keep up the camaraderie and language of the road at the table. But my father was different there, shrunk back into the quiet man I had always known. Once, after she had left the room, I was passing him when I suddenly found myself sprawled on the floor. My neck hurt where he had clattered me. It was the only time he ever struck me. 'That was man to man,' he said softly. 'Now don't.'

That summer the world seemed to be flocking to Laytown and Bettystown. Caravan parks appeared in fields where sheep had been grazing a month before. Corrugated-iron huts normally used to store fodder now served as shops, each one with racks of postcards outside.

'The bastard!' my father screamed. 'The tight-arsed, Pioneer –' my father glanced at the Pioneer pin on the

Laytown farmer-turned-shopkeeper who was staring at him from inside the hut – 'lapsed-Pioneer, drunken oul alcoholic!'

'They're lovely new postcards,' the shopkeeper said. 'Mr McHenry had them taken up there beside the sand dunes. I tell you, they're going down a bomb here, especially with the Northern shower. Sure my granny used to send home them postcards of yours on her honeymoon.'

My father crumpled the new postcard up in his hand. Barefoot children in swimming costumes were crossing the grass for ice-cream.

'When that bastard dies,' my father said, 'they're not going to bother putting an awning over his grave. They'll lay down an oversized *Quality Irish* envelope across the open pit and lower him through the middle of it.'

The children brushed past my father. Two of the girls were around thirteen with bathing suits that didn't quite cover their buttocks. They sensed me staring after them and giggled.

'Why in the name of Jaysus would they do that?' the shopkeeper asked.

'So McHenry can go out of this world as he came into it,' my father said, slamming the card down. 'Through a hole in a shagging letter.'

Once when my father's van broke down I had been sent to the processing lab where all the shots – which decency and the consciences of Irish chemists prevented being developed and returned to their takers – were blown up and pasted on to the walls. What husbands taking private pictures of their wives, or secretaries exploring the first topless beaches of Europe, knew that their images would wind up pinned to cubicle doors in the flooded toilets? Pezzani walked through every few hours, pausing to inspect the latest addition to the wall with either a sad shake of his head or a whistle and the words, 'Lovely girl like my mamma, very Italian tits.'

But I had never spoken to him before the morning in July when he opened the door of my father's van as we were about to leave the yard.

'All right, you get your wish,' Pezzani said. 'Today especially for you I shoot Bettystown and Laytown. But they have a better sell.'

He gripped the door handle and stared at me, then put his hand softly out to touch my face.

'But who is this lovely van boy? Very Irish with the freckles. The freckles is good. I take him from you for the day. He fucks the bush for me and maybe . . . who knows?'

His knuckles brushed softly against my cheek again.

'Very nice. A neighbour's boy to you? You sure he's fourteen?'

My father nodded. I wasn't sure if Pezzani could discern his unease. What I felt was pure terror. Pezzani was the fattest man I had ever seen. With my father work had been an adventure, now suddenly I wanted to be back in the safe anonymity of a classroom. I sensed that my father was unable to help me. He shrugged his shoulders and, with a warning glance to me, drove off alone.

Pezzani's van was tiny. There was a curtain dividing off the back where something heavy seemed to be stored. The steering wheel was almost between his knees. He drove with the window open, shouting *It's my road* at any motorist who refused to give way before him.

'Forty years ago I come to this country first,' he said as we sped towards Swords, 'all the postcards black and white. Trams, trams, trams. You think the whole of Dublin one big tram. I work for a good Irishman, I give him a good Italian grandson. When he finds out he gives me his daughter's hand. A bit late, I already have the rest of her. Now we partners I tell him. No more black and white. Colour, colour, colour. Because I have the secret of what the Irish love in their postcards. It is red and it no good in black and white. You like pictures, boy? Today I show you the secret of great pictures.'

I did like pictures, I told him, I even wanted to be a professional photographer when I grew up.

'Like me,' he said.

'No, not like you,' I said, with the naïve arrogance of a twelve-year-old. 'Much better.'

As he put his head back and laughed I could see how old he really was. The uneasy thought came to me, as so frequently it did when I came into contact with any strange man, that maybe he could be my real father. Often with tramps in the street or somebody deformed I would find myself unable to look away from them, searching their features with a quiet horror for any reflection of my own.

'Everybody, they want to be the great photographer,' Pezzani was saying. 'Even the man you drive with. Once he good photographer, but I stop him because he far better salesman. In the photographs he has no sense of how to use the red. Now you tell me, boy genius, the postcards you sell, what you think of them?'

The problem was that I liked quite a lot of them, but I felt it would be unsophisticated to say so. Also he had insulted my father. Working myself up into a passion I dismissed each image I knew Pezzani himself had taken as clichéd, detailing how I would have handled it, anxious to impress him. I stared out the side window, trying to hide my intense blushing as Pezzani laughed so much that the car kept swaying across the road.

'You want the real life, boy genius. Well, tough shit,

because nobody else they want it. They wanta the mountains and the lakes and the red. The postcards you really hate. I take them twenty-five years ago and still they sell in thousands. You know what sort a photographer you make, boy genius? A starving one! Now here we are, Bettystown. I take the photograph, you fuck the bush and watch and learn.'

We had pulled off the road on to the dunes. The van seemed about to stick in the sand but Pezzani powered it on, defying it to stall. We got out. There was a crowded beach below us. Pezzani lay down and beckoned me beside him.

'When the sun comes out of the clouds quickly and catches the water. That is the moment. The view is nice. See how the dune falls away there. Only one thing is missing – the splash of colour.'

He flicked the keys of the van across at me.

'Now get the bush.'

I looked at him. He pointed impatiently towards the back of the van, then turned to remove a lens box from the bag on his shoulder. I opened the van. There was a large fuchsia bush in a heavy clay pot tied up with ropes. I undid them and lifted it out, staggering under the weight. Pezzani had moved back to kneel on the next dune.

'Now you fuck the bush over there,' he said. 'No, wait, fuck it back more down the slope. That is good.'

The sun came out from a whorl of cloud and I heard a series of clicks.

'Now fuck the bush up to your left,' he called.

I lifted the heavy pot again, staggering as I tried to keep my footing in the sand.

'Fuchsia bushes don't grow in sand dunes,' I called back up at him.

'Neither does money. You just fuck the bush around, boy genius. Everybody loves the red.'

'It's not red, it's purple.'

'That's just reality,' he snorted dismissively. 'When I print it it's a red.'

Then it came to me. On almost every postcard which we sold this same bush popped up somewhere in the foreground: framing mountain passes on the Ring of Kerry, the sunset at Galway Bay or the view of Dublin from the Wicklow Mountains. I was hauling around the most famous bush in Ireland.

'What do you call it?' I said as I struggled back up the slope.

'Lire,' he clicked happily. 'My beautiful little red Lire.'

I put the bush down between the tufts of coarse grass. Two girls with candy floss smearing their faces had come up to watch us. Their dog barked excitedly and ran over to lift his leg against the clay pot. I kicked out and he retreated, staring back with hurt eyes.

'They're all fakes,' I said. 'Every single one of your cards.'

Pezzani changed the lens on the camera and laughed.

'You spend the summer fiddling my books, stealing my cards with your driver and yet you call me a fake. What do you want that I photograph? Children sitting in their caravans in the rain? All the litter and shite you people leave on the beach? I make people's holidays for them. They see my postcards again six months later and they see this beach the way it should be, not the way it was. What's so wrong with making people happy? Maybe you should give up the photographs and just stick to robbing me blind.'

'I . . . we . . . never . . .'

I imagined my father being sacked, and thought how I

had been tricked to come here alone with Pezzani so he could question me. Yet it wasn't my father's face, but my mother's which most troubled me. The shame she would feel, how she would blame herself even though she had no involvement in this. I knew that I would not be smart enough to be able to give Pezzani all the right answers. He laughed even louder at the look of terror on my face.

'You think I'm stupid? All you Irish love to fiddle. All day I have to go around pretending not to see this and that. I know everything but I let it happen. You have twelve of my postcards, you take one out and put a slightly faulty one in. Now you must sell twelve sets before you have a set free. So I let your driver steal two hundred dud postcards. But that day he has to sell two hundred sets of mine before he can sell sixteen of his own on the fiddle. He is making me a fortune, selling out of his skin so that he can fiddle a pittance.'

'I don't know what you're talking about,' I stammered, watching Pezzani enjoy my discomfort. He screwed the cover back on the lens and spread his hands.

'You afraid you be sacked, boy, but I like you. Now I teach you second lesson. You be good boy, do what you're told, then we never have this conversation and you go home a pound richer. Fuck the bush back in the van.'

The girls had gone away. The sun had retreated behind the clouds and it felt cold again. I had to climb into the van to tie the ropes around the clay pot. He stood at the door, watching until I was finished.

'Now you take those clothes off,' he said.

I froze. This was it, I thought, the purpose all along. Maybe he even knew that my driver was my father. By making me stammer and blush, Pezzani had trapped me into acknowledging that we had been on the fiddle. Now my father could lose his job. I felt that he knew I had been adopted and passed from hand to hand, and that this was somehow part of it. I put my hand on the clay pot, watching my fingers tremble.

'The light will be gone,' he said. 'Come on quickly, boy.'

My teeth clattered. I pulled the jumper slowly over my head. As I began to undo the buttons of the shirt I heard him approach behind me. I swallowed hard as I felt something being placed over my head. What if Mrs Lacey found out, I thought, could the agency demand to take me back? I put my hand up. It was a plastic bowl. I heard the snap of steel.

'Please . . . ' I said. A slight trickle of urine began to stain my underpants.

Then I felt it, the scissors cutting my hair along the rim of the bowl. He lifted the bowl off. My neck felt cold.

'Now we see those Irish freckles,' he bellowed cheerfully.

Reluctantly I began to undo my trousers. I half turned but he had climbed down and wasn't even looking into the van. He was shouting down at somebody on the beach.

'You'll find clothes in that bag,' he called back casually. 'They should fit you more or less.'

Then he was gone. The air felt cold on my legs. I opened the bag. There was a pair of old knee-length breeches and an old-fashioned boy's jacket from the west of Ireland. I put them on, feeling ridiculous and confused as I stepped out of the van. Pezzani was coming back up through the dunes, followed by the man who had been giving donkey rides on the beach.

'Beautiful,' Pezzani said. 'But why you put your shoes and socks back on? The bare feet, they are lovely. This was my very favourite postcard and you say you did not like it. So now especially for you I do a brand-new one.'

He climbed into the back of the van himself and began to root underneath the stained oilcloths. He emerged a few moments later with an old wicker creel which he placed on the donkey's back. He handed me the reins and we started down towards the beach. The young men playing soccer stopped to wolf-whistle after me. The Rolling Stones were playing on a radio. A straggle of children began to follow us. I kept my face down, furious with myself for blushing. Pezzani and the donkey owner began to haggle over money again. We reached the water's edge and Pezzani pushed me on until I was standing in the shallows with the donkey beside me.

'Now you gather seaweed,' he said.

'You are not serious,' I said, 'you're taking the piss out of me.'

Pezzani raised his camera.

'You Irish,' he said, 'almost as much as the red bush you love the freckled barefoot boy with donkey.'

I looked at him defiantly, refusing to move. He spread his arms out.

'What? You call it a fake? The donkey is as real as you and me. You want to be famous photographer, boy genius? Not a hope. But at least I make you into famous photograph. When you on holidays with your grandchildren you can tell them it is you on the postcard they are buying – *Aran Island Boy Gathering Seaweed for Kelp*.'

Chapter Six

Aunt Cissie must have had trouble walking by now, but her garden was still kept immaculate. The windows were painted the same cream colour as when I was young, the front door the same dark varnish. On summer days I knew she would still hang a tattered green awning over it to protect the paintwork.

It was the final week in March. The new car which Geraldine had bought had been sitting outside for ten days. Without telling her, I got in and drove off. I didn't want a fuss and didn't know myself if I would have the courage to drive the two miles to Aunt Cissie's. It was fourteen months since I had last made that journey, yet I knew that she would greet me as if it were only days. She put her head to one side when she answered the door, trying to disguise her pleasure. There was a scent of baking filling up the whole house and her hands were coated in flour.

'Speeding again I heard you were, you wee scut.'

I grinned, the trauma of the past few months being reduced to another childish prank. This doorstep was where I had always ended up when there was trouble.

'If you think I look bad,' I joked, 'you should see the bus.'

'Well, you weren't speeding to see your old aunt, anyway.'

'Is there any tea in the pot, Aunt Cissie?'

'That wife of yours not feeding you, Seanie? You'd better come in so and don't be bringing any of your oul cameras with you.'

The hallway seemed smaller and more dank than when I was last here. I remembered how big I once felt when I was able to jump up and flick on the light switch. I noticed that the same heavy switch had survived various rewirings.

'You have the house looking great, Aunt Cissie. It hasn't changed a bit.'

'Not worth changing it now when I'll hardly see another Christmas out.'

'You've been singing that song since I was twelve.'

She slapped me playfully on the arm and pushed me into the living room. From inside the kitchen I heard the heavy kettle being filled and the whoosh of the gas being lit. When she came out she had tried to put lipstick on without a mirror and it was smudged, highlighting the fine down of hair above her upper lip. There were traces of flour in her hair where she had run her hands through it.

The room seemed at once both familiar and exotic. A blessing from Pope Pius XII still hung on the wall. I remembered staring at the Latin inscription as a child. She selected and carefully wiped the best china, and as soon as I had taken a sup of tea she held the teapot out to refill the cup, almost pouring through my fingers when I held my hand out to motion that I had enough. I knew how disappointed she was that I had not called an hour later, when today's bread would have been ready. Her eyes followed mine to the faded photo of John F. Kennedy over the television.

'God, that man fairly made the bed shake,' she said, wry humour replacing the almost religious tones in which the household had once spoken of him. 'He was a new Daniel O'Connell, all right.'

I remembered the joke from her native Kerry that you could not throw a stone over an orphanage wall without hitting one of O'Connell's bastards.

'You have the piped television?' I asked.

'The best company in the world,' she said, 'after the women down in bingo. Especially the American wrestling on the satellites. Them would have been the boys to beat the Black and Tans. Did I tell you what I've won at the bingo since?'

'No.'

'Not even the price of the bus fare. It's a good thing I've the free travel pass.'

We both laughed. For as long as Aunt Cissie had not been going to see out another Christmas she had not even won the price of the bus fare at bingo. She stopped talking, that old smile on her lips as she tilted her head sideways in anticipation, knowing that I would not have called without a reason. I smiled back, suddenly embarrassed.

'Maybe I just called to see how you were keeping.'

'Pigs could fly, wee scut. You never just called to see me in your life. Say what's on your mind.'

I put the slender cup down. Underneath the tea leaves I knew there was the carving of a girl's face which used to fascinate me as a child when I was allowed to touch her china. I tried to think of a way to begin.

'I don't know what's been on my mind really since the accident, Aunt Cissie. All kinds of memories, and . . .' I paused. 'You know that I was dead for a few moments?'

The few people I had been unable to avoid meeting were either overexcited or dismissive about this. Aunt Cissie just nodded gravely.

'I find it's hard to adjust to ordinary life. Things have a way of playing on your mind afterwards. You know, with no parents or brothers or sisters it's hard to know what you're remembering or only imagining. It's only a little thing, but lately I've been wondering . . . we only lived a mile from the Botanic Gardens and yet I can't remember my mother ever setting foot beyond the gates. It was like she was frightened of the place. There had to be a reason.'

Cissie poured herself more tea. A butterfly had got in and flapped about in the lace folds of the faded curtains.

'Your mother was very . . . well, ashamed isn't the right word . . .' Aunt Cissie began, 'but uneasy about not being what she called your real mother. The way it was, after a while all of us forgot that you were adopted. Well, maybe not forgot, but you were just another little terror and she was another mother coping like the rest of us. We were all too busy with everyday problems, but your mother . . . she'd spend hours peering at you as a baby, comparing the way you reacted to everything with how our children reacted. She couldn't shake it from her head that you were not responding to her the same as a child would to his natural mother.

'She could blow the smallest thing out of proportion, your mother. She suffered traumas that I wouldn't even be aware of until they were over. It's hard for any mother with a first child, but when you're that insecure . . .'

Cissie looked at me.

'How old is your boy now?' she asked.

'Just three.'

'It's a magical age that.'

'I know.' I realized how disappointed Aunt Cissie must have been that I had not brought Benedict with me.

'You can't tell a three-year-old what's real and what isn't,' she said. 'God knows, it doesn't seem long since you were three. Do you remember the times I used to mind you?'

'You used to mind the whole street.'

'Sure you were more fun than the rest of them together.

A Second Life

Such a serious little face and the blatherings away out of you, your hands darting in all directions and everything said as solemnly as though it were the end of the world. *Mind me.* If there was a fly in the room you'd run into the kitchen, lip trembling, *mind me.* Same as if crowds came in. You were never really able for people. The kitchen to yourself, that was your idea of paradise. Every pot and pan out on the floor and you'd be running in and out, so serious about what you were pretending to cook that I almost expected to see cakes and tarts appearing in the pans you had arranged under the kitchen table. I never met a child with an imagination like yours.'

She stopped talking. It was hard to reconcile myself with the child she spoke of or to equate this old woman with the figure of the strong aunt I remembered.

'Why do you ask about the Botanic Gardens?' Her voice was quizzical.

'I don't know.' It was only half a lie. 'Like I said, maybe I've just had too much time on my hands to dwell on little things.'

Her husband had been among the dead faces in the kaleidoscope which had greeted me at that instant of clinical death. I thought of telling her how well and happy he had looked but knew that I never could mention the experience and she would never wish me to. It made me feel lonely again.

'I used to ask you who all the pretend cakes you were making were for,' Cissie said. '"Mamma, Dada, Auntie Cissie, Baba Seanie and the old man in the shed." One time when your mother was collecting you I told you for a laugh to go down and ask the old man in the shed if he wanted a jam or an apple tart. Off you went, racing down the garden as though somebody really lived down there. Your mother and I were sitting here in the kitchen laughing at your imagination when you came in, panting, your face so serious. "Jam tart," you said. "The bits of apple stick in his false teeth." I looked at your mother, wee scut. Three-year-old boys don't make up that type of remark. Maybe you had heard it somewhere else, but you frightened the wits out of us both that day. We never let you down near the shed again.'

I strained to remember the incident, but all I could recall was the bolted shed in the distance and the time that my uncle had kept a greyhound locked in it and he used to bring me down to see the wet tip of his nose sticking out under the crack in the broken boards. I had been much older then, six or seven. There was little I could really remember about the age she was speaking of, except that single image of sitting on a ridge of grass and poking at the loose earth where a worm was slithering back under the soil.

'I know it was just your imagination,' Cissie said, 'but at times it was frightening. The same summer you turned three your mother came over here in tears. She had brought you in to see her brother's grave, your Uncle Peter. He fought in the British Army in the war, you know. The Desert Rats. Had almost half his head blown off. I don't know how they patched him up or how he lived so long. One moment the man was sane, the next you'd realize that he thought there were other people in the room as well as you, soldiers he fought with, Arabs on camels and God knows who else. It was the first time your mother had been to the grave in the seven years since he died. She hadn't even told you what a grave was. I think she was going to explain to you about people getting old and going to heaven. She thought that you were gazing down at the flowers she had placed in the urn when you looked up at her. *That man has no ear.* Your voice was like you were saying that there was a big truck passing on the road. She grabbed you up in her arms and ran all the way home from the cemetery.'

'Maybe I'd heard them talking about him?' I said. 'Maybe I expected to see a man there?'

The sun had gone behind a cloud and it was dark in Cissie's parlour. The story unnerved me. Suddenly I wished I hadn't come to her house. Partly it had only been an excuse to see if I could get behind the wheel of a car again. I had been given my life back, so why couldn't I just accept it joyously without having to mull over every scrap in my past? It was time that I broke out of this limbo and got a grip on the present. Driving to Cissie's I had seen cranes dredging the Royal Canal as workmen restored the wooden locks at Binn's Bridge. I could have gone there this afternoon with Benedict and shared his excitement at the huge planks being lifted into place. That pain was starting again in my chest. I tried not to panic and to control my breathing.

'Maybe you did hear about him. That's what I told your mother too. But she was from one staunch Republican family. Her own brother, your Uncle Joe, was interned for being in the IRA for the whole war in the Curragh. Your granny had a map in the kitchen to mark out the German advances. Even at the start of the sixties his exploits in the British Army were hardly the centre of conversation.' She stopped. 'Listen, Sean, you were just a child. The cartoons were as real to you as the people next door. Don't start dwelling on these things now.'

'I'm not really myself since the crash,' I said. 'What I mean is . . . well, I still don't seem able to fit back into the life I had before. Maybe I feel that I've been given a second life for a particular reason that I haven't discovered yet, to find out things that happened, to make amends in some way.'

These were the words I should have been saying to Geraldine, which maybe I would have said if we hadn't the constant pressure of two children. But they even seemed foolish spoken to this old woman in this room where so much of my early life had been decided. They were thoughts I barely understood or believed in myself.

'For years I've half expected you to call like this,' Cissie said, 'but I always thought it would be to ask about your real mother. I often wondered what I'd say to you if you did.'

'My real mother is part of the jigsaw,' I said, 'but so are lots of other things. Often I think of my father out in his van or your husband on the buses ... life seemed much simpler for them back then.'

'That was only because you were a child looking in.'

'My real mother came from Laois. My parents told me once. She was nineteen, that's all I know.'

'There was more. Your mother thought of her every day. I think she haunted your mother and probably your mother has haunted her. It doesn't seem that long ago, Sean, but looking back it could have been another planet. We weren't brought up to question. That doesn't mean we didn't, just that we felt guilty for even thinking of doing so. Your real mother must have come from poor folk.'

'Why?' I asked.

'Because we were poor. I think the nuns thought wealth was genetic. No rich couple wanted to feel that they had a labourer's child in the family. They matched poor with poor and rich with rich down the line.'

'How did my parents know her age?'

'Your father and mother got a call to go into the agency in town. They had been waiting for almost a year and a half before it came. Forms, questions, inspections of the house. Everything was done through that Mrs Lacey who used to visit your mother for years afterwards. But there was a big nun from up some convent in the agency that day, a Sister Theresa. She terrified your mother, God knows what she must have seemed like to the girls she was in charge of. You were six weeks old in a tiny blue outfit. Your mother couldn't wait to take you away from that place. There were more forms to fill in but the nun started to interfere. She kept looking down at you, poking at your face. "A grand healthy child," she said. "You'll always get that from a girl of nineteen." Your father said that you could see Mrs Lacey wanted to be rid of her, but . . . the power they had back then . . . even she couldn't ask her to leave. You see, there was supposed to be nothing said about her, nothing at all.'

Aunt Cissie stopped. The tea was cold, but she took a sip. I was unsure if the shake had been in her hand from the start. She looked very frail suddenly. I knew that I was causing her pain.

'There was this awkward silence after she said it. For something to say your father stupidly asked if you had the girl's eyes. The nun smiled down at you. "If he has the eyes of a slut's son, then thank God he won't have the upbringing of one." Every Christmas morning when your father had his few whiskeys here, just the pair of us alone after your mother had taken you down to a later Mass, he used language like I never heard from him to curse that bitch of a nun.'

I felt that I had only to turn my head in the darkening room to see him again, the fire of logs blazing in the hearth and the way he would turn to look up with the glass in his hand when I came racing in with my mother after Mass to open the Christmas present from my aunt. I had tired her out enough. It was time to go, but I could not leave it alone.

'How did they know about Laois then?'

'They never told you? Your father even?'

I shook my head.

'Then maybe I shouldn't,' she said.

We sat for a few moments in silence. I think the presence of my parents had become very tangible.

'It can't hurt them now,' I said eventually, 'and it might help me. They're either dust and bone at this stage or else they've entered some kind of elevated state where such things no longer trouble them.'

I looked across at her. Her eyes had taken on all her old sharpness.

'What did your wife say when you told her you were adopted?' she asked.

I looked down again, saying nothing.

'Maybe they are dust or in this state of yours,' she said, 'but I'm not . . . and neither are you.' She stopped. 'Your father . . . he had years to . . . did you never . . .'

'As I remember it he always left anything difficult for you to sort out,' I replied.

'Are you your father's son?' Her eyes had that glint again.

'Geraldine . . .' I let the sentence hang. 'There's just you and me left now, Aunt Cissie. I want to find her, or at least sometimes . . . most of the time . . . I think I do. Help me.'

She reached back to the sideboard behind her and found her cigarettes. I watched her break the filter off one and light it.

'It was . . . I don't know . . . two . . . three months later,'

Cissie said. 'Your mother had changed your clothes as soon as she got you home. But she couldn't bring herself to throw that blue outfit of yours away. One night she looked at the stitching inside the leg of it. The seam was crooked in some way, doubled over. She undid the stitching. There was a tiny scrap of paper inside with a girl's name and an address.'

I remembered that day in the solicitor's office when Geraldine and I were buying the house and the deeds had been thrust briefly into my hands. I had flicked through them and suddenly come across a death certificate, showing how the house had changed hands a half-century before when a previous owner died in it. I had closed my eyes, trying to blot out the date of his death from my head, cursing my curiosity as I knew that I would never be able to feel easy sleeping there on the anniversary of that date. What thousand-times greater terror must my mother have felt, turning the folded paper over in her hand, knowing that she would open it even though she dreaded its contents? I looked at Cissie in the dusk and wondered if I really wanted to know myself.

'What was the name?' I asked finally.

'The address was of some small village in the Slieve Bloom Mountains.'

'What village? And what was the girl's name?'

Cissie looked down at the table where ash had fallen and scattered apart.

'It was a long time ago, Sean. She mightn't have told me and even if she did my memory might be wrong. If your mother had wanted you to know she would have left the address with her will.'

I knew that was all the information Cissie was going to tell me and knew by her voice how she felt she had betrayed a confidence. She looked up.

'There are ways of finding out these things,' she said. 'It's not easy. I'm not even sure how it's done. But if you really want to, then you will find her yourself in your own time.'

We remained silent for a long while before she got up and turned on the light. I knew that by now Geraldine would be starting to panic and trying to conceal it from Benedict. Ever since the night when he had found me crying on the landing the child had developed problems about sleeping alone. We had to sit in the room with him till he fell asleep, soothing him and trying not to get annoyed as he kept turning over to check that we were there. I was back sleeping with Geraldine, but three or four times every night one of us would have to go in to him, before his cries woke the baby, and hold his hand till he fell asleep himself. I rose to go.

'I hope I didn't upset you,' I said.

'Sure I know you inside out, wee scut.'

'I'll bring the kids over to see you soon,' I promised.

The amused disbelief in her smile was like that which I remembered from my childhood.

'If I had a shilling for every one of your promises.'

'I mean to come more often. It's just my life these last years. No matter where I am I'm always supposed to be somewhere else as well.'

'Bring them down this side of Christmas. I'll hardly see another one out . . .'

I kissed her on the cheek and squeezed her shoulders as though about to shake her.

'You old fraud,' I said, walking out into the hall. 'I bet you have to hire a truck to bring your winnings home from bingo. I bet you the other women have a contract out on your life. You probably have shirts in that wardrobe upstairs off the backs of every bingo-playing pensioner in Dublin.'

She cackled and pushed me playfully on.

'Curse of God on you,' she said. 'Can you not smell that bread burning?'

I opened the front door, surprised at how bright the twilit street looked after the dimness of the house. I remembered again how at every sign of trouble I had once run here. She came back up from the kitchen. Her bones had shrunk in recent years, yet I suddenly felt small as I loomed over her. I didn't want to leave.

'Before I go,' I said, 'you were going to tell me about the Botanic Gardens.'

'Have you no wife to go to?' she scolded.

'I promise, I'll ask you nothing else.'

She put her hand up to the wooden switch beside the door. In the flood of strong light the veins on her wrist stood out like lengths of blue flex. We were suddenly framed in the doorway against the evening. I would have photographed us like this from a long way off.

'After that time at your Uncle Peter's grave,' she said, 'any little thing had your mother's nerves on edge. You never remember being in those gardens at all?'

'No,' I said. 'Not till I went there myself when I was ten.'

'Your mother was a born walker. There wasn't a park this side of the city you were not wheeled through a hundred times. It was hard to keep the woman indoors when you were small. I remember once ... you could have been no more than a year old and my Patrick was just starting to walk ... we went down to Glasnevin. You were so cranky in the pram and yet when we went into the Botanics your mood changed. I think it was all the green leaves and buds overhead. We put down the roof of the pram and you were staring up, delighted with yourself, gurgling, laughing, suddenly dying to talk. You were like a different baby. And because of that your mother began taking you there every other day of the week. In the end she knew most of the gardeners by name.'

'Were there photographs taken of me there?'

I remembered those blank spaces in the family album which had always puzzled me.

'She destroyed most of them, but I have some. I told her I'd burnt them, but there was no need to. The whole affair was just your imagination.'

'Can I see them?'

Two women came out from a house across the road and called to her. She waved after them for longer than was necessary, then turned and shook her head.

'It's funny, Seanie, but I don't want you to. Already I feel I've betrayed her somehow. She blamed herself, you know, for not being able to have children. I think she felt worthless. It was all a woman was reared for in those days. Remember the games of football out on that street there? Twelve-, thirteen-a-side and every boy playing was from one of the houses between here and the corner. It was your father who was to blame. It was common enough in our family. Two uncles of ours were childless too. I wanted to say something, but if your father could never tell her the truth who was I to?'

There were cars tightly parked along both kerbs now, with hardly room for traffic down the middle of the street. I could recall those games, yet only as if they had happened to another person. The image of lunging against the fence at the end of the yew walk and waiting to be caught by a man's hands seemed no less real and no less imaginary as well.

'You learnt to walk in the Botanic Gardens,' Aunt Cissie continued. 'On that big grassy slope down to the pond.

You'd spend hours in the old wooden house among the trees, collecting sticks and dipping them in a puddle to pretend that you were painting the walls. After a while you knew your way around better than your mother did, toddling along in front of her, watching the men cutting the grass with their tractor. *The tractor loves Seanie,* that's what you used to say. *The Baba trees love Seanie.* Everything there had to love you. And everything there had to be yours. *My tractor is cutting the grass.* There was only one bit you didn't like. That little walk there with the old yew trees. You used to bawl if we went near it. I think it was the way the crooked trees slanted inwards, maybe you thought they'd fall on you. And there was only one bit your mother didn't like. The rose garden. At first she loved to sit there, but you began to drive her crazy, always pointing over to the corner and complaining, *My house missing. Bold man stolen my house.*

I pictured the rose garden, bordered by the Tolka House pub and Botanic Road on two sides and cut off on the other two sides by the river itself. It was linked to the main garden by a narrow bridge and was seven or eight feet below the level of the road which ran past the wall.

'Your mother asked me to go down with her one day and sit with you. You were getting more and more possessive about that little square of garden, getting upset if anyone else even came over the bridge to walk around it. I thought it was just like when you were pretending to cook in my kitchen . . .'

Cissie reached into her pocket for another cigarette and lit it, the smoke trailing from her hand as she imitated the gestures I had made as a child.

'. . . *Mammy Peg washes the clothes in the river, Mammy Peg hangs them there. The boys all sleep in the hay. My*

doggie sleeps in shed, my doggie bold doggie old man says.
It wasn't frightening or anything, if a tractor came along by
the river or you heard a motor bike over the wall you
forgot everything else. But it was . . . maybe if I had heard
you everyday . . . it would have got to me as well. I think it
was the word "mammy" that caused your mother such
upset, as if deep down you knew that she was not really
who she said she was. When we went to go you wouldn't
leave the rose garden. *Stay home, stay home,* you were
crying. There was an old gardener working on the flower
bed beside the bridge. To reassure your mother I asked him
how old the rose garden was. "As far back as the gardens
themselves," he said. "When I started here the scent at the
bridge in summer would suffocate you." Your mother
smiled at him, I think she had been half afraid to ask
herself. We were half-way across the bridge when he called
after us and pointed to the little semicircle of trees and
rocks on the other side. "You can see the old one there on
your way out," he said. "The biggest job I ever did, shifting
all the roses across to this side of the river the time we
knocked down Davitt's old cottage after the war and planted
the new garden there." Your mother had stopped. I could
see how scared she was. I asked him who the Davitts were
and he called them the best family that ever worked there.
Father and son with over a hundred years' service between
them. He began to point out how the wall by the road was
made up of bricks from their cottage. But your mother had
begun to run, with you pulling out of her arms, whining,
Stay home, stay home.'

Mind me, hold me. It wasn't myself as a child that I saw
in my mind but Benedict, who would be whining in the
kitchen now as Geraldine waited for me to come home. I
wanted to be there with my arms around him, protecting

him. I was not sure from what – the future, the past, or simply the fact that soon he would outgrow the secure innocence he lived within. Or was it simply that I still felt I could protect him at his age, bolt the door, read him stories, create a joy for him that would never be as absolute again? Maybe I just felt suddenly scared and slightly lost, and wanted to pretend that I could share in the totality of his joy with him. I patted Cissie on the arm, trying to let on that her words had not unnerved me.

'I shouldn't be tiring you like this,' I said.

'Away home to your wife and kids, wee scut.' They were the same jokey words as always but her voice was sad, barely audible.

When I went to walk down the path she pushed two ten-pound notes into my pocket, one for each of the children. I knew that she would have to do without her beloved cigarettes for a fortnight to make the money up. I tried to argue but it was useless. She stood in the lit doorway.

'Drive that car slow for a change. And you keep your promise to bring those children down to see me this side of Christmas, do you hear, or else I'll come back to haunt you.'

I stilled the tremble in my hand, swallowed and began to turn the steering wheel with caution and sudden irrational fear.

Chapter Seven

Something was always going to lure me back to work for the paper again. The funny thing was that I had thought of Frank Conroy just the previous week and remembered the promise which I had made the previous October to photograph his first child when it was born. Just before my crash I had heard through the newspaper that it was a girl and how Frank was totally engrossed with the child.

Yet when I turned on the radio that morning on the first of April to hear how a car had been dredged from the Shannon at Killaloe in County Clare with a man in the driver's seat and a four-month-old girl strapped into a baby chair beside him, I knew immediately that it was Frank. No names were given and the newsreader passed quickly on to details of the IRA bomb in London the previous day, but already I was waiting for Gerry's phone call.

Geraldine followed me upstairs after a while and asked why I was not going to the studio. I had my father's old camera bag out and was packing equipment and clothes for an overnight stay.

'I'm starting work again,' I said. 'I'll be away for the night.'

I could sense the fear that made her body stiff and answered her unspoken question: 'I have to get back behind a wheel properly at some stage.'

'Love, I don't like it. Be careful . . .'

'Don't . . .'

I didn't mean my voice to be as sharp, but I just couldn't

stand any fuss. I didn't want to have to think about driving the car until I got into it. Apart from the one trip to Aunt Cissie's I had let Geraldine do all the driving. I knew that my tone of voice had hurt her, but I was too tense to turn around and take her in my arms. Sinead was still in her high chair. Benedict was climbing the stairs to see what we were doing.

'What's the story you're working on?' she asked.

'Frank Conroy.'

'I thought the paper had dropped that story. Didn't he change his mind about publicity?'

'The body of a man and a four-month-old girl were pulled from the Shannon at Killaloe this morning.'

'Good Jesus. Were they named?'

'I just know it was him.'

'Why would he . . .?'

Benedict was tugging at her jumper, disturbed by the atmosphere in the room and wanting to be held. I couldn't answer her question. Geraldine picked him up. He put his arms out to me for a hug, bringing all three of us together. I remembered how, on the previous evening, I had gone up to check the children. I knelt on the floor beside Sinead's cot, straining in the half-light to catch the faint murmur of her breathing. For a few moments I had heard no sound. Every worry from the three months since the crash seemed utterly eclipsed, trivial now as I pressed my ear firmly against the white bars, holding my own breath and trying not to panic. Then the child stirred with a loud exhalation of air and I was flooded with unadulterated joy.

I had found myself smiling, almost wanting to laugh. Sinead's clear breathing seemed to defuse, at least momentarily, that residue of loss at my being brought back to life. I realized how desperately I wanted to be alive to witness every stage of her development until she too came to kneel in some room like this and feel the same sense of exhilaration. I had gone in to Benedict, who had kicked the quilt off, and tucked it carefully back around him. He stirred and looked up, still asleep, to murmur my name before his eyes closed over again.

Now I realized that, during those moments, Frank Conroy's eyes would have been staring blankly out into the black waters of the Shannon while his left hand still cradled the small fist of his daughter. I closed my eyes tightly, feeling Benedict lifting his head from the cuddle.

'Silly old Dada,' I heard him say to Geraldine. 'Why does silly old Dada look like he's crying?'

It was ten o'clock when Gerry, who had done the original interview with Frank Conroy, phoned with the news. There was no pressure on me to cover the story, he said, but the editor had felt that it might interest me. The sly fox, I thought wryly, he realizes that I know the wife and will be able to get good access to the house. He had had his chance to print the story six months before, and had been happy to let it slip past. Now he knew that the human-interest angle had to be covered. Gerry offered me a lift but I refused him. We agreed to meet up instead in the Railway Hotel in Killaloe at three o'clock that afternoon.

Geraldine said nothing when I was leaving. I confidently drove off, but managed only to get the car around the corner before I had to pull in. My hands shook like an alcoholic's outside an early-morning house.

I remembered a taxi driver I met once who described waking up on the morning that he began to work for himself to find that his whole body was locked rigid with fear, and how it had taken him hours to get the courage to simply lift his feet out of the bed. My body felt like a lead weight in the driver's seat. It would be another five or six months before the court case came up. Until then at least I still had my licence. It had been hard enough driving to and from Aunt Cissie's, but now the traffic lanes and roundabouts of the Nass dual carriageway lay ahead of me. I could almost hear my heart palpitating. What if I got a panic attack out there in the middle of the motorway? I wiped the sweat from my palms on to my shirt and started the engine up again.

I didn't know how much money Geraldine had got for what was left of the old car. Likewise she hadn't told me how much the new model had cost. We had some resources left from the settlement of the court case about my father's work, along with a small sum coming in occasionally from permissions and prints of mine that were still ticking over. The newspaper had kept paying my retainer, but I knew that I had to start making proper money again soon. I focused on money, bank balances, mortgage payments, to stay calm as I drove into the heavy traffic along the quays.

The cabin cruisers would be tied up in Killaloe, waiting for the end of the month to bring German and Italian accents. Cars would have stopped all morning, local people saying nothing as they stared into the waters of the river. Whatever people had thought of Frank Conroy in the final year of his life they had kept it to themselves. They would do the same now at his death. On the phone Gerry had said there had been no note left, that anyone who had met him in the hours before he drove the car into the river said that he seemed in almost manic good humour. I knew there would be former miners from Mullabeg on the quayside, men whose boots and shadows and bent forms I had photographed eighteen months before. That was when I had met Frank Conroy first, after he had been elected in his absence on to the local committee to save the mine.

If the Japanese factory had not closed in Galway in the same week then the media might never have even noticed the closure of Mullabeg coal mine. But job losses were news for that Sunday's papers and after months of anonymously fighting their case the fifty miners had found themselves the centre of a nation's attention for a weekend. There were only two coal mines in the country, both privately owned and both no longer useful to the ESB, who had used their low-quality coal for generating electricity. Agrina mines had already closed. The miners at Mullabeg knew that they had no hope of reversing the owner's decision. But they also knew that, except for those few young enough to leave, once the mine closed none of them would work again.

The interviews had been standard, the television crew asking the miners' spokesman who had just come off shift if he would rub some coal dust on to his face to look better in the shot. By the time he reached Gerry I could see the spokesman's nerves beginning to fray.

'You come down on safari from Dublin,' he said, 'but you people haven't got a bull's notion. If you want to know desperation, boy, then take a trip down that shagging mine with us. Because there isn't a man Jack here who hasn't cursed it every working day of his life. A crumbling black hell under the ground. There isn't one of us who hasn't knelt down there and prayed to God for someone to come along and close the place. All hand work. Not one tool in the place that isn't twenty years out of date. And the fact that we're out here fighting to save it . . . that, by Jaysus, is desperation. Because we'd sooner a black hell under the earth than to be walking around in a living hell on top of it. I see your paper in the shop every week. Singing the praises of rich gangsters in dickie-bows. So don't pretend that your paper gives a shite for us or will do anything to help us. Maybe you'd be as well off buggering over to do another of your big colour spreads on the Orphan McHugh and his shagging Country Club down the road. And you tell the poor orphan up in his castle that we know he's just waiting to level this place to build an extra nine holes for the Germans and the Yanks to hit golf balls over our graves.'

It was Frank Conroy who had stepped forward to deflect the man's anger away from us and back at the government for refusing to increase their subsidy to the ESB to use the coal. But the miners' spokesman was right. This would be a one-off feature on an inside page provided that no big advertisement came in before the paper went to press. The Country Club which Peter McHugh was building featured on the gossip page every week. When it opened there would be a two-page colour spread heading the supplement with a page of paid advertisements from suppliers congratulating him yet again. The miners had grinned at the nickname 'orphan', getting McHugh's measure, knowing there was more than one way to call a man a bastard.

When Gerry had finished the interview I slipped the roll of film into his pocket and asked him to get somebody on the picture desk to develop it. I hung on until the last of the media had gone. The owner had come down in his car. The mine had been in his family for a hundred years. The coal was low-grade, worthless to try and sell commercially when the ESB contract expired in two weeks' time. The miners and himself seemed to have a grudging respect for each other.

'He'll do all right for himself,' the spokesman said to no one in particular after the owner drove off. 'He'll do the deal with McHugh. But he won't do as well as he thinks he's doing. Once a bastard, always . . . eh?'

The light had gone. The gathering was breaking up, men heading back to their homes in Ballynahinch and Birdhill and Newport. Finally only four men were left. There was a small grotto to the Blessed Virgin over the entrance to the mine shaft. The light around her head came on with a faint electric humming. Frank Conroy had walked across to stand beside me.

'Tell him I'll take up his offer,' I said, nodding towards the spokesman. The other men heard me and looked across.

'Have you missed your bus or what?' the youngest of the men sneered.

'I'll go down the mine with you in the morning.'

'You already have your pictures,' the spokesman said. He had taken his helmet off and washed himself. He looked far older in ordinary clothes, his face used up, long past retirement age.

'I have the paper's photographs. Now I'd like to take my own.'

'The shaft gets narrow down there. You'll be crawling on your stomach at the coalface. You'll meet bigger rats than in Dáil Éireann. Now why don't you just forget it?'

It had taken me ten minutes to persuade them. They were scornful at first, convinced that I would not have the courage to show up the next morning. Frank Conroy offered me a bed in his house outside Killaloe, seven miles away. We stayed up talking till four o'clock. He was a civil servant in Limerick who had taken a week's leave to help out with the miners' action committee. That was how I still remembered him best, sitting beside the old range in his kitchen with a cat on his knee while his wife teased him about her having given up a good job as an interpreter in Brussels to settle down with him, only to find that he had been coerced on to every committee in Clare. Tidy Towns, Meals on Wheels, Tourism Taskforce, Community Watch for old people in isolated areas. And I could still see Frank – a massive, gentle figure – grinning sheepishly back across at her.

The Mullabeg mine shots were among my favourite photographs. Outside at the entrance I had used the twenty-year-old Nikkormat FTN which my father had left me with only a 50mm and a 135mm lens. At first in the low, strong winter sunlight I just shot the silhouettes of the men like ghosts dwarfed against the dust and broken asphalt of the yard. Down in the shaft their attitude to me changed. I was, briefly, a part of their underground world. Their problems seemed temporarily forgotten in that bond which existed there. Brilliant electric light and utter darkness existed simultaneously in the tunnels, figures perpetually shifting parts of their bodies between the two. They worked that day as though the mine would last for ever, aware perhaps that soon these images would remain as the only proof that they had existed as a body of men. Their features slipped in and out of focus as I clicked so that they seemed just one more integral part of the mine. I had used infra-red film, which made the black and white images of their faces and hands curiously pale.

Later I spent weeks in the darkroom bleaching and toning sections of the prints before I was satisfied. By the time I had finished, the mine was closed, the men living off their smallholdings and the dole. McHugh had bought the site. The gossip columnists said that it was rumoured he planned to use it for war games in a fantasy adventure playground.

Leaving Dublin my nerves had steadied on the motorway. I moved out from the slow lane, gathering pace, testing myself. The crash which I kept seeing in my mind was not my own but Frank Conroy's car as it sped along the quayside. At what point had there been no return for him – twenty yards, ten? There seemed to have been no witnesses to say if he had tried to brake before the water's edge or held the wheel tight, jerking his head back in that weightless moment before the car made contact with the water. His death I could try to understand and forgive. It was the small four-month-old corpse which filled me with total horror. *You stupid bastard, Frank*, I kept repeating as I drove along the deserted strip of new carriageway paid for by Europe to bypass Nass. I tried to think over the details of his story, but my mind would slip back to the two bodies under water. I knew it was that which was bringing me here, the betrayal of trust. I could not focus on the world of politics and news or anything outside my own obsessions.

Beyond Portlaoise I began to slow. It was ten miles to Mountrath. I had another fifty miles to Killaloe beyond that. I should keep going while my nerve lasted. Yet all the time I knew that I would stop, that this was another reason why I had agreed to cover the story. I reached the T-junction on the edge of Mountrath. The cars ahead of me swung left, taking the main road on to Roscrea. I indicated to follow them, then at the last minute turned right and took the narrow left turn into the Slieve Blooms.

There was a market on the side of the road. Wellington boots and overcoats for sale along with small plastercast statues of Saint Jude, Guns 'N' Roses T-shirts and ancient bootleg tapes of U2 playing in 1979 in Tullamore and Kilkenny. I stopped the car. My shoe dangled out of it for an eternity before I set foot on the ground.

I began to walk among the horse-boxes and stalls. I was studying each face as neighbours chatted or people leaned across the trestle tables to purchase goods. That old farmer might be my uncle, the woman with the child in the buggy a cousin of mine. As a child my real mother must have run around the stalls here, playing with women present who would still remember her. The odd person glanced at me. If my aunt's story was right then I had come home. Here for the first time I was standing among my own people. I felt short of breath again. I must have inherited some of her features. I wanted to shout, *Does anybody know my face? Can you tell me who I am?*

Maybe my real mother was still here, the wife of a strong farmer now with her youthful indiscretion long banished. Before I was born my existence had been written out of this place, as surely as if I had been aborted with gin and hot baths and buried in a shallow grave under the bog. Even if I found her here among these stalls she would probably deny my existence. I would be made to feel like a beggar, come to threaten the share-out of her inheritance among her proper children. Suddenly I felt anger. I wanted to kick over the trestle tables, to reverse my car into the stalls with their tacky coloured bulbs. I got back into the car. The noise of the wheels spinning on the gravel made people turn around.

'Fuck you,' I mouthed through the closed windows at them. 'Fuck every bastarding one of you.'

Beyond Roscrea I pulled in again. I had been speeding, recklessly overtaking, trying to shake the unexpected rage, which seemed to have been buried in me, out of my system. My breath was coming shorter again. I tried to fight it, then went with the breathing instead, feeling the tightness grip my chest, sensing my hands begin to flutter wildly as though made of rubber. My body was pushing against the seat belt. There would be burn marks on my neck. My rage was like a physical weight lodged against my ribcage. I screamed to expel it and kept screaming, my voice seeming to come back to me from a great distance. Gradually with each scream I could feel it lifting.

The slipstream of trucks rocked the car as they sped past. I opened my eyes. Bloated cows watched me from a field. I felt empty and yet strangely good. I was late. Gerry would be waiting for me now in Killaloe. I knew that Geraldine would soon be phoning the hotel and worrying if I was not there. I started the engine again. My father's old camera bag was on the floor beside the passenger seat. I touched it for a moment as though it were a good-luck charm.

Two weeks after Gerry's article on the Mullabeg miners appeared the mine closed down. I had not expected to hear from Frank Conroy again. Six months later I had half thought of calling to him when the Arra Mountains Hotel and Country Club was officially opened and I was sent down to do a portrait of Peter McHugh for the cover of the supplement. Some time after that an Italian magazine ran twelve of the Mullabeg shots and I sent a copy to Conroy as his was the only contact address I had for any of the men in the area.

It was last October when he phoned me. I recognized his voice at once although it sounded different. The warmth was squeezed from it. It sounded edgy now, anxious, hard to reconcile with his massive figure. He wanted Gerry and myself to travel down to Killaloe. He had a story for us which he didn't wish to talk about on the phone. Normally I told people that I was just a freelance photographer, I did not work for the newspaper. They should contact the editor directly or one of the reporters. But something in Frank Conroy's voice made me agree to travel the next day. He was not a man to contact reporters, not someone you could ever imagine feeling threatened by anything. All that night the memory of his voice disturbed me.

Gerry had been in Galway but agreed to travel from there to Clare. Geraldine had needed the car so I took the Cork train to Limerick Junction and arranged for a taxi to meet me. In winter the station, set in the middle of isolated fields, looked as surreal as ever. The taxi driver chose a cross-country route, avoiding the Limerick road, speeding through Doon and on into the Slieve Felim Hills.

'Do you know where you are now?' he kept asking, as though delighted with his orienting abilities. 'Do you know where you are at all?'

He had a countryman's inquisitive nature, perpetually glancing at the bag on the seat behind us and leading the conversation back to how few people visited Killaloe at this time of year.

'You'd be visiting a body down there, I suppose?'

'I suppose I would,' I had replied, amused at the game.

'Must be someone important now if you're taking a taxi all this way.'

I looked out the window, leaving him hanging, and tried not to grin. When I glanced back he was watching me slyly.

'The body you're visiting wouldn't go by the name of Frank Conroy, would it now?'

I didn't answer but the look on my face was enough for him to grin in triumph. He chuckled and braked to take a steep corner.

'I wasn't long sussing you now, was I? Ah, you're all right, you're with a friend here. But, by God, fair play to Conroy. He had us all fooled here. The best way, he was dead right. You'd have the Special Branch up your arse every day. Frank Conroy, eh? God, I had a good laugh. A few red faces on the guards around here. Listen though, mind yourself in Killaloe. There's a lot of sly, West-Brit bastards and informers floating around the kip. You were right to take a taxi. I'll leave you to his door so quietly now that not even his next-door neighbour will know you're here.'

He braked hard again and swung left down a narrow boreen, pointing to an old henhouse as we passed.

'That's where the boys had that dentist you kidnapped. Sure the whole townland knew it, the lads up and down to the shop there for Mars Bars and Twixs at every hour of the day. But nobody made a sound. The guards got here a week too late. The mean bastards spent two days, just for spite, taking every house along the road apart.'

The driver was getting more and more excited as he talked, the roads kept getting narrower. I began to grow afraid. I nodded occasionally but otherwise said nothing. Frank Conroy was the least likely IRA man I could imagine. I knew how often innocent people were intimidated into hiding arms on their land or pretending not to see movements in the fields behind their homes, but it was hard to imagine Frank Conroy not standing up to any thug. I felt uncomfortable and wanted to get on a train back to Dublin, but knew that it was unwise to ask the driver to change direction. If this was some sort of news story then it was a reporter's business. Why had I ever allowed myself to be dragged into it?

Outside Frank Conroy's cottage the driver winked when I tried to pay him.

'This one's on me,' he said. 'You can't be robbing a bank every day. *Éireoimíd Arís.*'

Gerry was already inside the cottage. The kitchen seemed far colder in the daylight. The range was out and a Superser was burning instead. Frank's wife was pregnant and looked as though she had not slept properly for weeks. Frank was talking when I went in and looked up, unsure whether to keep speaking into Gerry's tape-recorder or start again. His eyes looked disoriented and slightly frantic. I nodded for him to go on while his wife rose to make fresh tea.

His story was both simple and bizarre. Six weeks before, he had driven his wife into Ennis on a Saturday afternoon. They were looking for a smother-proof mattress for the wooden cot which he was making himself. He had left her in the department store and gone across to a newsagent's to get an ice-cream cone. There was a young Englishman in the queue with short hair who kept staring at him. The Englishman seemed nervous, sweating as he glanced around him. Frank nodded and reached into his jacket for his wallet. The Englishman had suddenly gone berserk. He produced a gun and thrust it against Frank's neck, shrieking for him to put his hand down, shouting that Frank had followed him on the train all the way from Belfast and was sent to kill him.

It had taken the guards five minutes to get there. The shop had cleared, just Frank left with the young man staring up at him. When the guards came in the man shouted that he was a British soldier and Frank was an assassin who had tried to murder him. The guards had moved slowly towards them, telling the soldier to stay calm, that they had Frank covered.

'You're okay, mates,' the soldier told them. 'I can handle this bastard myself.'

He squeezed the trigger just as the guards caught his arm. It jammed. Frank had closed his eyes, hearing the curses of the soldier as the guards overpowered him and then the screams of his wife, who had been attracted by the crowd and witnessed his attempted execution.

Yet it was not so much the fact of being nearly killed as what happened afterwards which most upset Frank. His first concern had been for his wife, in case the shock induced her into early labour. When the guards told him to go with them to the station he had been busy comforting her and said that he would follow them in a few moments to file charges. It was only when a guard took hold of him that he realized he was being arrested.

'Jaysus, lads,' he joked to them, 'sure half the shop here knows me. I'm after driving in from Killaloe. I was never within a spit of Belfast in my life.'

The guard silently twisted his hand behind his back to handcuff him and he was pushed into the back of a squad car with his wife crying beside him. People had been shocked by the incident, sympathetic towards him and furious at the soldier, but at the mention of Belfast and the sight of the handcuffs he said that he could sense the atmosphere changing. Figures in the crowd seemed anxious to avoid his eyes. There was a sudden suspicion present, almost a hostility as though the very mention of that taboo place name was dragging their lives into a distant conflict.

In the Garda station nobody seemed sure what to do with him. The building was quiet. His wife and himself were left sitting across from each other in a tiny room. Frank could hear the soldier start to scream again about everybody wanting to murder him and then the voice of a man, obviously a doctor, in the corridor.

'It's not something he needs to be given to calm him down, it's for the effects of something he's taken to wear off. The man's as high as a kite, he's stoned out of his head.'

Half an hour later there was the sound of a helicopter landing on the pad behind the station. Several pairs of feet moved quickly down the corridor and passed back a moment later. The helicopter lifted off, the soldier was gone. Their door opened and Frank's wife was told to leave the room. Frank had reassured her that it was okay, he knew several guards who worked there, they would vouch for him. While she waited in the corridor she saw a sergeant who was on the Tourism Taskforce with Frank. He backed away into the room he had come from when he saw her, his fingers flicking through the files in his hands as though he had forgotten something.

Frank was questioned for two hours about every aspect of his life. Again and again they returned to lists of people living around Killaloe or in Limerick and Shannon, asking him if he knew them. Some he knew because they were neighbours, two in Shannon because he had been at school in Listowel with them.

'Why do you know these people?' one guard kept shouting at him. 'You know their sort. Why do you keep mixing with them? Where do you stand in all this? What did you do during the hunger strikes? We have your measure, boy. Come on, talk to us.'

The door opened again. The guard who came in was a senior figure whom Frank had seen once or twice drinking in hotels in Limerick. He nodded to the men to leave.

'Children,' he said. 'God knows why the British keep giving guns to children and calling them soldiers. Only twenty that boy, a babe in the wood. You know they're strictly forbidden to cross the border on their leave. I mean they're barely allowed to go to the toilet alone. He had a T-shirt under his jumper, *Hitler on Tour, Europe, 1939–45*. I ask you now, babes in the wood and they're sending them up there.'

Frank said the man gave a companionable half-laugh and sat down at the table to stare at him.

'The boy saw one of his friends killed by a sniper,' he said. 'In the papers a few months back, but sure who could keep track? He's thrown the head a couple of times since. He was being sent home when he vanished. God knows how he wound up here. You're in the Civil Service below in the city?'

'That's right.'

'And they tell me you're a great man altogether. Up on every committee and action group in the county. Well, you know this is a bad business. Now, there are charges that could be pressed but sure the boy would get off on medical grounds. Anyway he's back across the border by now. The only people who'd gain anything from this are the sort of people who want to wreck the talks going on up there between our two governments. And I tell you another thing. You're on the Tourism Taskforce here. How many English visitors do we get a year? And never a bit of trouble with any of them. The English papers get hold of this, they'll take the side of that young fellow. The Brits will never admit to being in the wrong. They'll be making out that the boy was attacked by a mob of Provos. There'll be a lot of empty B&Bs around here whose owners won't think too kindly of you if you try to push this.'

'So I'm just supposed to forget he tried to kill me?'

'The Northern Talks are important to the powers-that-be, who have to be seen doing something in Dublin, and, far more importantly, tourism is vital to us down here. Now unless you want to side with saboteurs . . .?'

The man had smiled, his arm around Frank as he led him

down the corridor to his wife. But when they got back to Killaloe they found that the local guards had been sent to the house. Things had been put back relatively neatly, but every drawer and locker had been searched. Floorboards had even been lifted and the timber covering the entrance into the attic was broken into pieces. Those parts of the garden where late seeds had recently been sown were dug up.

Frank's wife said that what was most eerie was the silence along the row of bungalows. Normally children would be out on bicycles or playing in the gardens, but there was no sign of life from any of the houses. That evening no neighbours called. At Mass the next day they could both sense people's unease. Neighbours who would normally come over to say hello hurried off. When he drove down to get Bisto later in the day two men outside a pub winked and saluted him.

'There usen't to be a door in this town that wasn't wide open to us,' Frank's wife told us as Gerry put a new tape into the machine. 'Now, well most of our good friends are the same, but other people . . . I mean, neither of us is from here but everybody knows Frank. Strangers would be at this door night and day asking him to do favours for them. He was a soft touch for everyone, getting messages for people in Limerick, bringing lads from the college home in the evenings. How can everybody just decide they don't trust him any more? And then there are the others . . . these slimy old men who slink up to you, talking about *the lads* and *the cause*. We had made a good life for ourselves here. Some days I'm so sick I don't know if I want to bring this child into the world at all.'

Her last words in her Wexford accent on that tape six

months before were what haunted me as I drove into
Killaloe just after three. Gerry was already there, sitting at
the bar in the Railway Hotel.

'You old bollox,' he greeted me in his customary way.
'Heard you went and died on us. How are you enjoying life
second time round?'

'You get to lose your virginity all over again.'

'Wouldn't fancy that. It was hard enough finding a sheep
when I was twelve in West Cork, but I'd never get one up
the stairs of that flat of mine now. I say one thing for our
Frank. He had good timing, he got me out of having to
cover the aftermath of that bomb in London.'

He turned to catch the barman's attention. I smiled at the
bald patch on his head, looking at the tweed jacket which
he had been wearing since I first met him. That tattered
jacket had occupied the corners of so many of my
photographs: Gerry interviewing spokespeople after EC summits, covering the relief workers kneeling among the starving in Africa, blending into screaming crowds at by-election
counts around the country, always with that same quizzical
look as though he had just been beamed down from space.
It became a silent joke between us to ignore the PR people
anxiously hovering around at summits and gala functions,
trying to lend Gerry a dinner jacket. He turned back towards
me, holding out a drink.

'Poor Geraldine,' he said, 'only two and a half minutes to
spend the insurance money.'

When we went out the quayside was deserted, except for
the odd onlooker who stared for a few moments into the
depths of the water and then turned to walk past us
without speaking. The whole town was silent and indoors.
In my mind I saw the children being released from school,
exploding through the gates with no sound from their open

mouths. Flowers had been left on the wet stones. There was a note with one bunch which had obviously read *In loving memory of Frank and baby*, only somebody else had torn Frank's name from it. The car had already been dredged from the river. There was nothing to see. Gerry nudged my elbow.

'It's your baby.'

'What?'

'Your part of the job. Click-click time.'

I glanced down at the camera suspended from my neck, then back at him with a half-laugh. It was the first time that I had tried to use one since the crash.

'It's been a while. I'm half scared to use it. Can't see the point. That's funny, isn't it? The stupid bastard. I know what he's been through, but that still doesn't explain it. Why did he have to bring the child?'

The question tormented me. I had not been much younger than that child when I was taken on a journey too, given away, offered up by someone who might have loved me. Why? I lifted the camera and pointed the lens down towards the freezing water where Frank Conroy and the child everybody said he loved had died.

The kitchen was crowded with neighbours. Here and there the usual suspects from the media were interviewing people. I knew that no local person would mention the trouble in Ennis unless the journalists asked them about it. Even then it would be played down and made light of. Suicides were common in Ireland. If it were not for the baby nobody from Dublin would be here, even if his story was well known. A week after he spoke to Gerry, Frank had phoned me to say that he had changed his mind, the story would do too much damage to tourism in the area, he would ride out the storm.

I hadn't told him that the paper had been reluctant to cover the story anyway, the editor's words echoing those of the guard about playing into the hands of the Provos. Conroy had been filed away under C, between D for dangerous and B for better left unsaid.

His wife looked up and saw us, the anguish on her face momentarily changing to relief at a familiar face. I thought of Geraldine and how she would have sat too, if I had died, in a kitchen invaded by neighbours and relations. In a curious way I felt like a ghost coming in. I could imagine Frank travelling up through the water towards a cone of light, staring back at the open-mouthed bodies in the car. Would the child have journeyed with him? Or was there a journey to hell, the faces hissing, casting him down into blacker waters away from the light towards which the child floated, lost to him? Frank's wife stood up. I knew the town of Blackwater where she was from, could remember laughing as I was swung by my parents' arms in summer outside the green shop there with its holiday display of buckets and spades. How far away our childhoods were. I tried to pull myself together and put my arm around her.

'Everybody keeps taking photographs of me and the house,' she whispered. 'They just won't go away. I don't know what to do. Am I supposed to feed them or what?'

I looked down at her face. It was bewildered, in shock. She seemed like a child herself. I turned to Gerry.

'Get them out of here,' I said to him. 'Please. Tell them whatever you want, but just get them the hell out.'

I telephoned Geraldine to say that I would be home by lunchtime the following day. She put Benedict on the line. He said nothing but I could imagine his mouth almost biting into the receiver as he listened to my voice. I told him that when I got home I would finish building him a bird-table in the garden so that we could leave out bread together for the birds. Geraldine made me promise to phone her in the morning before I left. Later on, when Gerry was talking to Frank's widow, I telephoned Peter McHugh. I had to soft-soap my way through receptionists and secretaries but I knew that he would speak to me.

'It's bad news about Frank Conroy,' I began.

'You mess with the North . . .' He left the sentence unfinished.

'You know well he had nothing to do with the North.'

'Down here . . . the North . . . it's like Aids. Some people . . . they bugger their way through half the Artane Boys band before they get it. Others . . . they get a cut on their little finger and a dodgy blood transfusion. All winds up the same thing.'

'Listen, I want to talk to you about something personal. Will you see me in the morning?'

I could hear a door open in his suite. I imagined him staring at the assistant who had come in.

'I've appointments all morning tomorrow.' He paused. 'Fuck them. Come on over.'

I went back into the kitchen. There were two local women left with Gerry and the widow. She looked up at me.

'The same question. All day you're waiting, watching them build up to it as though they honestly expect you to know the answer. Why? Do they think I know why? I lived with that man every day . . . now you tell me. Why?'

Chapter Eight

The next morning as I drove from Killaloe towards McHugh's Country Club I remembered the first time that we had met, a year before. Normally I didn't work with Valerie, the paper's society journalist, but there was a lot of advertising built into the opening of the Country Club and so I had been drafted. Valerie had two articles planned: a bland, flattering interview to complement the advertising in the paper and a later mocking piece for the column she wrote under a nom-de-plume in one of the smarter women's magazines.

Within quarter of an hour I knew that McHugh had figured her out, although she was not aware of it. Anything he actually said would not affect the tone of either article. The easy soft-soaping charm with which he had greeted her began to settle into something harder. His eyes registered her condescension when Valerie asked if he had a favourite saint. He looked at her as he answered, his voice beginning to affect a broader country accent.

'The oul F saint himself.'

'Saint Francis?'

'No. Saint Franchise.'

She had the word written down before she stopped, too well bred to show her irritation. *Be nice to him,* the editor had told her. *Make him like you and remember, get lots of good quotes about the orphanage.*

'You're not a Mullingar girl, no?' he asked.

'No. Glenageary in south Dublin, why?'

'Ah, just your looks, you know.' His eyes took me in. 'Beef to the heel like a Mullingar heifer.'

I drove in through the gates of the club. The finished golf course was deserted. Even with reduced rates in April few local people could afford to play it. Saint Franchise had looked after Peter McHugh well. The bar and restaurant on the golf course and the running of the Country Club itself were all franchised out, as were the health studio and discotheque which were built on the grounds. It was the method of operation by which McHugh had bought up over twelve major hotels in the region. Smaller, would-be McHughs sweated to pay his mortgages for him.

On the day of the interview with Valerie, although the Country Club had just opened, the golf course was still being built. McHugh had let us walk it with him and the architect. We stood on a small hill at the proposed tee for the short par-three sixth.

'You've two choices,' the architect had told him. 'If you tee off from up here at the top of the mound then you get a nice elevated tee but the lake doesn't come into play. However, if you move the tee down there into the hollow it's a duller setting but a much more interesting shot right across the water. So I would suggest we move the tee.'

McHugh stared at the trucks unloading the tons of sand for the fairways and the men working to remodel the landscape.

'I like it up here,' he said. 'Move the lake.'

Valerie began to laugh. He turned to look at her.

'My office is that big window over there,' he said. 'I want to be able to see all the nice folk from Glenageary who condescend to visit us, making fucking eejits of themselves.'

Whatever success McHugh had got he had not got it from Dublin. Long after the national papers had announced that the showband scene had collapsed, he had still been packing people into the six ballrooms he owned in Clare and Limerick. The artistes he managed rarely bothered playing Dublin and their songs were even more rarely played on national radio. Occasionally skits on them were performed by alternative Dublin comedians on television programmes which nobody ever watched. The artistes themselves were too busy playing in vast packed lounge bars and hotels throughout the countryside. Twice a year McHugh travelled to Nashville and booked major country acts, which Dublin promoters thought too big a risk, to play in the last ballroom he had left, a huge and superbly equipped building at a crossroads eleven miles from the nearest town. The local radio station which he owned, and which broadcast from the ballroom, said that he had never yet lost money on an act.

He had been tolerating Valerie because this interview was another commitment which, as a businessman, he had to fulfil, but it was a game he was playing. Behind Valerie's politeness he knew of her contempt for him, and that her contempt was shared by most of those who read the society pages. But he also knew what most fascinated them and her. The glamour of a single word: money. Nowadays he made more of it every three months than most of those readers would make in a lifetime. And he knew that they were equally attracted and repelled by the fact, convinced that he had politicians in his pocket, was twisting by-laws and avoiding taxes. He was a bog warrior in pin-striped wellingtons; the redneck bogman their parents or grandparents had been.

And yet because of his money they would have been willing to let him reinvent himself overnight, in the same way they had done with themselves over a generation. All he had to do was simply behave like the country's other new aristocrats did. His wife should host fund-raising balls on Bloomsday for some suitably distant charity, he should buy himself an honorary doctorate and let it be known that he intended to use the title. But McHugh had no interest in appealing to them. Every remark he made to Valerie was aimed over her readers' heads, was meant to infuriate them and be chuckled at in the small cottages and new bungalows that were springing up triumphantly around Clare – clean, modern houses that, if ugly to the passing tourist's eye, were warm and bright to live in.

I had paid little attention to the interview until Valerie began to probe about his childhood. It was like watching a mouse who was not even aware that a cat was playing with her. His replies were sardonic, laced with references to cooking nettles during the famine and bringing cattle in to sleep among the boys in the orphanage on beds of rushes by the fire. But there was no humour in his eyes. They had hardened and grown watchful, they darted about the room and for the first time began to seriously take me in. For a moment our eyes made contact, both hostile and questioning.

'But seriously,' Valerie persisted, 'you must have seen great cruelty from the nuns and then the Christian Brothers?'

'No.' His voice was cold, without emotion.

'But you were beaten. Was sexual abuse not common in such institutions?'

'Devil the bit of it.'

'But a lot of Christian Brothers, confined like that and in charge of boys . . . surely there were some closet gays?'

'Gay?' He pretended to dwell on the word as if puzzled. He looked coldly at Valerie, ending the interview. 'Only people in Dublin had closets. We were too poor down here for that class of thing. We just left our clothes hanging out on the bushes at night.'

Valerie conceded defeat, not even bothering to write his answer down. She left and it was my turn to pose him for the colour shot which was to adorn the cover of the supplement. We had not yet spoken. He watched me open the bag as she left.

'You're the sly boy, eh? Slinking away there in the corner the whole time. Do you ever open your gob?'

'A good photographer is even better than a Victorian child,' I said, adjusting the lens. 'Neither seen nor heard.'

Reluctantly McHugh lifted his head in various poses as I asked him to, but no matter what way I tried it the photograph would not work. His eyes could not recover their professional charm. Before the camera he was more ill at ease and attempted to cover this up with an expression of animosity. He was posing for Valerie and the image he had of her readers. But his hostility was a form of defence which closed his face down and killed the photograph. Finally I lowered the camera and began putting in a new roll of film.

'Listen,' I said to him. 'This interview, right, it's a long one. So that means most people, they're not going to bother to do more than skim the whole thing. They're busy on a Sunday. This photograph though . . . every single person stares at the photograph. Now Valerie can use your words anyway she wants, but the photograph is yours to use. Every one of them is going to be looking into your eyes. Now you look back into theirs. This is how they're seeing you, those envious mother-fuckers.'

'Don't fucking sweet-talk me,' he said. 'Smart-arsed Dublin fucker.'

'I'm not a Dublin fucker.'

'Where are you from so?'

'Like yourself, McHugh, I haven't a fucking snowball's.'

He looked at me, then snorted. I clicked. The shot was better.

'What do you want?' he said. 'A hand-out? Fucking violins?'

'Do people always want things from you?'

'Cupped hands or silver begging bowl, they all want something. So is this your party piece, eh?'

'No. I've never told anybody before.' It was true. I had shocked myself by saying it. But holding the camera seemed to insulate me from the words. His eyes had narrowed, but I clicked anyway.

'I'm supposed to feel flattered, am I?'

'Did anyone ever tell you you were a contrary bollox, McHugh?'

He threw his head back and laughed. The shot was perfect, eyes alive, features open.

'Not to my face they haven't, not for a long time past. They tiptoe round me, boy. You know what the men call me in the village?'

'The Orphan McHugh.' My accent was wrong, but I got the sneering contempt into the word.

'*The Orphan's a Bollox.* Somebody painted it in big letters at the gate when I bought that oul mine last year. Jaysus, there were more managers and assistant managers down on their knees scrubbing away in case I saw it. It was a laugh. I went down myself the next night and painted it back, just to see them shitting themselves with their scrubbing brushes in the morning again.'

'Mind you, I'd great adoptive parents,' I said, quickly changing the lens, deciding to chance getting right in at him. 'You must have been as ugly as sin if they could find nobody to keep you.'

'Don't push it, boy!' The anger was instant and unguarded. I had his face tight in my viewfinder now. I managed to get three shots. I knew that he had been sent to be adopted by a family in America who had sent him back after six months.

'It's like life, adoption, eh?' I said. 'You only get one chance.'

'My time is money, boy. Get on with it.'

'A lot of people jumped you in the queue back then, eh?' I changed a roll quickly and began to click again. 'Think of the laugh they must have had, you trying to hire your first showband, getting turned down for loans from a bank. All of them wanting you to fail like they did, eh? Sick as dogs next Sunday they'll be, looking at your shaving mug staring out at them again. And how about those who were left in that orphanage with you? Staring at the paper as though part of the glory rubs off on them. Well, here they all are, trapped inside this lens, forced to look out at you. You look at them, McHugh, look back at them.'

I clicked rapidly again as I spoke. Seven shots were all that were left on the new roll. But I knew I suddenly had what I wanted by the way he gazed, as if transfixed, not into the lens but right through the lens. I held the camera steady until he lowered his eyes. He looked up again.

'The sly bastard, eh?' He pressed a button on his desk and a secretary's voice answered. 'Barbara, bottle of Whiskey. Middleton Very Rare.'

'How many glasses, sir?'

'Glasses?' He looked at me coldly. 'Who mentioned glasses? I haven't decided yet if I'm going to pour this cunt a drink or smash the bottle over his skull.'

Now, a year later, delivery vans were unloading in the car-

A Second Life

park of the Country Club as I parked. I walked into
reception and glanced around for a moment. Mostly
photographers look to see if their work is present; I was
checking that mine wasn't. In the past I had done commis-
sions for hotel and pub owners who wanted their image
framed behind reception desks and counters. McHugh had
no interest in ego, but something in the final shots I had
taken moved him. He had been persuaded to use one on his
Christmas card and sent me a copy. 'A right cock-up this,'
he wrote on it, 'they printed *Seasonal Greetings from Peter
McHugh*, when I could have sworn I dictated *Fuck you all,
envious sons of bitches.*'

That night, after the photo session, I made sure Valerie
had left and then accepted his offer of dinner. Later, in his
office, overlooking the half-built golf course, the vintage
Bushmills had died a quick death between us. With another
man I might have thought that it was the whiskey speaking,
but McHugh was somebody who never lost control. Sitting
there, with just a soft desk lamp on, so that the shapes of
moonlit trees and the huge dunes of sand and clay were
visible through the bare windows, he had given me the
interview which he would never give Valerie or any other
journalist. Perhaps it amused him that I would never use a
word of it; perhaps, despite ourselves, we both felt a kinship
there; or, maybe, he just felt like talking and figured that he
would never see me again.

McHugh had traced his mother first through a private
detective. She was a timid Donegal woman who was terrified
by his sudden presence. But he claimed that he had no real
interest in her. It was his father's name which he was after.
He got it from her with threats and used his contacts to
trace him to a building site in Coventry. McHugh had hired
a Rolls-Royce to drive him there from the airport. The men

had stopped work, awed by McHugh's expensive suit as the chauffeur opened the door for him. He barked out a name and the foreman pointed to an old man standing up to his neck in a ditch. McHugh walked over and picked up a shovel from the bank of earth. 'Daddy,' he addressed the old man and then split his skull open.

'What did you do that for?' the foreman had screamed at him.

McHugh claimed that he patted the blood on the rim of the shovel and put his finger to his lips.

'Just wanted to check if I had blue blood,' he said, and vanished back into the car.

I remembered the story again as the lift doors opened and McHugh came down into reception.

'The sly fox, eh,' he greeted me. 'What can I do you for?'

'You still think everybody wants something from you?'

'Bet your life I do, boy.'

'I think maybe you're right.' I mimed swinging a shovel. 'I have it in mind to check if I've blue blood in me.'

Three hours later McHugh was driving me to Kildorrery along the small roads which bypassed Limerick, beyond Ballyneety and Bruff. Most people we passed recognized the car and gave an affectionate half-salute.

'Peadar O'Donnell,' McHugh said. 'Class of a writer up in Donegal. A sound man by all accounts. Back in the thirties he gets this job, he's to drive some old bitch, Lady Syphilis Shortcock or the Dowager Stephanie Wellrode Backwards, around her absentee-landlord husband's estates. Everybody they pass salutes the car and the oul bag is wetting her knickers with happiness. "Isn't it mar-vull-ulous how the peasants know who I am and their respect for me." "If you'll excuse me saying, Missus," O'Donnell pipes up, "it's me they're saluting. I'm the local commandant of the IRA."'

McHugh banged the steering wheel with his palm as he laughed.

'Frank Conroy could have done with a few less people saluting him,' I said, and he grunted.

'I've no sympathy for the bastard,' he said. 'Your Da, my Da, at least they had the grace to bugger off and forget we ever existed. I don't care if the whole town goose-stepped up and down his lawn, it's no excuse. All this love he was supposed to feel, my arse. Maybe our Das would have gladly drowned us, but they didn't.'

'Maybe they hadn't the guts.'

He stared at the road ahead of him.

'Fuck all heroes,' he said. 'Thanks be to Christ for cowards.'

We drove through Kilmallock in silence and went right at the fork a few miles beyond it. We passed a round tower and began to climb again towards Coolfree Mountain. With every mile I grew more nervous. I had promised Geraldine I would call before leaving Killaloe but had not expected to get caught up with McHugh like this. I am not sure what I had expected to receive from him – advice perhaps, or simply a hard-man sneer that would banish all thoughts of finding her from my head. Instead he had confronted me, the way I had done when taking his photograph, forcing me to decide finally whether I wanted to search for my birth mother.

'You're either looking for her or you're not,' he had repeated. 'Now make your mind up.'

'I can't,' I replied. 'Part of me wants to, but I have my own life now. I don't know if I need to know her.'

'Bollox,' McHugh said. 'Then why aren't you out leading

your own life instead of sitting in that chair like a stuffed gnome?'

'I'm scared . . . don't know what I'd say to her.' I stopped and faced his cold gaze. 'All right then. Are you happy now? These last months it's gnawing away inside me, I have to find her.'

'Right,' he said. 'Well, fuck the church and the agencies for a start. Hiding behind this law and that law. They wouldn't give you the steam off their piss. You're invisible, you understand. Lots of people want you to remain that way. You're on your own from here on and the first rule is learn to grasp at any straw.'

He left me alone in his office and returned ten minutes later with two of the women who worked in the kitchens of the Country Club. Watching McHugh open the door for the women and find them chairs I was seeing a different man. It was as if all three of them were part of an invisible circle. He introduced them by first name only and said that both had had secret children in the fifties. The husband of one still did not know. Because he had asked them they had agreed to talk to me and he knew of two other women in Limerick who might also do so. One of those had spent the fifteen years since her husband's death trying to find her daughter.

The two women seemed uneasy at my presence and yet interested in seeing me. For an instant I saw them become mothers, looking me over, wondering how well I had turned out, momentarily substituting me for the blank space they carried within them. I found myself doing the same as I gazed back and wondered at how McHugh had got them to open up their past to him. They looked out of place in that huge office and yet were at ease with him there, treating him with an affectionate respect.

'Laois?' one of them said. 'She could have been sent anywhere. Maybe to work for a rich family in Dublin, maybe to a convent. Don't presume that you know. Even if the story about the address on the piece of paper is true, I can't believe that the nuns didn't change your clothes after your mother handed you over. It mightn't have happened the same day. There could have been a month, or even more, when you were with foster parents that you've never even heard of. That address, it could have been sewn in those clothes months before, it could have been anyone's.'

'It's all I have to go on,' I told them. 'I want to believe that it's mine.'

'The Catholic Assurance Agency,' McHugh said to the elder woman. 'They're the same shower who did you. Can you remember any girl from Laois where you were?'

The woman looked over at me. Her eyes were very clear, as though long ago she had used up her quota of tears and nothing would ever shake her composure again.

'If I could help you I would,' she said. 'There were lots of us. We were young, we were scared, we were made to feel guilty. I still feel guilty, I will die feeling guilty. I have four other children. After each one I still felt guilty. Maybe you could go back to the agency. They have all the records, they know. It may take years badgering away at them, but who knows, the law might change, you might get lucky. You see, at least you, the child, you have the chance. We, the mothers, we have none. We signed the papers, we walked out and they closed that door on our faces.'

'My father . . .' I said, 'the man that I called father . . . he asked a nun there if I had my mother's eyes. "If he has the eyes of a slut's son," she told him, "then thank God he won't have the upbringing of one." If I went near that agency I wouldn't be looking for my mother any more. I would be looking to see if there's an old nun lying in a hospital bed somewhere. I would be looking to put a pillow over her face.'

The women were silent. The intercom buzzed. McHugh snapped back that he was not to be disturbed.

'She might still be there,' the elder woman said, 'in whatever convent it was. Often the girls never left. It was like a gaol, they didn't know they had the right to leave. Where I was, there was one woman twenty years there. A priest had brought her there when she was sixteen. She never had a baby or anything, it was just that her parents had died and she was left alone in a house full of brothers. The priest thought she was a temptation in the parish. "What's keeping you here?" I used to ask her. Twenty years, working twelve hours a day in the laundry for them. A slave, never given a penny. She looked fifty or more, terrified that the nuns would let her go. When I hear these things on the news . . . Filipino girls locked up in Kuwait . . . I always think of her face.'

'There's a woman in Kildorrery,' the younger of the women said quietly. 'Years ago I was praying in a church in Limerick, Our Lady's altar. I was praying for Brendan . . . my child . . . I don't know what name they gave him. There was a woman kneeling beside me. We looked at each other. I knew, and I knew that she knew, that we were praying for the same thing. We didn't need to say it, just the look on her face.

'When I left the church she was waiting outside. She looked at me, then walked on and then looked back. You could see she was begging me to follow her. She stopped in the far corner of the car-park behind the grotto. As soon as I put my hand on her shoulder she began to cry. She had never told anybody, you see. She was from Laois. Said she had been brought to a convent in Sligo and then one in Meath. Said she had gone back to the one in Meath just a few years ago, she'd run away from her husband, hitching lifts off strangers to get there. Said there were girls who knew her, they were still there from her time, you see, working as skivvies, after they gave up their children they had nowhere else to go. Said the midwife, she used to only visit once a month. When her time came said it was the other girls who delivered her baby, whenever she screamed said a big girl from Waterford would slap her face.'

The woman stopped talking and looked around at us.

'In a car-park in Limerick, you see. Said it was the only time she ever told her story. What could I do for her? Byrne I think her name was. Said she lived in Kildorrery.'

'Had she a boy or a girl?' I said. 'Tell me.'

The anguish in the woman's voice was replaced by a kind of cold pity.

'There were dozens from Laois, dozens from everywhere, you see. Don't think you'll find her that easy. The woman from Kildorrery had a girl.'

It was half-one when we reached Kildorrery. McHugh stopped for directions, then drove on for a mile the far side of it. Outside the house I had stayed in the car.

'How do you know she will talk to you?' I asked McHugh.

'Listen, I'm Peter McHugh,' was all he said.

It was a whitewashed two-storey labourer's house of the sort built by the county council early in the century. The windows were painted a flaking purple. A cat stared back at me from the window-ledge. I felt like a child again, that summer when I had worked with my father, sitting for ever in the cab of the van outside some country pub, not knowing when he would be finished his business. The mobile phone began to ring, as it had incessantly on the drive over. I ignored it as McHugh had done, not even bothering to switch it off.

I longed to be gone from here. A part of my life which had been an intimate ache inside me was being thrust out beyond my control into public view. This was all too close and too fast. I was being forced to sift through a thousand lives without any certainty that I would even begin to glimpse the one I wanted. I waited for the door to open and yet another woman to appear, but when McHugh came out he was alone.

'She wouldn't talk so,' I said as he climbed into the car.

'She didn't talk much,' he replied, starting the engine, 'but she did talk.'

'I thought she would have come out.'

'She didn't want to have to see you, she didn't . . . I told her your date of birth. She has a daughter somewhere in the world who is seven weeks younger than you. She wouldn't do it when I was there, but if you want to see a woman cry then go up to that window.'

'I told you we shouldn't have just landed on her. Nobody knows her secret. She must have been terrified.'

McHugh released the handbrake and hit the accelerator hard. The gravel scattered beneath us.

'You want something,' he said, and it sounded as though his teeth were clenched, 'then you let nothing and nobody get in the way of going after it, boy.'

We were both silent for the first few miles. Passing the bridge at the hamlet of Bruff, McHugh asked if I knew how the place had got its name.

'When Saint Patrick came here the entire population of sixteen lice-ridden natives and a goat gathered to meet him,' he said. 'He took one look at the kip, leaned over the river and went Brufffff!'

A Second Life

McHugh leaned forward over the steering wheel, making a vomiting noise. The phone began to ring again. An old man holding up the corner of a building saluted him.

'Our friend in Kildorrery remembers that there was a girl from Laois in that first convent in Sligo who was due to give birth six or seven weeks before her. She was from somewhere up the arse end of the Slieve Bloom Mountains. She says she only remembers her because the girl's mother died when she was there and the nuns finally decided that she didn't look pregnant enough to be prevented from going to the graveside. They took her back to Laois, but the girl's father would not have her in the church. They let her visit the grave that evening when the churchyard was deserted, then they brought her back to Sligo.'

'Did she have a name?'

'If she had she wasn't telling.'

Something in McHugh's voice made me know not to look at him or continue the conversation. The story he had told me about finding his father was one of bravado. After being returned from America he had been thought of as handled goods, not suitable to be given to anyone else for adoption. He had spent the first fourteen years of his life in a gulag, along with orphans or the unwanted children of married people, never knowing what a glass felt like on his lips, being marched through some midland town in a uniform on Sundays, being hired out as cheap labour to farmers. When I had told him to stare into the lens, what ghosts had he seen there?

I had met men who survived those orphanages. You grew to recognize them, living alone in flats, unable to form bonds with people. You met them in menial jobs, in pubs looking for fights at closing time, banging against the doors of battered wives' shelters. Men who had never known what it was to trust another human being. How had McHugh achieved all this, what rage had pushed him to where he was? At night, when the expensive suits were hung in the wardrobe, what dreams might still haunt this man? Was that why the woman in Kildorrery had spoken to him? The phone rang. Something about the way he put his hand down for it made him a businessman again. Before he picked it up he glanced across at me.

'You're on your own from here on, Inspector Clouseau.'

Later that evening, the sacristan in Dunross closed over the heavy wooden door of the sacristy and blocked out the light. For a moment I was back in Dublin as a child, waiting nervously with a note from my mother to have a mass said, listening to the sounds of disrobing and the clink of brass before the priest came out. These days Benedict pointed out the spires of churches from the car window with the same interest as digger trucks and tractors. 'God's houses' he called them, asking loudly on the sole occasion I had taken him into one, 'Why is the God man not home?'

The sacristan lifted down the heavy register of births, deaths and marriages and opened it on the table.

'Journalist?' he asked again, slightly uncertain. 'What is it exactly you're looking for?' It was after five o'clock. There had been heavy rain on the way from Killaloe back up into the Slieve Bloom Mountains. From Roscrea I had taken the side road across to Kinnitty and stopped at every church from there, climbing up along the crumbling road high into the mountains. The tarmacadam had been corroded away by trucks and winter ice. In darkness it seemed that parts of it would be almost impassable. Churches were open and empty buildings, half lit by stained light. In Kinnitty an old man had pointed me to the priest's house, a quarter-mile away where the aproned woman who guarded his privacy had finally relinquished the key to the records and walked behind me suspiciously all the way back to the church.

Later in Killinure I had been unable to find a trace of any living person. Except for the fresh flowers on the altar, nothing suggested that a person had entered it in days. Finally a passing farmer had stopped to tell me that, apart from a priest who came from Dunross on Sundays to say Mass, it was deserted. Any records were kept in Dunross. I had driven across to Ballyfin church, losing my way on twisting boreens, before crossing the mountain again to finally reach Dunross.

I still hadn't phoned Geraldine. I had meant to after I'd finished talking with McHugh, but I had been so disturbed on returning from Kildorrery that I simply drove away from the Country Club. For years my adoption was something I never spoke of. I had not felt ashamed or disturbed by it, but I had simply refused to let it define me. Now, for a whole morning, it had been the central fact of my existence to everybody that I met. Whatever small success I had achieved in life, the way in which I had developed and grown as a person, all these things seemed stripped away. Instead I had become just one of the thousands of lost children from an age and a world I could not comprehend, linked by the iron bars of cots, by silent nuns of huge black habits, by the stigma of invisibility.

Since the crash I had been slowly learning to feel at home again with Geraldine and the children. Now that house and life in Dublin seemed so distant again. I had not told her that I wanted to trace my real mother, indeed I hardly could. I had not even consciously decided to do so myself. An impulse had simply taken over and I was still in the grip of it. There seemed no way that I could tell her what I was doing and yet I didn't want to lie, so all day I had kept putting off the phone call, even though I knew the anxiety which this would cause her.

'What is it exactly you're looking for again?' The sacristan in Dunross repeated his question, waiting for an answer. He held the heavy book open, his fingers idly turning over the neat handwritten pages.

'A story for the paper,' I lied. 'Life and death in the 1950s. We picked a couple of months at random, April and May 1957. See who was born and who died in a typical parish at that time.'

It took him several minutes to find the right page. The other parishes had yielded nothing except the horror of TB. The aproned woman near Kinnitty running her finger down the list of names, suddenly interested as they came alive for her, talking about being in school with the young girl they had buried that month. Her whole family had succumbed to the illness, one by one, the woman said, except for the youngest sister, and not one young man in the county would court her, even after the disease had died out, because of the stigma.

In Ballyfin the records had showed that an infant had died in April of that year, two young girls were born and an old unmarried farmer found dead in May. I felt foolish dredging through the records of each church, and still unsure if I wanted to find a lead that might help my search. If I really wanted to find my mother I might begin with the adoption agency or somewhere like Barnardo's. Almost certainly I would meet a stone wall, but at least I would have made the proper beginning. But I knew that I would never set foot in any of those places, not just because I would feel humiliated putting myself back at their mercy, but also because it would be too definite a course of action.

And that was why I was here, playing at being the detective, keeping the whole business at a safe distance. I suddenly wished to draw a blank here, for the pistol barrel to spin and click empty against my cheek, so that I might walk away, feeling I had brought this trail as far as it could go, and be able to return to my life in Dublin.

'Not a death in April or May of that year,' the sacristan said, scanning the page. 'A couple of births in late April if that's any interest to you.'

'No,' I said, turning away and searching for the car keys, 'that's fine. Thanks for your help.'

'Now that I remember it,' he said, 'there wasn't a death in the parish all that winter or spring. I was an altar boy then, we were callous, there was money for serving at funerals. The custom only died out recently of a collection for the priest after the funeral where how much people gave would be read out. It was the second of June before there was a death, when Mary Sweeney died.'

I stopped, wishing that I had left before he started speaking.

'How old?'

'Mary Sweeney?' He glanced down at the columns. 'Forty-nine. She was young to go.'

'Had she daughters?'

'Daughters, two sons, fine lads, one a priest now. A nice family. Over the road there, about a mile and a half down. A small farm they had. I remember serving the funeral well.'

'Is there anyone left here belonging to her?'

'What sort of story is it you're after again?' His curiosity had become tinted with suspicion. 'You know, your face is familiar if I could only place it.'

'The paper,' I said, 'you've seen it in the newspaper.'

'Have I? The Sweeney farm was bought over by a neighbour. Hammond. Holdings that size wouldn't feed anybody now. He has a herd of deer down there, venison for export and for some of the big hotels. It's funny, seeing them roam about in the fields. Most of the land is idle. Gets a grant from Brussels to keep it that way. A spy satellite up in the sky making sure it stays fallow. Wonders of technology, eh? You can't go for a shite in your own field without somebody watching it on a screen up in space.'

He stopped, remembering his language in the sacristy. I fingered the keys in my hand. It would be so simple just to walk out across the gravel and drive away. The woman in McHugh's office had been right. That scrap of paper could have been sewn into those baby clothes months before I was born. Even now Geraldine and I swapped baby clothes with friends all the time, children grew out of them so fast. Back then, in that convent or hospital or wherever I was born, there would have been nothing new or owned. A cot which other babies had lain in, sheets that had been washed a thousand times, faded clothes which had contained dozens of different tiny arms and legs. Even thinking about it made me feel vaguely unclean. But surely if the outfit had been washed and rewashed then the writing would have been illegible.

'Can you remember?' I asked. 'Were all of Mary Sweeney's children at her funeral?'

The sacristan looked up. I knew that he no longer believed my story but his hostility was gone.

'That was thirty-five ...' He looked into my face as though assessing my age. 'No. Thirty-six years ago. I remember getting a bit of silver into my hand. That's all.'

He waited for my next question, as though wondering if I

would keep up the pretence. I had gone so far that it was too late to retreat. My stomach felt sick. I had nothing to lose.

'You must have known the daughters?'

'I didn't know them all. There was a big gap between them, Mr ... What was the name again on that card you flashed there?'

'Murphy.'

He glanced down at the book. I felt he was trying to hide a smile. I could have withstood ridicule, but when he looked up there seemed a hint of pity in his eyes.

'Four daughters in the family. One married to a chemist down in Cork. Never comes here. The eldest went to the States before I was even born. The matron of some hospital over there, never married. Bit of a dragon by all accounts. You know the starched-knicker type yourself. The youngest two are away in England these years. Ellen, she comes home every summer. God, she's getting on in the years but there's a great bit of crack in her. The baby of the family I didn't know at all.'

'Why not?'

He shrugged his shoulders, as though the gesture should be enough explanation for me. I repeated the question.

'I was just a child,' he said. 'One day she was there, you'd see her passing on the road, the next day she simply wasn't.'

'What happened to her?'

'If a girl vanished back then, I suppose the adults talked. Children ... well there was no Doctor Spock books in those days. You opened your mouth you got a clatter. They were a good family, the Sweeneys, only family round here ever to raise a priest. They were well respected.'

'What was her name?'

He made a clicking noise with his tongue as he thought back, then shook his head.

'Like I say, I was just a child. Never heard much talk of her after.'

'What do you think happened to her?' I asked.

He closed over the register and placed it up on the shelf. He opened the door. The late evening light seemed sharp after the gloom of the sacristy.

'We're not children now are we, Mr . . . Murphy? We're men of the world. I remember *The Late, Late Show* coming on the air first. I didn't see it myself, you'd have had to walk a quare few miles across these hills before you'd find a television in those days, but I remember all the shouting and fussing when the bishop condemned a woman for mentioning that she wore no nightie on her wedding night. Bedad, I was watching it last Friday night and they had a bishop's mistress on, talking all about bringing up his bastard without a scrap of help from him.'

I drove off from Dunross church and turned left on the first side road. It was after six o'clock. I knew that Geraldine would be frantic by now. How long would it take the sacristan to lock up? I pulled in, my wheels half up on the overgrown ditch. I climbed out. Another mile down that lane the woman who might be my mother had lived. She would have walked past this spot a thousand times, barefooted perhaps in summer.

The hedges needed to be trimmed, a riot of weeds and wild flowers grew out on to the road. I picked a dandelion clock from the bank and closed my eyes, gently blowing the seeds apart, one o'clock, two o'clock, three . . . I was trying to see her as a girl of nine or ten, pausing here in the late sunshine to pick such a dandelion and blow either the time or the riddle *he loves me, he loves me not*. I could see her brother or maybe her father walking on ahead, driving cattle who lurched against each other and shat along the road, and his voice calling back for her to hurry on. I could see it so clearly that it frightened me. I kept my eyes closed, trying to retain the image, but it was replaced by what I now called the death face, that young man whose features still haunted me. His image had no right to intrude here. I opened my eyes and put my hand out against the side of the car. I pressed the button on the keys and the car bleeped repeatedly as I locked and unlocked the doors, as if the clean electronic noise could banish ghosts.

I reversed and drove back to the church. There was a stile in the stone wall of the graveyard. I climbed over and began to walk through the headstones. A woman passing on a bicycle looked across at me. I turned away, leaving the gravel path now, moving through the ranks of graves, trying not to walk on them. The largest stone was a memorial to two local youths, *Brutally done to death by British forces, July, 1921*. The more recent ones had photographs behind glass built into the black marble. The same family names were repeated over and over, alien names which meant nothing to me. Six times I came across gravestones with the word Sweeney on the back, each time the names and the dates were wrong. It was seven o'clock now, still two hours' drive to Dublin. I had to leave and yet I couldn't. Several times I had almost lost my footing in the half-light, but still I began yet another circuit among the stones and wooden crosses.

It was at the very top of the graveyard that I found the headstone. *In loving memory, Mary Sweeney, d. 2 June 1957. Also her husband, Michael Sweeney, d. 11 April 1966.* It was in granite, the letters slightly weathered. There were flowers which had long withered in a vase filled with rancid black water. I put my hand out to touch the stone and looked across at the lights of that valley of farms. And then the realization came to me that I had been here before. There were no longer any doubts in my mind that this was the grave of my grandparents. At this same time of evening, at this same spot I had been here, curled and almost formed, a five-and-a-half-month embryo in the womb of a woman whose first name I did not know. The graveyard as empty as now, another car waiting at the gate. But it had not been a family in Dublin which awaited me back then, but a driver and a nun and long miles of sobbing back to the gates of a convent.

I remembered a story Geraldine had told me of a newly married woman she knew whose husband had walked out when she was three months' pregnant. She had spent the next six months in tears, sitting on a chair in the hall, dividing up the days, telling herself that his key would turn in the lock when she had counted to a thousand and then another thousand. I often saw the woman's child in the park now, a nervous, troubled boy glancing fretfully around him. Geraldine always claimed that his anxiety sprang from those long months in the womb, sensing his mother's tears. What effect had this graveyard had on me?

I reached in for the small Pentex I always carried in my inside pocket and raised it to my eye. The view was framed, captured, within my control. For a moment I was ten years of age again in the Botanic Gardens in Dublin, with that same sense of the forbidden as I clicked. I lowered the camera and raised my head. I did not know if she had cried, granted her few moments alone by the grave when all the neighbours were safely gone, but I cried, like I had not cried in decades; for her and for me, the pair of us alone on that

June evening in 1957, for that long spring and summer when we were the one flesh, and for the ache of all the years since that we had been apart.

It was a quarter past ten when I finally reached the house in Dublin. Geraldine was standing in the lit doorway, Benedict asleep in her arms, in his pyjamas with a coat thrown over him. The street was quiet. Before the rain she had cut the grass for the first time that year. I could smell the fresh earth which she had turned over. Her face was lined, glazed. She looked exhausted.

'You're all right,' she said, 'you're safe. Oh, thank God, thank God. I kept thinking of Frank Conroy, what he did . . .' Then her face and her voice changed. 'You stupid, stupid, bastard.'

Chapter Nine

April had always been the month that Elizabeth loved best. It was when the garden began to offer true escape. Time to clear out the forget-me-nots and other early flowering biennials which were now drooping in the border below the window and to transfer the hardy annuals that were coming into flower. A decade of springs seemed to merge in her mind. Evenings of girls' voices squabbling cheerfully over their homework in the kitchen while she knelt to lift bulbs from the soil, or cut back the fuchsia and tend the barberry that was about to burst forth in a mass of yellow flowers. Twilights when the garden was lit by the open door of Jack's shed and she called out to him when the girls were dressed for bed. April was when she had always sworn that this year she would allow herself to relax and try to forget.

Elizabeth placed her hand against the cool window-pane and looked out beyond the wilderness of her garden. That April of 1966 had been when her father had died, the woman next door coming in to tell her that her sister Ellen was on the phone. *Come back to Ireland. Come with me. We'll face them together. It's been almost nine years. Nobody can keep you from your place at the grave this time.* Come back to Ireland. It had been nine years, she had thought that she had learnt to control herself. Pretending to Jack that she was going over for the funeral, pretending to Ellen that she would meet her outside the Gresham Hotel in Dublin, pretending to herself that she would not go missing again.

The deck of the cattle boat, a scarf round her hair as she

let the sea spray drench her. How could she have been so stupid as to let those thoughts take over? Paudi and her running away for the day, fleeing together down some laneway beside a school; the rickety green St Kevin's bus bumping its way up into the Wicklow Mountains; the café which served fancy ice-cream and had dance music on the wireless. And what a perfect gentleman he would have turned into, telling her of his life, understanding everything that she had been forced to do.

The sheen of his hair and his smile when she told him, *You're the only man in my life.* And how he'd be too shy to ask for another ice-cream, but she would know with a mother's instinct. The aproned man laughing as he carried the banana boat down to their table. *Will you come to visit me again?* Her finger touching his lips. *Our secret, Paudi, just you and me.* And then it would be time to bring him back, the bus plunging down towards that hateful city, parting, parting . . . no, keep him, run away with him . . . somewhere, find work . . . leave the girls, leave Jack . . . mind him. His imaginary, bewildered little voice asking, *Why did you sign me away, Mammy?*

And then, after she screamed, she had let some man on the boat take her shoulders, steering her away from the rails, asking no questions, just guiding her into the warmth of the steel corridor, and leaving her voice to fade out among the sea birds and the swell of the dark waves.

That April morning as the boat pulled into Dublin. Thinking of Ellen, who would stand at the steps of the Gresham. The doorman in his top hat calling taxis from the rank. People queuing to climb the pillar. How long would her sister wait? Until five minutes before the bus, then she could imagine Ellen cursing her as she ran towards that ugly new Busaras. But surely Ellen would have guessed, after all the times before? The way she had agreed to meet in Dublin and not travel over together on the same boat.

Even at dawn on the quays in Dublin, Elizabeth had kept up the pretence that she would join her sister in her own mind. Then she had thought of how her son would be waking soon, in a bed somewhere in this city. His bare feet about to touch the lino as some woman called up to him from the stairs. What name would she be calling him by? And who was that woman who had stolen her child? A witch, a demon . . . no, Elizabeth prayed to God that she might be a kind and good woman, that he might have a home where he would be happy. Very soon he would be walking to school. If she only knew which school she could stand at the gate and he would have to pass her. Nine years would have changed him, but what mother would not know her own child's face?

There were no fantasies now about afternoons in Glendalough. Just to see him would be enough, just one glimpse in a bunch of children. To know that he was well. She would give ten years of her life gladly for that. At night she still woke, haunted by the thought that if he died they would not bother telling her. She would try to shake the image, but it was always impossible. A grave, a tiny headstone that she would never know of. *Oh, Sweet Jesus in heaven,* Elizabeth thought, *that I may just be given a sign that he is well. Strike me down here, let me die the most terrible of deaths if it spares my son any suffering.*

People on O'Connell Bridge were looking at her. There were buses along the quays. She ran towards them and jumped on the open back of one. *I'm in your hands now, Jesus,* she prayed. *If it be Your will that You forgive me my sin and I find my son then You will lead me to him.* She watched the streets of passing faces, waiting for Christ to show her a sign. There was a Christian Brothers' school across from the terminus. She fought against a rush of joyful tears. *Sweet Jesus, Sweet Jesus, I beseech You that You may have forgiven and led me here.* She stood by the gate. A handful of boys were already inside the yard, schoolbags as goalposts, shouting as they chased a ball. A car drove in, a teacher who glanced across at her. More boys passed, one of them sniggering. Her lower lip was sore from biting it. She found that she could no longer pray. Her head felt dizzy. There was just the one word, *Jesus, Jesus.* Certainly she dare not pray to the Blessed Virgin who had conceived without sin. She was too ashamed. Only Jesus, a son, could understand. There was a brooch in her handbag, she took it out. *I offer up this pain, Jesus, for just one glimpse.* The hiss of her breath as the brooch pin ripped into her palm. Her teeth were clenched. *I offer up this suffering.* The boys were flooding past now, a blur of faces. *Jesus, grant this sinner a sign.* The teacher was coming out, she began to back away. He followed her, suspicious now. She stood on the far side of the road, glaring back at him. If he tried to push her further away she would sink this brooch pin into his heart.

Elizabeth's daughter Sharon came into the kitchen and watched her mother's palms pressed against the window. She seemed like a moth trapped there on the glass. They should never have given in to her wishes. They had responsibilities to her now just as she once had to them. Sharon's husband was right, the correct time had been after her father's funeral. It had been cruel to leave her alone here. Once the garden had started to grow neglected it was a sign. The bungalow still shone, but Sharon knew that inside meant nothing to her mother. The garden had been her real home, as the shed had been her father's.

A Second Life

It was Sharon's husband, Steve, who told the family about her father's wishes, the night they had waited for him to die in the hospital.

'Every Saturday I brought him there he said the same thing at half-time. He saw it happen once. I mean it's up to your mother, I'm just telling you what the man wanted himself.'

The nurse had called them in. Her father tried turning his head. It was that last surge of energy before the end, his voice not more than a whisper, but loud enough for them to hear his favourite song. *Spread your tiny wings and fly away, and take the snow back with you* . . . And that night, when the cars had driven back to the bungalow, it had been Sharon who took her mother into the bedroom, watching her take her good coat off and throw that old tattered one over her shoulders.

'Where are you going, Mammy? Answer me. We're all here. You can't just go walking out.'

Only when Sharon broke down had her mother stopped, sitting on the bed, rocking Sharon's head in her lap like when she was a child.

'Mammy, it's like we've lost you these days, like nothing matters to you. We have to decide about Daddy. He told Steve, I don't know if he told you, he wanted to be cremated.'

Her mother stroking her hair, softly singing that old song in Irish which she would never translate for them.

'Do you understand, Mammy? You have to decide . . . for yourself as well . . . when . . . when your time comes . . . I always thought, the pair of you . . . in a family plot . . .'

Elizabeth had stopped singing. Sharon raised her head.

'Your Daddy was a good man,' her mother said quietly. 'He always went his own way.'

146

Two weeks later the three couples had visited the Coventry City ground. Elizabeth had not gone, claiming that Jack had never wished to bring her there. Sharon knew that she was glad to be rid of them, to be left alone to haunt the roads around the estate in that old coat. Before the kick-off she and Steve were allowed out on to the turf. Some of the crowd behind the goal began to clap, realizing what they were doing. She was shocked by how meagre the ashes seemed, scattered there behind the byline. There was a sort of ragged minute's silence before the teams came out. After the kick-off it began to rain. Coventry had been well beaten by three goals to one.

It was getting late now. Steve would be arriving at the bungalow soon. Sharon watched her mother lift her hands from the window and turn the handle of the back door to try and push it open. Sharon put her arms around Elizabeth's shoulders.

'Remember, Mammy, we agreed to lock it. It's for the best. That night when we all came over, you even agreed so yourself in the end.'

At least that April of her father's death she had not gone back to the agency in Dublin. Not even to stand across the street from it. That first time running away, just before Christmas in 1963, she had stood there and watched a young girl arrive with a baby in her arms. The girl was already up the steps before Elizabeth found the courage to move.

'Don't . . .!' She ran across, screaming through the traffic. The girl had looked back, frightened, then disappeared through the door. Elizabeth sat on the steps, rocking herself, then gathered the strength to push open the door. The same colour was on the walls, the same strip of carpet across the tiled floor. In the alcove beneath the heavy wooden crucifix, there was a large crib with kneeling figures arranged around an infant. The strict glasses of the receptionist turned towards her, demanding to know why she wanted to see Mrs Lacey. She had refused to let her wait in the hall, then threatened the police if Elizabeth sat on the steps outside. Mrs Lacey was busy. She had no time to be seeing the likes of her. The receptionist grew more and more angry.

'What are you coming back here for? We sent you out that door without a stain on your character. We took you in. You went out of here as good as a virgin.'

Elizabeth had retreated and stood on the pavement outside, knowing that she was being watched from a window upstairs. Two women ladened with parcels steered around her, then glanced back, whispering. She went back across to the railings on the other side of the street. An old tramp was sitting there with a stained grey beard.

'Oh, stay away from that place, Mam,' he said. 'Pray to God and he'll give you a child of your own. You want no truck with the leftovers of every little whore and hussy in the country up leaving their bastards on the doorstep there.'

Five hours passed before Mrs Lacey came down. The windows of the building were lit now, the open door framed with light when she appeared. The woman slowly crossed the street. Elizabeth eyed her cautiously. She wanted to run, but kept her fingers tightly pressed for support against the bars of the railings behind her.

'Any talking we have to do we'll do out here,' Mrs Lacey began, 'and then you'll be gone on your way.'

'I want him back,' Elizabeth had said.

'Don't be daft, girl. The child is happy in a good Catholic home. What right have you to come here demanding anything now?'

'Paudi's my child. I want him back.'

'You know well he's not your child. You had no right to the child, even before you signed him away. That was just a legal formality. Do you understand me? He was always God's child. What right have you to cast your sin on to him?'

'I want a name then, or just one photograph even . . . something of his . . . a book, even a piece of clothing.' Elizabeth was determined not to break down. 'You know where he is. If you wanted to you could tell me.'

A car had swung in to park beside them, the driver in the black coat beeping for them to move. Mrs Lacey lowered her voice to a hiss.

'You're inadequate, do you realize that? It's not natural for you to want him back. Every child has the right to a proper home. What sort of evil person are you to deny him a chance in life? That's a wedding ring on your hand. What would your husband say if he knew about this? He'd beat you black and blue and you would deserve a good hiding. Any man with an inch of respect would take his belt to you and then turn you from the door. But we gave you a chance to start your life clean and now you have the cheek to try and deny that innocent child the same chance. You're selfish, do you hear me, selfish. If you had an ounce of natural feeling inside you you would never show your face here, you would let him alone to live a decent life. Now you've been up to enough tricks in the past . . .'

The woman stopped and looked away. A party of schoolgirls in green coats passed, carol singers chattering excitedly as they moved on to their next pitch. Elizabeth tried to contain the surge of hope within her. She wanted to ask, she . . . The woman turned back to her.

'Your family could have had you committed for that.

Any doctor would have signed you into an asylum and they would yet, if the right people asked them to. Don't think you're safe just because you're over in some pagan country. Think of going to prison, girl. That's a terrible place, but in prison you have a length of sentence. If you wind up committed then it's for life, girl, and don't think there's anybody going to come running with a key.'

Elizabeth never knew how she managed to walk a few paces behind the woman as she crossed back to her office. A car came down the road. Elizabeth stopped, hoping that it would plough into her. The driver beeped and swerved. *Unnatural, evil, selfish* . . . The woman stopped on the steps. She produced a handkerchief and handed it to Elizabeth, who wiped her eyes and tried to give it back.

'No, keep it,' the woman said kindly. 'Go back to your home now. It's Christmas time. You should be with your husband. We have given you a second life. Don't waste it. Have children of your own, children who will belong to you. Please, I'm thinking of your own good and of the child's good. When you look back in years to come you'll be grateful. And remember, the Lord in his mercy can forgive anything.'

'Just tell me one thing about him,' Elizabeth said softly. 'The colour of his hair, is he big or small . . . just something to take home with me. I have an ache . . .'

The kindness was gone. Elizabeth felt like a dog about to be beaten.

'You will never find him. We have the file on him. But we have a file on you, too. And we can find you, and your husband . . . and if you make a nuisance of yourself we can tell him. You're no spring chicken, think of that. What man would keep you? And you might not find it so easy to get a grip on another man with that body of yours that is used goods now.'

A Second Life

Elizabeth watched the woman close over the door. From the street corner the girls' voices began again: *Away in a Manger, no crib for a bed* . . .

Sharon came out from the bedroom with the bags. Her mother was at the bin. How could she have known? Sharon had waited until her back was turned.

'That coat is ancient,' she said. 'I've your good one packed here. Put it back in the bin . . . please, Mammy.'

'Have to wear it.'

'Mammy, please . . . you look like a tramp in it.'

'The coat he'll find me in.'

'What do you mean, Mammy? Is it like the coat you met Daddy in? But it's not the same coat, I remember you buying it.'

'How will he find me without it?'

'Mammy, we've been over this. Daddy is dead.'

'A crash . . . you can survive a crash.'

'Daddy wasn't in a crash, Mammy. Look at me, please. Just try to look at me.'

Sharon held her mother's gaze until after a few moments the eyes seemed clearer. For a moment her voice was like Sharon remembered it.

'Unnatural . . . evil . . . selfish . . . that's all I've ever been . . . what a woman told me.'

'Who told you that? What bitch? You're my mother . . . the best mother . . . for all three of us. I know Daddy would have loved a son, but . . . Who said those awful things? You're only imagining that, it's those painkillers. We could never have asked for a better mother. The first thing we'll do is phone Auntie Ellen in Reading, you'll like that. I have the bags packed, Mammy. Are you ready to go?'

Chapter Ten

All that week following Frank Conroy's funeral, the atmosphere between Geraldine and myself was tense. The evenings were getting lighter. I worked away at building the bird-table which I had promised Benedict, while he pretended to help me and babbled away about fixing tractors with his new imaginary friend, Gerry the Goat, who lived in his pocket. His words filled out the silences between his parents since I had been unable to explain my disappearance *en route* back from Killaloe.

I developed the shots of the quayside and Frank Conroy's wife and house, but it needed a photograph of the crashed car to make the coverage work. I brought them into Gerry in the newsroom and found that he had the same problem with the story. Whatever physical clues there were to Conroy's actions seemed to lead back to that afternoon in Ennis, but any phone calls which Gerry made to the police went unreturned. People in Killaloe who had claimed to witness the events when we had first visited six months ago, now denied ever seeing a soldier or a gun. The woman who owned the newsagent's had come around the counter to try and push Gerry out of her shop. The only quotes he got were the standard ones: 'A decent man . . . a loving father . . . the community in shock . . . a mystery to us all.'

Some people told Gerry that it was a copy-cat suicide, inspired by a former miner at Mullabeg who had driven his car on to a level crossing near Birdhill. Others claimed that Conroy had been drunk and unaware of what he was doing. But if no reference was made to Ennis, then repeatedly, and seemingly without any context, people kept referring to the absence of any trouble ever in the district with foreign tourists and how everybody was always made welcome in Clare.

'Will you print the truth?' I asked Gerry, surprising myself with the question. For over fifteen years we had worked together. I had never asked him such a thing, had never felt the need to. The question reflected some deep unease, not with him but more with myself, with what I was doing working here. What was true any more? Those faces I had glimpsed in death were still more real to me than the street I had just walked down. Gerry looked up.

'You know the truth, do you?' he asked. 'Does your little safari to the other side give you instant access to the thoughts of the dead? A guy gets into a car and murders his four-month-old daughter. I don't care what happened or didn't happen to him in the past, I'm not in the business of inventing excuses to put into his mouth.'

The words were angry. I knew that I had touched something raw inside him.

'You know when we print this,' he continued, 'there'll be two or three deaths later this month. The dominoes. No one talks about them. The more talk there is the more dominoes you get. Once upon a time we were happy to kill ourselves slowly with whiskey, now it's like everything else, we're in a mad rush to do it quickly. I've talked to Geraldine on the phone once or twice. She doesn't say anything, but you can hear it in her voice. The suspicion, ever since you came out of hospital, that you were trying to pull a similar stunt yourself.'

The dominoes. The porch of the church in Killaloe had been plastered with notices of helplines for girls who found

themselves pregnant. Almost one in every fifth baby in the
state was born to a single parent now. But where every
parish had once had a girl drummed out secretly at night,
now they had a house, the corner of a field, a bridge, where
an unexplained and unmentioned suicide had occurred in
recent years.

'What do you think?' I said to Gerry.

'You?' He snorted and looked down again. 'Not a chance.
I know you too well. If you had meant to do it you would
have taken the camera out of the car first.'

Increasingly now, my dreams were disturbed. I would wake
abruptly with a sense that somebody had been calling and
listen to Geraldine's breathing in the silence, which would
soon be broken by Benedict's crying out. The night after I
saw Gerry I dreamt that an award ceremony for best press
photographer was being held in Dunross graveyard. Smart
women in pink dresses and men in dinner jackets wandered
aimlessly through the headstones, wondering why the loca-
tion had been chosen. I stood on the path, trying to block
off the top corner of the graveyard. Gerry appeared at my
elbow in his tweed jacket and winked.

'I heard it was yourself picked this gaff. You've got some
sense of humour, dragging all these shites down here.'

He glanced behind me at the overgrown corner of the
graveyard, then looked back. His grin was knowing, suspicious, triumphant.

'So who've you got stashed away in there then, eh?' he
sneered. 'Come on, that's what you want, isn't it? The truth
to come out. People's little secrets, eh, out in the open.'

I put my hands out but he brushed past me. I knew that
he would find the grave immediately, but when I turned we
were both standing on the open parkland of McHugh's

Country Club, where the golf course was still being built. Scores of men laboured around us as the huge trucks dumped their loads of sand. A youngish man, stripped to the waist, grinned as he lifted the heavy wheelbarrow and began to push it up the planks that crisscrossed the low hill. I knew his face. McHugh was beside me. He pressed an old-fashioned spade into my hand and pushed me forward. I looked down, my clothes were ragged. My arms seemed younger, but more covered with hair. I was whistling though I knew that I cannot whistle. I looked up. The men were still there but the golf course was gone.

There was water behind me, a pond planted with fresh lilies. Beyond that there was grass and a river with cows grazing in the sloping field which leaned down to the water. I turned to watch the men again. Two huge pits were being dug into a sparsely wooded slope and a line of small trees waited to be planted. A horse-drawn cart came down through the older trees laden with brown earth. The driver cursed at me cheerfully to get back to work. I walked to the cart and began to shovel the earth down into the pit. The young man with the wheelbarrow stopped beside me. The barrow was wooden and rudimentary. There was a crackle of burning twigs and the faint tang of smoke. A toothless old man crouched among the trees boiling up a billycan. The young man lifted the barrow, his naked shoulder deliberately brushing against mine. I knew his face now, the sound of his breath as he had chased me beneath those moonlit yew trees. He grinned and I found myself grinning back, whistling that tune again as I dug the spade into the earth and shovelled it down on to the half-buried remains of Frank Conroy and his child.

I woke beside Geraldine with my hands out, trying to restrain my breathing. Sinead was sleeping in her cot in the corner of the room, the blanket placed over the curtains making it hard to decipher the time. My vest clung to me with sweat. I recognized the place in my dream, although it had changed. There was a bridge over the pond in the Botanic Gardens now. Those trees waiting to be planted were over a century old. Cattle still grazed there in the grounds of the Holy Faith convent. I had photographed that river secretly as a ten-year-old suspended from school. Snatches of the whistled tune lingered in my head, but even as I tried to piece them together they were gone.

Perhaps if there had been somebody to take the children away, even for one night, Geraldine and I would have calmed down in the weeks that followed. But our parents were dead, Geraldine's sisters emigrated to America and New Zealand. Sinead was teething, waking three and four times in the night. We brought her into the bed and she would suck her thumb for comfort, then sit up and play her favourite game of slapping our faces. Sometimes Geraldine would give up trying to get her back asleep and hand her a hairbrush. Digging the brush into Geraldine's scalp and brushing her hair gave the baby a soothing comfort. I would drift between sleep and waking, hearing Geraldine wince when the baby hurt her.

Soothers were threatening to damage the shape of Benedict's mouth. Yet he clung to them for comfort. We pricked it with a pin so that the suck would be less powerful and he might begin to tire of it. But he sat up regularly at night, crying out half asleep for me to drive to a chemist and buy a new one.

In the mornings we were both wrecked from lack of sleep. It was better not to speak to each other, since even a casual remark sounded like an accusation. Geraldine would be facing another day of Benedict blocking the baby's path when she tried to crawl and taking toys out of her hands, and of Sinead breaking up any jigsaws or train tracks which Benedict tried to make. And always I felt most disoriented in the mornings, filled with a panic that I would not be able to work if I got involved in the house in any way, beyond changing the first nappies and feeding them their breakfast.

It was always the extra three or four minutes that I had to wait before Geraldine took over that brought me to the edge of losing my temper. The house was like a trap. Unless I got out immediately, and was able to be alone in the car, my plans for the whole day would crumble. Eventually I would snap and Geraldine would be left, with the baby crying in her arms because she had seen me put on my coat and Benedict demanding to be held as well.

The irony is that I had nowhere to rush to. The photographs from Dunross graveyard lined the wall of my studio, each merging into the next as though the Pentax was capable of a wide-angle shot. I had finally managed to trace the negatives of the first black and white shots I had taken when I was ten. The photographs I was able to develop were blurred and crisscrossed with marks, but they were blown up and arranged on the wall as well. The two sets of shots confronted me every morning, representing questions which I needed to resolve. This seemed the only way I could do it: by sifting through images, rearranging them as though my life was a kind of jigsaw that, put in the right order, would eventually make sense. Apart from Dunross I had not photographed a single image for myself since the crash.

Three days a week I was back working for the paper. I was not selective any more, I refused no assignments. I gladly photographed heads in business suits launching new investment portfolios and models spicing up expensive varieties of ice-cream. Once I had resented being dragged away from my studio, but now I welcomed the monotony of this work.

At the start of May it was guilt which made me decide to visit my parents' grave. When I was a child they must have often discussed the possibility of me wanting to find my real mother. They were both dead now and there was the chance that she might still be alive. So why did I feel so strongly that I was betraying them? I was eighteen when she had died and twenty-eight when my father followed her.

He had gone to her grave once a week, with a small bottle of water and flowers from the garden she had carefully tended. Only once or twice at the beginning had I gone with him, standing among the stones in Glasnevin, watching him never bless himself but simply stare down at the flowers so that it was impossible to know if he was praying or talking directly to her. Our only conversation there had been matter of fact, about the condition of the grave and where to dump the withered flowers. His only other real outing of the week was still to see Shelbourne play in whatever hired ground they managed to find. The Shelbourne glory days were long gone, the crowds tiny. It was hard to know which weekly excursion was the most lonely for him.

After her death there had been three awkward years of me living on top of him and then another seven for him alone in the house. I had been working for the alternative magazine where I first met Gerry; photo-documenting the protest against plans for a nuclear power plant in Wexford, PAYE mass-action marches in Dublin, pirate radio stations which broadcast from cellars under snooker halls and were back on the air within an hour of raids by the police, the occupation of listed buildings which developers had bribed local councillors to rezone for destruction. Sometimes my father came up to the attic that had once been his darkroom. He'd scan the prints that were drying there and shake his head.

'Can you not even take one shot without these weirdos screaming in the background?'

'We can't all block reality out with a red fuchsia bush,' I'd snap back, taunting him.

I'd wait with my hands immersed in chemicals until he'd turn to go. 'You make him feel like a peasant,' Aunt Cissie told me once on the street. He had his grief to cope with, he deserved to be allowed do so without me. He was right, of course. Most of the people on the magazine were simply destructive, perpetually opposed to everything. More and more people drifted on to the editorial collective, meetings became an endless scrutinizing of text and photographs to flush out latent examples of sexism and racism. A flour-bombing raid was made on the Photographers Gallery for showing an exhibition of Jerome Ducrot's crushed nudes, while myself and the two other photographers who had been involved from the first issue took refuge in a pub.

The breaking point for Gerry and me finally came one winter's night before a production meeting. A couple in their thirties had been waiting at the door of the magazine's office in Rathmines with one child in a pram and another wrapped up in the man's arms.

'Listen, lads,' the man said to us, 'we're skint, we're going to be made homeless in a fortnight. There's a bit of a small ad here, but we haven't got a penny. Is there any chance you could stick it in for us free?'

I told him that we were on his side, we would even post them a copy when it came out on the following Thursday.

A Second Life

Inside I read out the scrap of handwritten paper to the meeting and was denounced. *Married couple; husband good handyman, can turn his hand to anything, wife good cook, desperately need caretaking or any other position. Anything considered.* Had I not read it, a shaved head wanted to know? How did I think it was possible in all conscience for us to print something like that? *Handyman, husband, wife.* One faction wanted to rewrite the ad and print it in an acceptable fashion ... *Two people cohabiting, one handyperson, one cook* ... another wanted to write to the couple themselves and educate them about how they were demeaning themselves.

I cleared my desk and went home. I knew my father would be in the pub. He was surprised when I joined him there. After several pints I told him what had happened. He laughed, then cursed them viciously. And then, as if slowing opening himself to me, the more we drank together the more he began to curse others too, people whom he had spent years defending against my charges: politicians, clergy, even Pezzani's poxy fuchsia bush. Here, in the pub, we were on neutral ground. I caught a glimpse into his generation who felt themselves besieged, forced to justify causes they had long grown to despise among themselves.

Four years after my mother's death Pezzani's postcard business had been bought over by an Australian company. The images were now printed in Hong Kong. Every corner shop had a special offer from some new firm developing films. That side of the Pezzani business had been rational-ized and finally closed down. By the time I moved in with Geraldine my father had been forced into early retirement. We were on our way to becoming friends, but it was Geraldine who bonded us together. She was perhaps the first choice in my life of which he approved. *Athlone Town,*

160

he had chuckled, the first evening they met, *John Minnock's penalty!* She laughed in understanding and he had been delighted. It became a running joke between them. Before she walked up the aisle in Athlone at our wedding he had squeezed her hand. *Keep your head high and don't let John Minnock take the penalty.*

Twice a week we called to take him drinking. In the corner of his favourite pub he became the man that I remembered driving Pezzani's van, an old-fashioned charmer. All that was missing was the waistcoat. When he died I found a photograph of Geraldine in his wallet along with one of his wife as a young woman. His will was simple. *To my son, Sean, who has chosen a career that will never support a family, I leave my entire estate with the greatest regret that it is not more to help them.*

I had not expected to be so devastated by his death. My work was just becoming known: I'd had a Dublin solo show, signed a contract for a book of photographs, been part of a group exhibition in Berlin. It was only when he died that I realized how much the impetus driving my work had been to please and reassure him. He left five thousand pounds in a bank account. I was infuriated, knowing all the things which he had needed in those last few years, how he had stretched his pension, denied himself cigarettes and that extra drink. Along with the money from the sale of the house he had been determined to leave me a lump cash sum. Along with the deeds to the house there were thousands of old contact sheets, good honest photographs of Dublin life in the forties and fifties. There must have been a moment when he put his camera down and lifted it again to shoot what Pezzani wanted instead. Maybe the year when he and his wife brought me home from the agency, the year that he took on the responsibilities of a family man. Now that he knew we were hoping for a child, he was determined to buy me that extra bit of time for myself.

Among the papers which I almost threw out there was a neatly folded agreement with Pezzani, made in the year that my father went to work for him. It was a contract to take shots for postcards with a tiny percentage royalty. I remembered asking him once if Pezzani had ever paid him for the postcards he had taken, and how my father had laughed at the idea of Pezzani parting with cash. My father was a meticulous man, his life's earnings were neatly detailed in notebooks along with tax certificates. He had just been paid his wages and a small commission as a salesman.

I tracked down Pezzani to an old people's home outside Bray. He sat out on a balcony, staring at the Wicklow Mountains. He seemed muddled at first, then his eyes became clear. He readily admitted to having cheated my father, chuckling as he remembered the confrontations between them.

'These Australian fuckers, they take the business, liabilities, creditors, everything on their shoulders. Wait, I know your face now . . . Aran boy with donkey . . . you go and do what Aran boys do with donkeys . . . you screw them good.'

It was the only piece of Pezzani's advice which I ever took. The parent company in Sydney ignored the first letters from my solicitor. I knew that it would be impossible to concoct a sum for back royalties and make them admit liability for it, but what I decided to demand – as there had been a breach of contract – was that the copyright and original negatives of my father's work be returned to me. Almost nothing of it remained in print. But I knew that, dated and minor as the few shots left in use were, they were intractably linked in with bestselling posters and sets of table mats of vanished Georgian doorways and public houses, which the company could not afford to scrap. I thanked God briefly for developers and easily bribed councillors who between them had ensured that my father's photographs could not be replaced.

It was only after three years, when the case got listed for court, that they offered to settle. For me the sum was enormous, for them no more than a few weeks' legal fees would have cost. My team had taken it on a no-win no-cost basis. When I paid off my senior and junior counsel I still had enough from my father's estate for Geraldine and myself to live on for several years. My solicitor declined his fee. He settled for a framed copy of his favourite photograph of mine instead – Dublin's most notorious gang leader dropping his trousers to the guards outside the Four Courts to reveal a pair of Mickey Mouse boxer shorts.

I remember leaving the solicitor's office and walking down the quays. It was summer. There was a rack of postcards outside a shop where a girl in an apron worked an ice-cream machine. It took me several minutes to find one of my father's shots on the rack. How small did I make him feel, mocking them as an adolescent? I would have given every penny of that cheque for him to be alive just for one second, for him to hold that piece of folded paper which nestled in my inside pocket. It was Pezzani who had cheated him, but I had inherited my father's wry affection for the Italian. I didn't know if he would still be alive but I drove to the nursing home. He sat in the same chair, still looking out at the Wicklow Mountains.

'He won't know you,' the nurse said. 'He knows no one but if we lift him from that chair he gets angry and cries out.'

A Second Life

I leaned down. His eyes stared ahead, not acknowledging my presence. The nurse thought I was crazy, but I persuaded her to let me leave the fuchsia bush against the balcony railings, forming a red foreground to frame his vision of the hills. Perhaps I imagined the flicker of a smile. I left the postcard on his lap, the address side up. Across it in black marker were the words, *I screwed them good.*

My parents were buried beyond the Republican plot in Glasnevin, near the locked side gate of De Courcy Square which Daniel O'Connell had built so that poor Catholic funerals could avoid the tithes on the Finglas Road, designed to keep them away from the main entrance. As a youth I'd often drunk in Kavanagh's pub there, the Gravediggers, which had a hole in the wall at which men had once knocked for porter while the grave they were working on lay half opened. I arranged the flowers I had brought on my parents' grave, then stood for a while, unsure of what to say to them in my mind.

Fifty yards beyond their grave the eerie wilderness which constituted the oldest part of the graveyard began. Although the ground had been cleared by weedkiller, a light mossy growth remained. The old crosses were capsized and crooked. There always seemed a hint of mist or smoke there. Old family vaults with stone angels had stood untouched for a century. The most modern object was a curiously shaped cracked green bottle, at the rusted gates of one vault, which had not held flowers since before the Germans laid siege on Stalingrad.

These were the tombs of the rich. Elsewhere just the stump of wooden crosses remained, or else nothing except a hint from the shape of the earth that bodies had been laid there. And beyond them, as I walked away from the grave into that silence, were railings; and beyond those railings people could be glimpsed strolling in the Botanic Gardens.

It was mid-morning. A man with a wheelbarrow of cuttings walked through green gates where smoke rose from a bonfire. A young girl was kneeling among the sample beds of vegetables, weeding with her buttocks arched high in tight faded jeans which were thrust unselfconsciously towards the graveyard railings. I felt like a voyeur but did not move. At that moment I was sure that even if she turned and looked directly out towards the rows of slumped headstones I would still be invisible. I raised the Pentax and kept clicking until I heard the film beginning to rewind itself.

These moments of feeling at a loss among the living were fewer now. But still when I went for my monthly check-up the doctors advised therapy. Everybody who had undergone this experience suffered this sense of loss, they said. They were natural and with professional counselling I could overcome them. But for me it was not that simple. There were things which I felt I should be able to remember, things that were important. I could not move on until I had confronted them. That face seemed linked to those remembrances. By now I was afraid to lose touch with it.

I got back into the car and drove the mile around to the entrance of the gardens. I slowed, while the car behind me beeped, and stared at the spot on the road where I had died, then swung left and parked outside the gates. Three hired limousines decked out with ribbons were lined up, drivers sharing a smoke while photographers arranged brides and grooms in poses among the flower beds beyond the gates. It had become the standard cliché for weddings on this side of the city.

I turned right and walked down by the Victoria

Glasshouse with its giant water-lily. Construction work was in progress on rebuilding the curvilinear range. They were cordoned off with plywood partitions. A crane lifted girders high up to a scaffold against a hundred-and-fifty-year-old stone wall. I went down steps towards the river, past the sluice gates of the millrace, by the hanging willows and the rhododendrons, and came to the bridge which led across to the rose garden.

I stopped, suddenly and irrationally afraid. I could hear Aunt Cissie's voice in her darkened living room. I strained to remember anything of this place, closed my eyes, tried to see if I could imagine it a century before.

There was growth on the pruned roses but few were in bloom yet. I read the names – *Sangria, Moulin Rouge, Fragrant Hour* – trying them out on my tongue. They sounded gaudy and cheap like the names of seaside boarding houses.

A sundial stood on a raised plinth in the centre. I had been here two years ago, before the World Cup, helping out a young staffer on a photo assignment of Irish football players modelling for the fashion supplement. I remembered lining angles up for him and posing the players, but insisting that he took all the shots himself.

A girl was waiting for a bus high up on the road beside the bridge. In the wall beneath her there seemed to be a bricked-up entrance. The river ran on two sides and the other wall, screened by bushes, formed the gable end of the Tolka House pub. I pushed the screen of branches back and walked underneath, then stopped. The outline remained of the roof and stone wall of a cottage. I looked behind me. I knew who I expected to see there with his mocking grin. I was no longer frightened. It was hard to describe what I felt. The dull emptiness of a man with amnesia shown his home. I pursed my lips and tried to whistle.

The man with the armband and walkie-talkie was leaning against an immense bloated tree whose branches sloped towards the pond. They spread out above his head in a canopy of lime-green leaves which darkened to a rusty plum colour where they were exposed to the sun. The base was warped and ugly like a circle of moss-covered toes. Benedict always pulled at my arm to hurry me past this spot. I waited as the sun went in, then came out again. A red-beaked bird moved among the clusters of reeds on the pond. I approached him, uncertain if Aunt Cissie had even remembered the name correctly, or exactly what questions I wanted to ask. Up close I could see the scars of amputations on the lower trunk of the tree, forcing the growth upwards. A tractor was disappearing through the thick foliage above us.

'Sorry, mate,' I began, 'but do you mind me asking, does the name Davitt mean anything to you? Here in the gardens?'

'Someone who worked here, you mean?' The man shook his head. 'Doesn't ring a bell. But maybe Peter patrolling over in the arboretum might know. Remembers back to when they used horses in the forties. Is this Davitt fellow anything to you?'

I shook my head, as he spoke into the walkie-talkie. For a moment I expected gardeners with walkie-talkies to appear from behind every tree. The man stopped talking.

'I have the man you're after now,' he said. 'There's a photograph of him up in the front lodge with six other gardeners taken just after the war. *The Grand Old Men of the Gardens*, it's called. Three hundred years of service between them. Head up there by the Chain Tent. Peter says he'd be glad to talk to any relation of Austin Davitt.'

I climbed up towards a circular wooden hut with a cast-iron bench inside it. The trees dropped away to the river and the high cemetery wall. The grass had been allowed to grow high there so that wild flowers could thrive. A squirrel watched for a moment, then bobbed out of sight. The gardener was old. He sat on the bench outside waiting for me. I knew I had no hope of lying to him.

'Listen, I didn't know this Austin Davitt myself,' I said. 'I'm just curious about something. Do you mind if I ask you some questions?'

'Work away,' he said. 'It will make a change from "Can I swipe some cuttings?" and "Will you take my photograph?"'

'How long did Davitt work here?' I sat down beside him.

'His whole life as far as I know. Maybe he trained elsewhere, but he was born in these gardens. Over there at what became the rose garden not long after the war. His father was a gardener here too, his grandfather for all I know.'

'Would many gardeners have actually lived in the grounds like that, reared their families here . . . I mean back in the last century?'

He threw his head back and laughed.

'Jaysus,' he said, 'how old do you think I am? The Ancient Shagging Mariner? I doubt it, but I wouldn't have a clue to be honest. Except for the apprentices, though they were an unruly shower of gougers by all accounts. They were housed up by the gate lodge. A damp old kip, you wouldn't keep a dog in it now.'

I had run out of questions. All I had left were snatches of what could simply be my imagination.

'One last thing,' I said. 'Those trees facing the pond? Did you ever hear any stories . . . maybe during the famine . . .

that there might have been a mass grave or something dug there?'

'No. Definitely not.' He shook his head. Then he thought for a moment. 'The soil down there though, it's not the original soil. That soil was too shallow really for an arboretum. I believe they did a lot of replanting after the destruction on the night of the Big Wind. They would have dug fairly deep trenches and brought good loam in.'

I stood up quickly and began to walk away. It was that feeling again, like in the rose garden. I needed to be alone. There were steps down to a public toilet.

'Are you all right?' he called out. 'I tell you one thing. I often think of those apprentices when I see some of the young slips of girls working here now.'

I stopped. I felt queasy.

'Why's that?'

'It was all lads back then. You can see the terms and conditions written down in some of the old papers up in the storeroom. Only four shillings a week to start with and you had to bring your own bed linen and cups and plates and God knows what. But I tell you, you'd put up with all that and more if there were a few girls serving out their time with you. Because it's written down in black and white. You were legally entitled to "the share of a bed with another person".'

His laughter followed me down into the toilets. I closed over the cubicle and sat down, raising my palms to cover my face. After a moment I looked up at the wooden door. There was a message in black marker: *I will suck you off and let you fuck me.* I took a pen from my inside pocket and scrubbed and scrubbed at it until the ballpoint broke and I was scraping at the wood with shards of plastic, feeling the splinters lodge beneath my nails.

Chapter Eleven

In our courting days there was a game which Geraldine and I loved to play. We would get off our bicycles and sit on a bench, remembering moments from our separate pasts which we now discovered that we had shared. The two we always returned to were the spring of 1973 and the autumn of 1975.

Dalymount Park came first: those four endless March nights, long before penalty shoot-outs were invented, when Shamrock Rovers battled it out with Athlone Town in the FAI Cup. Seven and a half hours of stale and dreadful football were spread out over those four nights, filled with the addictive monotony of floodlights and familiar faces. It was hard to remember what I had been doing there. I hated the smug hoops of the Rovers, so perhaps it was to annoy my father, who, like all Shelbourne supporters, was convinced that the Devil had been in league with the Hoops since 1904.

But once you had endured the first of those matches you felt somehow compelled to keep returning until the final result. Unknown to me, and years before I met her, Geraldine had been forty yards away in the Tramway End on each of those nights, hoisted on to the shoulders of her brother, her fourteen-year-old voice screaming out for Athlone. She claimed that there were marriages made on those nightly trips up and down from the midlands, and babies conceived whose births were notable for the protracted length of their mothers' labours.

A Second Life

Two years later I had been on my knees praying in front of the radio on the mantelpiece, while Geraldine strained to see among the bodies in the massed silence which covered Athlone. Twelve thousand pairs of lungs collectively inhaled, twelve thousand breaths were held and then, in a unison of disappointment, let go. John Minnock, after a superb game, had just stubbed a weak penalty kick towards the AC Milan goal.

That freak draw in the UEFA Cup lived on in legend, the might of AC Milan descending like gods on to the narrow streets of Athlone. Geraldine claimed that moments after the draw was made a Milan official had managed to find Athlone on a map and telephone the club. Her father had to run through the streets to the local chip shop, where the Italian proprietor was propelled through the rain to translate on the phone while the bemused queue at his counter waited for salt and vinegar.

During the match itself whenever the stars of Milan stretched their arms back to throw in the ball they found themselves shaking hands with farmers who had reached in through the wire fencing. For Athlone to survive with a draw had been beyond anyone's expectations, and yet Minnock's missed penalty had somehow soured the day. Geraldine maintained that a cloud had settled over the town just as his foot stubbed the ball and the cloud had never lifted since.

During the first time we lay in bed together we connected these pasts. It was in a friend's flat with yellowing wallpaper and an Ian Dury album cover stuck to the ceiling over the bed. The scent of the four joints he had left neatly rolled for us, and the hot ports I had made, mingled with that of the mince pies Geraldine had cooked, and which we had left heating in the oven until the smoke alerted us. She said that

I looked like Tarzan standing up on the table, in just my underpants, to hold the smouldering oven tray out the small window across from the winking signs for kebabs and late-night shops along Rathmines Road.

How hard we both found it to leave the bed that night for the cold of our bicycles chained together in the hall, when my friend's golf club on the floor could be used to flick the switch on the record player, and we could turn to each other's bodies in the hollow of the small mattress and forget the midnight hour when the door was locked at Geraldine's hostel.

Finally, at half-eleven, we had to cycle across the canal and down overlapping streets of emptying pubs – Wexford Street, Aungier Street, George's Street – and along cobbled lanes against the clock to find our way back to Henrietta Street before the nuns put the snib on the hostel door. At five to twelve our bikes were suddenly slowing, the back wheels ticking as we freewheeled along by the side of Bolton Street. The bicycles halted by themselves on the hill up to the hostel. It was a new relationship, both of us unsure of what to do next. My voice didn't sound like my voice. 'I will never be rich, do you understand that? Stick with me and you'll never have anything. My worldly goods are just two cameras, this bicycle and whatever condoms we have left.'

The queue outside the Register of Births, Deaths & Marriages stretched half-way down Lombard Street. But when the doors opened most people crowded into the ground floor for birth certs and I was able to reach the upstairs research room. The ledgers stretched back into the last century. They were arranged in a loose order on old shelving on the right-hand wall. Even in the middle of May the room was filling up with visitors – professional researchers, geologists, elderly Americans. There were four volumes for 1957. I took down the last one, R–Z. It held thousands of names with minute information. The surname and first name of the child, the date, the district where the birth was registered.

I ran my finger slowly down the Sweeneys, then paused before turning the page. Up until now I had been able to convince part of myself that this was a fiction. The address sown into those baby clothes could still have been a hoax. The trail I had followed could belong to somebody else. There was nothing to link me definitely to Dunross except for my own, possibly imaginary, feelings at that graveside. Maybe it was better to leave the whole business like this, loose and unconfirmed.

I already had a name and a life, so why did I need to impose a second one on to it? But what if there was no Sweeney listed with my date of birth? Then I would be no wiser than when I first began, but I would be free of this obsession, knowing that, except by trying to contact the agency, I would have no way of starting the search again. Suddenly I prayed for the first time in decades. Lord, if you exist, may I not find myself in here.

I turned the page. Four lines from the end the Sweeneys ran out. There was no one with my date of birth in 1957. I felt a sense of release. Some other child had been curled in that womb in Dunross graveyard. I was anonymous again. I stood up, then stopped with a sense of cold inevitability and sat down again. Midway down a page in the first volume for 1957 I found myself. *Blake, Sean,* with my date of birth and the names of parents who had not known I existed on that day. Months afterwards my details had been written in, backdated. How could I have been so stupid as to think that any trace of my first life would be left to stain the official records? An elderly American woman sitting beside me looked up. Her eyes seemed about to brim over.

'I've found my grandmother,' she said. 'She was born in Leitrim, 1873. I'm so excited.'

'I don't care if she was hatched out of the bog,' I snapped, before I could stop myself. She lowered her face. I knew she was now crying.

'I'm sorry,' I said, 'I'm pleased for you.'

She looked across at my trembling hands. The veins were blue on her wrist as she lightly touched my fingers.

'Ink and paper,' she said. 'Rows of names. Amazing something that simple could hold so much joy and pain for us.'

'Just what sort of project are you working on, Mr Blake?' The official from the Botanic Gardens turned the key in the curved oak door at the top of the stairs. We were in gloom for a moment before the door opened. Two high windows looked down over the bend on the road where I had crashed. A curtain of ivy had begun to encroach across the upper panes. The room had the same pervasive melancholy as old Dublin pubs on winter afternoons. The bookcases were ancient, the leather bindings on the volumes dating from the last century. The man waited for an answer to his question. The rain was loud and yet distant against the bare panes of glass. I stared out at cars slowing on the bend.

'I'm looking for a ghost,' I said.

'For the newspaper?' he asked, slightly anxious. 'Is that some sort of summer story?'

'No,' I said. 'I work for the paper, but this is private. Just for myself.'

I turned to see his reaction. He was impassive, there was no trace either of humour or anxiety in his gaze.

'Sometimes we bring our ghosts to places with us,' he said.

'Do you believe in them?'

'What's in our head is often as real as what's in front of our eyes.' He looked around at the shelves of bound records and files of old photographic plates. 'This is Bluebeard's room. The cleaners don't like being in here by themselves at night. None of them has ever seen Bluebeard, none of them will admit to believing in him or in ghosts, but if they're in here and that door closes he's more real to them than anyone outside.'

'What about you?' I asked again. He looked at me closely and I found myself staring at him. Both of us were trying to place the other's face.

'Listen,' he said, 'officially you're a journalist or photographer or researcher or whatever the hell you are. That's all I need to know for the daybook. You take your time, I'm downstairs if you want me.'

He stepped back and closed the door. I was alone with Bluebeard. I wondered how the cleaners saw him. A phantom pirate with a cutlass and black eye sockets materializing through the shelves of studies on the germination of orchid seeds. Or did the light sway suddenly, the room pierced with the tang of seaweed and damp salt? Bluebeard. If there was a Bluebeard it was probably an earlier version of themselves, one of the nameless women who gave Washerwoman's Hill its title, a stooped lost figure who had never found the exit.

I sat down with no idea of what I was really looking for. Searching through the Register of Births had been straightforward the previous day, but how could you start looking for somebody when you were not even sure if they had existed? All I had to go on were fragments from the aftermath of dreams.

A Second Life

I dreaded sleeping at night now. Always at some stage a dream would occur of being in a public place with Geraldine and the children – shopping in the supermarket, feeding ducks in the park – but as they walked on I would suddenly be confronted by a wall of glass. It was ice-cold when I pressed against it with my palms and their voices had become distant although I could still see them ahead of me. A sick feeling would enter my stomach as I cursed myself for forgetting that I had died. I would try to call to them but they walked on, Geraldine's head bent down to laugh with Benedict.

And then I would be imbued with a desolate sense of loss at being dead, as strong as that which I had once felt at being brought back to life. When I'd wake my breathing would be fast and I'd long for Geraldine to wake too and for her to hold me in her arms. *I'm alive,* I kept telling myself. *It's okay, I'm alive.* And always then I would find myself straining as if to remember some experience which had happened, which I knew had not been a dream but was not part of my present life, something which would have slipped away by the time I was fully awake.

I knew this sense of grief was healthy, it was a sign that I was coming to value the miracle of being alive. The spell of that circle of dead faces was being erased. The experience would never leave me but now I was focusing on this life. Every morning the feeling was tangible and utterly consuming. I would feel the nails on my hand to see how they had grown, the stubble on my chin after sleep. The pale light entering the bedroom was exotic. *I'm alive.* Again the phrase would be repeated like a mantra to calm my breath down. Benedict would stir in sleep at the noise of the milk truck or the postman. Always I found myself close to tears. And always that young man's face would hover as though trying to draw me back again into a malady of unease.

A Second Life

I knew that I had to track him down before I could fully re-enter my life again. Here, in the library of the Botanic Gardens, seemed as good a place as any to start. There were drawers of hand-coloured maps from the Royal Dublin Society; coloured plates under glass of sedge and perennial herbs; a set of engravings from the *Illustrated London News* recording the splendour of the visit of the Queen and her Prince Consort in 1849, while famine raged a discreet distance beyond the gates; ledgers and manuscripts which I could not decipher; and, finally, sets of old photographs.

I worked my way through these with a quiet terror. Time ceased to exist. I had no idea how long I had left before the bell was rung to close the gates. The rain grew in intensity and the room became dark. I switched on the light. In the pane of glass before me I could dimly make myself out, sitting at that high Victorian desk with my image superimposed on the cars passing outside. My hands shook as I lifted the photographs. Three men prepared to blast a tree stump in winter. The men's top hats and collars seemed comical as they posed in the deep snow with Nobel's newly invented dynamite and fuses. An anonymous group of workmen posed in 1913, the younger men kneeling, the older men with overgrown moustaches. A child in a pinafore knelt beside a sapling at the turn of the century. I recognized the tree from the position of the glasshouse in the background. It was still there, towering over its surroundings while, by now, that child had to be dead.

I turned over an old photograph of the pond in summer. The name *W. D. Hemphill* was stamped on the back with the date 1897. There were notes about the marsh plants grown at the edges of the pond and the aquatic plants which crowded the stagnant water. This was the landscape of my dream, but I was unsure now of how much detail the dream had actually contained and how much I was filling in from the photograph. A plantation of young trees was clearly visible on the slope where I had dreamt of working at a deep pit. I held the photograph up close to the light, peering at it with the sort of haunted intensity which had once consumed my work. I felt my breath quicken. My hands shook, I let the photograph drop. I sucked in deep breaths, trying to calm myself.

What if the doors were locked, the bell long rung, if I had been forgotten here along with the ghost of Bluebeard? It was irrational, but I ran to the door. Only when it was propped open with a chair did I return and quickly close the drawers. I tried not to run down the stairs. I just wanted to be out in the evening air, among the umbrellas and sodden overcoats, to be going home to my family like any ordinary man.

The private hospital was off the Malahide Road, an old landlord's house with a huge modern extension built on to the back. Gravel crunched on the path. Two nurses' aides cycled down under the low branches, the white of their uniforms flashing beneath their coats.

Throughout my childhood there had always been a fuss made about two callers to the house. The Avon Lady and Mrs Lacey – 'Mammy's friend from Cork'. Red and white sticks of rock were what I remembered most about Mrs Lacey's visits. Being called in from the garden and standing before her in the musty living room which we never used, knowing that I was on inspection without ever really knowing why. She would smile as she asked me questions and instinctively I knew how important it was to my mother that I smiled back. *Happy families.* Once she had brought me a packet of them, *Mr Baker, Mrs Butcher*. I was banished to the garden to arrange the cards out in families on the grass, while they talked on behind the closed sitting-room door and the freshly baked scones waited in the kitchen, covered by a spotless dishcloth.

Happy families. How happy my mother always seemed when her friend was gone. She would wave at the doorway till the woman was out of sight, then close the door and lean against it with her eyes closed. This was the part of the twice-yearly visit which I enjoyed most, when I could stuff myself with scones and my mother didn't mind. She was like a young girl, singing to herself, rustling my hair, shooing me to run up and take off those Sunday clothes. This is what friends are like for grown-ups, I thought, smiling faces to be afraid of.

After my tenth birthday it was different. My own terror was worse than my mother's. I would stutter when Mrs Lacey asked me questions, frightened – even at thirteen and fourteen – that she had the papers in her bag to whisk me away from my home. Yet my mother's fears and mine were separate, never to be hinted at. On the one occasion that I ever made a spiteful remark about Mrs Lacey, my mother had lifted the milk jug and flung its contents across the table into my face.

I stopped at the porch of the hospital. Three old women stared out from the bay window of the large front room. Their eyes possessed a kind of vacant hope. I stepped forward and rang the bell. There was the noise of a large iron key being turned, before I entered into the scent of wax and of waiting for death. It was Gerry who had tracked her down for me. He did not ask who she was and I did not ask how he had traced her. Now it was up to me to find a way to see the woman.

'You're not family?' the matron asked. Her office was

small, almost a cubbyhole under the stairs. There was the thump of feet above us.

'I'm not.'

'Mrs Lacey's family don't come any more. You might think that's cruel. They did look after her for as long as they could. But Alzheimer's, it's a wasting away of the brain. At first it's just forgetfulness, mood changes, then an inability to dress oneself, not to soil oneself. Most families ... well at that stage it's really better for all if there's professional help. Relatives do come but after a while the patients really don't know who they are. Sometimes it's just too cruel, people can't bear to look. Mrs Lacey won't know you, you know that, whoever you are.'

'I'd still like to see her, please.'

The matron took a sheet of paper from a drawer.

'And your name is?'

'Blake. My mother ... she was my mother's special friend.'

The hospital grew shabbier as we ascended the stairs. The matron had not looked up at the unexpected bitterness in my voice. She had been my mother's friend, a good and concerned woman, I was sure of that. But also the only person ever to have met both my mothers. The women in McHugh's office had told me that one person always oversaw each handover. My real mother would have placed me into Mrs Lacey's arms. The mother I had known would have lifted me from them. Who knew how long might have passed between those events, when I might have looked up at her with the same bewildered, unfocused eyes as Frank Conroy's child? Maybe I had been fostered out for a month or more while forms were sorted. She might have left me in other sets of arms and plucked me from them again.

I remembered a photograph from the collection of Father

Browne, a superb and unknown photographer who had wandered Ireland quietly for decades with his camera. It was of a baby in Laois in the 1930s, sharing a shabby pram with a kid goat. The child has no hair yet, but his face is already marked by poverty. He is sitting propped up by a tattered blanket, his eyes staring out in haunting bewilderment.

The matron opened the door of a ward and we walked past the six beds, through another door into the day room. None of the women there looked up at our entrance. Two nurses were trying to transfer a woman from her chair on to a commode. Beyond them, in the chair near the window, Mrs Lacey sat. Her hair had greyed, flesh hung in wrinkles on her neck, but I recognized my mother's friend. I hated myself for the stab of satisfaction I felt. She had never meant me any harm. For all I knew my real mother might have tossed me into a ditch without her. I remembered an assignment one winter, crossing a bog to photograph the shallow grave where an anonymous infant had been placed. My adoptive parents had shown me nothing but intense and unqualified love. How could I possibly feel a thrill of revenge?

The matron began talking to the nurses as I approached her. Her hands were agitated, but her speech was slurred. I knelt a few feet from her and tried to decipher the words. *Dinner, get the dinner, get dinner, dinner.* It was like an incantation which brought her no comfort. She leaned forward, staring at the floor, moving her head and hands like somebody who had dropped something but couldn't see where it had rolled. I spoke her name, softly and then louder. She never looked up.

Boys in from school, get dinner, get dinner. I spoke my own name, but there was no response. A nurse approached behind me.

'You can see the way she is,' she said.

'Can I sit awhile?'

The nurse nodded. I found a chair and sat across from her. A motionless woman behind me with her head thrown back repeated the words *Nurse please* in an expressionless singsong voice every fifteen or twenty seconds. I found myself listening for the phrase like a form of torture. Mrs Lacey's indifference to me meant that I felt free to stare at her. Despite the illness her profile still reflected how formidable she had once been. She stopped raving suddenly, as though aware there was somebody with her. We were silent, reunited again. There must have been moments when we had been alone thirty-five years before. Any bitterness was gone. If she had put her hand out to mine I would have taken it and cried like any son. I knew that this was as close to my real mother as I might ever come.

'Margaret Blake.' I kept repeating my mother's name. She had begun to stare at me.

'Get dinner, dinner, dinner.' Her voice was weaker with every repetition, like a record trailing away.

'Sweeney, Sweeney. Dunross. Sweeney. Laois. Sweeney. Margaret Blake.'

Her hands were making a different motion now, plucking at something, her knuckles white with effort. I repeated the names and the movements continued, growing in agitation until it seemed she was trying to pull the skin off her fingers.

'Tell him and you'll lose him. Tell him and you'll lose him.'

The whisper was so hesitant it took several moments before I understood it. The motions suddenly made sense. She was plucking at a baby's clothes, tearing open the seams. The nurse came back to my shoulder.

'Every day the same. Making dinner for her sons coming home from school,' she said. 'Three boys. All but one of them are dead now.'

Outside the hospital rush-hour traffic had crawled to a halt. Geraldine would have dinner ready, back in my real life where I was late again. This was her most difficult hour – the baby screaming to be fed in her high chair, Benedict blabbering about tractors, crying that he could not feed himself. She would have been alone all day, coping with them. Benedict was increasingly jealous of Sinead now that she could crawl. He purposely parked toy tractors in her way or tried to block her behind a chair, demanding that Geraldine put her back in her tummy. *Daddy's home from his adventure,* he would cry every evening as soon as my key turned in the lock, while Sinead would put her arms up to be lifted, reciting her two words, *Si* and *yeah*.

I owed it to Geraldine to turn for home, I wanted to do so. I got into the car and started the engine. I switched it off, then turned the key again and moved off. I drove across the toll bridge, where the noise of moored boats was like chimes in the breeze. Finally I came to the Pigeon House Wall. I walked out along the crumbling slabs of rock with the sea pounding on both sides. There was a deserted red tower at the end. Once, before we were married, Geraldine and I had walked for miles in winter to reach here, Geraldine convincing herself that the tower was a coffee shop. The huge twin chimneys of the power station split the sky behind me. There were a few tinkers' caravans parked in the distance, smoke from a fire, two children playing in a drizzle on a leather sofa with the stuffing pulled from it. Even the men who fished here had gone home.

Tell him and you'll lose him. It would have been Mrs

Lacey's job to ensure that no clue to my past remained. Had my mother asked her at once or spent years losing courage before blurting it out? And if my real mother had wished to abandon me, then why would she have left her name to be found? I stared out at a tanker entering Dublin Bay, tasting salt on my lips from the waves which splashed against the foot of the tower. How often as a child on holidays in Courtown had I thrown out a message in a lemonade bottle, my name and address stuck in the neck? I would close my eyes to imagine the distant white beach where it would be washed up. *Find me, son.* All of my life she must have been waiting, never knowing if it had sunk through the waves with smudging ink, or whose hands had prised the message open, to be discarded or treasured.

Ever since I had built the bird-table for Benedict the garden had been filling up with small birds. The day we erected it a warm, gusty breeze had made the clothes Geraldine was putting out on the line billow. Benedict sat on the step by the rockery leading down to the back lawn and painted away busily at the wooden base with an imaginary brush. 'No, Mammy, go away,' he had protested whenever Geraldine stepped out with more clothes to hang, 'we're busy doing an important job.'

Watching him I had realized how quickly school and the outer world would claim him. But for now this garden was the only universe he needed, the feel of being a fellow workman with his father, sitting in the spring sunlight wearing a plastic building-site helmet, immersed in the task of building a house for his friends who loved him, the birds.

Most days the bread blew off the bird-table or got soaked in the rain which swept in on perpetual raids from the Wicklow Mountains. But the nuts, which we hung in two wire-mesh containers, were a constant treat for the finches and wrens who had begun to visit the bird-table. From early morning a queue of small birds perched on the fence or hid themselves in the woodbine along the wall, occasionally flying down to scavenge for bread which had fallen into the bushes.

Beyond the end of the garden stood a row of old trees, in the tallest of which two magpies had built their nest. For hours Benedict and I would kneel at the bedroom window, playing 'I spy the pegs on the clothes line' and 'I spy Mick the Magpie's nest'.

Now, at the end of May, the nest was almost totally obscured by leaves, but Mick had become a more constant presence in the garden. The smaller birds would scatter in alarm as he landed possessively on the roof of the bird-house and waddled around to stare momentarily towards our window before taking off again. A few moments later, when the nuts had lured the finches back, Mick would land back again to chase them off. Lately Geraldine had begun to claim that fewer birds came back each time, but I took little notice.

It was half-seven that evening when I finally drove home from the Pigeon House Wall. I could hear Benedict shouting my name as I opened the hall door. He ran out from the dining room in his pyjamas, jumping up to be caught in my arms. I carried him into the kitchen. There were Lego and plastic farm animals scattered around on the floor. Sinead was standing with both hands holding the edge of the table. Her mouth was pressed against the wooden rim, trying to bite into it.

I was an hour and a half late. It had become a nightly event. Geraldine said nothing. Recently she had stopped asking me how I had got on during the day or even where I had been. I could see the tension in her shoulders as she stood at the sink. I joined her at the window with Benedict still in my arms, the three of us staring out at the flock of feeding birds. Mick the Magpie must have been on the kitchen roof above us, because he seemed to swoop from nowhere, his beak sinking into the coloured breast of a finch as the other birds flew off. Geraldine screamed as I swung Benedict round so that he could not see. The finch had fallen on to the grass. Mick landed on top of him and casually began to rip at his throat.

I thrust Benedict into Geraldine's hands. I knew how silly I looked, kicking the back door open, clutching the long bread knife. Mick flew up as far as the roof of the shed. The finch was not yet dead. I knelt and reached for a rock, praying that Benedict was not watching as I brought it swiftly down on the finch's head. There were flecks of blood on the rock and on my palm. I screamed as I flung the rock at the magpie. Mick flew as far as a neighbour's fence and settled there with a contemptuous stare. I knew that stare, those cold eyes. Every obscure force which threatened me seemed contained in that look. Geraldine was watching from the window, with Benedict's face pressed against her body. I screamed again as I flung the bread knife across the gardens after the magpie. This time he did not even budge, just blinked and looked impassively down at this intruder briefly careering around his kingdom.

Chapter Twelve

'You're back,' the official in the Botanic Gardens said. It was lunch time, the last Friday in June. How often in the previous six weeks had I passed those gates, slowed and then sped on again. I grinned and scratched my head. 'You seemed in a fierce hurry leaving last time.'

'It was Bluebeard,' I joked. 'I didn't mind him being a ghost, but you never told me he sang John Denver songs.'

The man took the keys down from the shelf behind his desk. I followed him up the varnished stairs again. He bent to insert the key and I knew where I had seen him before. Inside the room the ivy had been cropped back from the window.

'I don't think that Bluebeard is the ghost you're looking for,' he said. 'Do you want to be more specific?'

'I don't know how to be,' I replied. 'This is a personal business. It doesn't even make much sense to me.'

'You know,' he said slowly, 'the last time you were here I knew that I had your face from somewhere. You mentioned the newspaper, I thought I knew it from there. But it was Charlie out at the front gate who gave it to me. That crash at Christmas. It was you they pulled from the car, wasn't it?'

I stared out the window. In old movies the criminal always returns to the scene of his crime.

'I saw you too,' I said, after a moment. 'That bald patch of yours. At the gate. The pair of you standing together.'

'Sure you were in a coma. You looked dead to the world.'

'I saw you from the air, from a height. Can you believe that?'

I turned to face him. They had wanted me to go to counsellors, professionals. I had not even been capable of discussing it with Geraldine. Yet this stranger was the first person I felt able to talk to. He reminded me of the sort of men that my father had once drank with. He nodded his head slowly.

'Maybe I do,' he said, 'or maybe I just want to believe it. I've heard of that type of thing before. My own missus died eight years ago. She mumbled a lot at the end. Took a while to figure out. Names . . . dead names . . . like they were all crowding into the ward to greet her. Are you afraid of dying now?'

'Don't want to die,' I replied eventually. 'I really just want to get on with living, but . . . no . . . I'm not afraid of dying. You couldn't be after what I've been through. The thing is though . . . those faces your wife saw . . . what if there was one threatening one that you didn't even know, that you were afraid of meeting after you died? Your wife . . . how long did it take you to get over . . .?'

He took a packet of cigarettes from his jacket pocket and lit one. He held the packet out. I shook my head.

'You don't get over grief,' he said. 'You just learn degrees of forgetfulness. It still hits you, certain mornings years later.'

'Well then, what if you had died yourself?' I asked. 'What I mean is . . . like those astronauts who went to the moon . . . how do you fit back among ordinary things, focus your mind on everyday . . .'

'The same as we all do.' There was a sharpness in his voice which made me stop. I knew that this was what my father would have said. 'All of us pick up the pieces. We lose wives, husbands, kids even, we watch them die slowly in pain. It knocks the stuffing out of us until we just want to curl up and die. But we don't. We make ourselves get on with it. Now what have you actually lost?'

The accusation in his question made me think.

'I know what I will lose,' I said. 'A wife and kids if I don't get off my arse.'

'Then you're no *astronaut* come back from space.' My father would have built just such a sneer in the word too. 'They can send a dog to the fucking moon, can't they? If you've got kids, then you're a father and your job is to get on with living and working for them. It doesn't matter where you've been or what's happened to you, none of that stuff changes what you are.'

He looked away from me suddenly, and around at the crowded shelves, as though embarrassed. I thought of Frank Conroy, how those words would have applied to him as well. What must he have felt staring out into the dark freezing waters?

'It's one bizarre room this,' the official said, as though the walls had made him speak. 'I always thought so.'

'Listen . . . thanks.'

'You wouldn't want to be minding what I say.' He grinned. 'Just tell me one thing, will it help if you find this ghost of yours?'

'I don't know how or why,' I replied hesitantly, 'but I think I have memories inside me. Memories of this place that don't relate to me. Maybe I've inherited them in my genes, like features, maybe . . .' I looked around at the shelves of books. 'They frighten me.'

He reached his foot out and gently pushed the door shut, then took the keys for the glass doors of the top shelves from his pocket.

'The name is George,' he said. 'I don't know anything about that stuff, but I do know what's in this room and I'm in no hurry.'

We worked together through the early afternoon, George bringing up coffee and sandwiches at three o'clock. He had made no comment on the few selective scraps of dreams and memories which I felt able to tell him. He just kept opening drawers and files and producing more photographs. I had no idea what I was looking for or indeed what I might be looking at. The ghost of myself. A buried past which I had yet to fathom. This photograph he was showing me of a long-dead woman with gloves and an apron, could she have been my mother in a previous life? This man holding a pony harnessed up to the grass mower, could he have been me, or my father, or my lover? The image of the yew walk, which I had remembered or dreamt, came vividly back, the feel of a man closing on me, the strange thrill of knowing I was about to be caught.

My eye stopped at a Victorian family posed on a donkey cart outside the keeper's residence. The boy was in a sailor suit. I could be sure at least that I had not been him. My memories – if that is what they were – had the taint of poverty. I would have stood in bare feet to watch that cart pass, would have been taught to bow and call him *Sir*. Had I looked at him with hatred or even sexual longing? All I knew is that the face which haunted me held no room for servility.

'Let's start at the beginning,' George finally said. 'You say you had a dream of labouring down by the pond. Old Peter told you work was done there after the night of the Big Wind. Let's try to put a date on that.'

There were daybooks and accounts which had not been

disturbed for decades. We had to wipe the dust from our fingers before turning the yellowing pages. The cottage by the river was listed as being in the tenancy of Jeremiah Davitt. The copperplate writing of a gentleman approved his continued employment after his ninetieth birthday: *Noted for his generosity, he could mow before my grand-father first opened his eyes and is still able to cut round any man in the gardens.*

The early pages of the daybook for 1839 gave us the first inkling. A less educated hand recorded the *Aurora Borealis* as being clearly visible while workmen had struggled to rescue a policeman trapped under a fallen wall in the intense storm of the eighth of January. Local residents were listed who were given permission to shelter in the cellars of the keeper's house after the roofs of their own cabins were blown away. The corpse of a goat was found near the river after having been lifted by the wind from a field near Glasnevin village. Different hands noted which trees had been felled throughout the grounds. The meteorological readings listed the wind dying and then the depth of follow-ing snow.

Entries over the next few weeks were concerned with repairing the storm damage and complaints of the poor state of paths after fallen trees had been hauled away. Notice was given of the arrival of four hundred tons of gravel for resurfacing at a cost of sixty pounds. George and I had to search for half an hour before we came across the first references to work on the pond slope. Notice was given that the heavily depleted arboretum was to be extended. New trees were to be planted according to their needs for light and space and not their botanical order. A detachment of workmen was listed to prepare deep pits that would receive good loam to replace the existing shallow soil.

Rain clouds had gathered through the afternoon. Neither George nor I had noticed how dark the room was becoming. I looked up, suddenly wanting the place flooded with light. I put my hand briefly down on the page, wondering if it rested on what was once my own name among that list of men. George began to read out the detachment of work-men: *In charge, P. McArdle, outdoor foreman; workers, F. Goggins, P. McGovern, A. Drumgoole, E. McKenna, J. Davitt, A. Morgan.*

I closed my eyes. Jeremiah Davitt, a toothless old man boiling up a billycan as he crouched among the trees. What came back to me was no dream, but a memory from my own childhood. Being alone outside the back door at five years of age and suddenly running into my mother, scream-ing that the old man in the hedge at the end of the garden was staring out at me. A crouched figure with a puckered wizened face. Even later, playing there towards dusk at seven and eight years of age, the fear would return that if I glanced down quickly I would glimpse his face, concocted out of twigs and briars.

F. Goggins, P. McGovern, A. Drumgoole, E. McKenna, A. Morgan. Had I answered once to one of those names? But there was no other Davitt listed except for the old man. Then how could I have babbled on, as a baby, about that cottage being my home? George was staring at me quizzically.

'This must feel strange,' he said, 'trying names out for size.'

I had been doing that perpetually since my tenth birthday, taking the phone book down as a child, flicking through the pages, wondering which surname was my real one. There was a game which I had played where I dropped the book and told myself that if it opened three times in a row on the same page then the name printed at the top was mine. Only once had it worked. The name the book gave me was Mannix Motors. How many years had it taken me to stop looking at men and women on the street, as though something in their faces would tell me if they were my real father or mother?

'Where do we go from here?' I asked him.

'It's coming towards six o'clock,' he said. 'What about this family of yours?'

I knew that I should phone Geraldine and tell her I was okay. But once again there was the problem of how to explain where I was. I closed my eyes. The memory of that face returned, clearer than ever, watching me. *Fuck you*, I said in my head, *I will track you down. I'll go back home to my family without carrying you inside me. This time I'll put a stake through your heart and dispatch you to hell.* The face dissolved, out of reach again. I opened my eyes.

'I'm okay for time,' I lied to the official. 'I told her I'd be late. How about you?'

'Sold the house after the missus died,' he replied. 'I've got a one-bedroom apartment now. You know the type. Nice, secure, cold as a hotel. I'm in no hurry anywhere.'

The gates were closing below us, the parking spaces deserted. The forecourt was crowded in the Addison Lodge across the road as people began stopping for an after-work drink. After an hour traffic began to slacken on the road. The Victorian daybook, which we were examining, had a space for staff to sign themselves in and out. A rule at the front stated that after half-ten the gates were closed for the night and the staff locked away inside this private world.

Had I once walked through herbaceous borders on summer evenings to stare out the gates at the crowds of an earlier ale house where the Addison Lodge now stood?

Farmers returning to Finglas and St Margaret's pausing here beyond the city's edge. Had I stood by the water's edge near Davitt's cottage, later on in the dusk, to gaze out towards a laneway curving through fields which sloped down to the river? What was now called Botanic Avenue and back then, according to George, had been known as Slut's Alley. Had I spied on lovers from the lower orders walking out from the city? Or listened to the creak of carts heading up towards Finglas Bridge to turn left for Drogheda?

If my parents had brought me up to this room when I was three, would I have pointed out the sites of vanished cottages and mentioned the forgotten names of fields that were now filled with rows of neat houses, blathering away unconcerned in a child's voice?

George had climbed the stepladder to bring more volumes down. He blew at the dust which drifted across the room in a slowly dissipating cloud.

'Goggins, Frederick,' he said, finally tracking one of the workman down. 'Died 1843, in his sixty-second year. A bit old for you.'

'What do you mean?' I snapped, suddenly defensive. He closed the book over and leaned his head slightly to one side.

'I didn't mean anything. Just that all your dreams point to you being a young man back then. That's all.'

I felt embarrassed and exposed. I closed my eyes, the experience on the yew walk suddenly vivid again.

'I'm sorry,' I said, 'this is all . . . disturbing. I don't know how much I'm inventing and how much I really remember. It should be simple. The dead should just be dead.'

'I remember when I was a boy in Cork,' George said, 'we lived at the top of a large old house. You know the sort, stairs that creaked, pipes banging in winter. I used to lie awake, terrified that there were ghosts there. It's funny, but after you lose your loved ones you grow terrified that there are no ghosts, and you'll never see them again.'

'Is that why you're helping me?' I asked. He blew a second layer of dust from the leather-bound cover and then shrugged his shoulders.

'I don't know. I loved my wife. I suppose I want to know, or want to believe, that there's something more of her than just whatever's left in that grave by now.'

Neither of us spoke for a few moments. Then, in silence, we resumed working our way blindly through the old records in front of us again.

It was an hour later, when my eyes were aching and George had skipped on to later records, that we found another reference to the Davitt family. It was an entry for 1859, a reprimand for Charles Davitt, Jeremiah's son. He had allowed an inmate of the Richmond Asylum to be buried in his father's grave. It was regarded as unseemly and he was warned as to future behaviour.

The entry noted that:

Although it is a number of years since this inmate was dismissed from his duties as a labourer in the Gardens, the instructions that all staff were to avoid contact with him on pain of instant dismissal, and that gatekeepers should contact the constabulary if he made attempts to ever re-enter the Gardens, still applied at the time of burial.

George watched me as I read the words aloud.

'Do you feel anything?' he asked quietly.

'No.' It was an honest answer. The details meant nothing to me.

'The name Davitt is playing in my head,' he said. 'But it's not from these records. I remember seeing it over the years. But where?'

He climbed up to take down a bound index of nineteenth-century papers and specimen collections, and searched for several minutes before writing down a box number.

'You often get architectural students in,' he said, 'asking to see the original Frederick Darley plans for the glasshouses. There's an entry for *Davitt, J.* in front of him in the index.'

I watched him take out a high ladder which was resting against the top bookcase beside the door. He extended it, pushing the top of it against the trap door into the attic until the door was pushed open and the ladder rested on the rim.

'Hold it steady,' he said. 'I've been doing this for thirty years and I still hate heights.'

There was a light switch inside the attic. His legs vanished and I was alone. Suddenly I was afraid. What would George think if he came back down to find me gone? I had glanced towards the door when a voice said 'Catch!', and I looked up to see a leather-bound volume being tossed down to me.

The pages were stiff and the binding coated in a half-century of dust. George descended the ladder as I opened it. The date 1843 was stamped on the first page. I read the inscription:

These preserved herbarium specimens have been collected by Jeremiah Davitt to enliven the final years which the Lord in His mercy has allowed him to enjoy, and with a view to making himself master of that interesting aspect of Botany.

A Second Life

It is his wish that we should know each grass which we pass, so that they will afford us ample contemplation and wonder and lead us from Nature unto contemplating the Greatness of Nature's God. Jeremiah Davitt gives thanks to his ward, also of the Botanic Gardens, whose youth and energy was invested in collecting so many of these specimens.

I turned over the pages of the bulky volume carefully. The first half contained specimens of grasses with names and descriptions, while the second half held at least a hundred different specimens of mosses. There were pious remarks inserted by the old man throughout the text, all in beautiful copperplate writing. How many evenings had been spent in that cramped cottage working on this book by bad candlelight? Had he left spaces, waiting for his ward to come in after evenings walking in the local woods, clutching rare grasses and mosses?

But had this book also been his ward's path to nightly freedom, an excuse to be out after curfew beneath the stars, to keep rendezvous which the old man could never have dreamt of? An image came to me. A young man walking through a dark woodland, whistling as he held a rabbit whose brains he had just splattered with a rock.

I turned to the final page of the manuscript, where the hand of a gentleman had written in pencil, *Well done, good and faithful old servant, &c.*

George was watching me closely, obviously hoping the book might spark memories. I shook my head as I handed it back.

'It seems to prove there was someone close to the old man,' I said. 'But it's all just history to me. It means nothing. All I have is a face, and, if the dates are right, no photographs go back that far. You can show me as much stuff as you want, even find the name of Davitt's ward, but I don't think it will really prove anything.'

'Do you want to jack it in so?' he asked.

I almost said yes. I didn't know if it was tiredness, hunger or fear, but the longer I had spent in that room the more uneasy I had become about the whole search.

'No,' I said. 'If you don't mind let's push on. There may be things we haven't been through. When I leave I don't want any excuse to ever come back to this place.'

Another two hours had gone by before we found the name Davitt again. It was in another complaint, noted in 1844, from a member of the Dublin Society. George read it out, running his finger carefully along the lines of neat handwriting:

And can the Curator ascertain the truth of stories that one Mrs Martha Davitt has been running a public laundry from her father-in-law's cottage in the grounds, and drying these clothes in the Society's hothouses, the coal for which her husband is in charge of. And that furthermore Mrs Davitt's endeavours on her own behalf have been at the expense of the cleanliness of the apprentice's lodgings, not only in the basement of the Professor's house, but in a room of her father-in-law's cottage where she sleeps two young men in quite unsuitable conditions.

As I listened I remembered that when I was seven the boy next door had cousins who lived in a tenement down-town. Once I had accompanied the boy and his father there. It was a single room in a house about to be demolished. At night the three children slept in one bed while their parents squeezed on to the camp bed beside them. The mother had removed the television from the wardrobe after we came in, explaining that she was hiding it in case the knock had been from the landlord who might see it and put the rent up. The other children had settled down on the bed with crisps and bottles of lemonade to watch *The Man from U.N.C.L.E.*, but I had hovered beside the door, desperate to leave. The smell of stale air and dampness which pervaded the tenement was suffocating. I had felt claustrophobic and nauseated. Now, almost thirty years later, I felt that same nausea rise in me again.

'It stank,' I said. 'That shit-hole of a cottage stank.'

'What are you saying?' George put the ledger down.

My breath was coming fast. I closed my eyes. My chest tightened. I wanted oxygen. I opened my mouth wide to suck in air. I could see Martha Davitt's face, unwelcoming, threatening. I could sense the fear of her which had never left me.

'I remember that stinking smell,' I said. 'The curse of God on that smell of shit and spuds and damp clothes, and a stomach that was never full. That mean-mouthed old bitch and the feel of ice in winter on the scuttery window that never let in light, and having to run out in the freezing night to shit in the hollow by the river.'

I opened my eyes. George looked frightened now.

'Where are you getting this from?' he asked.

The nausea had passed. I felt afraid, then tried to calm myself. I knew that cottage. I had been frightened by a woman there as a child.

'Pass me that phone,' I snapped at George. It had a heavy brass receiver. At this time on a Friday night would she be at bingo? As I was about to hang up I heard a click and then her voice.

'Aunt Cissie.'

'Sean?' She sounded concerned. I never phoned her. 'Are the children all right?'

'It's nothing like that,' I said. 'Just a silly thing, I didn't mean to frighten you. Do you remember holidays in Wexford when I was a child?'

'That guest house outside Courtown your father liked? Mrs Byrne's. I remember her well.'

I could see it again as she spoke, throngs of midges under the trees and Ford Anglias parked on the gravel, rice puddings and custards and four beds in one large room.

'But there was another place that we went to once,' I said. 'When I was very young. Curracloe maybe, was it? A cottage we all rented.'

'No, Sean. It was always Mrs Byrne's. That was all we could ever afford.'

I looked across at George and then slowly around at the crammed shelves in the room. It felt cold. I gripped the receiver.

'I'm telling you there was another place.' My voice was almost angry. 'Some local woman was there to let us in. I was frightened of her. I remember it well.'

'Listen, Sean, love, I'm telling you now. Our two families shared that room in Mrs Byrne's every summer. There was nowhere else. Maybe you dreamt it. What's this about anyway? Is Geraldine there with you?'

I put the phone down while she was still talking. I took up my coat and rose, not even bothering to say goodbye to George. I ran down the stairs and stepped out into the forecourt. The gardens were in darkness behind me. A night bird was calling from a tree. The gates were locked. I began to pull at them, not caring how much noise I made. The watchman came out of the green doorway beside me.

'What's your hurry?' he said. 'Would you not think of ringing the bell?'

I rattled the gates again, feeling the steel digging into my palms.

'Just get me the fuck out of this place,' I screamed at him.

Chapter Thirteen

It was almost eleven o'clock when I left the Botanic Gardens, but I still could not bring myself to go home. I was frightened, nervous to be driving as I headed towards town, winding the windows down, flicking between the stations for loud music. How long was it since I had been out alone on a Friday evening? I forced myself to try and block out the last half-hour, to remember back to my single days.

Couples passed in bright clothes. The doors of pubs along Dorset Street were open, music coming from upstairs windows as people spilled out to sit on the pavements. The expectation of sex hung in the air, the memory of my youth. Back then I had loved to undress girls, to take my time and then let them undress me. It was well over a decade since I had known any other body except Geraldine's.

Gerry and I had shared the top of a house in North Great George's Street back then, but from the start I had borrowed friends' flats, knowing not to bring Geraldine there. She was somebody different from the other girls who had shared that bed with me, someone more serious, a new start.

Even though the flat was too big for him alone, Gerry had never left it after Geraldine and I moved into a house together. Since then different women had lived with him, young girls with long hair, and eyes which seemed slightly too large, as though bewildered to find themselves there. Gerry would have made a great photographer. He knew how to fade into the background of a crowd, until people had almost forgotten he was there, and let other journalists ask the obvious questions. Then, when almost everyone was gone, he would catch people on the hop with the most incisive grillings. I suspected that he used much the same technique for attracting women. When Geraldine once asked what he said to attract girls, Gerry claimed he never spoke to them at all, just licked his eyebrows.

I knew that Gerry would be in so I drove to the flat, rang the bell and looked up at the bicycle mirror mounted above the top window-sill to give him a two-fingered salute. The window opened and a set of keys just missed my head. He was waiting at the top of the stairs. I could see into my old room, littered with copies of American magazines and rows of books lined up along the floor. There was a reading lamp in the room behind him highlighting the old portable typewriter on his table.

'You never hear of computers?' I said.

He shrugged his shoulders and walked towards the shelf of bottles.

'You need some excuse to get stoned on Tippex. Shut up and drink this.'

I took the Southern Comfort from him and sipped.

'You look shite,' he said. 'Why aren't you at home?'

'You earn a small fortune, Gerry. You could buy an apartment, some nice palatial kip. What has you still living here?'

'It suits me.'

The view from the window had changed. The old parking spaces where lock-hard men with peaked caps once moonlighted were gone. They were building up those gaps in the street of old Georgian houses again, modern replicas of the houses they had demolished two decades before.

'It doesn't suit you,' I said. 'It suited what you were.

What we both were. Remember those early rezoning stories we covered, the time we were almost lynched when the builder found us at the next table in the restaurant he'd brought the county councillors to.'

Gerry grinned and refilled my glass.

'*Get your child a cowboy outfit for Christmas. Buy him Dublin County Council.* It was a great headline.'

'When was the last time you did a good investigative piece?' I asked.

'Things change. It's opinions they want now. Good, colourful opinions.'

'That's not news, it's gossip.'

'I've taken the King's shilling, is that what you're saying?' Gerry said. 'I've taken soup in church? Listen, we did our stint and we did it well. For ten years we did it. I'm not twenty-one any more. There should be little fuckers snapping at my heels, exposing this scandal and that. But they're gone. They're writing for the *Irish Echo* in New York or *Time Out* in London. You can only investigate when you've something left to find out. At this stage I know how the country works inside out. And you're old enough to, so don't pretend you don't. There comes a time when you simply don't feel outrage any more, you just feel that tired, stale old sickness. And after that you're only going through the motions, pretending to be shocked. All those stories we did, you ever notice something? Nobody ever went into their living room and took the gun from the drawer, nobody left their clothes at dawn on the beach. There are no Frank Conroys in Irish politics. Those same skulls that we exposed are still in power, blowing the same farts out of their same arses. Only now they've hired PR people to teach them how to fart properly.'

'I don't feel good about Frank Conroy,' I said. 'We let him down.'

'What did you do? Service his brakes?'

'You know what I mean,' I said. 'Maybe if we'd covered his story last year, even when he wanted us to back off. Even a few paragraphs slipped in that the other papers would have caught on to and blown up.'

'Do you really believe that?' It wasn't a question, it was an accusation. There was nowhere to hide from his stare. Slowly I shook my head. 'What's biting you about this, Sean?' he asked. 'There was a time when you just lived to take photographs. That was your real work. The newspaper used to be just bread and butter.'

'The death of a child ... it becomes personal to you. Maybe when he came face to face with it, the responsibility, sleepless nights, the pressure to provide stretching ahead of him. Did he really want to keep it? Twenty years ago they could have given it to the nuns. Nowadays that's not acceptable.'

'Everybody says he doted on the child.'

'Things are not always as they seem.'

'Don't give me that.' Gerry refilled my glass. 'You were smothered with affection. You always said you found your home suffocating as a kid, you were so well looked after. Anyway, the bottom line is that there was nothing we could have written to help him. You remember those searches after the dentist was kidnapped? Everybody who'd ever stuck their nose out on any issue was searched. Even the kid who delivered the census form to the Sinn Fein office. The Special Branch stopped him on the way out. He got home from work to find the floorboards up in his parents' house. Running the story might have been worse for Conroy. Once the finger is pointed, that's enough. There would have been a guard shining a torch up his arse every time he sat on a toilet bowl. And what would we have done? Made him some sort of media figure. The IRA hijacking him, Council of Civil Liberties hijacking him, everybody wanting a piece of him.'

'We might have told the truth.' The sharpness in my voice wasn't anger, it was fear. After all these years, how could I begin to tell the truth?

'Frank's wife was into the truth as well.' Gerry turned to root among the old papers on the floor behind him. 'She told it to the Brits.'

He found a British Sunday paper and began to read aloud:

The bombings in London this March claimed the lives of not one, but two innocent children. Twenty-four hours after IRA scum had murdered seven-year-old Tracey Reynolds – caught by the full blast of their car bomb – known Republican sympathizer, Frank Conroy, drove his new-born daughter into the River Shannon at Killaloe, Co. Ennis, Eire. Although police in neither country will officially confirm that Conroy was connected to the London blast, locals agree that it was his guilt at Tracey's death which led him to this act . . .

Gerry stopped.

'Do you want me to go on? No matter what we would have printed, by the time they got their hands on the story it was always going to be twisted around to that.'

'County Ennis,' I said. 'They invented a new county.'

'They're getting better though.' He threw the paper back behind him. 'They got the name of the river right.'

I drained the Southern Comfort again and held the glass out for a refill.

'Fill the fucking thing high,' I said. 'I need Dutch courage.'

Gerry watched me closely as he poured.

'Conroy's widow phoned the office. She didn't know the guy was a journalist. Claimed he'd been a friend of Frank's. She found a photograph of the child stolen after he had gone. Frank's sister in Liverpool got a brick through her window on Sunday night.'

'What will you do?'

'I have her version of the story written. We're using your photographs from the first session. They were still in the files.'

'Will it make any difference now?'

'The same difference it would have ever made.'

There were three rings of the bell. A lover's code. We both looked in the bicycle mirror. She had long red hair and had been riding an old black bicycle. I had not seen her before. I tossed him the keys.

'We're getting old,' I said.

He opened the window. I heard the keys fall.

'It's okay,' he replied softly. 'We're not doing it gracefully.'

We drank in silence for a few moments, listening to the noise of solitary footsteps coming up the stairs. There was a sudden burst of song from a party of girls on the street below. He reached across for my glass.

'What do you need Dutch courage for?'

'Maybe thirty-five years ago Frank would have been driving the child to an orphanage,' I said. 'I'm convinced of it. You see, you could do that then, the world wasn't built around children. There was a way out. We didn't count the same. We could be given away.'

Gerry was looking at me, not saying anything. I felt he would have stood there for eternity, patiently waiting for me to speak. I heard the clang of the bicycle being lifted around the bend of the stairs.

'A favour for old time's sake, Gerry,' I said, just before the door into the flat opened. 'Do one more investigative job. You have the connections. I never told you the truth. I was adopted. I want you to find an address for my mother.'

'Will you contact her?'

The girl entered and put the bicycle down. There were flowers in the front basket and a bottle of gin.

'I don't know,' I said. 'I can't make up my mind.'

The route I took home was circuitous, dodging possible road blocks. *Dead men* was how my father had always described empty bottles after a party. By the time I had left Gerry's the Southern Comfort bottle had joined their ranks. Yet I did not feel drunk, or at least the drink had not dulled the nervous energy which had my body on edge.

I thought again of my father. I remembered those first nights when Geraldine and I had taken him drinking, and the gaps which he had dropped in the conversation until he gradually realized that I had never told her the truth about my past. Once he had looked across at me. I held his gaze. We both understood how, in some way, telling her would have seemed a betrayal of his wife.

Yet there had always been a stage, every night we went drinking after that, when I found myself looking at him or discovered him looking at me, each of us wondering if the other had since told Geraldine the truth. Although we never discussed it between us, the longer it had gone on the more we had both felt trapped, sensing that Geraldine would be deeply hurt we had not told her. We were betraying her with our silence to avoid betraying a woman who was dead.

Maybe it was to explain this unspoken cage of guilt that my father had spoken so openly to us about his early years of marriage one night. It was a Sunday night in late May. Shelbourne had just survived relegation again. He had drunk more than usual. At first, when he began to speak, I thought that he was taking the decision from my hands and was about to tell Geraldine. Perhaps he had intended to and lost courage, or perhaps he was trying to open a way for me to tell her and justify my earlier silence, by explaining how my mother's insecurity still had a hold over both of us. Perhaps, even in some obscure way, he was trying to warn us how marriage can change people.

The world which my father spoke of was as new to me as to Geraldine, or at least the way in which he described it was. As he talked I could sense a series of images forming in my mind, like photographs which had been posed but never taken. The streetwise young photographer and the shy Mayo girl setting up home together. The deposit for the house leaving them poor, but still – in their childless state – with enough money for occasional excursions to the city pubs where his friends drank and, later on in the night, out in a convoy of cars to the bona fide pubs which he loved beyond the edge of the city, where the law then still allowed travellers to drink with impunity for several hours after closing time.

He described to us how those excursions grew less frequent, always ending in silences. The world of potato beds in back gardens and of prams creaking along the street had been exotic enough to interest him at first, as long as he could escape regularly back into what then passed for a sort of bohemia. But increasingly he found himself trapped into a stale monotony of life on that street, drinking alone in the local pubs where most men did not bring their wives, or walking out with his bride in the evenings to where the old tram lines into the city were being uprooted.

A Second Life

It didn't seem right to leave his new wife at home without a baby, but when he brought her out anything that was not banal in the conversation seemed to frighten her. She claimed that his friends from the time before he met her were peculiar. They stared at her and whispered behind her back, wondering what he was doing with her. And nothing that he could say would persuade her that they were just ordinary people, more real and honest than the safe, nondescript figures whom she leaned towards; that his friends welcomed people into their company without comment and felt nothing towards her except a simple acceptance.

He knew himself that she was different from the women who joined them there, women who put no pass on being in a public house all evening and even drank pints in pubs that would serve them. He liked that difference and the way that she was creating a home for them, away from this, in the suburbs. If she would only be willing to let him still occasionally pretend to be part of this other world. But for my mother all unknown people had been threats. She felt herself the centre of their curiosity, feared herself the butt of their jokes.

There were times when he knew that she overheard men making jokes to him about barber shops and parcels from England. He would have to answer back that no priest would rush him into anything, knowing that she knew the talk was about her not having children. 'At least they're not like your relations,' he would whisper, 'staring at your stomach every time they come to visit. They think we're being independent.' But still she pondered the most casual of remarks, going over phrases and looks in her head at night, constructing the worst possibilities from every brush with his past.

A Second Life

My father knew that she could sense how he changed in their company, grew more animated and relaxed like the man who had made her laugh in their courting days. At such times she would want him to put his arms around her in public, for them both to exist in a bubble within that crowded place, with only the muffle of other voices filtering through. She would not be able to keep up her smile, would grow frowny and worried as she watched him. She had little stamina and her limbs felt like weights that she could not rest until they were safely home together. He would catch her staring at him, her lips a straight thin line, eyes resentful and near tears. He would lose his smile as he looked around at the night just starting, with people cadging lifts to some outlying pub, and that old anticipation stirring within him.

In the taxi home he said that they rarely spoke. She would press against him, trying to communicate, while he stroked her hair and stared at the buildings sliding past, feeling more lonely than he had thought imaginable. They slept together, with a cold space between them. And when they woke, the previous night would remain like an unwelcome guest intruding on their lives in that childless house. At some stage the subject would be raised, their voices flare and then sulk into a silence which was left to slowly heal itself. And when he'd walk out for cigarettes later that evening he said that he always felt suddenly grey and middle-aged among those red-brick terraces, walking with a quiet melancholy, sensing that something had slipped away without him having noticed.

At the top of my old street he would turn for home with a last glance at the city lights spread out before him. I could imagine him walking back under the crazy paving of light cast by streetlamps that were caught among the shivering leaves of trees, and thinking of the pale line of her back in the bed, with the light out and the door ajar, her face troubled as she waited for his limbs to eventually slip against hers and try once more for the child who gave no sign of coming. And I could see him, after she had drifted to sleep, staring up, sleepless, torn in two.

The barmen had been shouting to clear the pub by the time my father finished talking. Geraldine took his hand.

'It must have been hard on you both, adjusting to each other. Then, after all your waiting, along came this fellow.'

My father had looked directly at me. He was challenging me to speak. I knew how difficult it had been for him to talk so openly about his life. Now was the time for me to tell Geraldine. I thought of how he must have felt, leaving the bright waistcoats behind in his van and walking back to that street which was always crammed with children – the girls skipping, chanting *Vote, vote, vote for De Valera*, the boys playing full games of soccer along the roadway or three-and-in against some gate. Winter evenings there were filled with shouts and summer nights of toys left littering every doorstep. What must they have endured before the decision to approach the adoption agency, and then during the long wait before the message had come for them to collect me? Everywhere my mother would have looked a swollen stomach must have mocked her, the midwife in and out of houses at all hours of the night. Inadequate, incomplete, a fifties woman who had failed in her duty in life.

Geraldine had looked over her shoulder. My father glared at me, nodding towards the door, telling me to leave with her. On our long walk home, we paused to buy chips, kissed in a damp laneway overhung with bushes, passed the last few lights of curtained bedrooms. That had been the time to explain everything. I never seemed to have as good a chance again.

It was after one o'clock when I got home from Gerry's. I had not expected Geraldine to be up, but she was sitting on the sofa with her legs tucked under her, watching some late-night film. She did not look up. Even a few months ago I might have made some joke about her finding consolation in the opened box of chocolates beside her, and after a few moments of stony silence she would have grinned and thrown a sweet at me.

But now I realized how distant we had grown, and how much I had hurt her over the previous months. Since the crash I had been so preoccupied that I had let our marriage slip apart without even noticing it happen. I had taken its strength for granted. I sat behind her on the edge of the sofa, unable even to put a hand out and stroke her hair.

'Benedict's been crying out for you in his sleep,' she said eventually, without turning her head. 'Ever since dinner-time he's been demanding that I produce you like a rabbit out of a hat. He has me all day. I'm boring, you see. He wants the excitement of his daddy condescending to visit us.'

There must have been nights at the turn of the year when Geraldine sat like that, staring blankly at the screen, tormented by the voice in her head which kept trying to fit the word 'widow' on to her. Attempting to be strong and think only of my survival and yet, for the sake of our children, having to confront the small wording of insurance policies and endowment mortgages. What pact would she not have made with the Devil to be able to know that six months later we would both be sitting here, alive in this room? But now, when that dream had come true, we sat, sullen and apart, like strangers.

'I was with another woman,' I said. It was an old joke but when she gave the standard reply there was bitterness instead of irony in her voice.

'No, you weren't. Your camera's still here.'

In the rays from the television the side of her face looked old suddenly. She reached forward to flick the set off and sat back so that her features were hidden by her hair.

'I keep asking myself. Was I blinded by love before or have you changed so totally in these last few months? Listen, Sean, there's nobody stopping you from leaving this house if you want to. But you've not lived here with us for months. There's just been a ghost of you walking around. Down in Athlone there was an old woman I used to visit as a girl. She was half daft, always talking about the fairies having stolen her child one night and leaving a stranger in its place. I'd grown up before I realized what she was talking about. A cot death. But you're like a stolen man, like somebody has stolen the husband I married and left a cold stranger in his body instead. Tell me I'm wrong, that you haven't changed, that you were always this big a bollox.'

'Bastard,' I said quietly.

'Don't be funny, Sean. I'm sitting here cold and stiff, and I'm not in the mood.'

'I'm not being funny,' I said. 'A bastard from birth, but I can't tell you whose. There's a law, you see. The adoption agency have the records safely stashed away from the likes of us.'

There was silence for a few moments, then she turned so that her face came into view. We stared at each other.

'How long have you known?'

'Since my tenth birthday.'

She lowered her eyes. There was shock there, but there was hurt as well.

'I'm sorry,' I said. 'I didn't think it was important.'

'Not important? Not for me . . .'

'No,' I said. 'I didn't think that it was important for me. I didn't want it to be important. I never told anybody, never even discussed it with my father. I mean, you wake up one day and find someone's after planking you down into the middle of a strange family without you knowing, and you're told, "Just get on with pretending to be part of them."'

'But your father loved you.'

'I know. And I loved him as much as anyone could love a father. And you loved him as well, as my father, and I never wanted you to think any less of him.'

'I wouldn't have.' The hurt was still there, but it had softened. 'It explains something though. The time Benedict was born . . . those forms I brought home about the history of illnesses in our families. I couldn't get a word out of you except no, no, no to every question. You kept getting so uptight when I pressed you.' She paused, as though the news was registering again. Her voice snapped suddenly. 'Jesus, I can't believe you never trusted me!'

She hugged herself as though she had just been slapped. I put my hand out and she shrugged it away.

'I'm sorry,' was all I could say. 'I'm sorry.'

'Does it hurt?' She looked up. Her teeth bit very softly into her lower lip.

'Like an aching wound I didn't even know I had until I started picking at it. I feel so unclean. I pick up Sinead, and I keep seeing myself, staring up at different faces, being passed around, called by names I don't even know. Do the fuckers baptize you twice, that's what I want to know? They've everything else worked out, your birth cert held and then doctored to leave no trace of scandal. I was six weeks old when my parents . . . what I've always called my parents . . . got me. I forgot to ask my Da, was the job done again. I mean the fuckers wouldn't wait that long to get their copyright on your soul.'

I was shaking now, anger welling up from inside me. It was Geraldine's turn to put her hand up to my lips and mine to flinch. Her hand followed my cheek and held it, calming me.

'These last few months . . .?' she asked.

'Searching for her . . . my mother . . . or trying to decide if I want to search for her . . . afraid of what I might find . . . that I might be rejected . . . thirty-six years . . . I mean maybe she has forgotten . . .'

'No.' Geraldine's face was close to me. 'No mother forgets. Not deep down, not inside. These last months, all the hours you've been missing, that you never talk about . . . is that all you have been doing? Tell me, you never talk to me any more.'

'That's the thing, you see, with being adopted,' I said. 'You could be anyone. You never know . . . never certain of anything. It's crazy, I mean . . . I have these memories, bits of dreams, things . . . like I lived before. Been trying to track down someone, lay a ghost, lay my own ghost. It's crazy. Ever since I died . . .'

'Don't say that word!' Her voice was scared.

'It's what happened to me. Face it. I've been so fucked up by it. You see, I'd no one to talk to. I couldn't . . . not you . . . because, you see, you'd feel that I didn't love you and the kids, didn't want to be here. I did . . . I do . . . but at first . . . it felt so good being dead, Geraldine, so . . . such a wrench to be dragged back to life. I felt so guilty for not being overjoyed. I came back changed, I came back shaken, imagining all sorts of stupid pasts and faces . . . but that's all over now . . . I'm just so glad to be home . . . to be home here . . .'

How long was it since I had cried? The taste of salt in my mouth made me worse, incoherent. Geraldine knelt on the floor beside me. She put her head down into my lap and I lowered my face, until it was smothered by her hair. I stopped speaking, but continued to cry, silently, almost impersonally, while her arms hugged my body. We stayed that way for a long time. Finally I raised my head. The tears had stopped. I stroked her damp hair and tried to smile.

'This is the closest I've come to getting a blow job in months,' I said.

Her voice was muffled by my trousers.

'The really funny thing is my father,' she said. 'The first time that I brought you down to Athlone to visit. You went out to the toilet in the hotel and he shook his head. "A lovely young man," he said. "One of the wonders of the world. After all these years when I thought that everybody who followed Shelbourne was a bastard."'

Her hair began to shake. I lifted her head up. Her eyes were wet but she was unable to contain her laughter. I pushed her gently back on to the floor and fell beside her, both of us laughing hysterically, with fresh tears down our faces. My stomach hurt. We would stop and then one of us would repeat her father's words. We were still laughing when I entered her, then we were suddenly serious, her half-pulled-off jeans still wrapped around one ankle, her legs raised in the air. She rolled on her side and then knelt on the sofa, with neither of us speaking, our bodies bonding together, shutting the world out. We remained that way for a long time after I had come, my cheek against her bare flesh where her blouse had been pulled up. We would have to check the floor carefully for shirt buttons in case Sinead put them in her mouth. Finally we rose. Geraldine had gone upstairs when the phone rang. It was half-past two.

'The very man,' a male voice said.

'Listen, you've got a wrong number.' The ringing had shattered my nerves. I was furious. 'Do you know what time it is?'

'Listen, I've found something else. Or at least I think I might have.'

I recognized the official's voice now. It was only three and a half hours since I had left the Botanic Gardens, but that room seemed so far away.

'You're not still at that?'

'There's no real doubt in my mind.' The man's voice was triumphant, giddy almost. 'Everything fits.'

'Listen, just leave me alone.' I tried to control the anger in my voice. I was terrified that Geraldine would come back downstairs. I knew that it was I who had sought his help, but now I resented him as though he was deliberately trying to destroy whatever peace I had finally managed to achieve. 'I've changed my mind. I've my own life to lead . . . my family. That other stuff was just my imagination. I don't want to know.'

But the man's voice seemed mesmerized, as if during all the hours peering at those heavy yellowing pages he had slipped into an altered state. I could not even be sure if he heard what I was saying.

'It's all in the records. I went backwards. This Jeremiah Davitt, well he found a young boy. During a cholera outbreak. The boy's parents had either died or abandoned him, but there's a pile of letters before Davitt got permission to raise the boy in his cottage. They gave you the name of the man whose land you were found on.'

His voice went quiet. I could see him, looking out at a

taxi passing along the otherwise empty street, blinking as though waking from a dream, with the absurdity of what he had just said dawning on him. He sounded suddenly tired.

'I'm sorry,' he said in a low voice. 'It just seemed to fit some of the things you'd said. I didn't mean any harm.'

'I know, George. Listen, it's late. Coincidences happen. There must have been thousands of boys starving. It has nothing to do with me.'

'I suppose you're right,' he said after a moment. 'You get caught up in these things. You start looking for signs, wanting to believe things. Fair play to Davitt though. He stood his ground when his family wanted nothing to do with the boy. He'd found him sitting on a ridge in some old potato patch riddled with blight. The letters say the child had been eating worms.'

There was a click as he put the phone down. I closed my eyes. Red, slippery worms. I could still feel the dull empty hunger. No, it had happened in my back garden. I remembered sitting there at home. It had to have been at home. I was conscious of the coldness of the room. I turned out the light and stood in the dark. I was frightened to turn. I felt he was waiting there, with that same knowing sneer. Only now I recognized it. How often had I photographed that look: on men standing in dole queues, cheap labourers waiting to be picked at dawn in the pub car-parks of Kilburn, kids with cropped hair and ragged pullovers jumping through street fires of unsold rubbish after the Ivy markets? That sneer was a badge of defiance, a defence for people with nothing else to fall back on.

I felt I had only to stretch my hand back to touch my own past. What did he want from me? *Search on.* The whisper was inside my own skull. The sneer was gone.

There was a pleading instead. *Stop dithering.* That was what I had been doing, burying myself away, playing at ghost-hunting to avoid risking the pain of my real search. George might not have left yet. I had only to pick the phone up to be told the name of this ghost. I could track down the records of the Richmond Asylum, find his grave. But I knew that, if he existed, this was not what he wanted. *Let the dead take care of the dead. Find her while you can.*

Slowly I put my hand back to touch the empty night air. A famished boy eating worms, a child abandoned. *What use are your tears? Search on.* I felt strong. My search wasn't over, it was just beginning.

'Thank you,' I said to the darkness as I turned. 'Whoever you are.'

Chapter Fourteen

His plane would have landed fifty minutes ago. She had phoned Stansted airport to confirm its arrival, from the only phone still to accept coins on the concourse outside W. H. Smith's. Now the electronic noticeboard in Liverpool Street station confirmed that the Stansted Express was due in eight minutes. She ordered another coffee, although she had drunk two cups already. It had been crazy coming here so early, crazy phoning Dublin airport to confirm that the plane had taken off safely, even the note she had sent him was crazy.

She began to drink the fresh coffee as soon as it arrived, feeling that the staff in the coffee shop were watching her, that they knew there was something furtive in her trying to pass herself off as an ordinary customer. Good God Almighty, what would she say to him? She had seen Stansted airport on the television once, space-age commuter shuttles zipping between the terminal and departure gates – no drivers, just a voice instructing passengers to hold tight and disembark. How different it had been on those nights in the fifties on the Dublin quays, leaning on the rails of the boat to see the shapes of cattle and sheep being loaded in the ship's belly. People didn't talk on planes, she knew that. Not like on those cattle boats, lurching out past the lights of Dublin harbour, facing into the dark and the future with only the handful of boys left on deck bothering to look back.

Her cup was empty again. It was a cigarette that she

needed, but it had been five years since she managed to give them up. She would not start again, even for this. She felt uncomfortable with an empty cup so she ordered again. The taste of coffee was making her sick. She sensed the girl who served her staring at the shake in her fingers. The schools were starting the autumn term this week; a party of girls in uniform emerged from the entrance of one of the platforms.

Two minutes to go. She could leave a note for him, she could cross the concourse and find the platform for her train home. *I would send a photograph, but I have a thing about having them taken,* he had written. She should have said more in her reply, not just *Meet me Friday, the third of September, one o'clock, Liverpool Street station, the coffee shop beside W. H. Smith's. E. Sweeney.* But what could she have said? A letter did not seem the right place. Would she even recognize him? Would she see a man stopping to speak to every old woman in the station, then finally eyeing her with disappointment? And what if he never showed up? Would she sit here, waiting for the next train and then the next, drinking coffee, becoming the butt of jokes among the staff? The lonely old woman pretending to have someone to meet.

She had written his name on a piece of cardboard in her bag. At one stage she had planned to stand at the entrance to the platform and hold it up, but then lost her nerve. It would be too sudden, searching every man's face, never knowing if one was going to suddenly touch her shoulder, or if he would see the sign confronting him and decide to walk past. She would not frighten him off, she would stay here and give him time to approach. He would need that as surely as he would need time to try and forgive her for this.

The noticeboard announced that the train was in. She

turned back to the counter so as not to have to watch the passengers coming out. After a few moments there was the bustle of people entering the open-plan café. A man's voice beside her ordered coffee. Her heartbeat seemed so loud she was suddenly fearful of collapsing. Then the voice called back to a woman, asking her if she wanted a Danish pastry. It was not him. She would have to turn. He would be expecting her to look out for him. He could not be expected to tap women on the shoulder. Why had she picked such a public place? But it was safe here, neutral. Not a place for public displays of anger or grief.

She turned and knew him at once. He had his father's eyes. She had never forgotten his father's eyes. But he had not seen her. He stood by the square of telephone booths, looking around. He was built like all her family, those were Sweeney shoulders. His expression was almost cold, disinterested, like a traveller mildly impatient between connections. But she knew that he wasn't. He was as frightened as she was, only the fear which caused her hand to shake was distilled so deep inside him that he seemed turned to stone. It would have to be her who made the first move. She got down, a little unsteady, from the stool. It was ridiculous, but she felt that the staff were watching, that she looked like an old woman trying to pick up a stranger. The station seemed to have gone silent. There was the muffle of a loudspeaker, but she could not decipher the words. He turned as she approached. His expression did not change but he leaned back against the phone booth as if needing support. She knew that he had not slept. He regarded her with the naked curiosity of a child. It brought back memories of dance halls. She swallowed and nodded yes to his silent question.

'What name was I given?' he said.

'Paudi . . . well, Padraig, but . . . Paudi.'

'Paudi.' He made the name sound different from any other time she had heard it spoken. He pronounced it slowly, like an unfamiliar word in a foreign language. 'It's Sean now. That's the name my . . . my parents . . . gave me. I've been thinking all the way here, I don't know what to call you. Elizabeth, Lizzy, Mother?'

'Paudi . . . Sean . . . your mother's dead. She died ten weeks ago. I didn't know how to tell you in the letter. Sweet child, I'm sorry. I'm your Aunt Ellen.'

Lizzy had been right, that was what was most painful. Every morning he had been a day nearer. And Ellen had never believed her. It was just that she never wanted Lizzy to over-build her hopes, so she had spent years being neutral, trying to deflate them quietly. The disappearances had taught her how dangerous Lizzy's hopes were. Time made no difference. If Lizzy had lived another thirty years the yearning would not have lessened. Indeed the sense of grief had grown in recent years. That night, after her husband's funeral, when the in-laws had called a doctor for her, Ellen had known those tears were for her son.

Once, in Dublin, Ellen had even looked up a private detective in the phone book. She had expected a man in some shabby office in a back street. Instead a woman in her thirties had welcomed her into a bright suite of offices in Fitzwilliam Square. There were people working on computers, some sort of machine printing out. It reminded her of the backdrop for the television *News at Ten*. The detective had shaken her head like some sort of professional counsellor. The grown child might have some chance of finding the mother, she told Ellen, but there was no way a mother, or a relative or friend of a mother, could discover any facts.

Ellen had stared at the private detective, wondering how often she had heard mothers hide behind those descriptions, 'a relative', 'a friend'.

'Have I half-brothers, sisters?' the man beside her asked. How long had they been walking like this? She was afraid to suggest they stop, and thought that perhaps he was too. If they stopped they would have to make a conscious decision to sit down together. She suspected that each was afraid that the other would refuse.

'Three half-sisters. Grown up. All married now,' Ellen said.

'Are they nice?'

'They are, they've done well, they're . . . ' She paused. 'I'll not say a word against them, but . . . you know the joke . . . the Frenchman up in court for necrophilia? Holds his hands out and says, "But your honour, I thought they were English."'

She stopped. They were on a corner near Shoreditch.

'God, that sounds awful,' she went on, 'but you know what I mean. They were . . . well, your mother, the older the girls got the less of herself she could see in them. They were strangers to her . . . '

'Did she tell them of me?'

'They wouldn't have understood. Listen . . . one time I was in their house after being back home in Ireland. They saw my passport. They were amazed it was green. They hadn't imagined the Irish would have passports of their own. Another time I was telling them about TB when I was a girl. They looked at me like I was daft. One of them said, "But surely you could get treatment on the National Health." Lizzy never encouraged them, maybe she was terrified what they'd find out, but none of them ever visited Ireland. They would not have understood.'

'I was just written out.'

'So was your mother . . . and maybe she got the rawer deal.'

It was the sudden bitterness of his words which made her voice sharper than she had intended. They were stopped outside a pub with closed curtains. She saw him glance at the notice on the blackboard. *Exotic dancers. All day. Every day.* He pushed against one door, but it was locked, then found one which opened and went in. She had no option but to follow. There were about eight men at tables or stools beside the counter. Each was alone, all immediately conscious of her presence. There was a carpeted platform with a spotlight. Two strippers in red and black lingerie chatted at the far end of the bar. A black bouncer stared at her, unwelcoming.

He had ordered a drink for himself. The barman looked at her. She asked for a brandy. He slammed her glass down, then glanced at Paudi, silently asking should he take for both drinks from the ten-pound note on the counter. She did not see Paudi nod, but the barman rang up the two drinks and put the change down. One of the strippers was approaching them with an empty glass in her hand. Her hair was dyed blonde, but close up her face made her older. She looked at Paudi, then down at her glass with little-girl eyes. She was saying something, but Paudi ignored her. She spoke to him again. He just stared at the bottles behind the counter. Ellen knew that the girl was going to approach her.

'Do you and your friend know what sort of pub this is?' she asked sweetly. The empty glass was still thrust forward. Ellen shook her head.

'I'm going to take my clothes off. Do you think you can stand the shock?'

Ellen opened her purse and shoved a five-pound note into the glass. The girl's smile remained fixed.

'Enjoy it. Nobody's ever given me a bad review. Not even dykes.'

The girl turned and walked back. Nobody had turned their heads but Ellen knew the whole pub had heard. The bouncer had taken down a microphone.

'For the delight of you gentlemen . . . even you gentlemen who don't look like gentlemen . . . the beautiful Joan will perform the art of strip-tease.'

Loud music began to play as the girl climbed up on the platform. Paudi still did not turn his head or acknowledge where he was, but Ellen found that she could not help watching. It was half-past two outside. Shoppers would be passing a few feet away, women collecting children from playschools. The girl was kneeling now, pretending to masturbate. Ellen grabbed at Paudi's arm, suddenly furious.

'Why are you doing this to me?' she hissed. 'Humiliating me. Humiliating.'

He remained still for a moment as though he had not heard, then his voice was so loud that the men began to look back at them.

'You had no right to lead me on. No right. You could have written. You could have said she was dead!'

The bouncer got down from his stool as if about to evict them. She tried to hush Paudi, but he pushed her arm away.

'Do you know how hard it was to come over here? Do you?'

'And how hard it was for me,' she answered, anger at him causing her to raise her voice too, even though the bouncer was now walking straight towards them. 'I could have just dropped a note, it would have been so easy. Said too late, pal, tough tit, written you back out of it like everybody else in my family did. Now stop humiliating me.'

'I'm humiliating both of us.' His voice had dropped. He turned to look at her. 'I feel unclean. Do you understand me? I feel like a piece of dirt.'

The booming music stopped and there was ragged applause. Ellen looked back and the platform was empty. The bouncer brushed past her shoulder and opened the doors. Dusty light came in.

'I had the contacts . . . the newspaper business. I could have found her, or at least tried to, any time in the last ten years. Did she want me to? Tell me.'

Ellen could still clearly remember the first time Lizzy had disappeared. Early December, 1963. The talk on the boat which Ellen took to Ireland was still of shock at the deaths of Kennedy and Pope John the Good.

'A breath of spring, he was,' the man who stopped at the rails beside Ellen said. 'They said to his Holiness, "Here's a closed envelope that no Pope has opened since the Middle Ages." "We'll put a halt to that caper," says Pope John, and off he goes into a private antechamber. Well, he comes out with a big long face on him. "I shouldn't have opened that," he says, and all the cardinals are looking at him, white as sheets. "It was the bill for the Last Supper."'

She watched the man move down the boat, looking for someone else to tell the story to, and wondered where to begin the search for her sister. It was only six months previously that she had found Lizzy herself, and that was only after a final tip off from a Ballyfin girl whose brother had seen a woman who looked like her wheeling a pram in Coventry. She had asked for holidays from the factory in Guildford and told the foreman to stuff his job when he refused her.

Ellen had spent a week in digs in Coventry, walking the

streets from early morning and riding on buses at random, before she caught a glimpse of Lizzy. She followed her for several minutes and still was not certain that it was her younger sister. The figure looked so much older, pushing the large black pram with a baby inside it and a three-year-old girl balanced on the edge of it, and holding the hand of a slightly older girl with ponytails who held up a whirling paper windmill. Only when the figure stopped at the kerb to look around at the traffic was Ellen certain that it was her sister.

'Lizzy, Lizzy!'

The figure seemed not to have heard and then, just as Ellen was about to reach her, she pushed the pram off the kerb and began to run while cars braked and horns beeped. A driver leaned out of his window to scream 'Stupid bitch!' after her, then drove on. Lizzy was a hundred yards ahead before Ellen could get across the road. She vanished down a maze of narrow red-bricked streets with the little girl screaming in terror as she was dragged on. The windmill lay on the roadway, flattened by tyres. Ellen ran, dodging and twisting down side streets, asking people if they had seen a woman running with a pram, occasionally catching a glimpse of her sister in the distance.

The houses ended abruptly. There was a large green space, a bombed wilderness still to be rebuilt. A dirt track had been laid by feet across it and half-way up the hill a cloud of dust betrayed the moving pram. Ellen began to run. There was a new estate at the crest of the hill. No names on the streets, just arrows pointing towards site numbers. Rubble lay on the edges of the pavements, the sound of hammering from the unfinished roofs of some houses. Ellen had run past the laneway when she stopped. She stepped back and stared. It was Lizzy all right, her eyes like those times she used to wake at home after nightmares. She was crouched behind the pram, her face pressed against those of the two little girls. All three stared at Ellen when she approached, as if expecting to be beaten. It was hard to know who was shielding who.

This much was certain, Ellen had thought on the boat back to Ireland that December, wherever Lizzy was running to it was not back to the fists of her father in Laois. The previous morning she had been called to the phone in the office to hear Lizzy's husband telling her she had vanished. There was a stammer in his voice which she had not noticed before. She could imagine him asking to use the phone in work, the secretary making him feel small as he shuffled in his overalls, the way so many of the English seemed to do when faced with authority. Subjects, not citizens. That was the root of it, she often thought. She remembered back to playing as a child among the blackened stones of the old hall near Coolrain, where Black and Tan Officers had been entertained, and feeling so proud that her father was among the IRA men who had torched that great building to the ground during the War of Independence. There was no way Lizzy would have even looked at someone like her husband before the nuns took her away to that convent. What had happened in there had crushed her spirit, and Ellen knew that it was this vulnerability which had attracted him. Up till now Lizzy had been easily managed, asking for nothing. Now as she listened to her brother-in-law's voice on the phone Ellen guessed that Lizzy had gone to Ireland and knew that he must never know why.

'Lough Derg,' she had told him. 'A pilgrimage. That's where she'll have gone. It's a Catholic thing, every five years. Fasting and walking with bare feet on stones. She wouldn't have known how to tell you.'

Ellen had imagined him nodding ignorantly, as the secretary watched. Catholics were as exotic to him as the pygmies in Hollywood movies. 'It will only be for a few days. Don't worry. She'll be back.'

She took a taxi with Paudi towards Hyde Park. He called on the driver to stop outside a large hotel. The Arab owners had restored it to look like a parody of colonial times. An Indian doorman bowed and opened the glass doors for them, a waiter who looked like an actor took their order for afternoon coffee. Ellen remembered how in her first year in London she had stood outside this line of hotels, never convinced they would serve her coffee, even when she had a full wage packet in her hand. 'You'll never be a lady,' her mother had always said, 'until you learn to drink coffee.'

Paudi seemed more at ease now. He had his grandfather's good looks, although it was difficult to match those features with his modern haircut.

'There was no day when she . . . your mother . . . did not think of you,' Ellen said. 'It's important that you know that. But what were her choices? Even if she had been English back then, or American. It was a different world. Maybe she could have kept you, but did you ever think what sort of life the pair of you would have had, and where would you have been able to have it? Not in Ireland, where every door would have been closed in her face. And probably not even over here. I mean, the English themselves were shipping unwanted kids off to Australia ten years after you were born. She was so young . . . how could a girl like her stand up to . . . '

Ellen stopped. There had been rules she had laid down in her mind on the train to London about what to tell and what to keep back. What Lizzy would have wanted him to know. She had never asked her sister.

'You say she sometimes ran away?' he said. 'How did you know where to find her?' Ellen watched the waiter return with a tray and take the credit card which Paudi had left on the table.

'Intuition,' Ellen said. 'Luck. I tried the churches first, maybe she'd be sitting in the back of one, but' – she paused and watched him look closely at her – 'that wasn't . . . really likely. Do you know how many primary schools there are in Dublin? Walking around from one to the next in the depths of winter. I remember that first time, I had a blister on my foot. I wasn't even sure if she was in Dublin. I'd only just found her in Coventry. Wondering if I had sparked off memories, if I was to blame for her going. I tell you, when you're forced to tramp a city you grow to hate it. That first time I found her by chance in Clontarf. Near the seafront. There was a whole group of young mothers waiting for their children to come out and she was standing a way off from them. You could see them looking at her, hostile, knowing she didn't belong. She never looked at them or back at me, just stared in through the gates, scanning every child that came out. If she had taken a step forward I think one of the mothers would have hit her. You know how it is with a school, all screams and noise for five minutes, then silence. I went up to her and took her arm. She didn't try to run away. Never spoke to me all the way back across on the boat. Like there was nobody left inside her body.'

'A stolen child,' he said. The waiter returned, bearing the card on a plate. Her nephew – the phrase sounded strange – picked it up and left a tip in cash in its place. Ellen fought against the sudden threat of tears. What Lizzy would have given for this moment. Those last weeks in the hospital, the skin stretched over her bones, one could see the pain she suffered. The only thing keeping her alive was willpower, the doctor had said. Lizzy didn't say it, but her eyes . . . She was staying alive to give him time to find her.

Her daughters had come, but she did not acknowledge them. They were good girls. She had not been easy, as a mother when they were growing up or in those last years when she let herself go, wandering about the streets. They did not deserve this ostracism. Ellen had tried to put her daughters' hands in hers, but Lizzy closed her fingers. Every last bit of strength being used up. Where had this young man been? Why had he left it so late? She cursed him silently for a moment. If only . . .

Ellen still went to Mass in Reading in order to see the other Irish women her age who had settled there. But it had long ago ceased to be anything for her other than a fairy-tale. Now when Ellen remembered those family rosaries in the kitchen, all she recalled was the numbness of her knees and the boredom. She was certain there was no world beyond here where her sister might one day meet her son. Lizzy's chance had died when the machine in the hospital made that rapid bleeping noise. She blinked and looked away, then back at him.

'What do you mean, stolen child?'

'Something my wife said. These last few months I've been distracted, like I'm being torn in two. She said it about an old woman talking of a cot death . . . a stolen child, someone different left in its place. Since I started this obsession about finding my real mother, that's what she called me . . . a stolen man . . . walking round like you said your sister did . . . ever since I survived an accident last year.'

Ellen put her cup down.

'Was it between Christmas and New Year?' she asked.

Paudi sat back. His face was white. He didn't need to answer her.

'Lizzy was woken up one of those mornings,' Ellen said. 'She claimed it was by the noise of a crash.'

It had taken Ellen so many years to prise the whole story from Lizzy that now it felt flat and unreal to be retelling parts of it again to Paudi on that sofa in the hotel foyer, while Japanese businessmen walked past, talking into mobile phones. Ever since his letter had come she had been rehearsing it, chopping and changing the bits that were best to leave out. She had known who the letter was from as soon as she saw it in the hall: *Private. Please do not open. Att: Mrs Elizabeth Wilkins. C/o Mrs Ellen Wyse.* A few weeks previously Lizzy's daughters had sent her some mementoes: a broken watch which she remembered her father giving Lizzy, cuttings from local Irish papers in the fifties, a cheap medal from the Feis Ceol. Everything else would have gone to the Barnardo's shop. She could imagine them perplexed by the last few possessions as though they exercised a sort of power, and then thinking of the way out – a parcel to Aunt Nellie.

It had been the same with Lizzy's ashes. Everybody had always presumed that she would share a family grave with her husband before it was discovered that he wished to be cremated. Now, when she was dying, none of the daughters had known what was the correct thing to do. Lizzy had agreed for them to be raised in the Church of England, but she was still a Catholic, even though they had never known her to publicly practise her religion. They could remember her praying when they were sick as children, long solitary decades of the rosary, but she had never set foot inside a church and refused to allow a priest near her in the hospital.

Increasingly in those weeks the girls had leaned on Ellen for guidance. There had always been nurses moving around the ward or visitors talking loudly around the other beds. Yet for Ellen it was the presence of the girls which made the subject impossible to mention. They had seemed determined to maintain the pretence of reassurance in front of their mother, which Ellen suspected was more for their own sakes than Lizzy's. Only when they were gone could the two of them talk openly.

'Burn me.' Lizzy's rasping whisper was almost indifferent.

'For the sake of the girls, a proper funeral ... a priest and mass ... Father Tom would come over ... you could make it up ... for your own sake as well. Deep down you know it's what you want.'

'I want Paudi.' Lizzy's eyes had closed. The words were barely audible. Ellen knew there was a touch of spite in what she was doing, running away one last time, showing that Coventry had never been her home. Ellen had never heard her use Tom's name in all the years in England. 'Burn me. Scatter the ashes anywhere.'

There had been almost nobody at the crematorium. It was done as Lizzy instructed. No speeches, no music. She had asked for no flowers, but at the last minute her daughter Sharon had driven to the old house and made up a small bouquet from Lizzy's flowers which had grown wild in the garden. They lay in a small blaze of colour on the polished wood as the coffin slowly vanished. Afterwards nobody spoke. It was as if they had been robbed of their grief. The urn was given to Ellen, as though the girls could think of nothing else to do with it. There was a meal in Sharon's house. Ellen had kissed her nieces, knowing that the cremation had left such wounds that she was unlikely to ever see them all again.

Two months later, just when those wounds were less raw, Paudi's letter had seemed the ultimate black joke. Ellen had placed the envelope on the kitchen table and spent the morning staring at it with terror. There was a box of matches on the kitchen window-sill. Twice she almost managed to find the strength to burn it. Her husband came in. *Won the pools, have you?* She put her hand out to cover the address, then went to the bathroom and locked the door.

I am taking the liberty of writing c/o your sister, as it has proved impossible to find an address for yourself. Because your sister returns home regularly, it was possible to discreetly obtain one for her. It is possible that by now you will have put me firmly away at the back of your memory, and – should you wish me to remain there – I do not wish in any way to intrude upon your life.

It's funny trying to write this letter because I suppose I've been writing one to you in my head all my life. But if you should wish to know something more of me, and of the two grandchildren you will not have known you have, then I would certainly be glad to either exchange letters or travel somewhere to meet you. I am now almost twice the age that you were when you gave birth to me. I have been a parent too. I cannot claim to know anything of the things you went through, because there is nothing I know of you except the slightest scraps. I know that you have not been home since you left Dunross, except just once for your mother's funeral. And I know, from the date on the headstone, that you were carrying me when you stood at her grave. I have since been in that graveyard and found the grave.

If you decide that we should meet then I don't suppose either of us will know what to say. I might have your hair or your eyes, but we will be strangers really. I had a good home. You should

know that. I was well loved. We were not rich, but I lacked for
nothing. But I believe that once you may not have wished to part
with me. There was a scrap of paper found like a message in a
bottle. This letter, in turn, is my message in a bottle thirty-six
years later. If it causes you too much pain or the years have
erased all feelings then simply cast it away. I would send a
photograph, but I have a thing about having them taken. Whether
you reply or not you will always be in my heart.

Yours sincerely,

Sean Blake

The doors of the hotel opened and a coach party of
Italians crowded into the foyer. Ellen looked across at him.
The coffee had gone cold. Both of them had been silent,
preoccupied by their own thoughts.

'We were never that close,' she said to him. 'There was
three years between us. Three years is a lot for children.
Our brother . . . Tom . . . there was only a year's difference.
You couldn't keep them apart. He even slept in with us girls
till he was four. Him and Lizzy, they insisted on sharing the
one plate at meals when they were young. Refused to eat
their dinner off separate ones. The pair of them giggling
away the whole time. Running wild in the fields. I had to
mind them. She was the baby, you see, and I was an elder
daughter. It was hammered home to me, my responsibilities,
even at the age of five. She could be the dancing pet, and
she was too, for half the parish and for me as well. In
school I'd own up to things that she and Tom had done,
wouldn't mind being slapped to save her.'

Ellen stopped. His eyes had a peculiar look, she thought,
like he was trying to retain and visualize every sentence.

'I never had to worry about myself, I knew that I'd get by
. . . with boys, with life. I was firmly planted, you know.

She was . . . well, it was hard to place where she'd finish up. With Tom it was easy. Though, well, it wasn't really. Back then . . . maybe it's the same now . . . it wasn't just a vocation you needed to be a priest. It was hard cash. You ever look at priests down the country? Big strong men, sons of big strong farmers with good land. As unlike Tom as you could get. When I came over here first I remember the signs, *No Blacks, No Irish.* Well, it was like that in the church, *No sons of labourers, No sons of the poor.*'

A lift door opened and the Italians all seemed to start talking together. A woman sat down at the next table and began to stare at them.

'An aunt of my father's helped,' Ellen said. 'His family never liked my mother, they felt he married beneath him. God, how that woman dreamt of shutting them up. The mother of a priest. She saw it as the makings of all of us. Being married into respectable families, getting . . . I mean, she wanted what was best for him, she didn't push it, but she had it in her head from the time he was a boy. Funny thing was, none of us knew him . . . I still don't . . . only Lizzy. The whole time he was either off with her or off by himself.

'Lizzy . . . she missed him badly when he left. She went a bit wild, but there was no harm in her. The pair of us cycling away to dances. She got a bit of a name for herself, but I think it was spite. Men that she'd led on and who got nowhere inventing lies for their friends. I can't tell you what happened. She was seeing someone, that's all I know. A couple of evenings I covered up for her, said we were out walking together, would arrange to meet her out beyond the lane. I remember she came running down from off the hills up above the high field to meet me once, her hair wild, scratches on her legs, and I couldn't get a word out of her.

Somebody promised her something . . . made her believe she
was good enough . . . with a priest almost in the family . . .'

Ellen stopped. Could she honestly expect him to understand that world? The farm next to theirs had been bigger,
but still so poor that it was often hard to put food on the
table. One evening Ellen had been invited to stay for tea.
The farmer had told Joseph, 'the boy', to get the table
ready. 'The boy' was in his eighties. He had taken out a
large white cloth which Ellen thought he was about to
spread over the table. Instead he had hung it from a wire
stretching across the room so the table was divided in two.
'The boy' had sat alone, out of view behind the cloth,
eating the same food as the family and their guest at the
other end of the table.

'When Lizzy got into trouble she never told me anything,'
Ellen continued. 'Sometimes I think if she had . . . well,
maybe I could have done something . . . or maybe I couldn't.
Tom was the only one really who might have helped. He
was home, that one week he was allowed out in the year at
harvest time.'

'What could he have done?' Her nephew leaned forward,
suddenly aggressive.

'Maybe nothing,' Ellen backtracked. 'Like what could
anyone . . . it was black and white in those days.' She
stopped. 'No. He could have got the name of the father
from her, he could have made my father go across and
confront the man's family. They listened to Tom. From the
day he left to go to that seminary it was like he was a priest
already. My mother . . . it was the good cups when he came
home, like he was a visitor. She was dying, she knew she
would never live to see him ordained. He could have done
something. It was to protect him that they were so brutal,
so that there'd be no trace of scandal, no talk of men

carrying shotguns across the fields, chasing after the father. He was allowed off scot-free. I . . .'

She stopped again. It hadn't just been Lizzy's tragedy. It had changed her life too. She had been the one left listening to the whispers, facing the silence of the house.

'All these years I never dared ask Lizzy who she told first, but I swear it was Tom. The way Lizzy would never talk of him after, even when she was dying. He must have told them. Maybe she asked him to or maybe he betrayed her, just thinking of himself. My father, well, he was a man of his time. I knew nothing until I came in from the yard and saw the blood on her face. I don't think my father had ever struck her before. Tom was just standing out of the way in the hallway, a long white face on him, not saying a word.

'There was a parlour we were never allowed into. My mother pulled her in there by the hair and locked the door. I couldn't get to her, I couldn't find out why. When I tried to shout into her my father hit me, then got my eldest brother to lock me in the shed. I kept screaming at Tom to help her, to help me. I could hear his footsteps turning away. All night I was there. When I woke up there was the noise of a car arriving, footsteps in the yard, the voice of a nun, then it was gone. Soon afterwards my mother unlocked the door. I knew that she was dying. My father and Lizzy were gone. I stood in that dark yard and I spat at her.'

Ellen's voice trailed off. She could see her mother's face in the old photograph which she was carrying in her handbag. The one they had found in her father's wallet. A young girl's face in the twenties, before thirty-five years of hard labour laid it waste.

'I stood at her grave,' Paudi said. 'I . . . felt . . . old bitch . . .'

'No.' Ellen grasped his hand tightly. 'You can't say that. You don't have the right.'

'Don't tell me what I have the right to.' His voice was angry. 'It was me as well, inside that womb, being kicked out.'

'Listen, Sean, you can't feel bitter. You were not there, not as a person. You don't understand. I've been bitter, for decades now I've been bitter. It cut our family into ribbons. My mother and I were never friends again, even when she was dying. My father . . . up to his death it haunted him, it came between us. Your own mother never went home. Tom's ordination . . . the whole parish were out with bonfires blazing and our family sullen in the church. People thought we were mourning our mother. We'd nothing left to say. My older sisters, brothers, we send cards every Christmas, not even a one-line letter. We're all bitter, trapped in our corners. There's been enough bitterness. I won't allow you to be bitter. You've got a duty to understand.'

Ellen took out the photograph from her bag. Paudi held it carefully, tilting it in the foyer lights as she told him about his grandmother. She could remember Lizzy and herself as girls in the kitchen, listening to their mother telling them about the locked box of Indian meal which had dominated her childhood. It was in that cabin outside Tullamore where their mother had spent the first decade of her life, waiting in the dark evenings with her baby brother for their father to come home. A drunk who mourned the wife he had beaten until her death, and whose only affection was for the greyhound who followed him everywhere. When he finally came home the box would be opened and a full scoop of meal taken out. The dog had first serve. Whatever was left over the two children shared between themselves.

'All she ever knew was hardship,' Ellen said. 'She had a mark on her shoulders where an aunt, whom her father had given her away to, beat her with a bellows when she was ten. It was a cruel world, they had a cruel humour. There was a spastic boy in the town. She often told me about running after him with stones. She built herself up, managed to marry above herself, got a man with some scrap of land. And I never saw her when she wasn't working, washing, digging spuds out of the frost with her hands. She lived for her children, to build us up, give us schooling, respect. What she did to Lizzy she did to protect the rest of us. My sister in Cork, she was courting then . . . that marriage would not have happened . . . my brother, he couldn't have gone back to the seminary . . .'

'You would stick up for her,' Paudi said.

'No. I cursed her into her grave. But what good will it do you to do the same? She was from another age, my father was . . . for your own sake, you've got to let that bitterness go.'

'But he wasn't, was he?'

'Who? What?' she asked.

'Tom. Your brother. He wasn't from another age. Where is he now?'

'Leave him. He sees nobody from the family. He's his own man.'

'I want to know where he is.'

'Cavan,' she said. 'Small parish. Kilnagowna. Lakes of pig slurry and sheds of battery hens. Leave him be. He won't want to know you. Nobody in the family will. They'd feel threatened.'

Paudi handed her back the photograph and asked to be excused. She watched him walk across the carpet to the toilets. The Italians had been checked in and the foyer was quiet when he came back. He walked stiffly. Water had been splashed on his face. Ellen became aware of how hungry she was, but was afraid to suggest that they eat something in case he made an excuse to leave. He sat down. Suddenly it seemed like an inquisition.

'Where was I born?' he asked.

'Sligo. Out the country somewhere. St Martha's.'

'How long was I there?'

'Six weeks.' Ellen felt suddenly drained. She was tired of talking, opening old sores. 'That time it was called *Waiting for the Brown Envelope*. They were your marching orders. Lizzy said that there was a Sister Theresa there who kept at all the girls to sign the forms.' Ellen tried to remember the invective Lizzy used to put into her impersonation of the nun's voice. "You've no rights to that child. He belongs to Christ. You can't deny him a Christian home." In the end it was Lizzy's decision to sign, but . . . she was nineteen. What sort of girl could stand up to them, could pack her bags and walk out those gates with her baby? You're miles from nowhere. Walking to a train station with every door closed in your face. There was one girl wouldn't sign . . . Sister Theresa screaming at her, gripping the girl's hand, crushing her wrist. Held her there for hours, Lizzy said, wouldn't let her wrist go until the girl signed.

'You cried a lot as a baby, she said. One night she was walking the floor with you. You were screaming. She lost control, hit you across the face. Your eyes wouldn't look up at her eyes for days afterwards.'

Paudi leaned forward and produced his wallet. Ellen began to panic. He was going to leave a tip and walk out on her. Instead he took out a photograph of two children, a boy of three being allowed to hold a baby in his arms. It seemed like a peace offering. She held it for a moment, then closed her eyes. She didn't want to look, it was not her who should be sitting here.

'Lizzy never forgave herself for signing,' she said. 'For years afterwards she used to dream that she had escaped from St Martha's with you. But she didn't. That was the terrible thing. She had the chance to and she didn't. She came back to the dormitory one morning and you were gone. She went hysterical. The nuns had taken you. You were being bathed and weighed. They told her to look on her bed. A brown envelope was there. She insisted on dressing you herself. She always talked about the outfit she dressed you in. They drove her to the station, gave her a ticket for Dublin. One of the nuns bought her chocolate. She cried all the way to Dublin. People on the train must have known. They left her alone. She always said your eyes were pleading with her. She had to stop looking at you and stare out the window, pretending you were already gone. Sister Theresa was on the train as well, up in the first class, having nothing to do with her. In Dublin Lizzy stayed in the carriage at Kingsbridge until she saw the nun pass, then she walked all the way in from the station. There was nobody with her. She told me she suddenly wanted to keep you. All the way walking into town she made plans to take the boat that night. Sean, the girl just didn't have the courage, she was little more than a child herself. Kept thinking she was being followed. She went into a draper's. She got thread and a needle. The only address she had was our old one in Laois. What use would that have been? She sat in a park, it must have been Stephen's Green, and resewed the hem so carefully nobody would ever notice. She felt they would be looking for her if she was any later. She kept showing people the address on the brown envelope and they'd give her different directions. It took her hours to find the house. There was a waiting room with four other girls in it. She was called into a room by a Cork woman. She signed a form, then the woman said to her, "Take a last moment now. Kiss your baby goodbye.'"

Both of them were silent, gazing at one another. Ellen

had expected to break down, but found her eyes were dry, her voice almost expressionless.

'I'm sorry,' she said, as if needing to justify herself. 'I have no tears left in me.'

Paudi took the photograph from her hands and put it back in his wallet. She had been waiting for the question.

'Who was my father?'

'I've told you enough now. Let sleeping ghosts lie, Sean. She never told a living soul.'

'She told you.'

Ellen nodded slowly. She felt that they would not see each other again. Paudi remained calm-looking, but she could sense that anger again which frightened her.

'We've gone this far,' he said. 'How do you know she would not have told me? I have the right to know.'

'I'm not sure if I have the right to tell you.'

'Do you know what this is doing to my life, to my family?' he snapped. 'I'm like a stranger to them. I want it sorted out now and finished. I won't be at peace until I know.'

She was silent for a few moments.

'You had a good father, you said so in your letter. One who loved you, who was good to you. Let that be enough, Sean. Why should a man who never gave you a moment's thought in thirty-six years get to meet you, when a mother who loved you all that time never did?'

He leaned forward. She knew that the conversation was over.

'Do you think . . . would we have liked each other?' He asked very quietly.

'Paudi . . . Sean . . . you're the one flesh and blood.'

Chapter Fifteen

I flew back to Dublin late that evening, intending to go straight home, but stopped at the bank of phones in the baggage terminal to phone instead.

'Where are you?' Geraldine's voice asked. 'You were supposed to phone me as soon as you met her.' Then her voice faltered and I realized how nervous she was. 'What's your mother like?'

'Listen, love,' I said. 'I can't come home just yet. I've things to sort out.'

'Where are you? Are you going to stay with her, or in a hotel?'

'My mother's dead, Geraldine.'

The line was quiet for a moment. I could hear Benedict crying to be allowed to hold the phone. There was an announcement on the loudspeaker as the luggage belt behind me began to move. Geraldine's voice was low.

'I'm sorry.'

'Listen, I'll phone.' I put the receiver down quickly before she could ask anything else. I had no plans, I just needed time alone to think and to grieve. I got the car from the short-term car-park and turned off the motorway, driving in the direction of Howth. The streetlights were coming on. Soon the coast lay to my right, a long wash of darkening water out to the cliffs of Howth Head. There was a hotel there where I had always wanted to spend a night. I could take a room in it, have the hours of night alone to try and rid myself of this anger. I would buy brandy at an off-licence and wake up shattered and fully clothed before dawn, my chest burning, my throat raw. I would drive home gingerly, too immersed in a hangover to feel anything. Then I would start my ordinary life again.

I had moved into the outer lane and indicated right at Sutton Cross, before swerving left in a chorus of car horns and speeding away back along the side roads to rejoin the motorway. I was still unsure of where I was going, just that I needed to keep driving. I headed towards the West-Link Toll Bridge that spanned the Liffey valley. I wanted open motorways, pure lines of unfeeling tarmacadam where I could open up the engine and speed.

I had not driven fast since the crash, but now I raced into the growing darkness, seventy-five, eighty, eighty-seven miles an hour. Occasionally I had to swerve back into the inside lane to overtake a truck lumbering along in the fast lane, but generally I had the highway to myself. I flicked the buttons on the stereo, wanting the loudest music. I felt at one with the car, my body shifting in the seat at the bends, my neck pressing at the headrest as I screamed the engine on. Nass was bypassed and then Kildare. Monasterevin lay ahead on the border of Laois.

The closer I came the more I was forced to decide on a plan. In America I would have had two loaded guns as I roared into Dunross. There would be a hamburger bar to spray with bullets, a siege, psychologists to explain my motives, an actor with good teeth to play me in the movie. Here, the miles of motorway paid for by Europe were petering out as I crossed the Curragh. Sheep grazed on the flat grass where thoroughbreds would be exercised at dawn, I was caught up in a slow convoy of local cars. I was scared. What could I say to anyone there?

But I kept going, slower now, on to Portlaoise and then

Mountrath, and then taking the dark, tiny roads which wound towards Dunross. I did not stop at the village. I came to the laneway which had led down to the Sweeney farm and pressed the mileometer to zero. I turned to face up into the mountains, finding my way along narrow boreens to beyond Roundwood, and then took that crumbling long road which crested the hills and fell away down through dark state forests to Kinnitty.

I knew where I was going now, although I was not sure of the route. It was a pilgrimage, a futile act of atonement. I wanted her to know that I was doing this for her, that somehow, in that state beyond the tunnel of light, she would be aware of how I was making this journey again. On through Birr, with the lights of late drinkers coming out from the town to dazzle me, and then Cloghan and the road across the flat bog to Ballinasloe. The roads were empty now. I had not slept for forty-eight hours, had eaten nothing since a hurried sandwich passing back through Liverpool Street station. I could so easily crash. I knew what face would be waiting for me now if I did, but it felt as if she was protecting me. I felt unearthily calm. I drove on, trying to guess what route the nun's driver had taken, imagining the silence which must have accrued in that car.

I realized that I had gone wrong, but found a side road which led to Athleague and then into Roscommon town. Flags littered the main street, advertising beer in the closed-down bars. One drunk sat alone on a bench, staring open-mouthed at the empty street.

I drove on towards Boyle. There was no moon, even the good roads were pot-holed. I was getting low on petrol. Tullsk, Ballyroddy, Ratallen Cross Roads. A girl with a bruised face staring out from a car window. Had she cursed me? Had she squatted in the fields, jumping into ditches, praying for a miscarriage? A girl with a bruised face carrying an embryo across a dawnlit landscape. Like prisoners handcuffed together. A low wall ran parallel to the road, there were lights beyond it. Even in the dark its shape betrayed itself as an asylum. I drove past, wondering if there were other girls from that time there still, signed away with the family doctor's consent, written out, turned slowly crazy while the world they had left withered and vanished outside the locked gates.

For over an hour there had just been static on the radio, now it came within range of some local station on that frequency. There was a burst of low melodeon music, a scratchy recording of a set-dance as I passed the ruined abbey at Boyle. I seemed to know the lilt from somewhere long ago, found myself trying to whistle it with a pensive gravity. The signal was going again. I could not be certain if I heard the name of the tune correctly, *An Lon Dubh*, *The Blackbird*, recorded by a John Kimmel or Kummel in 1919. There was just static again as I moved out of County Roscommon. The road climbed into the Curlew Mountains. I found myself nodding, once I think I even slept for several seconds. I wound all the windows down. The car plummeted towards the shore of Lough Arrow. I stopped at Ballinafad, climbed down to the lakeside and splashed the cold water over my face. The lake spread out into blackness. There was another mountain behind me. I knelt forward again and almost fell into the water. I took off my shoe, filled it, poured the freezing water over my hair. I started crying then, hunched there, with some night bird calling familiarly across the dark waters. I knew that I could have found her in time if I had bothered. I rocked back and forth, trying to shake the accusation from my head.

A girl with a bruised face who had glimpsed the sun rise

over this lake. A girl whose brother had been sitting down to breakfast as the car drove. A tablecloth laid, the good cups out. Bacon and black pudding which the other children would have to go hungry for. Off to read his breviary and fart in the yard while a family collapsed around him. Neighbours greeting him respectfully. I stopped, holding the shoe in both hands. Maybe he was my father? The thought lasted only a moment, but the image stuck, a penis jutting from a cassock. It was too neat, too simple. I knew that I was assigning my own sense of guilt on to him, but I would gladly have killed the man.

Anger made me suddenly alert. I climbed back into the car and began to drive. Four miles later the petrol ran out. The car slid forward for a hundred yards, then came to a halt. It was half-three. From here on I was unsure of my direction. All Ellen Sweeney could tell me was that the convent had been five miles along side roads from Castlebaldwin. She wasn't even sure if it still existed or what the building was now used for. I wanted to find a ruin, the empty sockets of old windows, tumbledown walls which I could deface. I pushed the car as far into the ditch as possible, took my father's old camera bag from the boot for safety and began to walk.

I could only pick roads at random. There was a whitening mist gathering and no sign of the lights of a house on any side. After two hours it had brightened enough for me to see a flat boggy landscape. I was so tired and disoriented I was unsure if I was dreaming. There was a figure coming towards me from a long distance off. He walked rapidly, hands thrust into the pockets of an old great coat. There was something menacing in his walk, the way his eyes never left me. I slapped my face, trying to wake myself. Suddenly I was alert to danger. The man was in his forties with a peaked cap and the stubble of several days. I remembered the taxi driver taking me from Limerick Junction, pointing out the safe houses which terrorists used. How many miles was I from the border? I looked around. There was nowhere to hide. He came within fifty feet of me and stopped. His stare was manic.

'I'm Barney O'Connor,' he bellowed. 'Do you know that?'

'No,' I said, trying to identify the shape of what his hand was holding in his pocket.

'And you haven't a snowball's in hell where you are!'

'No.'

'Hah!' He threw his head back and laughed. 'Well, I do.'

It was hard to imagine him lowering his voice to speak in a room. He cackled again and nodded towards my camera.

'Pictures, ha! Do you know what you want, boy? Something you'll not see in a day's march. Take a gander at them!'

His hand slowly came out of his pocket and held out a bundle of tightly rolled newspapers. He came closer and offered them to me. I knew better than not to take them. His eyes were bloodshot as they pressed close to my face.

'Hah!' he cackled again, and looked down at the papers. I unrolled them. They were month-old copies of an English tabloid, the *Daily Sport*. A girl in leather underwear grinned on the front cover. *We're off again. Watch her strip all this week*, ran the headline. I looked back up at him.

'Hah!' he cackled one last time. It was a laugh without humour, like a shout of pain. I nodded and began to walk slowly on, holding the papers carefully. After ten minutes I looked back and he was still there, a fossilized speck in the distance, staring after me. From there he seemed a ghost from another world and time. Only when he was totally out of sight did I feel it safe to throw the papers away.

I did not so much find the convent as the convent found me. From half-seven onwards a trickle of smartly dressed girls on bicycles began to pass me, some giggling to each other as they looked back. They were so bright they seemed unreal in my exhausted state. I could hear their voices calling long after they had vanished. A school bus passed and some cars with parents driving pupils, and then a blue Nissan Sunny came towards me from the direction of the convent driven by a young woman in her early twenties. She stopped and lowered the window. Her amused smile made me realize how bad I must look.

'God, if you could see the state of yourself,' she remarked gently. 'Is it St Martha's you're looking for?'

'How did you know?'

'Ah, the girls said a man with a camera. We're used to journalists here. Did your car break down?'

'Ran out of petrol.'

She laughed. It was the laugh of a confident woman, aware of her good looks.

'You know it's a far bigger country outside Dublin than you people in the media realize. You really should at least invest in a tankful of petrol.'

'How long has it been a school?' I asked.

'Oh, for ever.' She shrugged her shoulders. 'Twenty years . . . more.'

I looked around at the empty fields that were starting to glisten in the early sunlight, then down at my camera case.

'I am a photographer,' I said, puzzled. 'But how did you know what I was looking for?'

'Well, let's face it. St Martha's has quite a reputation. You don't take a step like we have without getting very used to calls from the press. The press and from parents all over Ireland, I might add. Some have their daughters' names down from the day they're born. Would you believe that one father even phoned from the labour ward? Of course, our senior girls winning the Aer Lingus Young Scientist of the Year Award three years on the trot put us on the map. But it's the interdenominational aspect that really appeals to parents today. It was a bold step, becoming the first interdenominational school run by the Catholic Church, but that's what our order is about.'

'What?' I said.

'Progress, risk, looking forward. We raised hackles here among conservatives, but we stood our ground.' She stopped and looked at my appearance again. 'I hope you're not expecting a full Irish breakfast though. The girls have decided that for this month the whole school is going vegetarian.'

'What do you mean, *your order?*'

She climbed out and opened the back door of the car. She wore a purple polo-neck and a white knee-length skirt. She held her hand out.

'Sister Anne is the name.'

'Sister . . .?' I let the camera case drop on the roadway. 'Well, fuck me.'

She laughed at my surprise and tut-tutted in mock horror.

'I'm afraid our activities have not quite broadened that far.'

I had a sense that the parlour was one of the few rooms which had not changed from the time I was born. The furniture was old, dark, beautifully kept. Two of the senior girls served me a breakfast of cheese, rolls and coffee. They chatted away, probing me about the role of political bias in Irish newspapers and the impact of new technology on the media. I had the impression that if I were a fugitive nuclear physicist dropped by parachute, they would have just as easily owned up to baking the rolls themselves and then quizzed me knowledgeably about new developments in molecular theory.

'Do you know what this building was before it became a school?' I asked them.

They looked at each other, then shook their heads.

'Just a convent, I suppose,' one said. 'You know, nuns in retreats, cut off from the world. There's old bedsteads and lockers dumped down by the river these years back. Must have been a lot of them here.'

I had no right to be angry with them, but I could not help myself.

'Did you never think to find out? To know what happened to girls your own age here back in the fifties and sixties?'

They turned, disturbed by my tone, and looked towards the door. Sister Anne had returned. She beckoned the girls to leave.

'Dubliners,' she said to them. 'Free-range eggs and black pudding with blood dripping out of it is what they want down here. All the things their wives won't feed them at home.'

I waited till the girls were gone.

'Very droll, Sister,' I said.

She placed my car keys down on the polished table.

'It was safe and sound where you left it,' she said. 'We took the liberty of filling it with petrol. Just in case you forget again.'

'Maybe I might have,' I replied sourly. 'Forgetfulness seems prevalent in these parts. How about you? Do you know what went on here?'

'Yes,' she said, 'I do.' She held the door open for me.

There was a hint of hostility in her voice. 'A long time ago. Before those girls or myself were born. Mother Superior will see you now.'

The Mother Superior's study overlooked a modern extension where rows of girls could be seen seated in classroom windows. There were framed photographs of former students receiving awards. The nun was older and dressed traditionally. She looked at me carefully as I entered. I sensed that behind me Sister Anne's eyes were hinting at trouble.

'Mr Blake,' she said, indicating a seat, 'a photographer.'

'That's not why I'm here.'

'I know.'

I looked at her in surprise.

'I saw Sister Anne driving you in,' she explained in a soft voice. 'You got out of the car. The way you looked up at the building. We get three or maybe four callers like you every year.'

'What do you mean, *like me*?' Suddenly I was defensive, as though a raw nerve had been exposed.

'I don't know how many of you there were,' the nun said. 'Babies who saw the light of day in this place. Sometimes it's the mothers who come back, sometimes the children. Just twice it was them both together.'

I glanced at the row of filing cabinets along the wall.

'You have all the records of this place here?' I asked.

'Only for the school.' It was the younger nun who answered from behind my back. From her voice I knew that she now regretted having brought me into the building. 'You know, two of the women TDs in the present Dáil were educated here. The signs are that at the next reshuffle we'll have our first minister.'

The older nun looked down for a moment at the heaped

trays of paperwork piled on her desk as if to hide her annoyance.

'Sister Anne is justifiably proud of our achievements,' she said.

'Yes? And how many TDs did you produce from us here in the fifties?' The force of my anger frightened me, although I knew that it was being used to cloak grief and shame as well. 'How many shagging Young Scientists were trotted out back then, eh? Or are you part of this collective amnesia as well?'

'Mr Blake . . .'

'Sweeney's the name!' I found that I was shouting. 'Padraig Sweeney. That's my name in those filing cabinets over there, or wherever else you've stacked your dirty linen. I'm another of your past pupils, so why don't you stick my fucking photograph up on your wall there? Me and the thousands of poor fuckers like me. Sister Fucking Stork discreetly dropping us down chimneys when the neighbours weren't looking. What about a photograph of my mother and all the other girls who were locked behind these gates?'

I kept smashing my fist into the palm of my hand as I spoke. I stopped and looked down, realizing how exhausted I was, how sickening and shameful it felt just to be there again. The nun asked Sister Anne to fetch me a glass of water and I heard the door close. When I looked up she was regarding me quietly.

'No, Mr Blake, or Mr Sweeney,' she said. 'As it happens I'm not part of what you call that amnesia. I was a novice at the time. From a poor family too. My life was no bed of roses either. I spent time here and in other places like it, Magdalene laundries in Athlone and Roscrea where women were locked up for life. Sometimes they had had children out of wedlock, or had been prostitutes, often – I realize now – they were just women who were in the way at home, ugly sisters who couldn't be married off or girls who were any way odd. The nuns in charge back then ... they were some of the most stupid and ignorant women I ever met. Not them all, there were some of the finest and most loving as well. But there were many others who should not have been in charge of a sweet shop, never mind ...'

She stopped. The fax machine in the corner had begun to print a message out. The phone rang but she ignored it and, after a moment, somebody outside picked it up.

'Sister Anne is right about one thing,' she said. 'If you have come here looking for records then I'm sorry but I really cannot help you. They're now in a central office in Dublin. Also under law your birth mother has the right to privacy ...'

'I've found her already,' I said. 'She had just died.'

'I'm sorry,' the nun replied, and bowed her head.

'Stuff your sympathy.'

'If I were you I would be angry too,' she said, raising her head and waiting until she had made contact with my eyes before continuing. 'Things were done badly here. You have every right to be angry. But often those mistakes were made out of ignorance, not cruelty. You have to understand, nuns back then, we were given no training, we entered the convent while still children ourselves, we knew nothing about the real world. Just because we wore a black habit we were put in charge of things, presumed to be able to handle any sort of situation.'

'The nuns here were bitches.'

'That's too easy, Mr Blake, and you know it is. At least we were here. Say if we weren't. What would have happened to your mother or to you? What would her family have done, locked her up, beaten the child out of her, buried you at night in a lake or a bog hole? Or say if they had kept the pair of you, what would the neighbours have done? Stoned the house, burnt the family out?'

'Led by the local bollox of a priest with his collar concealed for the occasion,' I sneered.

She smiled slightly and shook her head.

'When did a priest ever have to get his hands dirty back then, Mr Blake?' she said. 'A few words planted in a sermon. And who hid behind the priests, eh?'

'And who hid, or who hid . . .?' I mocked. 'Passing the buck down the line doesn't change anything.'

'No. We were at fault. We allowed things to be dumped on us, we questioned nothing. I pray every night for your mother and for all the other girls whose names I never knew. But I pray for those nuns as well. They could be terrifying, they terrified me in their loneliness. But they were victims too.'

I knew that she was sincere, but something in me had to cause trouble. Ever since learning of my mother's death I had kept moving about, not wanting to be still, not wanting to have to think. Now, in the stillness of that room, grief threatened to overwhelm me. I needed anger to keep it at bay.

'I want to see the room where I was born,' I demanded. 'That's not too much to ask.'

'At this time of day it is, Mr Blake.' The nun rose and walked to the window. She leaned her head against the glass and pointed to the side wing of the old convent. 'Those wards are classrooms now. A new term. Girls starting to study again for exams. I can't disturb them.'

'You won't, you mean.'

'Stay on till the school is closed,' she said. 'We have a visitors' room. You can sleep for a while and then after school I'll show you around the whole place. For now those girls have the worry of exams, their futures. How will disturbing them help your mother?'

'So you'll just wash away the past, eh?'

'No.' She turned back from the window to confront me. 'But I'll not have them imprisoned by it. And you can't let yourself be either, Mr Blake.'

'Sweeney I told you the name was!'

'Somehow when you walk back out those gates I think Blake will still be the name on your credit cards and your union membership and the school forms for your children. For right or wrong you were given a second life. I can't change that and I think you know that it's a bit late for you to try either.'

The door reopened. Sister Anne returned. She placed the water down on the desk. The Mother Superior beckoned her to leave. I heard the door close.

'I want to see where my cot was,' I said. 'Where I was taken from. I want . . . I want . . . it all back.'

I knew how irrational I sounded. All these years my mother had waited for me to find her. I needed to talk to someone, but I would not betray her by breaking down here. I closed my eyes, shocked at the violence which had been dwelling within me, waiting to get out.

'There was an old nun,' I went on, 'a Sister Theresa. A right bitch. I want to know where she's buried. I want to piss on that bitch's grave.'

'Sister Theresa is still alive, Mr Blake. You will have to wait for that privilege.'

'She can't be alive,' I said, 'I . . .'

'Why don't you go and see her,' the nun suggested quietly. 'I'll even bring you if you want. She won't know you. Most of the time she doesn't really know anyone. If you hate her that much then go and see her. Confront your demons, Mr Blake, you'll be surprised where they might lead.'

'Screw her.'

'Are you afraid?' the nun asked. 'All this hatred, what good will it do you to carry it around? Lay it to rest. See for yourself if she's a demon.' She paused and looked at me carefully. 'Can I ask you a question, Mr Blake? When did you discover that your mother had died?'

I looked away from her. I thought of getting up and walking out to wherever my car was parked.

'Yesterday,' I finally replied, and then, without warning, I began to cry. 'She had wanted me to find her. She . . . fuck it, fuck it!'

'Stay the night here with us,' the nun said. 'Have you got a wife? Phone her. Let her come down and collect you. Let her see this place too.'

'I can't.' I tried to get myself together. 'We have children of our own.'

'Then for their sake you must lose this anger,' the nun said. 'Sister Anne and some of the other nuns her age . . . well, they want to bury the past of this place. It's all petitions for human rights in Central America and for travellers' rights to halting sites. They don't want to be touched by what happened here. They're wary of people like you, like you can drag them back. That's wrong. You have the right to be angry for all that happened to you, but you can't let it ruin your life. Unless you rid yourself of this anger you'll just pass it on.'

I took a sip of water and sat in silence. What had I wanted here? I didn't want to admit it to myself, but I was frightened of confronting that old nun. The previous week I had read Benedict a bed-time story by Martin Waddell about two bears walking home through the woods and the big bear lifting the little bear to reassure him that the plod, plod, plod which he heard was not a plodder behind them but the sound of the big bear's footsteps in the snow. Benedict loved the story but then, later that night, had woken in terror, crying out, 'I don't like the plodder.' I had covered bombings and murders, I had sat beside Gerry when he interviewed Dublin gang leaders who had already slashed our car tyres as a warning. But this fear was different; it was like Benedict's, something irrational left over from my childhood.

'You feel guilt,' the nun continued, 'and that hurts. I know. Most nights I walk these corridors last thing. There's no real need, but I like to. Sometimes I open a door in the moonlight. Instead of rows of desks, for a moment I see beds and cots. I imagine I can hear sobbing. I was just a novice, I had no power. What could I have done to change anything? But I still feel guilty because I accepted that those women were fallen and depraved. And I am guilty too, we all are. Every last person who stayed silent, who didn't see and didn't want to see. Families who sent their collars down to be starched and their tablecloths made white again in the laundry. Over in our Retreat House in Sligo your Sister Theresa is dying. The younger nuns there, they think she's saintly. They won't welcome you, but you owe it to yourself to go and see her, then ask yourself, can you really heap all that blame on her shoulders?'

A bell rang in the corridor for the end of a class. There was a sudden throng of footsteps outside. The nun was staring at me, but I could not bring myself to acknowledge her.

'If I can't see the rooms,' I said, 'then can I walk in the grounds?'

'Would you like me to join you?'

'No.'

There must have been a button on her desk, because after a moment the door opened and Sister Anne appeared. I rose.

'Good luck with your search, Mr Blake.'

The nun held her hand out. I looked at it, then shook my head.

'I'm sorry, I can't,' I said.

She nodded. I followed Sister Anne down the long corridor in silence. There was a door open at the end of it. I glanced in at the old desks stacked together, the tied-up bundles of yellowing ledgers and files. A crucifix had been removed from the wall, but the outline remained where successive coats of paint had been applied to the bricks around it. There were two high windows. I stopped, while the young nun hovered impatiently beside me. A group of girls came down the corridor. I felt that if I tried to speak to them she would have pushed me into the room. We went outside. My car was parked on the gravel.

'I owe you for petrol,' I said.

'It's okay.'

I managed to make the young nun take the money, then looked around again at the high windows of the convent. Would my mother have come back here with me if she had lived? The nuns had not kidnapped her. They had been here when her family turned their back. What future could she have had as an unmarried mother, shunned by every person? The nuns would have felt they were giving her a chance to start again. She could never have had the other children that she did have, could probably never have married. And what sort of life would I really have had, carted about between a succession of cheap flats in London? For years I had barely acknowledged to myself that I was adopted. Surely now part of this grief was hypocrisy? If I were to be totally honest, was I not relieved that I had been spared that past and had known a cosy upbringing, wanting for nothing?

I remembered again feeling sickened as a child simply by the taint of poverty in the tenement I had been brought to visit. I remembered . . . no. I tried to block it, but once again the image came to me so vividly that I felt nauseated. A starving boy on a ridge of grass eating worms. I wanted to climb back into the luxury of my car and drive as far away as possible. Sister Anne was waiting for me to go.

'The nuns who used to live here,' I said, 'are they buried about the place?'

She pointed to a low wall bordered by yew trees. There was a cross on top of the small iron gate.

'How about the women who died here in childbirth or the children who were stillborn. Where are they?'

As she glared at me, I noticed the fear behind her hostility. If I had been an Aids victim, a rapist in prison or a leper in an oppressed foreign land she would have grasped my hand. She stepped back.

'This is a school,' she said. 'A school in which any parent would be proud to enrol their children.'

There were trees behind the convent which sloped down towards a river. Cows grazed peacefully there. I reached the water's edge and picked up stones from the bank, flinging them violently at the surface of the water. I mouthed every curse I knew, while the cows grazed placidly beside me.

Finally I stopped and began to work my way slowly along by the river, searching for the dump which the girls had spoken of. It was a mile beyond the convent. I had gone past before I realized what it was. The lush river-bank vegetation had almost reclaimed everything. Local people had, no doubt, long ago taken anything which could be reused. All that was left were bits of broken beds, the smashed wooden bars of cots and scraps of loose debris so discoloured that it was hard to know what they had once been.

There were six rolls of film in the camera bag. My hands were covered with nettle stings by the time I had shot my way through them. Once, I heard voices and hid among the long grass as if ashamed to be found there. When I had finished the last roll the sun was high overhead. Far off I could hear the shouts of young voices at volleyball. I felt more calmed. But still I knew I had to confront the nun who had terrorized my mother.

They were waiting for me at the Retreat House in Sligo. The middle-aged nun who stood at the doorway looked formidable. Before I was even out of the car she began to explain that Sister Theresa was frail and hardly able to breathe. She was in almost constant pain and any shock could kill her. If the Mother Superior of St Martha's had asked that I be allowed see her, then she would not stand in my way, but what possible good could it do me? Things that had happened in the past were bad, but they were part of the times the country had gone through. Sister Theresa would not even remember my mother. Nobody there now would deny that perhaps my mother had possibly been badly, or at least unwisely, treated, but could I not just let an old woman die in peace? I was tempted to turn back; then I thought of Benedict and Sinead. *For their sake you must lose this anger.* The Mother Superior had known how to get at me.

'I've come this far,' I said. 'I want to see her.'

'You've caused quite a stir,' she said. 'Sister Theresa has overheard the younger nuns talking. She wants to see you. She thinks you've come . . .' The nun stopped. 'She's confused. She'll be flustered now until she's seen . . .' She paused again, as if trying to decide. 'Mr Blake, you can have five minutes if you give me your word that you'll behave yourself.'

I was led inside in silence, up two flights of waxed stairs and down a long corridor. I could hear doors opening after I passed, and sensed that I was being watched. A young novice sat beside the bed. The old nun under the blankets was shrunken into a child's frame, her head pressed into the pillow as if already dead. She moved her head slightly towards me and smiled. Her whisper was barely audible.

'I am so pleased you have come to visit me, child. So happy for you. A fine man now. How well you've turned out.'

'Lizzy Sweeney,' I said. 'My mother was Lizzy Sweeney.'

The nun smiled again and tried to nod. The novice wiped her mouth with a tissue.

'A wonderful mother you must have had, a wonderful home. How well you look, such a gentleman come to visit. I remember feeding you, a sickly baby.'

She began to ramble, her breath coming hoarsely. The novice bent her head close to the old nun's lips. She looked up.

'She wants to touch your hand. She's thanking God for you.'

The novice held up the frail hand. When I took it I felt that I could crush the bones of her fingers with one squeeze. I leaned across her. I could feel the spittle already swilling about in my mouth. I looked into her eyes and swallowed it, then turned away. The old nun was smiling, her hand still held aloft, staring up as though I was still there. I could hear her whispering away, oblivious to the fact that I was gone as they closed the door after me.

'So pleased you have come to give thanks, child.'

Chapter Sixteen

There was building work being carried out on Kilnagowna Chapel. Scaffolding that was flecked with rust rested against the wall nearest the graveyard. The job had the look of being done by local men, unpaid, in their spare time. A long sweep of gravel led down to the single shop with its green corrugated-iron roof at the small turning. There was an old sign in miles for Virginia and a new green one in kilometres for the German-owned hotel which I had passed earlier. A truck sped by, heading for the border. The two young donkeys in the field behind the school yard did not raise their heads. An elderly man on a bicycle stopped at the junction beside the shop and stared up at me, immobilized, one foot on the tarmacadam, the other poised on the pedal.

It was half-six in the evening. I had pulled over in a lay-by several miles outside Sligo and slept through the afternoon, jolting awake at half-three with a queasy stomach to feel the car being rocked by the slipstream of trucks. I had rubbed my eyes, which felt as if a fragment of crushed glass had slipped beneath the lids, and started the engine. It was the voice of the nun from St Martha's, urging me to confront my demons, which kept entering my head as I found myself following an unspoken impetus, taking side roads through Leitrim and into Cavan, until eventually I found Kilnagowna.

I went into the chapel. A single crude spotlight blazed from the ceiling, highlighting the altar and casting the side pews into shadow. 'Confessions from six to eight,' the housekeeper had told me. 'You'll find a queue though. Father Tom is one of our own.' There was a double line of six people, waiting for the two boxes attached to his confessional. The sign above his door read *Fr Sweeney*. I had expected all the penitents to be old, but the two girls who knelt in the pew in front of me were in their twenties, while the young man waiting to go in next had a punk Mohican hairstyle which seemed incongruous with the black tweed overcoat he was wearing.

How long was it since I had queued like this to enter the darkness of a boxed space? I could remember my teacher's voice telling us how valuable this period of waiting was, our seven-year-old heads bowed as instructed while we searched our consciences for any sin which we might have hidden from ourselves. The faces of the girls in front of me were composed either in thought or in prayer. I felt angry for them suddenly. This man invested with the power to forgive or condemn, what understanding could they expect from him? I knew that I had no right to recruit them into a conflict of my own. Yet I sat there stiffly, watching them kneel, imagining his voice railing at them. An old woman came to kneel beside me. I motioned her to go past, but she shook her head.

When my turn came I entered the box and knelt because it felt foolish to stand. I could hear the whisper of a male voice granting absolution. I heard someone leave the far door and then the small wooden slot between me and him opened, casting a band of weak light into the box. I could see the outline of his cheek through the golden mesh. It turned so that I could see his lips as he puzzled at the silence.

'Do you not remember the words?' he asked. 'You're a stranger in these parts, I feel?'

'I'm a son come home.'

'Is it confession you want? There are people still waiting.'

I expected to see irritation on those of his features which I could glimpse through the slot, but his voice sounded genuinely concerned.

'It's hard to remember which sins are real sins. There's different leagues of them, aren't there?' I found myself sneering. 'I don't know what's been promoted or relegated since my day.'

'You have a lot of anger inside you. I don't know what you have done. Now if you wish me to hear your confession I will, but don't belittle this confession box because I have not forced you to come into it.'

'How is hatred rated as a sin?'

'First you begin by saying *Bless me, father, for I have sinned*. Then you tell how long it is since your last confession.'

'I asked you a question.'

'Hatred is a serious sin. Unchecked it can lead to acts of violence, destruction. Have you been involved with the men of violence?'

'I hate one man only. And not even for anything he did to me. It's for things he didn't do. For how the bastard betrayed his own sister.'

'I cannot allow language like that in the confessional.'

His voice was sharp. When I stared in through the mesh his eyes were looking straight ahead, keeping a professional distance between us. That is the face of my uncle, I thought, only the second blood relative I've seen in my life. In twenty or thirty years' time I may look like that. I wanted him to turn, to be forced to see me too.

'You had girls in before me. What sort of penance does a man as righteous as you give them for any falling by the wayside, eh? Twenty lashes of the whip behind the altar?'

He did turn now with a quiet outrage on his face. That is how I would photograph him, I thought, his eyes in shadow, his mouth slightly open in the light.

'What is it that you want?' he asked. 'A scene, the guards called? Well, I'm not giving you one. There are sincere people waiting to have their confessions heard. I'm closing this slot and I want you to leave the confessional. You do need help and if you come back ready to genuinely confess I will give it to you. You have more sins on your soul now than when you entered this box. Now go, my son.'

'Wait.'

The dim shaft of light narrowed as the slot closed.

'Am I? Your son? Or your father's? Or whose son am I? That's all I've come here to know.'

His hand stopped. There was an inch of light left. My anger had dissipated. There was a vague aftertaste of disgust in its place. I remembered my plans on the drive there to humiliate him. Now the closing light frightened me somehow. I wanted to talk, I wanted to know something, although I could not be sure what.

'What if the man you hated is a priest?' I asked. 'Maybe you hate him unfairly, there were others worse, but he's the only bullyboy you can lay your hands on.'

The box was filled again with the slanting light. I could not see him and knew that his head was leaning against the wood behind him.

'It is no greater sin than to hate any other man,' he replied.

'Limbo still existed when I was a child.'

'The concept of limbo has been long abolished.'

'Where do the bastards in a priest's family go?'

In the silence I could hear him breathing. Had he been expecting this moment for thirty-six years?

270

'Not many cars stop here,' he said slowly, then was silent again for a moment. 'It seems an isolated spot for a man to pick for his confession. Are there not priests in your own parish?'

'None that I would call father or uncle.'

There was another silence, then I heard his door open. From his low whisper I knew he was telling the few people left that he could not hear their confessions. I stared in at the empty box where so much of his life must have been spent. He returned. There was a click of the light switch and we were both in darkness.

'When people see the light out they know confessions are over.'

'I believe you.'

The sudden bitterness in my voice hurt him.

'I did not ask for your belief,' he replied.

'Maybe you feel certain things are best left in the dark?'

'This man whom you hate . . .'

'This priest.'

'Let's call him a man,' he said. 'Maybe you have him at a disadvantage, because he doesn't know your name or how much you know about him or what happened in the past.'

'There are bits of the puzzle I've yet to fit,' I said. 'Like, had you a hearty breakfast after watching your sister being dragged off in a car?'

He was silent for a long time. The dark was becoming claustrophobic. I wanted to claw at something, to break the tension.

'You have this priest down as a strongman, a bullyboy. What if all his life he was a coward?'

'Is that some sort of excuse?'

'No.' The voice in the darkness paused. 'Not for forgiveness. It's just important . . . to me . . . that you understand. What can I call you?'

'What did your sister call me?'

'I don't know.' The anguish in his voice was real, but it kindled only anger in me.

'Did you never *fucking* think to find out?'

'A coward. The less you know the safer you feel.' His voice was suddenly scared. 'Who sent you here?'

'Frightened that I'll bring down your good name, is it? Don't worry, I'm sick of you. Just answer one question and let me go. I want to know, for my children's sake . . . incest, family illnesses . . . if there are things that I should warn them about. Give me the name of my father and let me out of here!'

'I don't know,' he said. It was a whisper so low that I had to strain to hear it.

'You were the closest to her. I don't believe you.'

'A coward,' he repeated. 'The less you know the safer you feel. He was older, that's all I know. She tried to tell me, I stopped her.'

'Was it you?' I raised my voice. 'Tell me!'

He began to laugh, a low choking in the back of his throat. It sounded eerie. He stopped.

'If you only knew,' he said. 'Would that you were, or had thought you were, my son. This man you hate . . . this priest. He has the feelings of any other man. Same loneliness, same sense of growing old. Only thing he is denied is that which sustains other men. The sense of belonging in a family, of seeing children grow.'

'You said yourself nobody forced me into this box. Nobody forced you to wear that collar either.'

'What if over a thousand people packed the church grounds on the night you were ordained? What if there were pitch barrels blazing and two bands marching down the boreen to your father's farm? What if old men the length of the parish were telling you that the very thought of this day had kept them alive for the previous seven years?'

'And what if there was somebody absent,' I retorted. 'A vanished sister who had been down on her knees at eight months' pregnant scrubbing convent floors?'

There was silence, then a spurt of flame. He inhaled the cigarette, the red tip glowing through the wire mesh. He held the lit match for a moment.

'The girls you saw tonight and that young punk lad are about the only young people left in this parish,' he said quietly. 'We won the minor county final two years ago. The medals arrived only last month. Eighty pounds it cost to post them. Sydney, Boston, New York, Birmingham, Frankfurt. Just two of the team left in Ireland. Often I think the only way to get the repairs on this bloody church finished is to burn it down for the insurance and start again.' The match spluttered out. 'What do you know about those convents in the fifties?'

'What I've read or been told.'

'Well, I saw them. I was the young priest in the black robes sent in to hear the confessions of what they used to call fallen women. One woman I remember, she had skin that might never have been touched by sunlight. You wouldn't keep a dog in the condition she was in. I almost got sick in the confessional listening to her describe the tape worms which she was passing. It was God's punishment, a nun had told her, for giving birth thirty years before. So don't you try to tell me what those places were like. They were like everything you think and worse. This man whom you hate. Would it make any difference to know how much he has despised himself all these years?'

'Not especially.'

A small strand of smoke floated like a white ghost through the wire mesh towards me.

'You mentioned children,' he said quietly.

'I have two.'

'Do you think I might know their names?'

'I thought there was anonymity in the confessional.'

'At least are they boys or girls?' His voice sounded desperate.

'Putting them to bed sometimes, I sit holding my son's hand in the light from the landing. He asks me, "What was your Daddy like?" and I tell him about a quiet man who worked all his life selling postcards on a van. He likes the look of his face in the old photographs. One day I'll have to tell them.'

'Have you photographs with you?'

'In my wallet.'

The light clicked on. I could see his face close to the slot.

'Please, place one . . .'

'No.'

The light clicked off again. We heard the footsteps of somebody who had been saying his penance at a side altar coming down the aisle. They paused a moment. I knew he was staring at the box. The footsteps moved on. A church door closed with a soft swish.

'We are alone,' I said.

'Except for God.'

'I forgot. You made your choice.'

'The choice was made for me.'

'They would hardly ask for the presents back if you left now.'

'Funny thing is that I found him. No, not for years afterwards. It all seemed a charade for so long. Every five years a reunion with my old classmates and you could see it in them, the ones who had been so devout, you could see their faith hardening into something different, slipping imperceptibly away from them. They had become managers. All their talk now about parish building programmes and overdrafts. Yet for me, after fifteen or twenty years, I found that the charade had become flesh. That's funny, isn't it?'

'I didn't come here to laugh,' I said.

'Why did you come?'

'I've told you. I want the name of the man who left Lizzy Sweeney like that.'

'Can you not call her . . . what she was to you?'

'She was a stranger to me. I never met the woman. She died before I found her. Anyway, who the hell are you to tell me what to call her? Did you even try to contact her once since you watched her being flung out?'

'Not for years. Then I tried through Ellen, my sister. She didn't want . . . I can't blame her.' He went quiet again. I could hear his breathing in the dark. 'You say you didn't find her in time? It would have meant . . . I said a mass for her soul here on the morning of her funeral.'

'A safe enough distance, was it?'

An intense anger was consuming me. I had wanted him to be callous and evil, a substitute for the father who had never bothered to think of my existence, who – if he remembered my mother – remembered her as an early conquest to boast about some night in a pub. Now I wanted to put my fist through the grille and shatter that quiet despair in his voice. Yet I knew also that my anger was directed at myself. I could have found her in time. The accusation kept coming back. I opened the door of the box. The light still shone on the main altar. A few candles flickered in memory of the dead in front of a cheap statue on a side altar.

'Please wait. Please.'

I stepped out on to the side aisle. The station on the wall beside me depicted the Crowning with Thorns. The whisper came from the box again, near tears, pleading and yet dignified.

'I loved your mother. She was the only person I've ever been close to on this earth. Even if you have just come here to mock do not desert me yet. For years I've prayed that we would come face to face. I have no family. Since that day. I turned my back on every one of them. Call me any name you want, I don't care. Just stay . . . a few minutes more.'

I turned to face the closed door of his box.

'How dare you say that?' I shouted. 'Walk out that door with me then, *face to face*. Let's see you walk to that shop below and introduce me as your bastard nephew?'

'Why? So you can prove some point?' His voice had that same quiet tone. 'I am the confessor of that woman in the shop, I buried her husband, sat in the hospital with her when he died. Does your hatred of me mean that you have to hurt her as well?'

'You're a coward,' I taunted.

'Of course I am, I've told you over and over. Inside every one of us, if we're brave enough to admit it, there's a coward.'

I began to walk down the aisle, my footsteps loud on the waxed floor. I think I expected him to follow me. I reached the door and turned around. I felt smaller there and lost, looking back up the church. I wanted a response. I thought of those variety shows on television where the magician vanishes from his box. It was irrational but I could not help feeling that he was no longer present in that darkness. I walked back and stood by my open door. My footsteps were quiet this time, but as soon as I had stopped his voice came softly from the box.

'All my life I've knelt on the other side of this box too. Making false confession to other priests, never telling the truth. To anyone. Not even Lizzy Sweeney. Hear my confession first, then you can damn me to hell.'

'It was you who told me not to mock this place.'

'I came to know God only very slowly. Let me decide what constitutes mockery.'

'Come out here and face me.'

'No,' the voice said. 'The priests of this parish change, but this box does not. Often I think it is not us who absolve sins but these wooden walls which absorb them.'

I waited a moment, then got back into the box. I closed the door. I found that I welcomed the darkness too. Behind a thin partition of wood he was waiting for my permission to speak. Yet I stayed silent, all those years of buried anger refusing to leave me alone.

'Do you know what a bad confession is?' he asked.

I leaned my head against the wood and said nothing.

'I was eleven when I made my first one. A mortal sin. Every confession I have made since has been the same. You get young boys in this box. Week in and week out, the same banal prattling. Then one week their voices are different, you know it has begun. *Have you had any thoughts? Have you committed any actions?* The weight on those poor children's shoulders like they were the most shameful sinners in the world. "I hid under my sister's bed the night she had a bath . . . I read a magazine the boy beside me brought into school . . . My father sent me to bring the cattle in, I was alone in the top field."

'It's hard on any young boy to have to say that. But they come out. They kneel in front of the big wooden crucifix to say their three Hail Marys. Think how much harder it is for a boy to say, "I knelt in front of that crucifix, I gazed at those white limbs, the outline of bones on the rib cage. It was an occasion of sin.'"

'This has gone far enough,' I said to the darkness. 'I am not your confessor. Whatever you have to say come out and say it to my face.'

'Do you think I have not tried?' his voice answered. 'Afterwards you can walk away, you can damn me, but just listen now. There were two sorts of boys in Laois. Footballers and priests. I know it was not that simple, often the men with clerical collars were the biggest thugs on the playing pitch, but you know what I mean. When I was five or six my father brought me on his crossbar over the mountains to Birr. There was a hurley tied to the bar beneath me. A big field of young men stripping for the match behind the bushes by the river. I've never forgotten the feeling I had, that curious, marvellous joy. The way the winter sun gleamed on their ribs and their naked legs. It was the time of the emergency, rationing. One man gave me a piece of orange. I bit into it, felt the bitter juice on my tongue. I think perhaps I have never been that happy again. And on the way back, crossing the mountain in the dark, the road rutted and crumbling away so that the bike had to swerve between the pot-holes, I could sense my father's amusement and then unease as I talked away about how lovely the men were. And after a while we were freewheeling down by Roundwood towards Mountrath, neither of us speaking, with him annoyed and me not knowing why. And when the next Sunday came he brought my brother and you could hear them laughing and joking in the dark for over a mile before they got back into the farmyard that night.'

As I listened to him, without warning, the dream of the yew walk haunted me vividly again. Maybe it was the lack of sleep, but I had the sensation that, there in the darkness, if I touched my face I would feel a stranger's features. It frightened me. I tried to control my breathing. My hand had become a clenched fist. I tapped the knuckles against the wood as if to drown out his voice. He ignored the noise.

'You grow up and you're somehow different from other boys, gentler, not getting into as many fights. A time comes, your classmates are roaming in packs, hungry for the sight of girls and you're not with them. It's hard to avoid rumours of sanctity, especially when you find out how much they please your parents, especially when you want no other rumours started about you.'

I wasn't just listening to his words any more, I was reliving a memory of the same terror of exposure which he was describing. From somewhere in my past, some time which I was not conscious of, a sense of apprehension was overwhelming me. I felt younger, leaner, filled with a hunger unlike any which I had ever known. It was like waking from a dream beyond my ability to recall. I had the sensation of having dreamt of being in this confession box before.

'Take a small parish,' his voice was continuing. 'Two pubs, a shop, a church, a bridge to gather on in the evenings. You've got a city accent, so you might think of the country in terms of space. But a parish is a closed fist. Even walking out on the bog in winter you'll be seen. At first you think there is no other person like you in the world. You think you'll wind up in the asylum. Then one day you find out and the asylum is not your worry any more. You realize that long before that you're likely to be found battered to death.'

'So you hide behind the priesthood?'

My voice was sharp, almost a shout. There was silence from the other side of the partition. I wondered if there had been other cubicles like this for him, men who had not looked into his face either, the gush of water from the urinal behind them.

'Do you have anything but bitterness in your heart?' his voice asked. 'Would I have been better to hide behind marriage like most did? What husband would I have made for Lizzy, what father would I have made for . . .'

My fist smashed against the wood again.

'She was your sister! What are you talking about? What are you telling me?' I threw my shoulder against the door, ready to drag him from his box.

'No! Listen . . . it was not like that . . . there was nothing . . . your father was some flyboy, I'm not sure who, or if he forced her or she gave herself willingly or what. It was just my stupid, stupid plan to look after her . . . and you.'

His voice had dried up, as if he had touched something so raw that it was impossible to continue.

'Put your light on,' I said.

There was a click. I reached into my wallet and produced a photograph. I held it to the grille.

'The boy is aged three,' I said. 'The girl fourteen months.'

Several minutes passed. I expected him to ask for names or details of their personalities, but finally all he said was 'thank you' in such a way that I knew he had been crying. The light was switched off again. It was some time before he spoke.

'My parish had my vocation for me. We had had a runner who came second last in his heat in the Olympics. We had a man born above one of the pubs who had his own dance band on the road in the forties. But we had never had a priest. It was easier to go along with that than to face whatever other sort of future I might have known. I told myself that a priest is celibate. It would be no harder for me than for anyone else, I thought. Different and no easier, but no harder.'

That presence which I had felt in the darkness of my living room seemed close at hand again. I lowered my head, accepting that such a sense of affinity with his fear could not have sprung from my present life.

'The only trouble was,' he said, 'I didn't want to be a priest. I was an ordinary man, I just wanted an ordinary life with ordinary things. Lizzy, there was a special magic in her. There wasn't a boy in that parish without dreams of her. I wish you had seen her. Maybe . . . I have a photograph taken one summer up in the parochial house if . . .'

'No. Finish speaking and let me walk out of here,' I said.

'We were so close. I understood her. She would talk to me about boys she liked. Often I tried to hint to her, but . . . she would not have understood, nobody would have in that place, in that time. Leaving her was the only thing I hated about going away from Dunross. The seminary was no more lonely than life had been there. Life behind walls, not allowed to read a newspaper or listen to the wireless except for the All Ireland Final. I used to make plans to run away, but I knew that I never could. They told you, even if you hadn't a vocation, when you stood at the altar to be ordained God would give you one. A few years back they had these pictures on the news from Iran. Young boys in their bare feet holding up their holy books as they walked through the minefields to clear the way for the tanks. That was us back then. Blind faith was what we were taught. Trust in God, keep walking, even as your limbs are being blown off. But every evening in that seminary I prayed to God to show me a way out.'

I closed my eyes as he spoke. I was a tiny child again. I saw a sky of swollen thunder clouds, a ridge of wild grass, a blighted field of potatoes. For a moment I felt a wasting hunger as if everything inside me had been shat away. I watched my filthy hand reaching down towards the worm which had crawled out from the soil. The wind was freezing, I had just pissed the ragged pants I was wearing. I opened my eyes, trying to banish the image. I banged upon the wood with my palm, wanting him to stop, wanting to run out into the light and yet knowing that those disconnected memories would follow me. From the far side of the wood his voice carried on.

'Then one summer I was allowed home. Lizzy, she wasn't herself . . . worried, paler. I caught a glimpse of her once behind bushes beyond the far field. I thought she was using the toilet and turned away, then realized she was getting sick. I didn't understand. I asked her at dinner was she feeling better. The look she gave me across the table . . . hatred, terror. I couldn't explain it.'

Footsteps entered the church. He stopped and waited till they turned and faded off into the distance. I found I was trembling. My forehead was covered in sweat. I could see the face so clearly which had haunted my sleep, only it was no longer sneering. It was frightened and pleading. And now it seemed to belong to the voice on the other side of that box, as if – over all these months – it had been leading me here.

'I could never get her alone to talk to her,' he continued. 'Like she was avoiding me, avoiding being near any of us. One morning we were making hay in the lake field and I nicked my hand, knowing that our mother would send her back to the house with me to bathe it. "Tell me what's wrong," I said to her. "Whatever it is I can help." Gripping my hand tight, squeezing the cut, she started to cry as she told me. She was three months gone. This was God's sign, I thought, he's telling me the path to take, how to escape. With her I would have the strength. I started hushing her, telling her not to worry. The pair of us would go to England together, pretend that we were man and wife. I'd find work, I'd mind her, I'd mind . . .'

He stopped, as though frightened to say the word.

'. . . I'd mind you. I didn't want to know who the father was. You'd be mine. You'd . . .'

He stopped again. There was a noise like a rat scraping. It was his nails on the wire mesh. He did not seem aware of it.

'Lizzy kept shaking her head, terrified, saying no, it would be a greater sin to take me away from God. She couldn't do it, she would manage alone. I told her that it was what God wanted, I even pretended I had dreamt of it in the seminary. Eventually I calmed her down. I convinced her. She told me that she had tried to kill herself. She had gone to the man . . . your father. He had struck her. I put my hand on her hair . . . such beautiful hair. From now on I would mind her, she was to trust me. Every man in that parish dreamt of her, and I abused her far worse than the dirtiest old man ever could. We made plans, what we would bring, the route we would take. There was a mart in Mountrath in two days' time. We would set out as if going to that, be in Dublin before anyone knew, then on the boat to England. I can still remember lying upstairs in my room, hearing her singing in the kitchen. Sometimes I wake at night. I think I still hear her.'

The scraping had stopped. I had never known a silence as deep. It was hard to conceive of a world beyond the jumbled lives of this closed confessional. I do not know how long it was before he began to speak again.

'The evening before we planned to go,' he said, 'I waited

for our mother to send her out down the lane with the bucket for water. I knew it would take her four minutes. I could hear my father joking with her as he scraped his boots out in the yard. It's what I've always been, you see. A coward. I told my mother Lizzy was pregnant. I went up to my room and closed the door. I lay on the bed with the pillow over my head, but I could still hear her screams after she came in. She was calling for me to protect her. That awful thud of my father's belt. I came down and stood in the hall. All I had to do was open the door and the beating would have stopped. But I did nothing. She vanished behind one set of walls and I went back to the safety of another set of walls. Sweet Jesus in Heaven, not a day has passed since when I've not . . . Sweet Christ . . . Sweet Christ, what I did to her.'

He ceased speaking. My eyes had grown used to the darkness. I could see the shape of his hand pressing against the wire mesh.

'Are you still there?' he asked, his voice suddenly fearful. I tapped very softly on the wood in reply.

'People come in,' he said. 'And they think everything can be forgiven. I don't believe it can. I give absolution to dying people. It means so much to them. And I feel so privileged to give them that peace of mind. But I know that when I am dying I will turn my face away from the priest because there are some sins that you bring with you to the grave.'

I opened the door of the confession box. If I drove quickly enough back to Dublin I might be in time to read Benedict stories before snuggling him down in the bed. I wanted to put my arms around him and Sinead and Geraldine. I wanted bright lights and noise and music and streets filled with people.

'Will I ever see you again?' he asked.

'I don't believe so.'

'It would never have worked,' he said. 'Legal documents, jobs, birth certs. God knows what I spared you, but I did it for myself.' He paused. 'No matter how much you hate me, it will always be less than how much I hate myself.'

'What do you want?' I asked. 'It is not in my gift to condemn or forgive you.'

'I condemn myself. It is in your gift to try in some way to understand.'

He had taken his hand away from the wire mesh. I turned and placed my fingers lightly against it. I could feel the slight pressure where his hand pressed on the other side. Long after I had driven away, when I had passed through Navan with the lights on at the dog track and the straight flat road had consumed me between its lines of unblinking cat's-eyes, I felt that he was still sitting there, his fingers pressing on that wire mesh, trying to cling on to the last trace of human warmth.

Chapter Seventeen

On the first of October, the night after I had finished working on the St Martha photographs, I took Benedict to his first football match. I knew that he wouldn't last the whole game, so I waited outside until almost the end of the first half before going in. After a twenty-one-year absence, Shelbourne were in European competition for the second time in a row, now as FAI Cup winners. Two weeks before they had lost the first leg away in the Ukraine to Karpaty Lvov by an unlucky late goal.

I had been intending to go to the second leg alone, but on the radio before leaving the house I heard from Tolka Park that Shelbourne had already pulled a goal back in the opening minutes to level the tie. I lifted Benedict up into my arms as Geraldine was about to undress him for bed, ignoring her protests as I pulled on his coat, and told her that we would be back before ten. He turned to wave back at her, then put his arms around my neck, delighted to be carried off on a late adventure.

It had always been a source of pride for my father that he had brought me as a child to every home game which the Shels had played in Europe. That was back in the glory days of the early sixties, when we lost to Sporting Lisbon and Barcelona. There was little that I could remember of the games, except the joy of being allowed to stay up so late. But I could still clearly recall the night in 1964 when my father was in tears. It had been on the only occasion that Shelbourne ever won a European tie, in the Inter Fairs

Cup, as it was called then, against Belenenses, back before away goals counted double. Shels had drawn one-all away from home and then had a scoreless draw in Dublin. The tie was settled in a play-off match at home, with Ben Hannigan and Mick Conroy scoring the goals which put us through.

There had been a storm that night, lightning splitting the sky, rain spitting down like darts of crystallized light in the haphazard floodlights, as the huge crowd screamed around us. To me it felt like the electric storm was pulsing through our bodies as I swayed on my father's shoulders, and began to cry at the end too, because he was in tears.

The glory didn't last long: we were beaten in the second round by Athletico Madrid. In my mind that had always seemed the start of the end for Shels. There had been just one more brief outing, seven unsuccessful years later, in the UEFA Cup against Vasas Budapest in 1971. I had been a teenager then, still screaming behind the goalmouth with my father and his friends as Shels' late chance of a winner rebounded off the crossbar in the one-all draw which knocked us out. But the sensation had been different, I had wanted to be off with my own friends, and was relieved, after the match, to leave the older men to relive their pasts over pints in the Hut Bar.

The Vasas Budapest game had been staged in Dalymount Park, Shelbourne not having a real home ground of their own. Since then they had been forever on the move. Twenty years in seemingly terminal decline. Itinerants, nomads. Spells in Tolka Park and out in Ringsend, years of playing in the wilderness at Harold's Cross dog track, struggling to avoid relegation every season, always rumoured to be on the verge of extinction.

Two decades lit by the brief optimism of occasional cup

runs, and by the memories of greying men who talked about the Sundays in the fifties and sixties when the whole of Dublin was stilled by the roar of a local derby with Rovers or Bohs. Giants like Ben Hannigan walking up from Fairview among the crowd with his boots on his shoulder, straight off the boat from England after the long trek home from watching Manchester United at Old Trafford the previous day, and ready to impersonate the Dennis Law salute after each goal which he would score that afternoon.

My father's heroes. The memories of those winning salutes and of that solitary win against Belenenses had to keep him warm on those empty terraces right up to his death. Years later I found a shot among the files of negatives in the sports department of the paper. It showed three figures standing together on the open terrace of Harold's Cross stadium. On every side there is empty space. Without even needing to develop it I could recognize my father in the middle, shouting himself into a faded old age.

The only terrace he ever felt really at home on was here in Tolka Park, and he had not lived to see the revival over the last three years. Shelbourne returning to actually own their first ground since 1895, turning it into the best stadium in Ireland, and finally, last year, bringing the championship back to Tolka Park.

This year they had almost succeeded again, losing in a play-off to Cork. But they had won the FAI Cup instead. In 1939 they had won the cup and the Second World War started. In 1963 they managed to do it again and Kennedy was assassinated. I could imagine my father shaking his head with a wink and remarking that it was no wonder I had crashed.

When Benedict had tired of staring at the huge television cranes which leaned across the stand from outside the ground I picked him up in my arms again. The steward at the turnstile nodded at me to lift him over. We entered into a tumult of noise and I placed him up on my shoulders. We were on the narrow terrace at the Drumcondra End, the only part of the ground where it was still possible for spectators to stand. Even though my father could have sat in the stand for nothing he had always insisted on standing at a Shelbourne match. I knew that this terrace was where he would have been now if he were alive.

Being there among the crowd with Benedict on my shoulders made his death painful again. Benedict was restless, thrilled to be out so late and yet frightened by the closeness of the crowd. I lifted him down and carried him in my arms up to the corner overlooking the river. There was some small space there. He ran among the rows of plastic chairs, pulling the seats up and down, then turned to stare in wonder at the full moon, so pale against the darkening sky that it seemed more like the shadow of a full moon, which watched over the Ballybough End. It was still one–nil for Shelbourne. The cry began again. *Shelbourne! Shelbourne!* How long was it since I'd heard a crowd so large chanting that? Not really since those far-away matches when I had been able to fit on my own father's shoulders among the terraces of standing bodies and smell from some corner the scent of hot Bovril.

I sat down and Benedict tumbled on to my knee, tired of the novelty now and wanting to be held and told stories. Shels were pressing forward frantically, always about to break down the Ukrainian defence. They won a free kick from outside the box. Ken Doherty lay on the ground, the Ukrainian player was booked.

'Benedict visits the farm,' Benedict suggested as a story title. Mick Neville took the spotkick from thirty-five yards.

It struck the underside of the crossbar and was scrambled away. Benedict banged on my knee with his hand as I rose to join the chorus of screams. 'Hello, farmer. What's your problem?' he said. 'Is your tractor broken? Me and Gerry the Goat will fix it.' He stopped and looked up excitedly, tugging at my jacket. 'Silly Daddy shouting. The farmer says his tractor's broken and me and Gerry the Goat are going to fix it.'

He began to busy himself with imaginary spanners and wrenches, waiting for me to improvise a story around him. The French referee blew for half-time. I stilled his hands.

'No,' I said. 'A different type of story tonight. About Dada's Dada. Will I tell you about when your dada was a little boy like you and my dada would bring me down here.'

'Is Benedict in it,' he asked, doubtfully, 'and Gerry the Goat?'

'Eh, Gerry the Goat is,' I said, and Benedict was sufficiently appeased to decide to settle down on my lap and listen.

'Long ago,' I began, as the crowd started to drift towards the Ballybough End, 'before Gerry the Goat came to live in Benedict's pocket he used to play for Shelbourne Football Club. That was long ago when I was a little boy and my daddy . . .'

Once Gerry the Goat popped up at the far post to head home a winner every few moments Benedict was happy to listen, and soon he even forgot about the goat. He snuggled down deeper into my lap, asking me questions now, demanding that I retell incidents from the story again, with his grandfather suddenly becoming real for him.

I had blown up an old photograph of my mother and father when they were young and hung it in the downstairs bathroom. So far he had shown little interest in it, but now he wanted us to go home so that he could look at the faces. The thought came to me again, if I had died in that crash, what would he have been left with to remember me? Geraldine's stories would not have been enough. I hugged him tightly to me, flushed with the sudden euphoria of being alive.

Perhaps it had been inevitable that I would have crashed again on the way home from Cavan, with so much tension over those few days and so little sleep. I had wanted so badly to be back home with Geraldine, to turn the corner of the street by the cherry blossom trees and glimpse the light on in our kitchen window across the row of gardens.

All that evening it had been threatening rain. Beyond Kingscout it had come with ferocity, the wipers barely able to cope as the road filled up with surface water. At Dunshaughlin I decided to skip across to the Ashbourne Road, down that twisting by-road through Ratoath, hoping to save time. I saw the sign for dangerous bends, slowed slightly and then sped on. I was half an hour from home when I rounded the bend and braked as I hit the pool of water. Once again the world broke down into slowed motion, the crash happening in distinct stages. But this time it was different. Outside the Botanic Gardens I had watched the accident occur, numbed into a mesmeric fascination. It had felt like a preordained event, a rendezvous which I had been racing to keep.

But now I watched with pure horror, scrambling at the steering wheel as the car spun, willing myself to live. For the first time in a year death became a genuine and absolute terror. The memory of those welcoming faces was banished, their warmth had become the coldness of the grave. I fought against meeting them with all my strength.

There was a crash and I was jerked back. The car had spun off the road, narrowly missing two trees as the boot ploughed into a gate. There was the tinkle of glass as the rear lights shattered. The boot burst open. I had closed my eyes, bracing myself. I opened the door and stepped out into the rain. One of the back tyres had burst. With the heavy clouds the road was almost dark. There was no traffic. I was utterly alone. I hunched down, shaking. Then gradually I had felt the shock dissolving into a sort of euphoria. I was okay, I was still alive. I had just almost written off my second car in a year, but I didn't care. The wheels had missed those trees by only a matter of inches. The windscreen should have shattered, the car turned over. I had come so close to dying once again. I lifted my head into the rain. It tasted like champagne. A truck came round the corner and slowed. I held my hand up and he stopped to give me a lift. I was so giddy the driver thought that I was in shock, but I simply wanted to celebrate the miracle of my survival.

The garage in Ratoath had sent a truck out to collect the car. I phoned Geraldine from Healy's pub to tell her that I would be home in an hour in a taxi. She kept asking me if I was at the airport and where was the car.

'From now on you do the driving,' I had said to her. 'Listen, I know it's late but keep Benedict up, just this once. Show him a video or something. I'm just dying to get home to you.'

Dying to get home. I remembered the phrase again as the referee came back out for the second half. I closed my eyes, reliving that sickening feeling as the car spun, then hugged Benedict tighter on my knee before lifting him up on my shoulders.

'Hang on tight to Gerry the Goat,' I said. 'This is where your grandfather would have brought me.'

I walked down the length of the pitch and then up into the heart of the die-hard Shelbourne fans standing among the seats at the back of the Ballybough End. There were other children there, even younger than Benedict, their fathers knowing that they would not remember it but wanting them to be able to say that they had been there. Benedict was jaded now but I could sense the crowd's adrenalin starting to work on him. Twenty minutes into the half, Neville won the ball and released Brian Mooney. He moved forward, Ukrainian defenders backing off him, and then, from thirty yards, he unleashed the finest right-foot drive I had ever witnessed. It curled in unbelievably under the bar. I threw Benedict up in the surge of screaming bodies and caught him in my arms. He was frightened by the deafening noise.

'It's okay,' I said, barely knowing what I was saying. 'Your granddaddy's scored!'

I looked up at the sky, which had turned a deep blue. The first Shels goal Benedict had ever seen. He would not remember it but was unlikely to ever see one better. The third goal came after seventy-six minutes, scored by Izzi, a young Italian who worked by day in his uncle's fish and chip shop. After that Shelbourne struck the bar again and then began to run their way at will through the Ukrainian defence. Against Belenenses in '64 we had scraped our way home, but here was Shelbourne not just beating a European side but destroying them.

It was a decade since any Irish side had won in Europe. My father had followed them all – even the dogs of Shamrock Rovers – when they played in Europe. How many dreams had he built around a night like this? Not even a break-away goal by the Ukrainians two minutes from the end could alter the magic quality of the night. The crowd began to whistle for time.

I took Benedict down from my shoulders. He curled up against my jacket. I must have been his age or younger when my father first brought me here, his friends pressing sixpenny bits in my hand, plying me with bars of chocolate which they told me not to mention to my mother. His friends had known who I was. That was why I had always been made to feel special as a child here. Now I realized that I had not just been adopted by him but, on the Sundays when I was taken here, by every one of those men.

The whistle blew and the ground erupted. Old stewards that I recognized from my father's day were dancing and blowing kisses at the crowd. Nobody had left the ground. The crowd stood as one to applaud the Shels off and this time Benedict was excited by the noise and happy to climb back up on to my shoulders to join in the clapping as well.

I waited for a few minutes among the coloured seats as the crowd pushed their way out, then began to make my way down. A hand gripped my shoulder, an old friend of my father. He hugged me in silence and I nodded in understanding. The stewards had opened the gates in the wire fence. I climbed in and lifted Benedict down on to the floodlit turf. More than gravestones or visits to graves I knew that this was how the father who had raised me would wish to be remembered. Benedict ran about on the grass, excited by the magic of the floodlights which sketched in four shadows around him. The terraces were almost empty. A scarf had been dropped by one of the kids running after the players. Benedict raced towards me. I caught him up in my arms and put the scarf around his neck. The steward carrying the corner flags stopped, obviously recognizing me.

'A great night,' he said, then nodded towards Benedict. 'He looks the spit of your oul fellow. God, your da would have loven' to see tonight. Anyway, as long as this young scut is around your da won't be gone from the world.'

'You know that I was adopted,' I told him.

'Listen, son,' he ruffled Benedict's hair as the child buried his face shyly in my jacket, 'I don't care if you came down the Tolka in a bubble, this young fellow here is the spit of your oul man.' He winked. 'Come on the Shels, eh!'

I waited till the steward had gone, then walked down towards the empty terrace at the Drumcondra End. If ghosts existed, I knew that my father would be standing on those concrete steps. We had baptized Benedict for the sake of Geraldine's family. For me it had been an empty experience. But now this passing on of a name seemed real and wonderful as I walked towards the wire fence. I wanted my father to know that it was his name which Benedict was carrying, and that, through all my grief for my real mother, it was being carried with pride. *He's yours,* I was saying in my mind, *not some nameless bastard who ran away.* I reached the goal mouth and lifted Benedict up like a trophy for his grandfather to see.

Benedict was exhausted when we left the ground and I had to carry him home, trying to avoid the bustle of the pubs and the trucks still speeding along Drumcondra Road. He laid his head against my jacket and dozed as I cut through the back lanes, across Ormond Road and up by the side of All Hallow's College. We came to the gates of Drumcondra church. Benedict roused himself for a moment and demanded that I carry him over. He grabbed the railing with his fist and stared in at the moonlit headstones.

'The strange place,' he said. 'Remember we used to walk there, Dada. The big tractor lives behind it.'

He let go and leaned his head down again against my jacket. He was becoming heavy in my arms. Those March mornings seemed a life-time ago, when I had stood here, afraid to venture out into the world. I had not brought Benedict back since then, but there had been evenings, coming home from work over the past weeks, when I had stopped the car to walk here or in some other forgotten graveyard on this side of the city, finding myself trying to decipher the headstones and wondering.

Once I stopped at Grangegorman to walk among the ruins of the old Richmond Asylum. Beds lay rusting on the grass beside an old opened wardrobe. I closed the wardrobe over with a huge bang. The birds on the window-ledge above me did not budge, perhaps possessing an immunity passed on over generations to noise, screaming and terror.

I had never contacted George in the Botanic Gardens again. But any time that I passed the gates there at night I glanced up towards the window of that room in the front lodge, as if expecting him to still be there, peering through those records. There were other avenues I could still use to try and unlock what was in my head – hypnosis, holotropic breathing sessions – but I knew that I never would. I had this one life to lead now, this one name that I would pass on to my children.

I remembered Aunt Cissie's story of my mother bringing me to my uncle's grave to try and explain about life and death, and how I had terrified her by describing a man in the earth with no ear. Maybe I had seen it that morning in a comic, perhaps I had just been babbling? Every evening now on our walks together Benedict gabbled on about Gerry the Goat and penguins from the zoo who visited the house when

I was at work. Those figments were as real, and unreal, to him as the footballers we had seen on the floodlit pitch. Who could take seriously what any child that age said?

And so, in the end, what did my dreams and fragments of memory mean? Were they just the babblings of the child I had once been, just half-recalled snatches of events which could have as easily been imagined? Ever since that night in Cavan the young man's face which had haunted me was gone. What came into my mind now, as if in its place, was the profile of my uncle in that dark box, the unshaven side of his cheek through the mesh of gold wire, the desperate pleading in those eyes for release. Could one face really have led me to the other? Or had I simply been living out those last nine months in a state of delayed shock after coming so close to death?

There was a movement among the tombstones: a ginger cat stretched himself and then crossed the gravel path. *The strange place.* Having died once, death – as against dying – could never frighten me again, and yet I still had not found the courage to explain what the word meant to Benedict. I looked down at him, now sleeping in my arms. His was a world without death or age, an infinity of fresh mornings which I felt so privileged to share. We were sleeping better these nights. He no longer cried out, but simply climbed in beside us in the night and lifted his head to wake us with a gentle 'boo' at half-seven. Soon Sinead would discover this pleasure and clamber in from her cot as well. Let her come and join our raft of love sailing through the night. These last months had taught me to treasure every kiss and sleepy caress, every push and elbow against my back.

Lately the word death had entered Benedict's vocabulary of its own accord. He used it without fear, wanting to know if the butterfly in the sandwich of Mr Jeremy Fisher was dead. But he had not yet connected it to people. One day the question would come and although I would explain how many thousands and thousands and thousands of days lay ahead for him, I knew that his innocence would never be the same again.

Until then these old slabs would just be funny stones, this gravel path simply a bed of loose pebbles for him to play with. But years from now, long after Benedict and Sinead had made their own way in the world and remembered just occasionally to call or write home, I knew that I would find myself coming back to quiet places like this. I would sit with Geraldine in the late winter sun on that bench inside the gate, and walk across the grass among those stones, still reading those worn names and wondering, still half believing that I might close my eyes and suddenly recall snatches of another self whom I might have once been.

I paused at the corner of the street to watch the light shining in our kitchen window. Benedict stirred and I pointed it out to him. How bright it seemed. He looked around at the dark roadway, a little scared by it, and asked to go home. Geraldine had biscuits and hot milk waiting for him. His face looked exhausted after the short sleep, but he was too excited by the big adventure to be cranky.

I had left the St Martha shots in an envelope for Geraldine to look at. She had laid them out on the kitchen table. How long was it since I had worked on photographs with that utter engrossment, dreaming of bleached shades of colour, waking up knowing exactly where the crop should occur? For the past month I had been living just to get back into the studio every morning. I had bleached the negatives, blowing objects up and cropping them closely.

Even with the speed at which I had taken the photographs

that afternoon by the river I was surprised at how I had intuitively worked so many complex elements into each composition. There was a disturbing ambivalence about the colours, the blue unpolluted river and lush high grass drawing the viewer's eye into a pastoral setting, to be then confronted by the intrusion of discoloured objects which no longer looked like themselves. The brass tops of beds, rusted by twenty years of weather and now embroidered by a lattice of green waterweeds. The distorted reflection of the broken wooden bars of a cot lying half in and half out of the water. The springs of an old mattress consumed by flowering nettles. Camouflaged by time, they betrayed the secret of their past only slowly. Mainly I had focused in on single displaced items: the knob of a locker half buried in the earth, the sole of a tiny child's shoe turned the colour of earth, the cheap emptied frame of a picture. Almost all colour had been drained from the shots. They were man-made objects, but so old and distorted as to seem part of the earth. Yet although the earth had almost claimed them, they still clung to their identity and past. Once they had been precious. How many of us had woken from our first sleep behind the broken bars of that cot, how many mothers had gripped that bedstead in terror and pushed their child into life?

Finally there had been just eight images with which I was happy enough to bring home to show Geraldine. These were an elegy for the forgotten, the only monument to my true past which I could leave. But they were also my way of coming to terms with that past. For long periods in the darkroom I had just sat and cried for the mother I had lost, or else had been engulfed by the most intense of angers. Then the impersonal photographer would take over again, finding the shape in the image, coaxing it to life. In those long hours alone in that darkroom I had gradually allowed myself to remember and to accept.

Geraldine had put on a tape of songs for Benedict. There was a noise on the baby machine and we both instinctively listened for any sound of Sinead shifting in her cot. But the machine had just picked up the noise of somebody passing on the street. Geraldine followed me into the kitchen, where I stood staring at the shots, and nuzzled against my shoulder as if to say that she understood.

'They're wonderful,' she said, 'I'm proud of you. I always was.'

'These last months I know I've not been easy to live with.'

She kissed the back of my neck softly.

'You'd swear to God you ever were. Sensitive souls the pair of us. It's no wonder poor Benedict hasn't a chance.'

'What would my mother have made of them?' I asked. 'I mean the mother who raised me. My da I think I can square, but would she think that I betrayed her, searching like that?'

'As you often say yourself about people,' Geraldine said, 'she's either just ashes and bone now or else she's in some higher state where . . . well, where these things seem very different to her.' She paused, a hint of nervousness entering her voice. 'He called when you were out.'

I fingered one of the shots on the table for a moment.

'I hate him,' I said quietly, 'for what he did to her.'

'Sean, it was you who phoned him. You started it, he phoned you back.'

'I know.'

'Have you decided what you are going to do?'

I nodded and reached my hand out to touch her shoulder. Benedict had followed us into the kitchen and tugged at my arm. He held out his empty palm proudly.

'Look,' he said, 'Benedict takes a picture of Gerry the Goat.'

I leaned down to inspect the tiny fate lines crisscrossing his palm and smiled.

'It's lovely,' I said, 'you captured him just right.' In a year's time he would have started school. I hated the thought of losing him. I had a memory still of my own first day, the terror as the black robes of a nun reached out to take my hand, the way my mother had been reduced suddenly by her power. The question came again, what if I had died in that crash? He was so young. There was nothing he would have remembered. I wanted this moment to live on. In years to come we might argue as fathers and sons do. When he reached my age I wanted him to be able to look at my face now and know that I had also felt the same things as him. There was just my photograph on a passport and another on my driving licence. Geraldine and I had fought bitterly before our wedding when I told her I wanted no photographs taken. It was the same fear which had lasted since my tenth birthday and made me always need to be in command, safely behind the lens, the irrational fear that I would look different, that the camera would somehow expose the lie for everyone to see who I really was. I looked across in at my father's old camera bag lying behind the couch.

'Benedict,' I asked. 'Will you take a photograph of Dada?'

He screwed up his face, peeped through his fingers and made a clicking sound, then held his palm out again to show me.

'No,' I said. 'A real photograph. I'll teach you how to do it.'

I took the camera out and, placing it on the chair,

showed him how to look through the viewfinder. He was tired and for a long time kept pretending he could see, then, by the look on his face, I knew that he had discovered how to look through it. Geraldine watched, stunned and amused.

'Jaysus,' she said. 'I've seen everything. Hang on there. I think I still have my wedding dress somewhere.'

I walked over to sit on the carpet beside the wall where I knew that I would be in focus. I stared at the lens and found that my throat had gone dry.

'Show him how to press the shutter,' I told her. 'Go on, hold his finger for him.'

Every time the camera flashed Benedict looked up and laughed, then bent again in deep seriousness to peer at the condensed image of me. He shrugged Geraldine away, wanting to do it himself. His delight made me smile as I stared into the lens. Suddenly I was not afraid of it any more. This was how my son saw me, this was who I was. A father sitting on a floor to amuse his child. In my studio there were thousands of contact sheets, but I knew that these were the shots that I would always keep with me, that he would find with my will after I had gone. Benedict looked up and laughed again.

'Get Sinead down,' I said to Geraldine. She looked at me. 'I know that we'll be up half the night snapping at each other when we can't get her back asleep. But go on, please. Just get her down.'

I put a new roll of film in the camera and set it at automatic self-timer. I brought Benedict over and sat back down with him on my knee.

'Now,' I said, 'Gerry the Goat is going to take our photograph.'

The camera flashed by itself. Benedict jumped, unsure

whether to laugh or cry. He looked back at me and I smiled to reassure him. He stared at the empty space behind the camera with huge eyes. Geraldine slid down beside us with Sinead still asleep in her arms. The camera flashed once more. Sinead blinked once, then closed her eyes again and began to suck her thumb. Geraldine snuggled in closer to me. The camera flashed again and this time Sinead opened her eyes wide and gave a gurgling laugh. Benedict turned, delighted, and banged excitedly at Geraldine's shoulder.

'Mammy, Gerry the Goat is taking our photograph!'

He laughed and we laughed with him as my father's camera flashed on to the end of the roll by itself.

Chapter Eighteen

Briefly oblivion had come again in that ward, followed by the dulled pain which drove her back. There were lights hovering above her, and beyond the lights there were faces waiting for her to die. Lizzy had wanted them gone, she wanted to be alone now. For almost forty years she had always been alone. Ever since the day they had waited for the Dublin bus, the family gathered beside the nettles in the ditch, and Tom going away from her, with his new suitcase and freshly cut hair, and the fear which only she seemed able to sense in him.

Above her the lights blurred, merged into each other. The beam became so bright that it burned against her eyelids and dissolved into a core of darkness. The drip in her arm began to hurt, along with the skin which had broken down her back. The pain pulled her briefly back to consciousness. It felt like a thread of copper wire twisting its way through her body, holding her there still when she should be gone. Darkness waited, emptied now of the screams of souls in hell or the bliss of paradise. Such childhood promises had long died. She knew that it was darkness now which she would welcome, a numb release from those years of waiting and of hope.

How long was it since the last injection? Time . . . what could time mean here? Those faces blurred above her now, becoming as indistinguishable from each other as those years of waiting had been, those decades of bitter hope. An eternity of afternoons lost in that kitchen when the girls were at school, with well-bred voices on the radio for comfort. The sharp black-handled knife for scraping the carrots passing so close to her wrist. *Peel the potato, peel the potato, don't let yourself dream.*

She found that she was there again at the sink, staring out at the shed which her husband kept locked. The radio went silent, then it blared out ceilidh music. She turned and the whole kitchen vibrated to the hiss of static. She was forty-one. She let the knife drop and stared down at the fortune lines along her palm. Forty-one. That made him twenty-two, wherever he was, whoever he was. There was a mirror, which her husband used for shaving, beside the sink. She picked it up and stared in, squinting up her eyes, trying to make her features young and masculine. She closed her eyes. *Lord or Devil, Demon or Christ. I don't care any more. Anyone, anything, whatever Your price; when I open my eyes let me glimpse my son.* She held them closed for so long that she grew afraid. Then she opened them. They were wild as she stared at herself. She closed her eyes; the face that she saw in her mind was Tom's. Lizzy dropped the mirror, hearing it shatter from a great distance off. She bent to pick up a shard and let it prick the skin on her thumb. The afternoon was heavy with rain clouds. She smeared the blood in the sign of the cross on her forehead and her breast, then closed her eyes ready to make a pact.

A gloved hand reached out from behind to cover her face. A rapist, a burglar, her son. He had her body now, pressing hard against her back. She fought against the grip of his hand but he was so strong, suffocating her, smothering her nose and mouth. He opened his fingers wide and fresh oxygen was pumped in. She could see through his knuckles now, they curved in hard smooth plastic. Each noisy inhalation of breath drew her back into the mesh of pain. The faces were still there, still waiting. Strangers, daughters, the low babble of their English accents. The noise of tears reached her, the noise of water trickling down the rock face beside the ruined houses of that abandoned famine village. She was lying there by the broken mossy walls on the hills above Dunross. The dominion of fields had long ended and here only the scrawny mountain sheep grazed. Her nineteen-year-old eyes closed to feel the sun's warmth, as she lay with the flower-patterned dress blown up over her thighs by the wind.

Fresh grass, rushes in the streamlet, midges in the air. The ground was swaying, below the cliffs the bog was a shimmering black sea. And when she opened her eyes to gaze up the sun was blazing down upon her and overhead a silent vulture hovered, black wings outstretched, his shadow flickering over her as he bided his time to swoop. His face was the face of the man who had used her body here. She opened her mouth to scream but there was a plastic mask blocking her, a hand which pressed down against her face. She heard a cricket chirping in the rushes, the noise growing unnaturally loud before it dissolved into the ticking of a watch on the nurse's wrist. Then the copper wire twisted inside her again. It tore through her flesh, her body jerked and fell.

Where had she landed now? She smelt the turf against her hair. She was twelve, lying upon the bog that summer noon after Mickie Black had left for America. Her limbs were jaded from the dancing all night in his parents' house, from the long walk among the crowd going all the way with him to the station, their singing drifting away into silence in the dawn light. That quiet platform of older girls and boys. Like deaths, these perpetual going-aways to Boston,

Chicago, New York. Mickie Black's kiss remained against her cheek long after the train had departed and the families traipsed their way out on to their holdings on the bog. Men cutting turf, throwing the wet sods up for their children to stack.

And then families had stopped as if a siren had sounded across the flat landscape. The sun high and merciless as they ate and lay down to rest. Beside her Ellen has drifted into an exhausted sleep. Lizzy turns on her side to stare at her sister's breasts beginning to press against her dress. Her own eyes close, then open to stare at Tom sitting a small way off, separated from the other lads but watching them. And now the whole bog stops to watch Ellen rise, still in a deep sleep, and begin to dance the steps from last night, her eyes closed, her face expressionless, limbs jerking with precision as she skims across the surface of the bog.

The noon sun grew in brilliance, lighting up the dancing girl until she burst into flame. Still Ellen danced on, burning as bright as the sun and then splitting up into four shimmering blurs which came back into focus. The copper wire twisted in Lizzy's bowels again, cutting against the lining of her stomach. Those same four lights shone above her, those same watchers who would not leave her alone. The mask was being lifted away for a moment and brought steadily down over her face again. The pain was utterly engulfing, then the pain just ceased. She could see a wedding ring on the nurse's fingers holding the mask down, and the black wires attached to it which stretched away into the machine.

Only gradually did she realize that she was looking at the wrong side of the mask, and could see her own sunken face in the bed and then the nurse's hat as she began to press buttons and the watchers moved forward, the lifted their heads back to reveal smudged tears like the silver tracks of snails.

Briefly Lizzy wished to stay and watch, but already the sweep of movement was carrying her away. She seemed to have reached the ceiling and begun to glide along it. There was no sense of fear, just a bemused and disconnected fascination. Below her the figures moved in the corridor; a trolley passed beneath the undusted top of a lampshade like a toy train under a bridge. Then the hospital lights were gone. It was dark out in the car-park, dark above the city. That warm darkness wrapped itself around her until she was spinning within it. All the pin-pricks of light below her were shrinking into a speck which flickered out, as her head turned, like a baby's in a womb, to point through the darkness towards a vast luminosity.

She felt herself being buffeted about in that warm black tunnel. The light beckoned her, drawing her slowly upwards. She knew that she had to decide whether to allow herself to be dead or to try and pull herself back down into that pain. He had never found her. Already everything else in her life seemed distant, but that yearning remained, trapping her in the tunnel between two worlds. The light had drawn nearer, it seemed now to have become a globe of speckled faces. People whom she had never thought to see again. They filled her with a sense of well-being, of coming home. How had she managed to live for so long in that loneliness without them? She knew that all she had to do was pass through this globe where the faces now merged into a core of brilliant light.

But how could she leave her son? The thought made her fight against the pull of those vibrating faces, and then she saw him there. The only face left unblurred. For a moment she thought that it was her son, then a sense told her that it could not be. Yet it was somebody close to him, someone who could almost be him. She remembered the stories of John the Baptist, the one who was sent ahead to prepare a way. At first the young man's face seemed surly, then he smiled as if to reassure her. It was a smile of welcome and recognition, before he vanished into the swirling globe of faces which she felt herself plummeting upwards to break through.

They came apart and she found that her feet were walking across the mountainside now. Trees in the valley below began to change colour until they took on the shades of autumn. The ground was warm, although dew was starting to drench the lush grasses at her feet. She came to the top field above Dunross, the dry-stone wall which her whole family had laboured to build. Lizzy sensed that the young man was walking somewhere beside her, guiding her although she could no longer see him. Her father waited at the gate where a sheep dog barked.

'You'll like it here, Lizzy,' he said to her. But she was frightened of his anger still. She climbed the wall and jumped down, knowing that her father was following. Her mother was waiting for her by the top wall, leading into the lake field which overlooked the church and the two shops in the village. The woman waved and opened her arms, but Lizzy backed away, and turned to find that she could now see the young man beside her. Again for a moment she thought that it was her son, but he shook his head. He was in the likeness of her son, that was all she knew, and had also somehow the gentleness of Tom. His feet were bare, his clothes ragged, but he was welcoming her, taking the place of someone else who could not yet be there.

He held his hand out and she accepted it. She looked back, but discovered now there was only darkness behind her. After every step the ground which she had covered seemed to vanish. Would she run out of earth and heather, meet a similar darkness coming from the other direction towards her? The thought did not terrify her. How long had she been here? She knew that time meant nothing in this place that was somewhere between worlds or states or oblivions.

Her father and mother walked with her as well, a small distance off, waiting for her to decide to call them. Cloud shadows passed quickly across the ground, the sheep dog had vanished.

They came to the wall of the lake field and looked down at the two cars arriving to park beside the blue car which was already outside the graveyard. A small group of people got out. Her sister Ellen looked well, pointing out landmarks to a frail old woman beside her who was smoking. The solitary figure in the blue car got out. She could recognize him, even though thirty-six years had greyed and saddened him. He fingered his stiff white collar as if about to take it off.

And she knew at once who her son was as he walked over, hesitated and then shook Tom's hand. He picked up a young boy who ran towards him and climbed over the stile in the wall into the graveyard. The child gazed around him, pointing excitedly towards the tractor which had stopped in the field across the road. Tom opened the gate so that the young woman could wheel in the buggy into which she had placed a sleeping baby girl.

A fourth car had pulled in, a Merc driven by a man in a suit with broad shoulders. He opened the back door and two women got out. She knew by their faces that they were mothers like herself. They stood awkwardly, a small distance off. The farmer had stopped his tractor in the field and walked to the gate. Several women had come out from the post office. The small group began to walk up the graveyard.

And the funny thing was that it seemed like I could almost feel my mother's presence there, for the first time in my life, as we left the gravel path and began to make our way carefully among the graves. Behind me, my two aunts walked together in silence. Cissie and Ellen. How much pain they had both witnessed from the two women who were my mothers. Gerry had taken off his jacket. For him that was a rare mark of respect. He walked beside my uncle Tom, who seemed unable to control the tremble in his hand. I had not expected Peter McHugh to be here, and had only left a message at the hotel on the last moment at Geraldine's suggestion. The two women, whom I had met in his office, walked beside him. I wondered if their husbands knew where they were. I don't know why, but I had dropped a note as well to Frank Conroy's widow. She was emigrating to Canada and I did not expect her to come, but thought in some small way that it might help her to know.

Perhaps it had been the sight of Tom, who had not returned here since his ordination, sitting alone in his car, which caused the local women to gather outside the shop. But when I looked back I found that they were following us from a distance. The farmer and some other old men were walking behind them. We reached my grandparents' grave. A strong autumn sun cast shadows from the crooked stones. When I looked down at the grass I could still see the motionless shadows of over a dozen villagers blending with those of the stones. I stared at them. My own father might even be standing here. They were all of an age to have known my mother. I knew that each of them was now aware of who I was. Ever since my mother had vanished in that nun's car they had known of me. How often had I been spoken of in whispers in that shop or out on those mountainsides?

Benedict was slightly frightened by the circle of people. Aunt Cissie came to lift him out of my arms and soothe him with her gravelly voice which had so often soothed me. Geraldine pushed the buggy back and forth as Sinead sucked her thumb in sleep. I nodded to Aunt Ellen, who took the urn from her bag and placed it into my hands.

It was the strangest sensation. The urn weighed little more than a new-born baby. It was the same time of evening as when I had first searched for this grave, the time of evening when my mother had been allowed to stand here briefly, carrying me inside her, and mourn alone. There had been no words spoken on either of those occasions and there were no words which could be said now.

Some of the local men were glancing at Tom, perhaps expecting him to lead them in prayer. But he kept his eyes fixed on the urn in my hands. I looked down at the grave of my grandparents. Autumn leaves had blown in to cover the grass. My friends and my families stood in silence. The local people remained at a distance, the men defensive and slightly hostile, the women staring at me with frank curiosity.

I opened the urn and began to scatter the ashes. The wind blew some of them off the grave before they had time to settle. I knew that before dark they would have been blown into every corner of that graveyard, some out on to the road where the tyres of cars and trucks would carry them off into villages and farmyards, and others lifted high by the wind, tossed out into the fields and up towards the empty darkening hillside where sheep grazed.

A Second Life

I wanted her to know that I had brought her home. Momentarily I felt empty and foolish, standing there in silence with that empty urn. Then I heard footsteps approaching. I did not look up. I knew that the local men would still be standing awkwardly in their places watching as their wives placed their arms gently about me. I leaned my head forward. It touched some old woman's cheek which was damp with tears. I nodded in understanding, feeling the arms of the women pressing against me, each one taking away my pain with a mother's quiet and certain caress.

Dermot Bolger was born in Dublin in 1959. His often controversial novels of Irish life, *Night Shift*, *The Woman's Daughter*, *The Journey Home* and *Emily's Shoes* (all published in Penguin), have received many awards, and his plays (published together in Penguin as *A Dublin Quartet*) have been presented in Ireland, Britain, Australia, America and Europe, broadcast on radio and television and received such prizes as the Samuel Beckett Award. A poet and publisher, he founded the Raven Arts Press and, more recently, New Island Books, and has been at the forefront of promoting a new generation of Irish writers. He is the editor of *The Picador Book of Contemporary Irish Fiction*.